DEDICATED TO MY FATHER BERNARD HEAGNEY
(1912-1982)
... and the untold thousands of other poor children
like him taken from their homes and scattered around
the world as indentured servants by the British
Home Children program for nearly a century.

JOHN HEAGNEY

Traveler

John Heagney

Cover image

The Heagney family farm Dunamore Cookstown,
County Tyrone, Ireland

Part I

The Home Place

JOHN HEAGNEY

1
July 13, 1920

"It's a weapon! The glass is a goddamned weapon!! Smash it in his face and run like hell!!!"

Barney Ned's eyes shot open in the diminishing wake of another bizarre dream.

Lying there in the dank, gathering dawn as his sisters slept beside him in the loft, the boy scanned the roof thatch a few feet above his head trying to glimpse the field mouse that skittered about unseen and would remain so this morning. He listened for rain that had tapered off to a drizzle an hour ago, casting a misty pall on another basalt-grey Tyrone morning.

Moments later, shaking off the lingering wisps of sleep, the boy pulled on his trousers and turf-caked brogues, descended the loft ladder and scuffed the few steps from his parents' small cottage to the barn door that wasn't so much wood as the memory of wood, long ago lashed together by his grandfather or uncle or someone not of his clan at all, to keep livestock in and thieves out.

Tugging the rope handle as the door scraped open, the boy -- called Neddy by his mother -- ducked at the barn's threshold although he was just a shade more than five feet tall. As his eyes adjusted in the dim light, he pushed aside a wheelbarrow and rusted hoe to grab what became a scythe in the retreating darkness of sunrise.

The barn, which in another time and place would be described more accurately as a shed, was a derelict affair filled with a riot of castoffs and farm implements in varying states of function. A slumping three-legged dining table, a murky shard of mirror, milk cans, a stack of drying peat, a tapestry of cobwebs and, at this moment, two farm cats. One of them lazed on the table near long-forgotten, half-buried remnants of a Blessed Virgin plaster statue no larger than a child's hand. The other climbed atop the clutter and disappeared through a large gash in the barn's roof.

A disagreeable swirl of pasture fog, midges and barnyard muck greeted Barney Ned as he headed back to the cottage, leaning the scythe beside the door and entering.

At the same moment, his father, Edward, emerged from the parents' sleep nook behind the fireplace and took a seat at the hearth-side table. Edward – who also went by Neddy in his younger days before growing into what he considered the more grand-sounding adult version of himself – was a slight-framed Ulsterman with powerful hands and a face leathered by four decades of farm life, alcohol and tobacco (more the latter two than the former one). Hunching over a thick slice of soda bread and tea, he rolled the first of dozens of cigarettes he would smoke that day. A habit deplored by his wife, Moira, and one he had refused to abandon so often, she wearied of harping about it years ago to keep the peace. He lit the cigarette and coughed as he inhaled, smoke rising like a veil to the brim of his ever-present pork pie hat then dissipating into the room.

"Boyo," rasped Edward, coughing and already in bad spirits for having risen so early after a very late night before, "You've man's work to do ..."

"Leave him be, old man," Moira scolded as she climbed

down the ladder from the small loft, where the girls were stirring. "'Tis you who should be doin' man's work and a lot of other t'ings 'round here."

"Ach, woman," Edward growled, brushing a cigarette ash from the oil-clothed tabletop. "What d'ya know about man's work? Leave it to us men."

"Sweet Jaysus, if I left it to men of yer sort, we'd starve," she shot back, slamming an iron skillet on the cooker, which she lit with a wooden match. "And just what will ya be doin'?"

"Important t'ings and that's all ya have to know."

Tea in hand, Barney Ned headed for the door.

"Neddy," Moira called, looking up from the fry pan, "where ya goin"?

"I've man's work to do ..."

"Not on an empty stomach, ya don't ..."

But the boy was already outside and moving to the far end of the barnyard, where he looked down on the small lower pasture, much of it in bog and useless for planting. The fog was beginning to lift so that Neddy could glimpse one of the family's six cows grazing near a partially collapsed, stacked-stone wall bordering Kinnigillian Road, which stretched to the crest of a hill, then disappeared into the endless patchwork of pasture and glen. A rolling palette of celadon and myrtle, honeydew and forest green rising and falling this way and that toward Cookstown, Belfast and who knows what beyond.

Standing there, hand cradling the teacup, he couldn't shake last night's unsettling dream and, again, the night visitor who, for nearly a year now, had been a regular nocturnal companion. Approaching the cottage on foot, stopping near the barnyard gate and always dressed in a manner the boy had never seen before and was at a loss to understand. And no wonder. The apparition appeared in white linen trousers, huarache sandals, a billowing flowered shirt, neatly styled grey hair and sunglasses, all crowned by an outrageous Panama hat and punctuated with a long cigar planted between his perfect, white teeth. On one of their early meetings, Neddy asked his name. The stranger replied, "You can call me Traveler. It's as good as anything else."

They always talked briefly at a distance about this, that and the other thing before Traveler walked on, but never without leaving behind a curious tidbit of wisdom or advice. It was always the same ... until last night. Last night, the meeting ended ... with a warning.

"I can't tell you more than this," Neddy recalled Traveler saying, his voice filled with uncharacteristic urgency. "He can't hurt you if you use the glass as a weapon. This isn't a joke, boy, so listen to me: *It's a weapon! The glass is a goddamned weapon!! Smash it in his face and run like hell!!!*"

As Neddy absently sipped his tea, trying to untangle Traveler's latest riddle, he failed to hear his father's approach.

"*BERNARD MCKENNA!!*" Edward's bark cut the morning air, startling the boy who knew his father only used his full Christian name when agitated. "Get on wit ya b'fore th' day's wasted. Now, tell me again, you'll be goin' where t'day?"

"To Squire Loughran's," the boy replied, locking on his father's eyes.

Edward's voice dropped to a whisper as he clamped the boy's upper arm. "An' what'll ya be doin'?"

"Askin' fer time on th' rent," he replied.

"Good. Grand," Edward said. "And what ...?"

The boy was silent.

"And *what* ...?"

"I'm to keep th' secret b'tween us men."

"Aye," said Edward. "*Our* secret."

As Edward loosened his grip, Barney Ned turned toward the cottage, handed the cup to his father, strode across the barnyard, grabbed the scythe, pulled on his cap and headed behind the barn. There, he began slashing at the seemingly endless tangle of ragwort, spear thistle and wild oat clogging the path that lay before him for a hundred feet toward the chicken coop. As he swung the scythe with increasing fury, Barney Ned fancied himself a Fenian freedom fighter mowing down the British army with every swipe of his blade. An avenging angel delivering retribution for those poor souls martyred in the Easter Rising.

After an hour of vengeance, the carcasses of thistle and weed lay in his wake as Barney Ned pulled on his sweater and headed back toward the house. He placed the scythe in the barn and yelled toward the cottage. "I'm away," he said.

Moira rushed to the door, stepping into the barnyard. "Neddy! Where ya off to in such a hurry wit'out a t'ing on yer stomach?"

"Man's work," he again parroted his father, grabbing the bicycle he called Packy, and heading toward Loughran's as Moira, resisting another call to breakfast, shook her head and went inside.

It had been two years since his younger brother Packy died from influenza along with 25,000 other Irish souls ... men, women and children ... leaving behind the bicycle he had been building for nearly a year. Actually, less a bicycle than a cobbled contraption consisting of a rusted handlebar, white front-wheel fork and a slightly battered rim missing a half dozen spokes. Several months before he died, Packy added a handlebar bell, although it didn't work.

Packy always admired his father's rickety, two-wheel banger and the posh ones parked outside the church on Sundays, but also knew he had scant chance of owning a bicycle himself. The one time he took Edward's bike for a jaunt down Kinnigillian Road, Packy was beaten so severely, the welts from his father's belt took nearly a week to disappear. So, combing roadsides and ditches, farms, pubs and nearby town sites, he scrounged through trash and thistle for parts to build a bicycle of his own.

When the boy died, Edward threw Packy's bicycle in the stream behind the chicken coop, sending Neddy in a panic from barnyard to rushing water, where he frantically dove in and pulled it out, collapsing on the bank breathless and sobbing. In his mind, this wasn't *just* Packy's bicycle, it *was* Packy, his dream, his soul, and from that point on, Neddy would be his guardian, the protector every big brother should be ... should have been ... even in the face of the virulent killer that had extinguished his brother's life.

In death, the two became inseparable as Neddy took Packy wherever he went in the Tyrone countryside, scraping and rolling as best it could on adventure after adventure that his little brother was unable to experience.

"Neddy, can I go?" came Bridget's delicate voice and the fawn-like footsteps of his young sister racing after him. "Can I?"

"No," her brother said, "Get on wit' ya."

"Please?"

"No, I says. Now, be off," he commanded. "There's no place fer a wee'un like you. I'm away t'do a man's job."

"But yer not a man, now, are ya?" Bridget smiled, eliciting a glower from her older brother, who tried his best to appear cross at this tiniest McKenna, a rusty-topped flurry of freckles and innocence who worshiped her brother so deeply, she believed anything he said, including gems Neddy fabricated out of whole cloth. Take, for instance, the time he shared with her the secrets of certain bodily functions.

"D'ya know where burps come from?" Neddy whispered to his rapt sister in the darkness of the cottage loft one winter's night, "Well, they're God's way of lettin' venial sins out yer body. An' mortal sins? Th' real bad uns? They shoot from yer bum as hot 'n' smelly air biscuits. They smell so bad an' burn ya fer sinnin' against Babby Jaysus."

The child hadn't yet embarked on the decades-long indoctrination by the Catholic Church, so she had scant understanding of sin, let alone their formal classifications. But if Neddy said it, the shared information was not only valuable but, in a word, gospel.

Presently, Neddy was looking down at Bridget standing in the middle of the farm lane as he repeated, "G'wan. Get ya home," and continued walking away.

Bridget stopped following Neddy, but before turning back to the barnyard and into the cottage, she watched her brother for a good long time until he passed the road bend and was gone.

"Well, Packy, this should be good craic," Neddy said, starting off again toward Loughran Manor five miles away, buoyed by being chosen by his father for the important and manly job of rent negotiations with Squire Loughran himself, although, at the time, he didn't realize why. But Edward knew. Edward was well aware of the rumors. The whispers that Loughran had a soft spot for children, especially young boys. So, Edward reasoned, Neddy's request for rent leniency would be difficult, if not impossible, for the squire to deny.

Far down the road, Neddy approached the Loughran property for a first look inside its walls and the sprawling 18th century Georgian manor house within.

The boy had read about such grand houses in books at the parish school, but never believed they actually existed. Yet, here it was, on a winding poplar-lined lane, behind ornate iron gates three times his size. The manor house spoke to him in the contemptuous language of wealth and privilege, representing everything unattainable to a culchie like him. The message was clear and wrapped in a lush mantle of stone and ivy.

He continued past the main entrance, along the towering white-washed outer walls, as his father had instructed, and to the narrow foot path that led to the stables where the estate manager's office would be found. He left Packy just inside the wall and headed toward the stable office.

"I'm here on important business," he announced to the manager, who peered at the boy across his desktop and over his wire-rimmed glasses. "I'm here to see Squire Loughran."

"Are you now?" the manager responded, slowly laying down his pen. "And what might that business be?"

"That's fer th' squire an' him alone."

"You're Edward McKenna's boy, are you not?" asked the

manager who recognized Neddy from Sunday Mass.

"Aye," Neddy replied.

"So why isn't your father here to discuss this important business?"

"He is otherwise enstaged," the boy struggled to quote his father precisely.

"You mean engaged? Otherwise engaged?"

"Aye ... that."

"Well, young mister, I'm afraid Squire Loughran ..."

"... Will be more than happy to talk with you," came a voice from the doorway behind Neddy.

Wheeling around, the boy confronted Loughran himself. Virtually filling the doorway, he was a walrus of a man standing nearly six and a half feet tall, although the final six inches were obscured by the top of the door frame. As he ducked into the room, Loughran's massive stomach preceded the rest of him by several seconds, swathed as it was in a gold brocade waistcoat tucked inside a velvet jacket with enough fabric to construct a passable tent. His white hair was thick and unruly, flowing over his collar in perfect collaboration with a white VanDyke beard that was as finely manicured as the manor's lush grounds. Neddy stared saucer-eyed at the squire, unaware that his mouth hung slightly agape as he drank in the sight of this outsized dandy.

"So, important business, eh?" Loughran repeated, his breath heavy with drink.

"Aye, sir," said the boy.

"And that business would be ...?"

"Rent," Neddy blurted, forgetting the speech his father had prepared for him.

Loughran said nothing and instead studied this shabby child in front of him. A farm boy with shit-caked shabby shoes, wearing a shabby sweater and a frayed shabby cap. And, most likely, about to make a shabby argument for not paying rent because his shabby father, who drank too much and worked too little, didn't have the intestinal fortitude to speak for himself. So he sent a boy to do a man's job.

"Rent?"

"Aye, sir. Rent," the boy straightened, assuming his best manly posture.

"Well then," Loughran began, again looking the boy up and down, "this must be taken to my office for a proper discussion and a proper libation ... between men."

Although Neddy didn't fully understand, especially the squire's reference to a *proper library,* when Loughran motioned toward the manor house, he followed. He followed up the flower-lined path from the stables, past the manor house's towering portico, through the massive front doors, across the marble entrance hall and into a cavernous room lined with floor-to-ceiling bookcases that he decided must contain all the books in the world. There were large ancestral paintings of long ago Loughrans in military regalia, powdered wigs and unsmiling, ruddy faces. A gleaming silver chandelier hung from the center of the ceiling above two hunt-club-leather sofas framing a fireplace that could easily house a cow or two.

Without speaking, Loughran went to a sturdy table of decanters beside a massive alder-wood desk decorated with gold embellishment and lavish scrollwork at the far end of the room. He selected a Waterford decanter, pulled the crystal stopper and poured the contents into two of the poshest glasses Barney Ned had ever seen. He handed one to the boy and sipped from the other.

"Rent," Loughran repeated. "What about the rent?"

"Well, our family has an embarrassment," said the boy, suddenly recalling some of his father's script, "so we kindly ask fer a consideration."

"Drink up, lad," Loughran said, motioning with his glass.

Neddy took a sip and winced at the fire on his tongue. "Poitin," he thought, instantly recognizing the legendary mountain dew, distilled from potatoes by the devil himself and consumed a few months back with his friend Brendan to the point of stupification. Stupification that left him brainless and almost mortally ill, wandering without reason or direction in a pasture he normally knew so well he could almost name the blades of grass there. Stupification so acute he would later recount how he threw up meals from years past and would have needed a rally of spirit just to die.

Pouring a second glass of poitin for himself, Loughran began undoing his waistcoat, removing it and his velvet jacket in one motion, slowly approaching the boy while grasping the carafe. "C'mon, boy. Drink up and we'll talk about the rent."

Loughran again drained his glass, poured another and slid the suspenders off his shoulders.

Confused by the squire's impromptu disrobing, the boy stammered, "We ask fer a consideration ..."

"And a consideration you shall have *if* you give *me* one," Loughran replied, as he started undoing his trousers. He drained the third glass, placed it on the desk and grabbed

Barney Ned's arm in a single fluid motion.

The boy recoiled, struggling against the large, beefy hand. "Hey! Let go a me!!"

When the squire held fast, trying to drag the boy closer, Neddy, finally grasping Traveler's frantic warning, swung the glass in his free hand and smashed it into Loughran's face sending crystal shards and poitin flying toward the landlord's eyes. Screaming, Loughran reeled against the desk, then to the floor clutching his face. "You've blinded me!"

But Barney Ned was already through the library door, out of earshot and barely noticing the manager standing there. He tore down the path to the wall, where he retrieved Packy and ran without stopping all the way home.

By the time, the boy reached the barnyard, he was sweat-soaked and staggering with Packy in tow. Not knowing what to do, he scrambled through the barn's rear window hoping no one would find him in the dark. He collapsed in the wheelbarrow and waited. When the cottage lamps were dimmed and he thought everyone was asleep, Neddy crept into the cottage to find Moira unexpectedly doing end-of-day chores before going to bed.

"Neddy," she said, scowling and obviously flustered by his long absence. "Where in God's name hav'ya been?"

Having already started climbing the loft ladder, he turned slightly. "A long day, Ma," he said. "I'm knackered. Can I tell ya in the mornin'?"

"Aye," she said with a scowl, "but I'm not the least bit pleased."

Crawling into bed, he heard Bridget stir next to him.

"Neddy?" Bridget whispered. "Ya smell."

"Aye," her brother responded and fell into a fractured, uneasy sleep.

2

Betrayal

When Barney Ned opened his eyes in the half light of dawn, he lingered beneath the bed clothes for a few extra minutes, going over yesterday, trying to untangle exactly what had happened. Spotlit in a thin shaft of light from the rising sun, a spider frantically plucked its web as if playing a silken harp in the low-hanging thatch as Neddy listened to the small chorus of breathing from his six sisters still asleep in the bedding next to him. One let out a tiny snarl as she rolled over in half sleep and fell silent again.

"I'm arseways on this," he thought, "and I've kilt th' landlord to boot."

Below, he heard the clatter of dishes and could smell cigarette smoke. His father was up and had to be told of yesterday's failed excursion. Taking a deep breath for courage, he threw off the covers, pulled on his trousers and shirt, grabbed his shoes and descended the ladder barefoot.

"So, boyo," Edward began, hearing his son on the ladder, but not looking up, "ya had a late night, did ya? Well, did ya take care of th' man's work? Do we have a pause in th' payment or not?"

At that moment, Moira entered the cottage and caught the tail end of Edward's question. He fell silent when he saw his wife, focusing on his tea and bread, then taking a drag on his cigarette.

"What payment?" she said, walking toward the cooker, her apron doubling as a sling bulging with eggs and a few bricks of turf.

Edward mumbled. "Don't worry yer head."

"And where were ya 'til all hours?" Moira asked Neddy, depositing the eggs on a weathered wood bench near the cooker. "Ya had me quite bothered." She turned her attention momentarily to the small fireplace in the far wall of the room. From decades of turf fires, the white-washed wall ascending from the firebox to the rafters was sooted black. Ashes spilled onto the cracked tile hearth and hard-packed dirt floor beyond. On her knees, she carefully arranged a small stack of turf atop a crumple of newspaper and lit the fire.

Again, Moira asked, "What payment?"

"Rent payment," said Neddy, his throat dry as chaff as he broke the compact with his father, incapable of lying to his mother.

"Shut yer gob!!" yelled Edward, slamming a fist on the table.

Barney Ned swallowed hard, finally answering his father, "Not."

"What payment?" Moira slowly stood. "What are ya on about?"

"Whaddya mean, not?" Edward turned in his chair. "Did ya not do what I told ya? *Exactly* as I told ya to say to th' squire?" Now, Edward was standing, taking a step toward the boy.

"Th' squire?" Moira frowned. What ...?"

"Da, I tried ... "

But his father's powerful fist glanced off the side of the boy's head and he stumbled back against the ladder. Moira screamed in protest from the fireplace, grabbed a turf brick and flung it square in her husband's face, knocking him back into the chair.

"There's more where that came from if ya hit Neddy again," Moira warned, another brick already loaded in her left hand. "Now ... *What's this about?!*"

"'Tis yer fault," Edward yelled at the boy. "Yer fault if we lose th' farm. Ya bollixed it all. I give ya one simple ..."

"But, Da, I tried, I did ... and I kilt th' landlord."

The cottage fell silent. The father. The son. The holy terror of a mother and the McKenna girls looking down from the loft.

"Ya did what?" Edward asked in a half whisper.

"Kilt th' landlord," the boy repeated, too frightened and ashamed to recount the more sordid details of the previous afternoon and his flight from the manor.

"Jaysus, Mary and Joseph," Moira rasped through the fingers covering her mouth while blessing herself with the other hand, as she started connecting the dots, suddenly fixing a furious gaze on Edward. "What have ya done, ya old eejit?!!" screamed Moira, suddenly realizing what Neddy meant by "man's work" yesterday morning. "What have ya done, ya filthy scunner!! Are ya daft?"

"I'd no choice," Edward almost whined an admission. "We canno pay th' rent an' th' squire would've t'rown me out fer askin', and where would we be then?"

As his mother's incendiary tirade fully engulfed his father, Neddy stood mum in the crossfire, trying to unpack his father's cryptic response, but answers wouldn't come until the next day.

For Moira, however, everything was quite clear. This seemed to be yet another unbearable cruelty of a truly desperate few years that had taken the life of their youngest son Packy as the influenza savaged the island, Britain and the whole of Europe. Then, with the comings and goings of rebels and soldiers in Tyrone, daily life itself had become an uncertainty. Just last month, a squad of Black and Tans raided Malachy Ryan's farm down the road, grabbing up the poor man and some of his livestock, shipping him off to God knows where as a suspected Fenian. They still didn't know what became of him. But in the moment, it paled when compared to a father sending his son into the lair of a known bugger of boys to avoid paying rent, a deplorable conspiracy ending in murder.

But Loughran wasn't dead, although his family may have wished him to be.

The manager had stood in the manor house entrance hall watching as Barney Ned fled through the front door, across the garden and out of sight. He coldly turned back toward the library and surveyed the room, as Loughran screamed, blood streaming from his face, shattered glass and poitin sprayed across the floor.

"I'm blinded! I'm blinded! That little bastard!"

By now, Loughran's nephew had joined the manager and the two spoke briefly before moving deliberately toward the squire whose trousers were more off than on as he lay on the floor next to his discarded waistcoat and jacket. Pulling Loughran's trembling hands back from his bloody face, the nephew examined the gash on his uncle's cheek and pulled a shard of glass from an eyebrow. His eyes were bloodshot, but not bloody and the squire recognized him immediately.

"You're not blind, uncle," the nephew said flatly, "but you are in a world of trouble."

It had happened again. Just like the other times. The other boys. The other families silenced and, now, another one was about to be.

Although Loughran was heir to a sprawling ancestral estate, now greatly diminished from its original 8,000 acres but still large enough to support scores of families working meager stakes and paying rent, he was far removed from the daily operations of crops, cattle and mining. In fact, he did little more than drink and peacock through local villages, making his presence known as the foppish face of the Loughran clan, much to the family's chagrin. It was the nephew and manager who primed and polished the lucrative business functions, day in, year out. And it was the nephew who always cleaned up Loughran's indiscretions and contained the damage.

At about one o'clock the next day, Loughran's crimson Rolls Royce Silver Ghost limousine rolled to a stop on the farm lane outside the McKenna cottage. The family fell silent as Moira carefully pulled back the curtain from the tiny front window for a glimpse. When the squire's nephew strode across the barnyard and knocked on the door, there were collective palpitations inside.

Greeted by a nervously smiling farm wife – her husband nowhere in sight – the nephew was surprised by the relative calm in the wake of yesterday's violence. There seemed to be no outrage. No signs of disturbance at all. Almost immediately, he entertained the possibility the boy may not have told his parents about the squire's attempted assault. Encouraged, he took a chance.

"I'm here to see master McKenna to discuss important business," the nephew announced to Moira who was mortified by her son's impending arrest as two small children hugged her legs in the doorway.

Before she could respond, Neddy emerged silently and was face to face with the nephew, ready to be taken away for the murder trial that most certainly would come.

"I wish a word with you in private," said the nephew who ushered the boy toward the gleaming Rolls. Just outside the barnyard gate, they stopped and began what appeared to be an earnest discussion, although the family could not hear what was being said. Edward insinuated himself between Moira and the open window, straining to hear, but turned away with no more insight than before.

"I dunno see a constable," he said hopefully to Moira, lighting a cigarette and sitting down at the table. "And I don't t'ink th' boy can be arrested wit'out one."

Back at the window, Moira saw Neddy and the nephew appear to conclude their business with, incredibly, a handshake. The nephew slid into the back seat and motioned for the driver to leave. At the last moment, the nephew called after Neddy who was already halfway across the barnyard.

"Remember, boy," the nephew said, "not a word."

Neddy gave a slight wave of acknowledgment and entered the cottage.

Edward, Moira, Bridget, Colleen, Nuala, Rose, Eileen and

Sissy were stone quiet even minutes after Neddy was inside, but watching his every movement. The boy walked to the cooker, grabbed the tea kettle and poured himself a cup.

"Th' rent's done," he said staring down at the flowered cup while stirring in three teaspoons of sugar. "'Tis done fer good."

"What d'ya mean, done fer good?" Moira broke the family's silence. "What were ya on about wit' young Loughran and what has it t'do wit' rent?"

Neddy had already absorbed the fact that the nephew's offer, curiously, was made *to him* ... not his father. How, in a strange and convoluted way, he *had* accomplished the "man's work" his father had wrapped in a conspiracy hidden from the boy's mother. But what his young mind couldn't grasp was his father's need for secrecy and the positive impact yesterday's near tragedy with the squire would have on the family, on his sisters and mother for decades to come. Equally elusive was an answer to his mother's question about the rent deal and its genesis. So, he simply replied, "'Tis not fer me t'say." A moment later, allowing, "But th' squire's nephew an' me-self agreed on ... *a consideration* ... and because of it, we don't owe rent fer th' rest of our lives."

"But why would he do that?" Moira asked, slowly answering the question in her mind "... unless ... did th' squire hurt ya ...?"

"Did he what?" Neddy's eyes narrowed, confused that his mother could possibly know what happened at the manor house.

"Did he try ... as neighbors say ... before ya ... kilt him?"

"I didn't kill nobody," Neddy pushed back, "... and what

do th' neighbors say?"

"Not a t'ing," Edward lied. "Ya didn't kill him?"

"I did not," Neddy repeated. "What do neighbors say?"

Moira whispered, barely able to articulate what most parish adults knew, choosing her words carefully. "He's an eye fer hurtin' boys," she said.

His mother's reference was lost on the 14-year-old, whose carnal knowledge was limited mostly to what every farm child witnesses with livestock, and from the bizarre inaccuracies shared among virginal pubescent boys. This was beyond his scope of knowledge, but as he linked what his mother said to the blur of events from the past day, the pieces began forming a horrifying picture of betrayal by his father.

"Ya didn't kill th' squire?" a relieved Edward asked. "T'ank God."

Turning to his mother, who had been kept from Edward's dark plot, and then to his father who hatched it, Neddy asked, almost pleading, "Da ... ya sent me there knowin' he hurts ... boys like me??"

"But nothin' happened, did it?" Edward said offhandedly with a shrug.

Neddy stood still, the room buzzing, his thoughts jangling as he replayed his father's pact with this new, disturbing perspective. He silently turned to the table and cut a slice of bread, carefully placing the knife on the oil-cloth. "Not a word," he repeated, stepping outside as the sun poked through the clouds for a moment, disappeared then emerged again, casting a lacy shadow on the barnyard and cottage.

3

The Secret

In the coming weeks, the incident faded from all conversations, taking its place as just another wound shared by Moira and Edward. But this time, Neddy was wounded as well. And like the scores of wounds suffered during their years together, this one didn't prevent the responsibilities of farm life returning largely to Moira. After years of a marriage that had traveled from promise to disappointment to resignation, she knew not to rely on Edward beyond the most trivial expectations as he busied himself with his *man's work* in and out of the village pub. She also knew not to ask too keenly about that work because she feared it had to do with the uprising.

For Moira, it was more important and increasingly difficult to keep the farm running and putting food on the table for her seven children. Even with their help, she still was left to grind the meal, sharpen tools, cook, clean and generally maintain the household. For the most part, she mended and washed the clothes, supervised the children's chores, dried their tears, mediated their squabbles and ensured they attended school and church.

Moira knew all there was to know about farming from roof thatch to water-pump repair to harvesting and where to borrow a horse and plow during the planting season. But for all that knowledge, there was one thing she didn't know that could hurt her and her family the most. Her husband and father of her children, as she suspected, had put the family farm, her family's very existence, at the epicenter of the rebellion against the British Empire.

Here in a bucolic stretch of Northern Ireland, miles from Belfast and light years from Dublin, amid rolling countryside and flax fields, wind-lashed loughs and dense forests, surf-pounded shorelines and vast bogland, Edward McKenna concealed a nationalist rigor as explosive as his temper, a smoldering hatred of British cruelty, subjugation and neglect handed down from father to son going back generations to before the Irish Republican Brotherhood.

4

Contraband

As its engine fell silent, the truck rolled to a stop about 50 yards north of the McKenna barnyard on Kinnigillian Road. A gale whipped through the trees as three dark figures emerged silently and met with another carrying a kerosene lamp near the chicken coop. They spoke briefly and disappeared behind the structure. Moments later, they re-emerged and began unloading cargo from the truck bed. They worked for close to an hour, handed a few shillings to the man with the lantern and left.

Several days later, the process repeated, only in reverse. Once the truck was loaded, money was exchanged and the three men drove away. This nocturnal back and forth continued on and off for months before hitting a pause just before Christmas.

One night, Moira could hold her tongue no longer.

As Edward wheeled his bicycle into the barnyard and leaned it against the cottage wall, he retrieved the lantern from the basket on the handlebars, extinguished the flame and returned it to a spot on the floor next to the door. He took off his jacket and stubbed out his cigarette before crawling into bed.

"Wher've ya been?" Moira asked, always repulsed by the late night stench of lager mixed with tobacco.

"Out is all," he replied.

"Doin' what?" she pressed.

"Lookin' after th' chickens," he said., "Savin' 'em from foxes and gypsies."

"Rubbish," she shot back. "Do foxes drive lorries?"

"Don't be daft, woman," Edward said, rolling away from her and pulling the bed clothes tight around his shoulder. "Don't be daft."

"Yer dancin' wit' the devil y'are, Edward McKenna," she said rolling in the opposite direction. "What am I t'do when they take ya away in chains or worse. You'll be leavin' me t'do it all on me own."

"Ya won't be alone," Edward yawned. "Ya have th' boy."

5

Bearing Fruit

As the barren months of winter slogged on, there wasn't much to expect from this rocky, boggy excuse for farmland. Even occasionally sending the children to work on larger farms for day wages did little to help the family's dire financial situation. At best, their patch of Ireland provided subsistence farming. At worst, it was unsustainable for a family of nine. Moira knew it. Neddy knew it. Edward knew it but didn't seem to care. Even what little money he picked up on the side from his late-night adventures with contraband didn't ease the family's plight as it mostly went for drink and gambling. Some found its way to the children for shoes or shirts, but not much and not often.

This time of year, Neddy, now 15 and seeming to grow by the day, was at school where he excelled at numbers and geography. But by the time he arrived in class, the boy already had worked three hours around the farm. Several more hours awaited him after school. Such was his life, so that at the end of the day, Neddy fell into bed, sometimes without undressing and was asleep before anyone else in the cottage.

However, on this night, he seemed to drift in and out of sleep uneasily. Dropping into the depths then snapping fully awake. But sleep finally came … and the first real dream in weeks.

This time, Neddy was in the barnyard, Packy leaning up against a wall, when he heard footsteps on the gravel farm lane. Looking up, he saw Traveler not 10 feet away with cigar smoke swirling about his head. He planted his hands squarely on the barnyard's low stone wall, leaned in and warned, "They're coming for the guns. You have to get rid of the guns …"

"What guns?" Neddy asked. "I don't know of no guns."

"Your father knows about them. So do the British," Traveler said, "and they're coming. Hurry, for God's sake! Head for the chicken coop and get rid of the guns in the root cellar, but don't cover your tracks …"

Suddenly, Neddy was awake and the night was still except for a chorus of crickets and an intermittent east wind tousling oak branches against the cottage walls. Traveler's warning didn't make sense. "Get rid of the guns in the root cellar but don't cover your tracks …" What does that mean? he thought. The root cellar? What root cellar?

The embers in the turf fire were still aglow, so he figured it couldn't be later than maybe midnight or a little after. While there remained enough brightness in the Irish twilight, Neddy knew it would be full dark in an hour or so, maybe as late as 2 a.m.

He eased down the ladder, snatched the matchbox by the cooker and retrieved the lantern by the door. Stepping outside, he rounded the barn and headed down the path toward the chicken coop. Heavily shaded in the half light, he lit the lantern, held it high to get a better look at the coop and walked around its perimeter. Seeing nothing, he got down on his hands and knees, looking beneath the coop, as it was raised off the ground about 18 inches. Still nothing. He walked to the far side toward the barbed-wire fence at the rear of the property.

There, the lamplight illuminated a disturbance in the underbrush, as if it had been pushed aside then pulled back into place. Beneath the spread of thistle, he saw the corner of what appeared to be a wood plank. Several feet to the left was another corner of what now most certainly was a sheet of plywood. He found the full edge and yanked on it causing the plywood to give way enough to open a small gap in the ground cover. Moving the lantern closer, he could see there was a deep depression in the ground. Stranger still, there was a fresh rope handle and new hinges attached to the plywood.

Setting down the lantern, he used both hands and all his strength to pull up the plywood and let it flop on the ground, opening up what he had always been told was a dangerous dry well that now had a set of fresh wooden steps. Descending into the darkness slowly illuminated by the lantern, he saw fresh support beams on the ceiling and walls and what appeared to be ... a rifle barrel. Then a box of pistols. Then more rifles. A half dozen crates in all. Nearly 40 guns and several dozen boxes of ammunition forming a small arsenal.

His heart sank as he thought back to when he play-acted Fenian rebel with the scythe and weeds on the chicken coop path, unaware how close he was to the real rebellion and the real killing.

But what to do? Traveler's message was clear. The Brits knew of the guns and were coming for them. "Holy mother of God!" Neddy realized. They would also be coming for his father. For the girls. For the family.

If they found the guns, they would burn the farm and jail his father ... or worse. Unless, Neddy did something with the guns first.

Dig another hole somewhere? Burn them? Scatter them in the bog in the south pasture? None of it would do. The guns still could be found unless they were gone. Gone completely from the farm. Unless they were *moved*. Almost instantly, Malachy Ryan's farm up the road came into focus. The widower Ryan was in the lock-up already, snagged by the British for being a suspected republican. They took him away along with a few of his pigs, but in what condition did they leave the house?

Neddy grabbed the lantern and headed to Ryan's farm. Much larger than the McKenna cottage, Ryan's house had a slate roof and a second floor, as well as a full cellar actually *under* the house. Unexpectedly, the front door was ajar, allowing Neddy to walk right in. He went to the kitchen, where his eyes fell on a crucifix and a framed lithograph of Jesus hanging on the wall opposite the kitchen table. He paused momentarily to consider the sin he was about to commit, then scanned the shelves for preserves of fruit or vegetables and found two, both opened and filled with mold.

He quickly found his way to the cellar stairs easing his way down, guiding himself by the moonlight streaming through a cellar window where coal was regularly emptied during winter months into a large wooden bin by the furnace. And then ... there it was. An entire wall of preserved fruits and vegetables, jellies and smoked fish, sausage and dried beef. Jars by the score, neatly assembled on wood shelves attached to the wall.

"T'ank, God," he sighed, taking a moment to bless himself. "Lord, forgive me," he whispered.

Moments later he was back down the road and into the barn, where he tossed aside a tangle of tools, dug out the wheelbarrow, was down the path to the chicken coop, then to the dry well that was now a root cellar.

He grabbed a crate of pistols, which was heavier than he expected and struggled, half pushing, half carrying the box up the steps until he was outside. He loaded the wheelbarrow with pistols and several boxes of ammunition to begin the tedious transfer of weapons to Ryan's house, replacing them in the root cellar with jars of preserves and dried meat. Back and forth he went for hours. Sometimes just three or four rifles at a time. Guns for strawberry jelly, bullets for a fine looking ham until shortly after 3:30, as he made his last run to Ryan's and was halfway across the barnyard when ...

"Neddy?"

Startled, he spun around to see his mother's dark silhouette in the doorway and almost dumped the last load of firearms. A pistol slid silently off the wheelbarrow into the dirt undetected.

"What's all this?" she said, slowly making her way toward her son and putting a hand to her mouth as she realized the nature of his cargo.

"Let me explain," Neddy began. And he did just that, in great detail ... but not all details.

"But how d'ya know they're comin' fer th' guns?"

"Don't worry about that," he said, "I just know."

Without another word, Neddy completed his final run and began returning the brush to the plywood, when he stopped. "Don't cover your tracks," he thought. "Don't hide th' cellar? If this was a root cellar, why would someone hide it? That has to be what Traveler meant." Securing the plywood over the opening, Neddy brushed away the makeshift camouflage, leaving the lid in plain sight. He returned to the cottage and quietly scaled the loft ladder, easing onto his straw-filled pillow without waking the girls. Moira had returned to bed, as Edward began to stir.

"Why are ya about so early?" Edward said through the pillow covering his face.

"Just to pee," Moira replied, crawling back under the covers.

For once, she was the one with a secret because Edward was no wiser for the grand operation that had taken place. No wiser that his clandestine role in the uprising has been transferred to a neighbor's cellar.

Moira was beyond sleep and remained awake for more than an hour, her anxiety at full throttle, until her ears were filled with rumbling engines and growling men's voices followed by heavy boots on the ground and the cottage door being smashed from its hinges. The entire family was jolted awake with a blur of uniforms, helmets and weapons rushing into the cottage.

In that first chaotic moment, Moira shook Edward awake. "Don't mention guns to th' Brits!"

"Wha ..." Edward snorted, snapping awake.

"Dammit, man!" rasped Moira who never cursed. "Don't mention th' GUNS!" At which point the uniforms were at their bed, pointing weapons in their faces.

"DON'T SHOOT!" the couple begged in a desperate duet, arms thrust toward heaven, all the time hoping they wouldn't be visiting there soon. Neddy cautiously eased down from the loft, catching the attention of a soldier, who swung around, bringing his rifle to bear on the young teen, then lowering the muzzle, seeing no threat.

"Edward McKenna?" the obvious group leader barked.

"Aye," Edward almost shrieked.

"Where are the guns? NOW!"

Quickly heeding Moira's last-minute admonition, Edward shouted back, "What guns? Ya want me shotgun?"

"No the guns ... THE I.R.A. GUNS!!"

"I.R.A.??!! Saints preserve us, *NO*!! What would a loyal subject of our dear king be havin' wit' th' I.R.A.??" Edward pleaded, mustering his best outrage as Moira focused on the ground.

A hand the size of an Easter ham reached down and grabbed Edward's nightshirt, practically ripping it from his shoulder, drag-walking him to the barnyard where he first saw the three army vehicles and nearly a dozen heavily armed soldiers.

"Where is the root cellar?" came the next demand.

Edward instantly thought, "I'm a dead man."

Still gripped by the long arm of English law, he led the squad behind the barn, down the chicken-coop path to what appeared to be a plywood door in the ground. Edward was stunned at the brazenly visible gateway in the dirt, obvious as a prostitute in a convent. Edward, shaking almost uncontrollably, began praying.

Two soldiers were on the plywood and pulling the rope handle, tearing open the root cellar and dropping to the subterranean dirt floor without benefit of the wooden steps. There was the sound of rustling, of broken glass, then silence.

"Toss down a torch," came a voice from below, and a flashlight was passed through the opening. More silence, followed by the sound of boots on the steps. A helmeted head slowly emerged and a shrug. "Nothing, sir."

"What do you mean, nothing?"

"Well, there are jars of fruit, vegetables and dried meat, but no guns."

Edward couldn't believe it, but worked to conceal his

complete surprise.

"Where are the guns, McKenna?"

"And again, I'm tellin' ya there's ... no ... guns."

By now, the girls were in the barnyard, still in their night clothes and encircling their mother like a small clutch of white votive candles at the feet the Blessed Virgin statue in church. Their faces dimly illuminated by lamp light, seemed to flicker in the night breeze. Neddy stood just outside the cottage door, still fully clothed but barefoot.

"Search the house and the barn," shouted the leader, dispatching a half dozen soldiers who took little care as they rifled for weapons. Glasses and plates, pots, pans and furniture rattled and crashed. The ancient barn door collapsed from its hinges and the frantic farm cats snarled and hissed as they scattered into the night. For 20 minutes, the chaos continued until the unit reformed around their leader to report ... nothing found.

Their leader continued looking about, momentarily settling here and there on other potential hiding places, and as he did so, Neddy's eyes fell on the errant pistol that had fallen off the wheelbarrow. His body stiffened as a nauseating chill swept over him.

"Sweet mother of God," he thought, mind swirling with an unexpected, possibly horrific, ending to this search. How could he have missed it? The pistol was 15 feet behind the leader, just inside the gate on the edge of a weed patch and half buried in dirt, but still recognizable in the half light.

Neddy edged slowly toward the girls until he was standing next to Rose. He leaned in and whispered, "I need ya to start cryin' and run to th' wall just left of th' gate."

"Cryin'? Fer what?" Rose whispered back, not unlocking her gaze from the soldiers and her father.

"Don't matter why," Neddy whispered more urgently, "just do it. Run."

Rose was momentarily still, then began to wail, startling everyone including the soldiers. She shook and sobbed and ran toward the gate with Neddy in close pursuit.

"Now, look what ya done," Neddy scolded the soldiers, as he bolted past them, catching his sister just inside the gate, a foot from the pistol. He grabbed and hugged Rose, guiding her toward the ground as he whispered, "Sit ya down. Now!" Slowly, brother and sister collapsed to the weed patch as Neddy came to rest atop the pistol. Rose, still blind to the need for these dramatics, but fully committed to her role, buried her face on Neddy's shoulder, continuing to whimper as her brother wiped away her imaginary tears.

Watching the impromptu performance play out, the unit's leader refocused on the search and his confusion how a usually rock-solid informant had been so terribly wrong. The group stood there for several long, empty moments, looking at each other for answers that wouldn't come. Most wore military uniforms, weapons still at the ready. A young girl sobbed in her brother's arms on the ground. A Madonna-like farm wife stood encircled by tiny acolytes. And one scared Irishman in a rumpled nightshirt, counted his blessings that he didn't soil himself in the commotion.

Not much was said from that point on, as the soldiers put up their weapons and climbed back into their vehicles ... unexpectedly empty-handed. The engines roared again, but without the drama of their arrival. As they pulled out of the barnyard, Edward rearranged the nightshirt on his shoulder and began waving, "God save th' King! God Save th' King! Rule Britannia!" Then under his breath, "... ya pieces of shite."

Edward was more than a little flummoxed while simultaneously elated at the serendipity of the situation as he watched the army unit disappear down the road.

Still shaken but quiet, the girls retired to the cottage and climbed to the loft with the soft urging of their mother, who turned to survey the damage left in the wake of the British assault. Smashed dishes and pottery, scattered utensils, an overturned kitchen table, a crippled chair, pots thrown, clumps of clothes like discarded souls on the floor. Quietly, she set about reestablishing order to the room.

Meanwhile, Neddy walked to the barn and seeing the destruction there decided to address the clutter and repairs in the morning. Instead, he headed for the stream behind the chicken coop and chucked the pistol into the racing current before returning to the cottage, where Edward sat at the table, oblivious to the mess, and rolled a cigarette. "Jaysus," he said, lighting it, "What th' fuck was that?"

Neddy didn't know where to begin with his father, who was wildly superstitious and heavily invested in banshees, leprechauns and folklore legends. That included Finn McCool, the Gaelic behemoth who Edward swore built The Giants Causeway with his bare hands, planting thousands of basalt pillars hundreds of feet high along Ulster's Wild Atlantic Way. Maybe Da might accept that his son moved the guns – replacing them with fruit and vegetable jars – saving the family after a mysterious Traveler warned of the weapons-store raid in a dream. That could work, couldn't it?

"Ya want me believin' *what?*" Edward squinted at Neddy, sitting across from him at the table. "A gypsy tells ya ..."

"No, Traveler ..." Neddy corrected him.

"Right, right. A traveler, then. A traveler walking on th' farm lane ..."

"Not *a* traveler," Neddy said. "He wanted to be called Traveler. Just Traveler."

" ... Traveler all dressed in white ..."

" ... and th' shirt wit' flowers," Neddy added.

"... and flowered shirt and a gypsy called Traveler, walkin' on our farm lane, tells ya not only that there are guns ... in a root cellar that was supposed to be a secret ... but th' bloody English are comin' fer 'em?"

"He also said I had to get rid of th' guns."

"Aye ... and ya had t'get rid of 'em."

"Aye," Neddy nodded with a satisfied smile.

"And just where did th' guns go?" Edward cocked his head slightly (sarcastically, if that's possible) as he waited for the reply.

"Ryan's cellar."

"Ryan's cellar?"

"Aye, in place of his jars of preserves that are now in th' dry ... um ... root cellar."

Washing a hand across his face, Edward shook his head, exasperated. "When th' I.R.A. come fer th' guns an' find fruit what am I to tell them? They were moved because of what a ghost ... no ... a *gypsy* named Traveler told me son in a dream? I know their mind. They've no sense of humor and they'll murder me where I stand."

Moira's eyes widened. "Not if ya tell 'em first that ya

saved th' guns by hidin' 'em from th' English."

A moment later, a grin came slowly to Edward. "That just might work," he said. "That *could* work, it could. They'll be collectin' th' guns next week, so I'll tell 'em ..."

"No ... no ... *NO!*" Moira protested. "Today! Ya havta tell 'em *today*! Th' raid happened t'day so ya must tell 'em t'day an' appear dithered *t'day*! Why would ya wait a week to tell th' I.R.A. our farm was raided???"

Edward got dressed, jumped on his bicycle and headed for The Speckled Hen, the village pub owned by Seamus McGrahan and his cousin Johnny. They inherited the establishment when old man McGrahan – *God rest his soul* -- died on the short end of a wager involving consumption of prodigious, and fatal, amounts of Jameson's and stout. Although full details are sketchy, the circumstances also involved a peat bog, a riding crop, a rake handle and a mule, something Seamus and Johnny refused to discuss.

As pub proprietors, the McGrahans were exposed to people of all rural persuasions, some with specific skills especially in demand during these troubled times. It was rumored that some of that ilk actually frequented The Hen, but no one ever admitted it. Edward, however, knew precisely where to go when he entered the pub and quickly exited by a rear door. He walked to an adjoining garage that smelled of kerosene, slurry and stout to find Johnny seated at his desk, a greasy half-sheet of plywood atop four saw horses. Edward grabbed a piece of paper and pencil there then scrawled a quick note: *Terrible scuffle at the meet up. Cupboard is bare.* Without a word, he pushed the note toward Johnny.

Johnny read it, frowned and wrote, "*Wexley at 2.*"

As Johnny ran inside the pub to make a phone call. Edward was back on his bicycle headed for Wexley Cross Road, a heavily shaded narrow lane about eight miles away. He arrived shortly after 2 p.m. No one was there and 20 minutes passed without a contact. Finally, a horse-drawn cart clopped toward him, wandering side to side, carving lazy arcs in the dirt before stopping.

"Mother Hubbard," the driver offered the counter code to "cupboard is bare."

Under normal circumstances, the bare cupboard code confirmed the successful transfer of munitions from the McKenna farm to I.R.A. intermediaries. That's why the driver seemed confused.

"There's not been a pick up, so how can th' cupboard be bare?" the driver quizzed Edward, as the restless horse strained against its bit, jostling the cart back and forth about a foot.

Looking nervously north and south on the road, Edward placed his hand on the horse's muzzle and, gently stroking it, said, "Th' Brits raided th' farm this mornin'."

"Jaysus Christ! How th' fuck ...?"

"Dunno," Edward said, raising a hand to comfort the driver, "and they knew about th' root cellar ... "

"Christ, fuck and a milk cow!!" yelled the driver so forcefully that his cap fell off.

"... but th' guns are safe." The driver fell silent, waited a beat, grabbed his hat off the seat and not quite grasping the story, asked, "They raided th' root cellar, yet the guns are safe?"

"Aye," Edward smiled. "All they found were jars of preserves and dried meat."

Edward proceeded to lay out, in precise detail, the

comings and goings earlier in the day. How *he* had learned from a mysterious source – whom he was not at liberty to identify -- of the impending raid and how *he* had devised the clever swap of guns for gooseberry jam between the root cellar and the interned Ryan's place. How *he* kept his head and called the English soldiers "pieces of shite" to their faces, ordering them off his farm. How *he* was the hero of this nasty, but successful, chapter of the rebellion.

He retold the story late that night when the black truck rolled past the barnyard and the three men went to the root cellar under the light of Edward's lantern. When they inspected the jars and grabbed a ham for themselves. When they went to Ryan's cellar for their final gun run to retrieve the weaponry, unsure whether or not the Brits or Ryan would return or whether Edward could be trusted ever again.

In fact, for decades, Edward would recount the heroic tale to his weary brother, a fellow Fenian, long after the trucks stopped coming to the farm, long after his children were grown and the rebellion won. In fact, Edward wanted his legend to carry well beyond his demise with a headstone epitaph that stated boldly, *Hero of the Irish War of Independence (1919-21).* However, after Edward died, Moira had other ideas, editing it to read: *Was drunk during the Irish War of Independence (1919-21).*

6

Night Visitor

About a week after the great pistols-for-produce kerfuffle, Traveler gazed skyward for the longest moment in

Neddy's dream. Pushing back the brim of his Panama hat, he scanned the path meandering toward the stream behind the chicken coop, then the upper field toward the Cowley farm. He looked down the lane in one direction, then the other, almost as if memorizing the landscape, tree by tree. The birches, the elms and hawthorns, junipers and oaks and scotch pines. He glanced down at his white linen trousers and flicked a thistle from the right leg. Nearby, sheep bleated randomly as sheep are prone to do. He straightened his red Hawaiian shirt with several swipes of a hand, brushed a fly from a yellow hyacinth printed there and lit his cigar. A skylark raced by on a wind gust that would carry it effortlessly to its home meadow.

Taking a drag and letting the smoke slowly spill from his mouth, Traveler contemplated the cigar in one hand, adjusted his sunglasses with the other and finally spoke to Neddy.

"You know, I've always loved the idea of this place. Especially in the morning," he said. "Nothing like it on earth."

"How did ya know about th' guns?" Neddy asked. "How did ya know about th' raid? About Squire Loughran? About everything before."

"Quite the mystery, isn't it?" Traveler smiled, again looking skyward, this time following a hawk. "No doubt about it. Absolutely love this place."

"How do ya know these t'ings?" Neddy persisted. "I've lived here all me life and I don't know none of it."

"Your lack of knowledge, lad, is because of your age and provincialism ..."

"Me what?"

"Lack of experience and travel, the failure to look

beyond your nose," Traveler teased. "But that will change when you travel to other places. Far away places."

"Like Belfast?"

Traveler laughed gently. "Maybe. Maybe farther than that."

Neddy studied Traveler, trying to figure out where he was from. To listen for a hint in his accent. It certainly wasn't a brogue, but at the same time, it was. Yet different. His manner certainly wasn't Irish. And his clothes? Quite odd and *definitely* not Irish or English or anything else he knew.

"Tell me," Neddy became more strident. "How did ya ...?"

But Traveler was gone as Neddy was jostled awake by his mother.

"Neddy, come quick," she shouted, "Flora's calvin'."

Calving was quite the event on poor farms like the McKennas' and meant more of everything. If it was a heifer, more milk, cheese, cream and the income from selling them to Cookstown milk agents who represented Belfast dairy processors, not to mention the possibility of more calves each year. If it was a bull calf, it could be castrated and raised for beef or if kept intact to eliminate the need to find a bull for mating, although feeding a bull for just six pregnant dairy cows a year might not make economic sense. Either way, each calving could inch a farm and the family that worked it closer to self-reliance.

At this farm, however, nothing seemed to move the needle. While Moira was the engine that kept the farm going, Edward fancied himself more a gentleman farmer – what the locals called *fur coat and no knickers* – content with an image but without the hard work to earn it. That was evident several years ago when Moira fell ill with bronchitis and was laid low for nearly a month. It didn't take long for the situation to go off the rails on all fronts from paying bills to corralling children for chores, culminating in the death of Maisie, the family's most productive dairy cow that died of mastitis because she hadn't been milked for more than two weeks.

"At least we've beef fer th' winter," Edward mused matter of factly, gazing down at the carcass and casually rolling a cigarette. "She needs butcherin'." Moira, near recovery, was already off her sick bed, fetching a knife, saw and cleaver.

And today, Moira was perfectly in the moment, supervising this calving, bolstered by Neddy's help and that of oldest daughter Rose. As for Edward, he was front and center at The Speckled Hen, well on his way to being flutered for yet another night.

Fresh hay had been strewn in one of two pens in the barn as Flora, already in the early stages of labor, settled in and was moaning. Checking on her repeatedly in the midst of other chores, Moira closed the barn door six hours later, returned to the cottage and announced the birth of a fine, healthy heifer.

Now, it was time for dinner. Colleen helped Bridget peel potatoes, slicing them into quarters and dropping them into boiling water. The green onions had been chopped while Moira skimmed cream and scooped a large dollop of butter from the churn. With a bit of salt and elbow grease, the *champ* was ready.

Potatoes had been a dietary foundation for the Irish

stretching back to the roots of memory. At times, the sole source of food for the poorest Irish at every meal for lack of corn, grains, meat and poultry their entire desperate lives. But the McKennas never tired of the starchy tuber, by choice. In fact, they considered champ a mainstay and even a celebratory treat for special occasions such as a calving.

As the family finished dinner and began clearing dishes from the table, they heard Edward outside singing *Brennan on the Moor* raucously off key, followed by the jangle and thud of his bicycle falling on the ground outside the door.

"... *bold, braaaaave and unduunt ... undaunted was (urp!) ... was yer man ... on th' moooooooor ...*" as he barreled through the door, taking a woozy step or two, righting himself with the assist of a chair. Trying to focus on the lamplit faces staring back at him, Edward doffed his pork pie, walked to the pot of champ on the cooker and plunged his hand into the remnants, stuffing his mouth and wiping the rest on his trouser leg before stuttering off toward bed, continuing his song, now an almost imperceptible garble, "*... she pulled a bloaded ... loaded blunderpis ... blunderbuss from underneath her goat ... coat.*" The next sounds were of Edward crumpling face first into the mattress followed by loud, wet snoring.

"Come, girls," Moira said, gathering the last of the dishes, "oﬀ to bed wit' ya. Mass comes early an' chores come earlier."

7

Church

At 5 a.m., the small McKenna army attacked the farm

on virtually every front. Colleen tackled the chicken feed, while Nuala gathered eggs. Eileen slopped the pigs, Sissy carried water from the pump, while Bridget picked flowers for the table. Rose helped Moira with breakfast while Neddy released the other cows into the lower pasture. Wearing his father's Wellingtons brought back from The Great War, he headed for the bog with a wheelbarrow and slane to cut peat. This Sunday, even Edward pitched in to milk a cow, having learned his lesson with Maisie.

After returning with the peat and stacking it in the barn to dry, Neddy approached the cottage and noticed Packy was looking poorly, leaning against a barn wall. It had been more than a week since they last played together, and several rains had soaked and splashed him with mud. Neddy fetched a bucket and pumped fresh water into it. He carefully ran an old rag across Packy's rusted handlebar, continuing down his fork and then meticulously cleaning the remaining spokes on his lone wheel.

"There y'are, Packy," Neddy smiled. "Good as new."

"Leave that t'ing be," Edward said in passing, entering the house with a bucket of water to wash up and shave before mass.

Neddy took a last swipe at a farthing-sized patch of shine on the handlebar's otherwise rust-pitted surface, then went inside as well.

Neddy only had two shirts, another pair of trousers and a soiled wool tie given to him by the parish priest. Standing in front of a small mirror hanging by a cord nailed above the hearth, he changed shirts and his trousers, then fashioned a necktie knot the best he could and combed his thick brown hair with the fingers of his right hand. He rubbed a smudge of dirt from his chin and decided he was in top form for the church walk, until he spotted mud on his shoes. Heading out the door, he stopped and hoisted each shoe to the back of his trouser legs for a final shine.

The family strolled the mile and a half, two-by-two looking like a small clutch of ragged nuns, down the farm lane to Ballyronan Road with Neddy and Packy trailing close behind. Several carts and carriages passed and a single automobile, owned by the McGrahans, with Johnny seated next to Seamus at the wheel. Edward tipped his grey Sunday bowler at them as they passed, but they didn't acknowledge him although he had helped finance their vehicle over many years.

The fact that Neddy hated church was a secret shared only with his sister Rose, herself a bit weak on the catechism. "Ach, Neddy," she would scold, "ya mustn't let anyone hear such sacrilege, 'specially ma. It would kill her ... then she'd kill *you*."

That was a fairly accurate assessment. As a child, like many Irish girls of the time, Moira had entertained thoughts of becoming a nun. Partly because of her deep faith and partly as a way to escape the poverty of farm life. But then came Edward McKenna with his easy talk, deep blue eyes a person could get lost in and a smile that made her light in the heart and flustered to the core of her being. To young Moira, he seemed almost magical ... until he wasn't. Then it was too late. And to this day, Moira still wondered what taking a path to the convent might have been like as she always admired the parish nun, so pious and proper and in control. Black habit and veil flowing in the wind like an ecclesiastical banshee. An outsized rosary dangling from her waist and ending in a large silver crucifix resembling what she imagined as a key to the very gates of heaven itself. And with her face framed in virginal white, the nun was, to her mind, authoritarian perfection.

Neddy thought differently, bristling at the unflinching, unchallenged authority wielded by the parish priest's partner in crime, Sister Assumpta. Not so much an angel of mercy as a grim reaper of sin and retribution in God's name, the nun never smiled, at least never as far as Neddy could recall. Making matters worse, Sister Assumpta, a parish school teacher, relished name-calling for those who fell out of favor. Neddy was forever "Mister Flipity" for a series of minor infractions, and would be flailed with a pointer or yardstick like a recalcitrant mule at every opportunity. As a result, while Neddy loved learning, especially from textbooks, he hated school and in turn, hated the church.

He endured the beatings in school and the interminable liturgy of the mass because he couldn't openly object to either, and both were becoming unbearable. As he sat in the pew amid his family and the faithful, amid the chest pounding and bead counting, amid the mindless regurgitation of sanctified chants, amid prayers *to* the canonized and prayers *for* the certainly damned, amid the dissolving of sacred wafers on tongues of the confessed, he fidgeted in his seat.

"Be still or I'll cuff ya," Edward whispered, elbowing the boy in the ribs for the third time as Colleen and Sissy stifled giggles and Moira cleared her throat as a warning to silence the girls as she listened to the homily.

Finally, "Dominus vobiscum," the priest droned and,

like drones themselves, the congregation responded, "Et cum
spiritu tuo."

Another mass had ended and Neddy was liberated from
the spirit-crushing ritual for another week ... unless he was
somehow forced to attend confession the following Saturday.
For Neddy's first prayer of the day, as mass ended and the
absolved sinners emerged to sin again, he implored the saints
that he be spared the confessional, waiting in that dreadful,
dark abyss until Father Haney slid open his tiny window of
salvation to stare deeply into the very pit of his soul.

Neddy's father was the first to leave the church,
escaping outside for a smoke. As Edward finished rolling his
cigarette, Father Haney approached him. "Edward, have you a
moment?"

Wondering which of his transgressions had caught the
attention of the clergy, he cautiously responded, "Aye, father."

After the walk home, the McKennas put away their
Sunday clothes and eased into the one day of the week each
could claim as theirs, except, of course, for Moira, who was
on duty without respite. But even her work was somewhat
diminished on this day of rest, allowing her a quiet, albeit
short, stretch to herself as the children ran about outside.
She loved to read, a lifelong passion too often sidelined by the
realities of the everyday. As a small child, she would listen to
Sister John Joseph, the parish nun who read to the youngest
children until they learned to read themselves.

The nun noticed early on that young Moira was a
particularly attentive child. As Sister John Joseph read books
to the class, Moira's hazel eyes were always intense and
focused, unblinking for long stretches, as she absorbed tales

of saints and martyrs, miracles, redemption and the Lord. So it was an easy decision for the nun to give the child her worn copy of the daily missal and a Catholic Bible upon Moira's first holy communion. The girl started reading the missal that night, continuing to read it and the Bible again and again for decades.

Now, Moira retrieved the missal from her small bedside dresser, opened it and sat near the hearth to read, only to be interrupted by Edward.

"I wanted a talk wit' ya once th' children were away," he began. "Did ya see th' father talkin' t'me at mass t'day?" He held out a leaflet.

Moira studied the page's large photo of smiling, well-dressed boys doffing their caps and cheering on the gangway of a huge steamship. A second photo showed another group of teenaged boys, again in jackets and ties, huddled around what appeared to be a sea captain on the ship's deck. Then her eyes fell on the wording:

Canada Welcomes British Boys
FREE PASSAGE TO CANADA

Free Farm Instruction.
Previous Experience Unnecessary.
Employment Assured.
Good Homes. Good Wages.

CUNARD LINE TO CANADA
Regular Sailings to Canada from LIVERPOOL,

SOUTHAMPTON and BELFAST

"To secure an opening from which to build up a career is the ambition of every boy, and these openings are very few in this country. But in Canada, where opportunities still abound, it is doubtful if there can be found any to equal that provided by farm life.

"One of the great demands in Canada today is for British boys between 14 and 17 years of age and for whom special arrangements have been made for placing in suitable farm homes.

"No previous experience of farm work is required, providing they are in good health, willing and honest and will adapt themselves to farm work."

Looking silently at Edward, Moira had stopped reading, although the wording continued to the back of the leaflet, describing supervision of the boys by the Catholic Emigration Association in Canada, paying wages from 26 to 30 pounds a year and how treatment of serious medical conditions would be paid for by the church.

"Father said he got this from Monsignor Connor of th' diocese himself. 'Tis a scheme between Rome an' th' English," Edward explained. "All th' way from Rome, I tell ya. And th' boy could also go to Australia, if he wished."

"The boy?" Moira's face reddened. "Our boy? To Canada

or Australia? Are ya mad? He's never been to Belfast let alone halfway around th' world. Have ya shown this to Neddy?"

"I was waitin' to see yer t'inkin' on it," he said.

"Well, here's me t'inkin'," Moira said, crumpling the leaflet and tossing it into the turf fire. "I warn ya," she said. "Not a word to Neddy."

Edward raised his arms in surrender as he backed away, having been at the gates of Moira's wrath too many times before to proceed further.

Moira forgot about the missal and walked outside to check on the girls. Neddy was off somewhere with Packy and would return in his own good time, she thought. And he did, after a successful hunt for bicycle parts netted him a single pedal, excavated from the McCowan's barn.

Moira checked on Flora and her calf in the barn, deciding that they could be released to the pasture tomorrow. But for now, it was time for dinner as she gathered the family to the cottage, adding more turf to the fire as it began to rain.

The thunder made it difficult to fall sleep that night and the girls fussed more than usual, finally settling down shortly after 9 p.m. Neddy lay awake on the bed clothes, locating above his head the spider web that had grown to the size a dinner plate illuminated by the light of the waning turf fire. Several insects had already been ensnared and preserved in tiny silken cocoons for future spidery meals. Soon, Neddy was asleep and watching Traveler's approach.

"Fine morning, don't you think?" Traveler mused, producing a cigar out of thin air, squinting into the sun. "Great day for a walk ... or a drive ... or a trip to destinations unknown," he said, forming a globe in the air with a flourish of his hands. "You should try it some time."

"Try what?" Neddy asked, swatting at a swarm of midges buzzing near his face.

"Trips to faraway places," he smiled. "Foreign lands. Like *Gulliver's Travels*."

"Like what?"

"*Gulliver's Travels*, lad. A travel adventure of sorts, written for the most part in Cookstown by an Irish fella named Jonathan Swift. An author. A poet. The director of St. Patrick's Cathedral in Dublin. Loved the book as a kid. You should look it up. How's Flora doing?"

"Fine, I guess."

"And your Da and Ma?"

"Grand," he lied about his father.

"No visits from rebels or the army lately?"

"You're askin' a lot of questions," Neddy said suspiciously.

"Just curious is all. Any visitors from America?"

"America?"

"Yeah, you know. Cowboys, Indians, broke the English king's heart about 150 years ago? That America."

"No. No American visitors," Neddy said.

"Just wait," Traveler said … and was gone.

8

The Return

Tommy Ryan thanked the farm-equipment sales agent who had given him a ride from Cookstown to the Ryan property off Kinnigillian Road. Tommy had waited almost half the morning for his father to meet him at the rail station, fully aware that Malachy was known for being late to most everything. But completely forgetting the arrival of his son from America seemed totally out of character, so Tommy reluctantly set off on foot. The sales agent noticed Tommy walking unsteadily on the road near the station and offered him a ride after learning the Ryan farm was near several farms on his schedule. Besides, the agent said, he would enjoy the craic.

Tommy's growing agitation turned to deep concern as he walked up the farm lane to the house and found the front door slightly ajar. Opening it, he stepped into a parlor thick with disorder and musty air. Tommy cleared his throat constantly as he surveyed the scene. A lamp broken on the kitchen floor. Several chairs overturned. The cellar door was open and when he descended the stairs, Tommy noticed what he always remembered as fully stocked shelves half empty and several jars smashed on the floor. Returning to the kitchen, he saw unopened mail scattered across the floor under the table. Leaning down, he picked up a letter with United States postage and an address in his handwriting. It was the letter he mailed to his father five months before saying he was heading out from New York and would be home ... Feb. 16. Today.

"What the hell ... ?" he thought, then called, "Da?" Silence. Again, "Da? Are ya about?"

He opened the back door and looked toward the barn for activity and then to the adjacent pasture. But the barn, barnyard and pasture were quiet and the livestock was missing. Tommy began to panic. "Da! Malachy Ryan!!"

Nothing except the fading echo of his own voice.

Thinking for a moment, he settled on the McKennas.

Crossing the barnyard, his breathing labored from his trot down the farm lane, Tommy saw Moira leaving the cottage.

"Mrs. McKenna, a word?"

For a second, Moira didn't recognize the gaunt young man who had left for Canada eight years before. Then her face lit up and she stepped toward him, arms outstretched. "Tommy? Tommy Ryan?"

They embraced briefly, then Tommy spoke. "I've been to the house ..." Moira's face darkened. "It's open and no one's about. Where's me Da?"

"Taken," Moira said softly. "Taken by Black and Tans months ago."

"Months ago? Taken fer what? Taken where?"

"We only know what we hear from people," Moira began, "but he was taken away to Belfast ..."

"Why? Why was he taken?" Tommy's voice became more urgent, his responses now punctuated with intermittent coughs to clear his throat.

"The English t'ink he's I.R.A. ..."

Tommy was silent. "Certainly, he's no love of the English, but a Fenian? I can't abide that. I've gotta get back to Cookstown fer the train to Belfast."

As Moira talked to young Ryan, a wave of guilt came over her as she considered the stock of preserves and other food stuffs purloined from the Ryan farm and now sitting in the McKenna root cellar. She hoped word of the guns retrieved by the republicans from the Ryan farm hadn't been discussed in the wrong circles, seeming to confirm in some minds that Malachy Ryan was, indeed, a gun runner for the rebels. Such talk could be fatal.

"There's no way to get ya there today," Moira said, "so before ya go back to yer house, at least stay fer a meal here."

At first, Tommy declined, but after a little coaxing, he admitted to being tired and hungry from the day's journey and accepted the invitation.

One of Ryan's hams had been pulled out of the root cellar the day before and was sufficiently carved, masking any specific place of origin. There were fresh cabbage and potatoes, and Rose had baked a rhubarb pie earlier in the day. There were tea and scones, Ryan's strawberry preserves in a bowl on the table, and the warmth of an Irish family that Tommy had missed since leaving home and ultimately working on the docks of New York Harbor at the mouth of the Hudson River in Manhattan.

"So, Tommy, when did ya go out to America? I dunno the year," Edward said.

"Well, I actually left here fer Montreal in Canada about eight years past," Tommy said, as Edward's eyes lit up and Moira shot a warning glance across the table. "I lived there a couple years, but got the chance to go to America fer work."

"America?" Neddy chimed in. "Ya live in America?"

"The land of opportunity," said Tommy with a laugh that descended into a jagged, wet cough. "Sorry, I've had this chest cold that doesn't seem to want to quit. In Montreal, I worked fer a shipping company as a longshoreman, but the company liked me work and offered to make me a stevedore superintendent if I was willing to move to New York. I jumped at it."

"So ya didn't like Canada?" Edward probed closer to Moira's point of no return.

"Not a'tall. Not a'tall," replied Tommy. "I liked Canada just fine and parts of it remind me of Ireland. The food is good, the people are nice ..."

"An' the girls are pretty, to be sure," Edward pitched in.

"And pretty girls, but none as pretty as those here at this table," he said to a chorus of giggles.

"So, you're an American?" Neddy continued.

"Not yet, but I hope to be as soon as I can apply fer citizenship." Apologizing again, he hacked strongly into a handkerchief, soothing his throat with a gulp of tea. "Caught this on the ship on my way over, I guess," he lied.

"Are ya glad ya left Ireland?" Edward asked, again tempting fate.

"Overall, yes. Very glad," Tommy said, "until today."

"Don't worry," Moira leaned forward. "Things will turn out fer ya and yer da."

"An' don't ya worry about Cookstown; th' McGrahan boys will drive ya," Edward offered, not at all sure he could deliver as promised. But that was Edward for you.

In the morning, Edward and Tommy walked to The Hen where Seamus, indeed, agreed to the Cookstown road trip. After fueling up the Vauxhall, he and Tommy set off on Dunamore Road, while Edward settled into the pub for the afternoon ... or so.

As Neddy finished working on Hazel, the squat but high-producing milker who calved last spring, he poured milk from the bucket into one of the large metal cans to be collected late that afternoon on their way to Cookstown, then Belfast for processing.

9
Revelation

Neddy grabbed his small satchel containing a few sheets of paper, a pencil, a sandwich of the dinner ham, an apple and *Introduction to Geography* borrowed from the parish school and to be returned today.

The McKenna children arrived for class just in time for a special announcement by Father Haney. "After school yesterday, we received a box of books from the diocese and we're very excited to say each of you can take one for your very own when classes are over today," the priest said excitedly. "Jaysus has blessed us with this wonderful gift and we hope you enjoy them as much as we enjoy giving them to all of you."

Sister Assumpta was quite subdued that day, threatening Neddy with the yardstick only once, visibly restraining herself from an actual strike, making the day's lessons almost enjoyable.

In the afternoon, when the nun pulled her hand from a hidden pocket in her habit and grabbed the school bell's wooden handle as if it were the throat of a small child, to signal the end of the school day, most of the class exploded from the door, scattering like bird shot in all directions without glancing once at the books piled on her desk. But not Neddy. Once he saw the stack, he focused on possibilities to be explored in the book on top: *Gulliver's Travels.*

Grabbing it like a starving man after a bowl of stew, Neddy stashed the book in his satchel and headed for the door. Father Haney was on his way in and Neddy nearly collided with him. "Slow down, child," the priest said sternly, "there's no need to be in such a rush."

But Neddy ran home to start his adventure with Gulliver.

And what adventures there would be during the next week. Lands where tiny people called Lilliputians prepared for war with their neighbors wielding itty bitty swords, firing off pin-sized arrows and navigating sailing ships no bigger than a scrub brush. Or Brobdingnag, a land of giants. There was a flying island called Laputa, where everyone did nothing but think; and a place called Glubbdubdrib, where Gulliver could talk to ghosts of historical figures. When Neddy read that, he immediately thought of his father who would be keen to sit down for a pint with the giant Finn McCool. And, of course, there were the Yahoos, a brutish race of human-like creatures controlled by a refined race of highly intelligent, talking horses called Houyhnhnms.

Each night, as Neddy read by kerosene lamp in the barn, he couldn't wait for sleep to discuss the book with Traveler. But two nights passed. Then five. Then seven and no Traveler. Neddy even reclaimed his geography book from the parish school, so he could locate Gulliver's fantastical countries on the world map, all without success except for Japan. Then, finally, Traveler strolled into his dream again.

"Where've ya been?" Neddy asked Traveler, curiously irritated as he walked out to greet him at the barnyard gate for the first time ever.

"I've been what is called M.I.A. ... missing in action, incommunicado, out to lunch," Traveler said, standing on one foot and touching his nose with a finger. "Had to do this for a cop once in the middle of a highway."

Traveler was having great fun, but poor Neddy didn't understand most of what was said, leaving him completely befuddled. "I'm not sure ..."

"Vacation, lad. I've been on vacation ... to Lilliput," he joked. "A great *little* getaway, but a piece of advice: Don't lie down and fall asleep. Woke up one morning tied to the bed."

"A what? I don't ..."

"Yessir, although you'll call it a holiday," Traveler explained, "a vacation is when you get paid by other people to relax, to travel or do nothing at all. Everyone in Canada gets one. Some get 10 weeks. Americans used to get vacations, but that was before Republicans and an unrealistic work ethic made them almost impossible."

"America has Republicans?"

"Not Republicans as in the Irish Republican Army, the American Republicans are ... oh never mind. No use spoiling your dream. I think I was trying get into your thick skull that Canada is the place to be because of their vacations. Oh, and universal health care. And maple syrup. And good manners. Now, where was I?"

"Lilliput. Ya went there? "

"Um, no," Traveler replied. "That was a joke."

"When I looked in me geography book, I canno find it on th' maps," Neddy said. "I canno find most places Gulliver went to 'cept Japan."

"Of course not, Neddy my boy," Traveler said, "because they were made up. They were fantasies in Jonathan Swift's head. Like these dreams."

"But th' dreams are real," Neddy insisted.

"No," Traveler contradicted, "only the things I tell you are real. Look, do you honestly think a real person could do this?" And instantly, his tropical ensemble became a powder-blue, polyester tuxedo with broad velvet lapels, ruffled shirt front and cuffs, all complimented by a velvet bow tie that resembled a mutant butterfly. His hair was suddenly brown and shoulder length, styled into a perfect Prince Valiant pageboy. "God I hated these monkey suits," Traveler said with a grimace, looking down at his purple patent-leather loafers. In the next instant, he was back to his pina-colada best and, in fact, was sipping a pina colada. "Ah, better."

Lighting a cigar, Traveler pulled his sunglasses to the tip of his nose, looking straight into Neddy's deep set eyes, the playfulness gone from his voice. "Look, Gulliver's travels were fantasies," he said, "but you'll have a real chance to travel to real places just as incredible. There will be people you'll consider giants as well as people so small and petty you'll wish they would disappear. If you're smart, you'll walk away from them before they can damage your soul. There will be mountains higher than the Wicklows or Bournes and great seas with stretches of water where you will lose sight of land for weeks on end. You will see incredible cities and warm beaches with sand so soft and white, you'll swear they were made of sugar. All waiting for you. Waiting for you to grab every opportunity to travel, to explore other countries ... like Canada. To be honest, my boy, there's nothing for you here.

There never will be. You don't want to waste your life, dying on this farm, never having really lived. Here, read this."

Neddy took the leaflet and looked down at the bold headline:

Canada Welcomes British Boys
FREE PASSAGES TO CANADA
Free Farm Instruction.
Previous Experience Unnecessary.
Employment Assured.
Good Homes. Good Wages.

CUNARD LINE TO CANADA
Regular Sailings to Canada from LIVERPOOL, SOUTHAMPTON and BELFAST

"And what's this?" Neddy looked up, puzzled.

"It's the future," smiled Traveler, dropping his cigar in the dirt and crushing it out with his sandal. "Your future." Then, with a tip of his Panama, Traveler was gone.

Neddy was awake and unsettled. There was no reason to doubt Traveler's word, not with his record of foresight and prophecy. But leaving home? Leaving his family? Pure rubbish! The more Neddy thought, the more anxious he became as he threw off the bed covers and a sheet of paper fluttered to the floor. He looked down in the dim light, picked it up and saw:

Canada Welcomes British Boys
FREE PASSAGES TO CANADA

Neddy shuddered and dropped the leaflet. His hand trembled, but not from the cold rain slashing against the roof thatch or from the gale outside. He was frightened by the thought that somehow last night, Traveler had crossed what he always thought was an intractable boundary between dream and reality. He gave Neddy the leaflet in a dream, yet there it was on the floor. And being real, was the prospect of leaving and betraying his family real as well? The proof was there beside his bed. He leaned down, snatched up the leaflet and folded it inside *Gulliver's Travels*, where it would stay. Neddy dressed and started his chores before heading off to school.

10

Dead End

Tommy Ryan had been gone for more than a month, overwhelmed by the infuriating bureaucratic maze in Cookstown and Belfast then Cookstown again, attempting vainly to find word of his father. After pulling up at the McKennas' barnyard gate on a jaunting cart he borrowed from a chum of his father's in Draperstown, he began coughing as he climbed down from the seat, clamping onto one of the cart wheels to steady his descent and regain his balance.

"Are ya all right?" Moira asked, drying her hands on

her apron as she approached the cart and grasped his arm. She thought Tommy looked terribly pale, thin, his eyes were red-rimmed and his shirt was damp, unusual for such a cold afternoon. He was woozy as a drunk, she thought, but smelled no alcohol on his breath.

"No, no, I'm grand," he said, wiping his mouth with a handkerchief, then mopping his brow. "Just a bit tired from the ride out here."

"Any news on yer da?" Moira asked.

"I was about to ask the same," Tommy replied, already suspecting the worst. "I've been almost out of me mind with worry since I left here. I've been to the constabulary to the army, to infirmaries, hospitals and jails. I've been in and out of government offices all over Belfast. No one knows a thing. No one's heard a thing. Fer Christ's sake, no one's even heard of me father."

"Ya look knackered," Moira said. "Why not sit fer tea. I've just baked scones earlier. Come ya now inside."

As Moira set a kettle on the cooker, she sent Bridget to the barn for cream.

Tommy was exhausted, wheezing until his breathing finally fell into a shallow rhythm. Bridget returned, placing the cream pitcher next to the teapot. She smiled at Tommy, and he at her, as she sat near him on a small stool that Neddy had fashioned from scrap wood.

A turf fire took the bite from the afternoon chill as Moira asked, "So what are ya to do now?"

"I dunno," he said, "and with each day ..."

"Have ya talked to Johnny McGrahan?" she asked, thinking of the pub proprietor.

"Aye, right before Seamus drove me to Cookstown and ..." but before he could finish his sentence, Tommy began coughing so fiercely his face flushed and the veins bulged on his forehead as he rose and staggered to the barnyard. Moments later, he returned, sweating. "I best be away as I'm feelin' poorly," he apologized, punctuating almost every sentence with small, gurgling barks.

Moira noticed specks of blood on Tommy's handkerchief and agreed, "Aye, that would be best. Get ya home fer a rest and I'll bring tea later."

As Tommy walked to the cart, Bridget followed. "I hope ya feel better," she said. Tommy paused, crouched to give her a hug and a kiss, then gently brushing aside a curl from her forehead said, "Don't worry, I'll be fine."

11

Holy Hell

Tommy died within the week. He hadn't contracted the tuberculosis on his trip home, but more than a year before while working the New York docks. Despite efforts to stem the disease's spread starting in the 1890s, it remained a devastating fact of life in New York's poor areas, especially among dock workers along the Hudson River.

Moira noticed Bridget's lethargy almost immediately Monday morning. Usually the first of the children out of bed, dressed and foraging through the bread box, Bridget was quiet and barely touched her eggs.

"Ma," she complained, "me head hurts an' I'm feelin'

poorly."

As Neddy walked in from the barnyard, Moira put a hand to the child's forehead, which felt hot to the touch. "Why don't ya try finishin' yer breakfast ..."

"I canno'," Bridget said, glancing at Neddy then pushing back from the table and vomiting on the floor. She started to cry, worried she might be scolded for making a mess and for the sins she obviously had committed, although she could recall none of them. "Neddy, I'm sorry fer sinnin' against Babby Jaysus," she sobbed, seeking some sort of absolution from her brother.

Neddy was momentarily confused by her outburst until he remembered that late night in the loft and his fabrication about sins, God and expelling stomach gas. Moira cradled the child in her arms and soothed her, turning quizzically toward Neddy.

"Rose," Moira whispered, "please gather a blanket an' pillow and set it by th' fire." As Rose arranged the bedding near the burning turf's warmth, Moira pulled Neddy aside. "What was Bridget on about sin and Babby Jaysus ... all th' time lookin' at ya?"

Neddy looked down at the floor. "I may've told her once that air biscuits and burps were God's way of lettin' ya get rid of yer sins against ..."

"... Babby Jaysus?" Moira finished the sentence. "Ach, Neddy. How could ya ..."

Neddy moved toward Bridget on the floor, sitting down next to her, gently snuggling the blanket around her shoulders, then stroking her hair.

"Ya don't have no sins, not now, not never," said Neddy,

his voice thick and his eyes suddenly welling with tears, not for his sacrilegious fabrication but at the sight of the sweet child by the fire, now ashen with illness and trembling with chills. "You're th' grandest girl an' best sister ever. God loves ya. Babby Jaysus loves ya. An' so do I."

Bridget lay quietly, her eyes partially closed, her breathing shallow.

For the entire day and into Tuesday, Moira encouraged Bridget to eat, but could only coax from her a few sips of tea and bites of bread. On the second night, Bridget developed a skin rash and had a difficult time sleeping, so that by early Wednesday, Moira told Rose and Neddy to keep a close eye on Bridget as she pulled on her shawl and headed out into the rain. She hurried to the parish church and caught a glimpse of Sister Assumpta stepping down from the altar after early mass.

"Sister," she called to Assumpta, a sister of Mercy trained to teach but also to tend to the health of the poor, "I need yer help."

After Moira shared her concern about Bridget's condition, the nun suggested they pray and an offering be made before returning to the McKenna farm. The two women knelt in the empty church as the nun prayed aloud.

"Almighty and eternal God, you are the everlasting health of those who believe in you. Hear us for our sick servant Bridget McKenna for whom we implore the aid of your tender mercy, that being restored to bodily health, she may give thanks to you in your church through Christ, our Lord."

As she left the church, Moira reached into a small coin purse in the pocket of her apron and dropped a ha'penny in the poor box by the door. The pair walked briskly to the farm and found Bridget as Moira left her, lying on bed clothes by the fire. Rose stood as they came through the door.

"Hello, sister," she said with a slight bow of her head. A moment later, Neddy walked in from the barnyard with fresh milk and, seeing the nun, doffed his cap. He filled a pitcher, then turned to leave.

"I've somethin' to do, but I'll be back in a dash," the boy said to Moira as he pulled on his cap and walked outside.

Tending to Bridget, the nun asked the child to stick out her tongue. Then, feeling her forehead, she asked, "Do you hurt anywhere?"

"Me legs an' me chest," the child said.

"Have you anything to eat today?"

Moira answered, "Tea an' part of a scone."

"Did that sit right with you?" the nun asked Bridget.

"Aye," said Bridget, whose dry throat triggered coughing that shook her tiny body.

"I'm thinking it's the croup," the nun diagnosed. "A lot of it is going around the parish. I'd keep her warm and give her honey for the cough. If it returns, have her breathe in steam from a pot of boiling water. She'll be fine, but prayer is the real medicine she needs."

Sister Assumpta motioned to Moira and Rose, and the trio dropped to their knees beside Bridget as she drifted off to sleep. Blessing herself, the nun began, "St. Gerard, who, like the savior, loved children, and by your prayers, freed many from disease, even death, listen to us who are pleading for our sick child. We thank God for the great gift of our daughter and ask Him to restore our child to health if such be His holy will. This favor, we beg of you through your love for all children and mothers. Amen."

Whether planned or by happenstance, Neddy entered the cottage just as the prayer ended. He shook the drizzle from his cap, walked to the dining table and carefully set down a small bouquet of Red Clovers and Buttercups, Bridget's favorite flowers. He poured water into a small jar, slid the flowers into it and arranged them just so, before placing them on the hearth next to Bridget.

"I heard these flowers callin' me from th' pasture," he whispered in her ear. "They said, 'Take us to Bridget an' make her feel better.'"

"Flowers don't talk," Bridget objected weakly.

"Ach, but they *do* speak when they needta," Neddy assured her. "They speak to let us know they're to be taken to someone very special when they're sick."

"Like me?"

"Like you, to be sure," he smiled. Then, plucking a buttercup from the bunch, he held it under the child's chin. "Let's see if ya like butter."

Meanwhile, the nun had left, promising to telephone a doctor at Tyrone County Hospital in Omagh. However, when she returned to the church, Sister Assumpta encountered several women from the Sodality of the Blessed Virgin Mary, who wanted to discuss plans for the next meeting. The phone call was forgotten.

When Moira returned to Bridget's side, the girl was shuddering beneath the blanket, complaining of a severe headache. Moira was becoming frantic by mid-day Wednesday, knowing that the doctor wouldn't show up until early evening. Bridget's condition was worsening by the hour and Moira was helpless to ease the child's pain or do anything to improve her condition. Rose and Neddy had taken to sleeping next to Bridget on the floor, while the other girls took turns checking in on their sister, climbing up and down from the loft throughout the night.

Edward hadn't been seen or heard from for nearly a day.

Early Thursday evening, when Dr. Campbell finally arrived from the hospital, Bridget had been dead for three hours.

After a preliminary examination of the child's body, the doctor suspected meningitis, but needed details from the family to help confirm a cause of death. However, Moira was so grief stricken, she could barely utter a coherent thought, even as she was comforted by Rose. Instead, Dr. Campbell turned to Neddy who filled the role as best he could.

The doctor jotted down symptoms experienced by Bridget and when they occurred. He also asked if the child had come into direct contact with any people outside the family recently. Neddy mentioned the nun, the parish priest on Sunday and Tommy Ryan. The name was immediately familiar to the doctor as he had assisted with the young man's post mortem examination at the hospital, finding that he died from meningitis associated with tuberculosis. It was the vital diagnostic link.

Edward was at The Hen when he heard of Bridget's death several hours after it happened. He broke down and, out of pity or a sense of obligation to a loyal customer, Seamus McGrahan pulled Edward a pint in the child's honor. Edward downed it and ordered another. Then another.

The next afternoon, sitting in the cottage with Bridget's tiny body laid out on the dinner table, Moira sobbed quietly, lovingly running a hand over the hem of her daughter's white dress that had been worn by two sisters before her. It was her church dress and now it would be the dress in which she would be laid to rest. Moira's second child dead in two years.

As friends and neighbors arrived for the wake, Maggie McDaid and Kathleen Duffy helped organize the tea, cakes and much of the food, while Kathleen's husband Ian made sure there was poitin, whiskey and other substantials. Pipe tobacco was set out as Ray Lynch and his cousins from Armagh gathered in the barnyard with their fiddles, pipes, a squeeze box and a drum. Soon there were dirges and jigs swirling into the night. Music rising and falling with the mourners' laughter and tears.

In a corner of the room hidden behind the tangle of adult legs, sitting alone on the floor against a wall, Neddy tightly embraced the small stool he had built for Bridget. Its seat on which he had carefully carved her name now spotted with his tears amid the mourning and merriment. He couldn't move (didn't want to, actually); his gaze fixed on the floor near the hearth where his sweet Bridget had taken her last breath.

Packy had died in an Omagh hospital bed in the middle of the night, so Neddy had never seen another person die, let alone someone so close to him, and was struck by the ease of it all. One moment, Bridget was there. The next moment she wasn't. Of course, her body was next to the fire as it had been for days, but *she* wasn't in it. Her laughter, her innocense and everything else that made her Bridget ... were ... suddenly ... gone and would never return. He never felt so empty and so alone.

As the evening wore on, the din was wearing on Moira. She grew increasingly morose, then angry at an unfeeling God. Angry for the death of another child. Angry for a husband who hadn't yet shown his face since his daughter died. But her greatest, most virulent anger was to come.

Driving in from Omagh, Dr. Campbell arrived to pay his respects and sought out the grieving mother who had yet to leave the side of her daughter lying on the table.

"Mrs. McKenna," he said, "I just wanted to tell you again how terribly sorry I am about the death of your daughter. Once I received the call yesterday ... "

Moira looked up slowly, directly into the doctor's eyes. "Yesterday? T'ursday?" she repeated.

"Yes. Sister Assumpta called yesterday afternoon and I came out as quickly as I could, although ..."

But Moira was already across the room to Father Haney and Sister Assumpta who were talking to Joe McClaren by the door. "You rang the doctor on T'ursday afternoon? T'ursday afternoon??"

"I ... I ... did ring him," said Sister Assumpta, unaccustomed to being questioned about anything, recoiling slightly at what she perceived as a brazen tone.

"On T'ursday afternoon??!" Moira repeated, her eyes ablaze knowing the nun had left the cottage early Wednesday promising to make the call.

"Uh, Yes," she said defensively.

"*T'ursday afternoon*???!!! Knowin' me sweet Bridget lay *dyin'*???!!!" Moira let fly her rage, resisting the urge to smash Sister Assumpta's face, she unleashed a double-barreled shove to the chest with such force it knocked the coif, wimple and veil of the nun's habit sideways so it appeared she had two heads, unmasking a thin thatch of white hair and a bald spot in the middle of her scalp.

As Mary Doyle screamed, Father Haney stuttered backwards into a chair, knocking into Minnie O'Brien's glass of poitin that spilled into John Flynn's fiddle sending it crashing to the floor. The nun awkwardly straightened her habit as she fled the cottage with Moira in pursuit. Only when Neddy grabbed his mother around the waist and restrained her did the mad chase end allowing the nun to careen through the barnyard gate and away.

The wake was over with people scattering like panicked escapees from a collapsing building. Within minutes, the cottage, the barnyard and the farm lane were empty. The McKenna girls sought refuge in their loft and were huddled under the covers, some falling asleep, others whispering to each other, except for Rose who laughed until she wept as she looked down on Bridget. There, amid the calamity was that tiny angel, quiet and serene. Her white dress as pure and innocent as her young departed soul that left the cottage and this world, as tradition dictated, through the open front window.

Moira and Neddy remained outside for several minutes watching the Gaelic gaggle retreat into the night, listening to the diminishing ruckus absorbed by the darkness. Neddy studied glow-worms in the trees behind the barn, imagining the luminescence was Lilliput at night, lit by hundreds of tiny lanterns. Moira just stared toward the south pasture before closing her eyes, tilting her face toward the stars and inhaling the sweet night air. When she opened her eyes, she motioned to Neddy, "Come you," she said. "We must talk."

The turf fire had settled into a crackling glow as Moira put a kettle on the cooker for tea. "I'm sorry," she finally said

"Fer what?"

"Fer ... everyt'ing," she said, quickly wiping a tear from her cheek with the back of her hand. "I'm sorry fer Sister Assumpta. I'm sorry fer losin' Bridget. I'm sorry fer losin' Packy. I'm sorry fer a father who t'inks more of his drink than he does of his family, of his children, this farm ..."

"Ma," Neddy protested, "the fault's not yers ... 'cept maybe fer th' sister."

Moira smiled slightly, finishing the tea and passing a cup to Neddy. "But 'tis me fault because I brought ya into this hard world an' made ya watch it fall apart. Yer a good boy, y'are, and there's more than all this." She swallowed hard. "There's nothin' fer ya here. There never will be. Ya don't want to waste yer life ..."

"... dyin' on this farm, never havin' really lived," Neddy completed her sentence from memory, repeating the words spoken by Traveler in his dream.

Stunned, Moira asked, "How did ya ...?"

But Neddy was already climbing to the loft, going to his mattress, opening his copy of *Gulliver's Travels* and retrieving Traveler's leaflet. Down the ladder, he held out the folded sheet of paper. Moira glanced at his face then unfolded the leaflet. She almost swooned. "But I burned this," she said, confused. "I watched it burn. Where did ya get it? Did ya get this from Father Haney?"

"Traveler," he said quietly. "This and every word ya

said."

While Moira believed fervently in heaven and hell,
limbo, purgatory and a universe of saints and martyrs, her
belief system never crossed the border into the supernatural
beyond the realm of miracles. But she did believe in Neddy
-- the good boy, the intelligent boy, the honest boy -- who
would never lie about such things. Did she believe in Traveler?
No. Divine intervention? Yes.

"I'm not sure how or why this came to ya," she said,
looking again at the leaflet, "but 'tis a sign ... from Jaysus. 'Tis a
blessed sign that ya have a chance fer better ..."

"But, Ma, what'll ya do wit'out ..."

"I'll be fine," she assured Neddy laying a hand on his.
"The girls will be fine."

And fine they would be. All of them. Colleen and Nuala
would become wives and mothers, married to fine young men.
Nuala in Londonderry. Colleen with her husband and children
in Cooktown near her sister Eileen who became a nurse. Sissy
studied to be a teacher and lived in Dunamore, while Rose ...
well, Rose would move to the new Irish Free State, to Dublin in
fact, and be elected eight times to the lower house of the Dáil
Éireann, the Irish center of power.

As for Moira, she would continue running the farm,
even after Edward died, eventually living with Eileen and her
family, enjoying her children, grandchildren and two great
grandchildren, although she never got to see her grandson
across the Atlantic.

"God will find a way," Moira assured her son. "He
always does. Come. Let's to bed. Mass will come early and
we've Bridget to bury in th' mornin'."

Despite the wreckage of the wake, Father Haney celebrated the funeral mass for Bridget early the following day as the McKenna family, including Edward who finally arrived home just hours before, prayed and mourned and wept for their daughter, their sister, the innocent wee girl missing her front teeth with a smile that crinkled her nose and lit up not just her face, but the faces of everyone around her.

The anxiety Moira felt entering the confessional earlier that morning had been lifted by Father Haney, who also had heard the disturbing confession of Sister Assumpta before. After Moira concluded her confession with the mortal sin of laying hands on a nun in anger, the priest told her to offer an act of contrition and handed down her penance: "One Hail Mary."

Following the mass, Moira and Neddy approached the priest. "Father," Moira began, "we need ya to tell us more about th' scheme to Canada fer th' boy."

The mechanism was engaged.

12

Preparations

The next week, Neddy received an official letter in the post containing an application from the Catholic Emigration Association in Belfast. It read: "Application Form for Youths desirous of Emigrating to Canada under Free Ocean Passage Scheme." The application was a detailed request for personal information from date and place of birth to a vaccination certificate, father's name and the applicant's farming experience ("Attending cattle, pigs, etc.," Neddy wrote.). In fine print, it requested "your birth certificate, a small recent full-face photograph and two references."

Father Haney sent a letter to the association: "This is to certify that Bernard (Neddy's formal given name) McKenna is a child of this parish, of responsible parents. I am pleased to state that he is a steady, industrious boy of excellent character. I have no doubt but he will give every full effort in any position he is capable of filling."

The parish-school's principal teacher, John Hunter, followed suit. "I have much pleasure in certifying excellent character borne by Master Bernard McKenna. He has been a most attentive, obedient and diligent pupil. His father and mother are respectable people. Therefore, the boy's home training has been good. I have no doubt that, if given a chance, he will become a credit to himself and his parents."

As the paperwork slogged through bureaucracies of the church, the British and Canadian governments, various emigration and immigration societies and associations, Neddy and the family prepared for his departure and his agreement to serve three years of indenture to an unknown Catholic Canadian farmer. However, an obstacle remained.

In a letter addressed to Neddy, the Catholic Emigration Society's secretary wrote, "Dear Mr. McKenna: It will be quite necessary for you to supply yourself with some kind of an outfit before proceeding to Canada. I would suggest that you make application through your Parish Priest to the St. Vincent de Paul Society saying that you are being granted a free passage to Canada on condition that you get a suitable outfit of clothing."

Neddy wrote Father Haney the same day.

"Dear Father," his letter began, "as I book the free immigration scheme, my father is poor with six more children in the family. He cannot supply me with sufficient clothes that I need to be wearing for Canada. I remain yours, Father. Bernard McKenna."

Going to the church two weeks later, Neddy retrieved the brown paper parcel secured with jute string and ran home, anxious to see its contents. Cutting the string, he unfolded the ensemble on the dining table. It was a well-worn wool suit with drooping natural shoulders and three parts: the jacket, matching waistcoat and trousers. Also in the parcel was a white shirt with a frayed area on one tip of the collar, and a necktie. The confusing item to Neddy was in a trouser pocket: a thin metal object resembling a two-pronged straight pin. He laid it on the table while stripping to his underwear and pulling on the suit piece-by-piece. The jacket sleeves were a bit shorter than his arms, while the trousers and waistcoat were acceptable if someone didn't pay close attention.

Edward helped with the necktie, instructing the boy how to create a proper knot. Then, reaching for the object on the table, Edward slid the collar bar beneath the knot and secured it to each side of the collar. Neddy stepped to the corroded mirror over the hearth and was amazed at the gentleman looking back at him.

"A man o' th' world," came Moira's voice from the cottage door. "Ready fer anyt'ing an' anyone."

Three days later, Neddy was on his way to Belfast shortly before dawn. Aside from the cardboard suitcase covered in faux leather he would carry on his journey,

Neddy also took along Packy, lashed by a length of rope to the running board of the McGrahan Vauxall. Seamus had volunteered to drive the boy to the boat, following final embraces with his parents and sisters outside the barnyard gate.

There, he hugged and kissed each sister, lingering in a hug with Rose. "Write when ya can," she whispered in his ear. "I'll be keen to hear yer adventures an', who knows? Someday, I may wind up in Canada me-self."

Edward shook Neddy's hand firmly, wishing him a safe journey.

Moira stood back from the goodbyes until they were finished, finally approaching Neddy and handing him a knotted napkin. "Scones and biscuits fer th' trip," she said, her eyes already moist with loss. "You'll be hungry and 'tis a long way to Belfast." Then she wrapped her arms around him so fully he thought for a moment his back would break until he realized it was his heart. He closed his eyes in the embrace, neither of them saying a word and neither of them wanting to let go.

"'Tis time," said Seamus. "We've a boat waitin'."

With a final survey of the barnyard, the cottage and the family, of the farm lane, the barn, and inhaling the last memory a turf fire, Neddy climbed into the passenger seat, gave a final wave and disappeared in a swirl of dust down the road and away.

As Seamus navigated the late-morning streets of Belfast, heading toward the docks, Neddy was gobstruck by the energy of the passing city with its wide streets, its smokestacks and factories, its exhaust fumes spewing from automobiles and trucks, its crush of people and maze of wires carrying electricity and phone calls along building fronts and across rooftops, coursing through the air toward the hills and mountains ringing Belfast Lough.

The docks were unlike anything Neddy had seen before and his arrival at the offices of the Canadian Pacific Railroad, which owned the *R.M.S. Sea Empress* that would carry him to Canada, was the most exciting moment of his life. He stood outside the office, looking up at the towering cranes swinging massive pallets of cargo into and out of holds in a half dozen ships lining the harbor. He listened to a growling symphony of trucks and people and horns and whistles and trains amid departures and arrivals as lovers, friends and families waved handkerchiefs of farewell as anchors were hoisted.

After a final thank you to Seamus for driving him to what would be his next chapter of life and shaking hands, Neddy pulled back with a pound note in his palm.

"Fer yer travels," Seamus smiled.

Neddy touched the beak of his cap in silent appreciation and was inside the office and in line with other boys, many looking like him and all carrying small suitcases for the trans-Atlantic voyage. They all looked essentially the same except no one but Neddy had Packy by his side.

Approaching the crisply uniformed Canadian Pacific agent, Neddy presented his boarding pass and all the documentation that had been given him. Dipping his pen in the inkwell set in the desktop, the agent filled out a red tag with "B. McKenna, St. George's Home, Ottawa, Canada c/o Mother Frances Euphemia" and attached it to his suitcase.

"Don't lose the tag," he said without looking up. "The

nun will need it when you land." He then handed him a rail pass that would take him from Montreal to Ottawa, stamped his boarding pass and waved him through the gate until ...

"Wait. What is that?" the agent asked, pointing at Packy.

"'Tis a very special bicycle," Neddy responded.

"Well, it's not quite a bicycle now, is it?" the agent said, arching an eyebrow. "It looks like junk to me. You can't take it with you. Sorry."

"But 'tis a bicycle," Neddy insisted.

"Get on wit' ya!" yelled another boy somewhere behind him in line.

"I don't care if it's a horse's arse," the agent insisted, "you can't take it onboard."

Neddy stepped away from the desk and stretched to his full height struggling to see the Vauxhall, but Seamus was blocks away already, headed home.

Neddy froze, unsure what to do. He couldn't take Packy, but he didn't want to leave him here. He had to do something quickly or they might sail without him. So, looking down at Packy, he took the only option open to him. He loosened the wire attaching the bell to the handlebar and slipped it into his jacket pocket. He then walked to the far end of the building away from foot traffic, where he carefully leaned Packy against a wall, gave him a final loving stroke of his hand and proceeded to the gangway.

JOHN HEAGNEY

Part II

The Voyage

JOHN HEAGNEY

13

May 9, 1921

After a series of hasty check-ins, there were greetings and the birth of short-term, shipboard acquaintances with other farm boys from Donegal to Antrim to Roscommon, Leitrim and Tyrone. There also was the coarser lot of city chaps from Dublin, Cork and Londonderry, as well as a smattering of girls going off to be domestics, all of them on deck as the liner pushed away from the docks and began gliding out of Belfast Harbor into the lough, the Irish Sea, then to the open waters of the Atlantic for the ten-day voyage to Montreal.

Although the boys and girls aboard the *Sea Empress* were from towns, villages, cities and counties scattered across Ireland, once aboard ship they shared a common bond that would come to be known as the British Home Children program.

Called a "scheme" by its organizers, the British Home Children program targeted boys and girls between the ages of 14 and 17 with promises of a better life by way of free emigration to Canada, Australia, New Zealand and South Africa. During its 80-year lifespan, the program -- administered by the British government, the Catholic Church and at least 50 other associations and religious sects -- ensnared more than 100,000 children of poverty. While most children came from poor homes and farms, where parents were sold on what amounted to retroactive family planning, Canadians were deceived and told the children were orphans

without families. They were assured this was a charitable --
and in many cases a church-blessed -- program. A religiously
ordained balm to systemic poverty, illness and desperation.

The reality was a philanthropic effort that went terribly
wrong through incompetence, poor planning, avarice
and religious zeal that created a global network of human
trafficking.

Still, the promises *were* enticing. Good wages. Job
training. Paid healthcare. Fine homes with loving families.
But most important, free passage to a world of opportunity
that didn't exist in the rural farms or urban mean streets of
Ireland and the United Kingdom.

The only price of passage was the child's freedom. After
parental permission was obtained (or not), children, some as
young as 4, not 14, were bound to an agreement of indenture
that could last indeterminate years into a murky future.
With that labor contract, the Catholic Church (in Neddy's
case) promised parents their child would be placed with good
Catholic families with good moral character, all under the
watchful eye of church administrators.

The promises, too often, played loose and easy with the
facts.

Many children were sent to abusive homes and
subjected to physical, sexual and psychological abuse.
Beatings, rapes and starvation were commonplace. A number
of children ran away. Some committed suicide while others
were murdered. Some were sent back across the Atlantic.
Others, indeed, arrived at good homes the literature promised
after processing through temporary group homes in either
Montreal or Ottawa. And now, another voyage to uncertain

possibilities was under way for another group of Irish children on the *R.M.S. Sea Empress.*

Neddy was at the rail, chock-a-block with a strapping farm boy named Mick from Westmeath who was the size of a small steer. Beside him was a slight Donegal lad named Eamon, who spoke with a lisp and was missing part of an ear lost, it turned out, in a dust-up over a local girl whose name he no longer remembered. As most of the assemblage peered into the spray and wind toward a new life ahead, Neddy could only look back toward the ever diminishing skyline of Belfast until it was the size of Lilliput, then gone.

The *Sea Empress* headed north and Neddy wanted to experience everything about the journey. He broke from the throng and slowly navigated through the sea of gawkers to the ship's prow. There he watched the Irish coast glide by on the port side and Scotland to starboard. He stood for hours into the late afternoon until passing Scotland's Mull of Kintyre Lighthouse. And because it was a crystalline day, he glimpsed Malin Head on the Donegal shoreline to the west as the ship finally broke free into the Atlantic Ocean.

Neddy had never been on a ship ... or a boat for that matter ... unless you count a few outings aboard Will McCarty's skiff on Lough Fea fishing for pike. But this was exponentially different, like riding a huge sea beast that rose and fell and rose once more with the sea currents, carelessly tossing about the more incautious passengers as it sliced through the waves.

By the time, the Atlantic leg of the journey began, Neddy was nearly alone, as many boys had gone below to find their assigned bunks. Even in Seamus's car on the road to Belfast, Neddy began doubting his decision to leave home, leave his family, leave behind everything and everyone he ever knew for a world filled, in his mind, with blank, nameless faces, unknown destinations and unwritten experiences.

The air was filled with sea spray and melancholy as well as a chill unlike anything he knew in the pastures and woods of Tyrone. He turned up his coat collar against the gusts then thrust his hands into the coat's pockets for warmth. His right hand fell on something familiar: the last of his mother's fresh-baked biscuits. But just as he began taking it out of his pocket, the ship lurched to port and Neddy went down. Then, the ship rolled to starboard making the wet deck a slide into the open sea. Kicking like a frantic crab on its back, trying to gain traction, Neddy slid inexorably toward the edge of the ship when the collar of his suit coat tightened, nearly strangling him, as Mick from Westmeath muscled the boy back from oblivion and flung him across the deck and against a mast.

"Nearly a goner," Mick said flatly, looking down at Neddy. "'Tis a long swim to Canada."

"Aye," Neddy said, gasping for air as he tried to collect himself off the deck, first by rolling on his side, then to his knees, finally pulling himself up by degree with both hands on a railing. Then recognizing Mick from earlier. "Glad to meet ya."

"Aye," said Mick dispassionately, turning back to the sea churning by.

Neddy hung on tightly, looking now for his suitcase, which he located against a bulkhead about 20 feet away. He inched along the bow until he reached the suitcase, carefully unlocking a hand from the rail and grasping the suitcase handle. His pulse was returning to normal as he took one last look in the general direction of home before finally heading below to his bunk. The ship lumbered toward Canada with its cargo of waif laborers indentured to a future somewhere over the horizon.

The *R.M.S. Sea Empress* was an aging passenger liner pressed into service as a troop ship during World War I, then converted back to regular transatlantic service between Belfast and Montreal following the war. At 15,000 gross tons, it had two funnels, two masts and an average speed of 18 knots during the ocean crossing, though at times it could reach speeds of 22 knots. The ship carried 310 first-class and 470 second-class passengers, while the lowest levels of the ship ... and passenger list ... were reserved for the 729 souls and Neddy McKenna in steerage.

Exhausted and still wet from his topside ordeal, Neddy joined the other boys in the men's section of third-class, a boiling caldron of bodies tall and small, large and thin, pale and strong, sickly and robust all seeking individual space in a maze of metal bunks stacked three high and going on for what appeared to be acres. The low overhead was dark and dripping with condensation, punctuated by occasional bare light bulbs that provided just enough illumination to navigate the grid of bunk stacks. The fact that he would be sleeping in a place with real electric light exhilarated him. Above Neddy's head was a tangle of pipes and wires like the circulatory system of a mechanical leviathan whose pulse was driven by unrelenting, grumbling diesel engines.

Standing at the door to the third-class compartment, Neddy was transfixed by the sight of so many people in such tight quarters. Nothing in his life came close to this experience, except maybe the frenzy of the Belfast waterfront earlier that day. But rather than being overwhelmed, Neddy found this ... *all of this* ... exciting. As he picked his way through the throng, being jostled and jostling others, all he wanted to do was find his bunk. Section 4, bunk 17.

Section 4 had been set aside for the 93 boys traveling under the auspices of the Catholic Emigration Association and the British government, which paid for their passage. Neddy's group of 13 boys, ages seven to seventeen and tagged for St. George's Home, were scattered throughout Section 4 as they had been scattered throughout Ireland. They came from Ballinlough to Belfast, Mallingar, Hythe and Ennis, Ballyporeen to Londonderry ... and Dunamore, Cookstown.

After a chaotic search and several miscues, there it was. The middle bunk of a three-tiered stack, one of many that lined the entire starboard side of the ship's hull. Climbing the stack's ladder, he found a straw mattress, a thin blanket and a life preserver for a pillow. There also was a fork, large spoon and a workman's lunch pail, which contained several utilitarian inserts, all standard issue for steerage passengers.

Neddy would find soon enough that the meal pail, made from the cheapest tin, was his most essential tool as it was the only conveyance to hold the stews and gruels ladled out at meals three times a day.

The body of the round pail was about eight inches in diameter and six inches tall with the dual purpose of soup bowl and wash basin. Nested inside it was a small tin dish for meat and potatoes, while its lid, when inverted, served as another small bowl for vegetables or what passed for them.

Fitting atop the lid was a tin cup for drinks.

To prevent theft of these valuable items, passengers
either had to carry them wherever they went in steerage or
secure them in some manner to their bunks because when
lost, there were no replacements. Another challenge was
trying to keep the pail and its tin components clean, as soap
and towels were unavailable unless the passenger brought
them onboard before the voyage. Complicating matters even
further was the single warm-water faucet serving all 730
third-class passengers, forcing most to remove grease with a
handkerchief, if they had one, or rinsing the utensils in cold
salt water, then drying them in the sun. But because the tin's
quality was so inferior, salt water caused the entire meal kit to
rust quickly, making them unfit for food.

While the bunk offered barely enough space for Neddy,
his suitcase and meal implements, he was elated. Tonight,
he thought, would be the first time in his life he had a bed
all to himself. A thought that thrilled and, at the same time,
saddened him. This also would be the first time he could
remember going to sleep without the chatter and giggles, the
whispers and whimpers and finally the soft gentle breathing
of his sisters lying next to him as they slept in the loft. Again,
he thought of the home place. He reached into his left coat
pocket and felt the bicycle bell he rescued from Packy on the
Belfast docks. Then when he thrust his other hand into the
right pocket for his mother's remaining biscuit, it was gone.
Probably lost in his life-and-death struggle with drowning
that afternoon. Was Packy's bell a talisman that had saved
his life? Was the lost biscuit the price of his salvation or just a
lost biscuit? Either way, it was gone. The last direct, relatable

vestige of his mother.

He slung the suitcase onto the bunk and was about to follow suit when a voice from below said, "I'm glad ya din't drown."

It was Eamon, the lad from Kilkenny with whom he had shared the ship's rail and a last look at Belfast earlier that afternoon.

"Aye," said Neddy. "I'm glad me-self."

"I dunno howta swim," Eamon confessed.

"I do, but I wouldn't fancy swimmin' back to Ireland," Neddy said with a wink.

They both laughed, then fell silent watching the chaos generated by hundreds of same-day arrivals trying to adjust to their new reality. At least the reality of a 10-day ocean voyage on an old passenger ship taking them to the New World.

Their arrival in Canada would pose an entirely different set of challenges.

14

The German

The dinner bell rang at precisely 6 p.m. and everyone in third-class was instructed to go to the dining compartment, a large windowless space providing a few rows of long tables and benches to serve the huge numbers of people flooding through the doors. Two tables at the end of the room had four large metal pots filled with steaming liquid brought by stewards moments before. Although the hall was better lit than the sleeping quarters, there was a darkness here that had less to do with light and more to do with the odor of rotting food in every corner and linked directly to the galley staff, who were less than astute when it came to cleanliness either at their work stations or with their personal hygiene.

Neddy and Eamon stood in line with meal pails and utensils at the ready and soon stood opposite a rather rotund German server armed with a massive ladle and an unkempt handlebar moustache caked with food and snot. "Move along, move along," he repeated over and over to the immigrants filing past his station.

"'Tis soup," Neddy said, turning to Eamon.

"I'm not so sure," Eamon piped in, after watching The German ladle slop into an old woman's pail. Apprehensive, she paused to inspect its contents.

"Move along. Move along. Eile! Schnell!" barked The German.

The boys' pails were filled with soup, some of it sloshing out of the ladle onto the floor, joining older ladle miscues from days, maybe weeks before. The boys moved quickly to a spot open at a table nearby. Moments later they heard The German.

"Es is fertig!" he yelled at a young woman, "Fertig! Done!! No more."

The food ran out while people were waiting in line and entering the dining compartment, pails, forks and spoons in hand.

"You too slow to eat," The German taunted a boy who was maybe five or six, as his mother, placing a hand on his shoulder, imploring quietly for something to eat.

"You slow," The German almost smiled, "you hungry."

Neddy got up, grabbed his pail and half a slice of bread. "Here," he said, grasping the boy's pail and pouring half of his soup into it. "Not much, lad, but ..." The mother moved to thank him, but he already had returned to the table and began to eat.

Eamon didn't look up, as he spooned the soup into his mouth and immediately spat it back into his pail. "What sorta shite is this?" he said, quickly wiping his lips with a sleeve but unable to clear the foul taste. "I've smelled better t'ings in me barnyard."

Eamon stormed back to The German. "'Tis pure rubbish," he yelled, holding out his pail, filled with a barely warm, brackish wash of indistinguishable vegetation, a piece of potato and several rancid chunks of floating fat and gristle passed off as beef.

Smiling, The German responded, "Ja, und ees only rubbish you vill get."

"Outta me way," came a coarse baritone behind Eamon as he was firmly moved aside. Spinning around for a confrontation, he found himself face to face (actually face to chest) with Mick, Neddy's topside savior. "Ya won't be likin' this shite," Eamon warned, baking off.

Mick offered his pail to The German, who looked at Mick and sneered, "Fertig! Done!! No more."

Before Mick could respond, Eamon pushed his pail into Mick's hands. "Couldn't eat this shite anyway."

Mick followed Eamon back to the table, where Neddy downed the last of the stew and soaked up the remaining liquid with a bread crust. Eamon looked at Neddy in disbelief, but Neddy just looked up and said, "When yer hungry, ya eat what's given ya."

When the meal was over, the boys headed topside again along with several hundred others in steerage. During the voyage, third-class passengers were segregated into cramped open-air deck areas near the bow and stern, both littered with unused or broken gear, ropes, lines and masts fore and aft. While providing fresh air, the areas were capable of accommodating only a fraction of the steerage passengers at a time. The hour or so after meals was a favorite time to congregate with men and boys in their cramped forward area, while single girls and women were grouped with families and children in a similar area aft, adjacent to the crew quarters.

This segregation of the sexes was a moral imperative, a vestige of the Victorian Era's hypocritical rules surrounding sexual decorum and modesty. But the day-to-day reality of third-class life for single women and girls was quite a contrast to the protective fantasy creators of those of rigid moral edicts envisioned. Blame fell, for the most part, squarely on the ship's officers and crew.

Openly referring to those in steerage as cattle or swine, the ship's staff certainly didn't consider third-class passengers human after years of seeing their undulating ragged masses and mealtime stampedes with kicking and shoving and gouging to reach food before the supplies ran out. They also never thought that when people are treated and housed like cattle, they may start acting like cattle.

And with the crew's easy access to the female sleeping compartment, is it any surprise that rapes and molestations of every stripe were common aboard ship? Quartered as they were with families, single women and girls were denied

privacy to change, bathe or sleep without the very real fear
of attack. Any time of day or night, the crew, single men
or libidinous husbands could hunt their innocent quarry, a
situation well-documented by undercover journalists and
government inspectors of the time. But nothing was done by
the shipping lines who laid down the moral guidelines then
promptly forgot them.

Even younger, weaker boys were victims of attack, so it
became obvious very early in a sea voyage for the vulnerable to
travel in numbers.

It had been a long day for Neddy by the time he crawled
into his bunk to sleep shortly before 8:30. That was when he
realized the steerage compartment lights burned 24 hours a
day, so there never was the nocturnal darkness of his loft at
home. There also wasn't that wonderful scent of wet earth
after an evening rain or the stone quiet of the farm in the
middle of the night. Instead, there were the sounds of young
boys crying, of people vomiting, of snoring and snorting, of
gamblers angry with a bad turn of the cards, of voices praying
while others sang or talked about home. Every so often there
was the sound of a tin whistle, fife, drum or squeeze box.

Despite the new universe of sound, Neddy finally
dropped off to sleep ... and Traveler.

"Quite a day, lad," Traveler said, lighting his cigar as he
stood at the side of Neddy's bunk. "Quite a bit to process."

Oddly enough, while Traveler was bunkside talking to
Neddy aboard the ship, Neddy was standing in the middle of
the barnyard outside his parents' Tyrone cottage, yet still was
able to see, hear and talk to his visitor as if they were only feet
apart.

"I don't understand ..." a confused Neddy began.

"Remember, it's a dream, your dream, so anything's possible," Traveler smiled, adjusting his sunglasses. "So, you're feeling torn right now, aren't you?"

"Aye," Neddy responded. "Not sure ..."

"... if you've made the right decision to upset the apple cart ..."

"What apple cart?"

"It's a turn of phrase, son. You wonder if you made the right decision to leave your life behind and start a new one ..."

"Aye," Neddy agreed.

"It really hit you when you found the biscuit in your pocket, didn't it?"

"Aye," said Neddy, a bit surprised that Traveler knew his deepest feelings. Then again, it *was* Traveler. "But I lost it. The biscuit was the last t'ing me Ma touched before me leavin' home. The last t'ing from home I could hold on to."

"That's not exactly true," Traveler said, casually blowing a smoke ring.

"'*Tis* true ..."

"'Tis *not*," Traveler mocked. "You, my friend ... *you* ... are the last thing your mother touched before you set out. *You* are the thing she hugged so tightly. *You* are the thing she held onto for dear life. *You* are the thing she held to her heart and filled yours with her love. The biscuit was just a biscuit, but your mother's love for *you* is something that will never be lost or can ever be taken away."

Neddy started to cry for the first time, quicky wiping the tears with his sleeve.

"Believe, me," Traveler said softly, "you'll have

doubts about your choices a lot during your lifetime. It's an important part of growing up, which you'll also do a lot of in years to come. You never stop growing or questioning or worrying, if you're normal. People who don't question themselves are people to avoid because they believe they're always right ... and rarely are. Worse yet, they're never open to new ideas, new people, new customs, new beliefs and experiences. How boring is that? How dangerous is that? You're not one of those are you?"

"I'm not?" Neddy responded apprehensively.

"Of course, you're not. You're here, aren't you?"

"Aye, I suppose."

"Look at it this way: you made the decision to seek a new life, so you can't dwell on the life you left behind. It's done."

"But what of th' people?"

"They'll always be with you as wonderful memories, except maybe for that bastard squire ..."

"Loughran."

"Him you should forget ... but won't. For now, you need to look ahead. But be very careful in the coming days, especially with a truly dangerous crew member you run into. There's a storm ahead and he's in the middle of it. Just remember that the decks can be quite slippery, so grab the rail as hard as you can. I can't say more."

Traveler was gone and Neddy was awake. He could see early daylight through a porthole and heard Eamon stirring.

"You okay?" Eamon whispered

"Fine. Why?"

"I thought I heard ya cryin'"

"Just a dream."

To guarantee a spot in line, the boys headed to breakfast before the bell sounded on their first full day at sea. A line had formed already, but they would be fed.

While Eamon had slept solidly, he awoke a bit nauseous. Neddy's sleep was fitful as he stirred several times, hearing unfamiliar noises in the night. Probably most concerning was the constant groaning of this sea beast in whose belly he was an apprehensive passenger. Then, of course, there was Traveler.

Although Traveler's nocturnal visit contained his typical blend of banter with sage advice, he also dropped one of his warnings into the conversation. At this point in time, Neddy took Traveler's cautions to heart, given his track record of saving the boy's hide or the hides of his family. His problem each time was trying to divine what Traveler meant. "Remember that the decks can be quite slippery" was a reference to the frightening lesson Neddy had learned topside on Day One. So why state the obvious?

"I wonder what shite we'll be fed t'day," Eamon mused as they entered the dining compartment after the breakfast bell sounded at precisely 6:55. With a total lack of hot water or soap, the boys' meal pails and forks had received just a splash of cold sea water as a rinse before air drying. The German was there again at the serving tables, wielding his ladle like a conductor's baton orchestrating a dissonant concerto of gruel. "You like this," he said to Eamon before pouring a stream of the glop into his meal pail. "Stick to your ribs," he laughed.

"Stick it up your arse," Eamon responded, leaning down

for a sniff and deciding it didn't smell as bad as it looked, although the taste was something else again. The same could be said of the ship's coffee. Neddy never drank coffee, opting for tea instead, but Eamon was a veteran of the stuff ... although never anything like this.

Ground coffee of questionable heritage and age was poured by the pound into a large metal vat and joined by sugar and powdered milk. Added to this unholy blend were gallons of water ... sometimes sea water by The German ... and heated to a boil, then ladled into each passenger's unrinsed tin cup.

"C'mon, Neddy," Eamon urged, "I t'ink you'll fancy coffee once ya try it."

Neddy's cup was filled and he took a cautious sip. "Sweet mother of Jaysus!! I'm poisoned!!" he screeched after spitting the liquid to the floor.

"Ach, lad!" Eamon laughed, "'Tis not as bad as all that." He put the cup to his lips, took a mouthful and swallowed confidently. "Fuck! Fuckin' FUCK!! What in the name of all the saints ... !!??" He dumped the contents where he stood. "It tastes like divil's pis."

Neddy broke out laughing. "Never tasted divil's pis, so I wouldn't know."

Neddy laughed and Eamon fumed as they left the dining compartment for the deck area. The boys stood at the door squinting into a steady light rain, which discouraged Eamon and most others in men's steerage from going outside. Not Neddy, who immersed himself in the damp chill as it reminded him of home. The rain was somehow comforting.

For several minutes, Neddy paced the deck area thinking of the farm and what his mother and sisters might be up to, but didn't give his father a thought as he already knew he'd be at The Hen. Then he noticed a ladder leading to the deck above. He wasn't sure whether or not he should ... or was permitted to ... climb it, but climbed it nonetheless.

Pausing atop the ladder for a moment, he took a short, measured step, then another and another across the wet wood planks until he reached the rail and clamped both hands to it. Despite the inclement weather, the sea was relatively calm, dotted with occasional white caps. Seeing the wind gauge whirling wildly on the superstructure, he faced into a moderate wind, produced most likely by the ship's forward progress, and looked upward to see smoke billowing from the ship's stacks like an undulating black genie from a lamp. The deck was empty toward the bow, but in the other direction, there was a lone figure, like him, standing at the rail. A woman.

He began moving in her direction, hand over hand on the rail and once within earshot, ventured a greeting. "I'm Neddy McKenna from Tyrone," he yelled into the wind.

Startled, but seemingly unthreatened by the safe distance between them, she took a long look at Neddy, then without responding turned to the sea again. After several minutes without a reply, Neddy started to inch his way back toward the bow.

"Mary McCarrick from Galway," she said without looking at him, "and I can take care of me-self. I've a knife." Pulling back a fold in her shawl, Mary exposed a five-inch blade at the end of a black handle.

Neddy whistled. "I've no doubt," he said, thinking of his sister Rose, who stood about the same height and could pack a massive wallop when Neddy rankled her. "Can I come closer so we don't have to shout?" he asked, adding, "As long as ya keep that cutter in its place."

"Suit yerself, but keep yer distance," she warned. "Remember, I can take care of me-self. I've six brothers."

"So can I. I have six sisters," he countered, not yet ready to let go of Bridget.

She tried unsuccessfully to stifle a smile, but quickly composed herself.

"Where ya off fer?" Neddy asked, watching her woolen shawl flap in the wind like a bird straining for freedom. Her red head scarf tight around her raven hair framing a face with fine skin, delicate features, a strong chin and the deepest azure blue eyes crowned by eyebrows that reminded him of two broad pen strokes. A handsome young woman to be sure.

"Philadelphia City," came her reply.

"In America?"

"Where else would it be?"

Confused, Neddy replied, "But we're to Canada. Did ya get on th' right boat?"

"I'm not daft, boy," she bristled. "'Tis th' right boat. Said so on me ticket. I'm to take a train when we land," Mary said, "then on to Philadelphia city."

"A train?" Neddy mused. "Never been on a train."

"Nor I," Mary replied. "Never been on a ship previous, either. And yer bound fer where?"

"Aye, where's a good question," Neddy sighed. "I guess I dunno. I start in Montreal, Canada, but then, 'tis up to th' Church, I t'ink. Farmin's all I'm good fer. And you?"

"I'm to be a house maid," Mary said.

"A house maid, ya say," Neddy said, reminded immediately of Loughran Manor. "So, you'll be livin' in a grand house?"

"I s'ppose," she said, pulling her shawl tighter around her shoulders as a frigid gust tousled a lock of hair escaping the head scarf like a recalcitrant child. Glancing at the dark clouds, Mary turned away from the railing and said, "I must be off."

"Right, right," Neddy replied.

"Eddie, is it?"

"Neddy," he corrected her.

"Neddy," she repeated as if filing it away, then turning to leave.

"Can we talk again?" Neddy called after her, surprising even himself for his boldness. "Maybe after dinner or breakfast t'morrow?"

She paused to consider this fella, shivering in the moist sea air, dressed in a rumpled suit, its jacket collar torn, hair whipping about the perimeter of a cap kept from taking flight by a left hand clamping it to his head. Pulled low against the rain, the hat shielded what Mary determined was a kind face she would have thought melancholy if not for the broad disarming smile. "After dinner," Mary said and was gone.

As Neddy came in from the rain that had weakened to a light mist and intermittent sun, he walked into the steerage compartment and was immediately greeted with, "Hey, runt!" from a bunk not far from his own. At first, he paid no attention, then the voice yelled again. "On deck in the rain again? Don' ya ever larn? I won't be savin' yer arse next time, ya bloody plank."

In a lower bunk one section over from Neddy's, Mick was barely visible until he swung his legs out to the floor and stood with a pronounced thump, unfolding to his full six feet, three inches. Neddy smiled despite the verbal abuse.

"Never thanked ya, proper," Neddy said, thrusting out a right hand to shake.

Mick's right hand swallowed Neddy's in a fleshy, authoritative grasp that was firm, but not overpowering. Neddy was impressed. One thing Neddy's father Edward taught him was how to judge a man's character by his handshake. "Yer handshake is who y'are an' how to show yer a man," Edward instructed, "an' not some lagrachán who squats to pee. Grab a fella's hand like 'tis yer last shilling an' don' let go 'til he does."

Problem was, Mick's father taught him the same lesson, so both boys stood for a long while locked in gripmanship, entangled like two pump handles vainly attacking the same dry well and neither willing to surrender.

Finally, Neddy gave in, relinquishing his grip and slowly extricating his hand from Mick's huge paw.

"Thank me fer what?" Mick replied.

"Fer what? Yesterday. On th' deck. Me nearly slidin' off ..."

"Oh," Mick said. "t'ink nothin' of it. Nothin' a'tall."

"Still ..." Neddy's voice trailed off. "So, where ya headed?"

"Nowhere," Mick said. "Just restin'."

"No, I mean when we get to Canada."

"Me papers say St. George's Home," Mick said, retrieving an official-looking document from his suitcase. "See?"

"Aye, me, too," said Neddy, examining the letter and noticing the red tag on Mick's suitcase. "Where's home?"

"Kilbeggan in Westmeath."

"Never been."

Mick laughed, "No one has."

"Family?"

"Just me Ma an' me two brothers," he said. "Me Da died this year past of consumption. He worked th' distillery, but now that's done an' times are tough. Ma thought th' Church scheme to Canada was best fer me, so here I am."

Neddy knew he first learned of the free passage from Traveler, but opted to go with a far less bizarre explanation. "Me ma told me about it, too."

For the next hour or so, Neddy and Mick swapped stories of their homes, friends, families, parishes and schools that were part of growing up until yesterday. Neddy found that, like him, Mick, a full two years older, had the same misgivings about leaving home, but also was excited by what he might find in a new life. By now, they were shouting to each other as the noise of steerage rose steadily throughout the day and into the night.

Fact is, there was no quiet in steerage. Never a minute. Never a second. There was constant clamor of specific then indecipherable noise, precise then unclear conversations, human and mechanical din at all hours. Even the inescapably foul odors of urine, vomit and excrement, of unclean bodies and filthy everything else grabbed the conscious mind like a scream. All of it a soundtrack for endless boredom, sloth, graft, anger, depravity, desperation and, yes, even hope as the 730 third-class souls on this voyage looked forward to its end ... almost from the moment it began. On this first full day at sea, the waiting already seemed interminable for people who had labored their entire lives in fields, factories and foundries, sweatshops, cottages and kitchens. For the Catholic majority, inactivity was a sin ... and now, everyone was a sinner.

As for Neddy, he found some escape reading *Gulliver's Travels* and a geography book he had purloined from the parish school back home. He also had struck up what was certain to be transient friendships in Eamon and Mick. And, then there was Mary.

15

Irish Chicken

After dinner near sunset, Neddy wandered onto the bow and waited until the crowd thinned before climbing quickly up the ladder to the deck above. Looking toward the stern, he noticed a number of people, but none who looked like Mary from a distance. He waited at the rail, looking out at the calm sea and noticing stars just beginning to reveal themselves in the darkening sky.

He waited more than an hour, but no Mary as the evening deepened. She never showed that night, but Neddy was back to their meeting spot the next night, gambling that she might show.

After several minutes at the rail near twilight, Neddy saw Mary emerge from a doorway onto the deck and walk toward him. As she neared, something was wrong. Her shawl hung loosely about her shoulders, held close by a clenched right hand. She was without a head scarf, allowing her hair to whip about unbridled in the wind. Her expression was flat, troubled, he thought. Then he saw what appeared to be a smudge in the middle of her forehead.

"A bit early fer Ash Wednesday," he joked as he approached.

She didn't smile, holding up her free hand to stop him at a distance. "I fell, is all," she said quietly. "I'm a bit of an eejit at times wit' me feet gettin' tangled an' all, especially wit' th' ship rockin' as 'tis."

"Aye, I'm a wee bit of a lump as well," He responded. "I've a bruise on me shoulder from a fall yesterday. Actually, I was t'rown against a mast ..."

"Oh, no ..."

"Nah, 'twas a good t'ing," he smiled. "A big fella, Mick, grabbed me collar and tossed me like a flour sack back from the railing to keep me from goin' over ..."

"That's how yer collar got torn?"

"Aye," he said.

"Give it here," Mary held out her hand. "It needs mending."

"Oh, ya don't have ..."

"Give it here ... now," Mary said sternly, reminding Neddy a bit of his mother. Obviously not about to win a battle of wills, Neddy peeled off the suit coat and handed it to Mary, who said she would return it the next day before dinner. But she didn't.

Neddy was at their spot on the deck, a good half hour before dinner, waiting for Mary and his jacket until he was chilled and had to retire or miss the meal.

"Where ya bin? 'Tis time to eat," Eamon said as Neddy climbed the ladder and into his bunk. "Gone to get me coat. Ya know that cailín I was on about ..."

"The one from Galway?"

"Aye," Neddy said. "She took me coat to mend and was to return it today. But she never came."

"Just like a woman," said Eamon, shaking his head. A head shake based on absolutely no deep experience whatsoever with the opposite sex except for what he overheard his father mutter under his breath hundreds of times behind his mother's back. He thought it would be fitting here. Suddenly, "The dinner bell!!" Eamon shouted, "C'mon!"

Scrambling for his meal pail and jumping from his bunk to the floor, Neddy quickly caught up with Eamon despite a 20-foot lead and having been almost fully absorbed into the throbbing scrum of passengers shoving and jostling through the single doorway like threading a thick cable through the eye of a needle into the dining compartment. Even at this early stage of the voyage, the boys resolved to be among the first wave to reach the long wooden tables, where aproned ladle-laden stewards manned large metal vats of food to be slopped into awaiting meal pails. Eamon and Neddy were not about to be denied, while those who were too slow, too weak, timid or old would go hungry.

The German entered the meal compartment hefting a vat of pungent stew onto a long table at the end of the room. At first glance, the vat's right handle seemed to be wrapped with a rag, but it actually was a makeshift bandage on The German's right hand. When he saw the steward next to him take notice, he said, "Burnt on de stove." He then reached for a ladle on the table and began stirring.

He looked up from the vat and saw the boys in line. As they approached, The German quietly retrieved something from his billowy trouser pocket beneath his apron and slid it into the ladle before carefully dipping it into the vat, then into Eamon's bowl.

"You don't like zeh meat, so I get sumzing special, yust for you," he grinned as Eamon took his dripping pail and began to walk way.

"Jaysus Christ!!" Eamon screeched, dropping the pail and spilling its contents, including a rat's head, on the floor.

"Eest Irish chicken!" The German roared. "Haha, haha, Irish chicken!!!"

"Ya cunt! Ya fucking Jerry cunt!!" Eamon lunged across the table, but The German's ladle became a cudgel as he smashed the boy on the side of the head, sending him reeling. Neddy caught Eamon before he fell, but both of them fell out of line as other people rushed to fill the gap and wouldn't let them back in.

Someone yelled, "Back of th' queue," which grew quickly into a chant by others in line. The opportunity for food was lost. But as Neddy and Eamon headed back to their bunks, Neddy heard a tiny voice. "Here," it said.

Looking down, Neddy saw a small boy holding out his pail. Neddy smiled, recognizing him from earlier in the day. Softly declining the boy's offering, he replied, "No, I'm fine."

Although a ship's officer saw the entire incident with The German, he surmised it was just another example of low behavior by the rabble, and looked the other way, casually surveying the hungry crowd before pushing his way out of the dining compartment and back to the officers mess. There, the steam table offered up Shepherds pie, Cornish pasties, steak-and-kidney pie, bangers and mash, hearty wheat bread and blood pudding. Hot, brewed fresh coffee was dispensed from the spout of a gleaming steel urn and hot water stood by for several varieties of tea. There was a serving tray of blueberry scones.

Back in their bunks, Neddy and Eamon talked with Mick, who was leaning against the vertical rail of the bunk stack.

"Saw what happened back there," Mick said.

"Cunt Hun," growled Eamon.

"Take this," Mick said, producing two slices of stale bread and handing them to the boys. "Granted, 'tis no rat's head, but it'll have to do."

Cramming the bread slice whole into his mouth, Eamon said, "I'm going outside." Mick followed, but Neddy stayed behind.

The *Sea Empress* was cruising at about 18 knots, making good time for such an old diesel-powered bucket that would be sold to a Norwegian concern in the next year or so and scrapped. For now, it proved serviceable for the sole purpose of crossing and re-crossing the Atlantic to transport undesirables ... hundreds at once and thousands over time ... away from Great Britain. It's why the crew referred to the ship as *The Rubbish Bin.* But to the people so mocked and disdained, stacked like turf in a barn, the *Sea Empress* was a large wondrous carriage taking them away from desperation and want, from unemployment and workhouses, slums and failed farms to something better. Something that was once a dream, but now was oh so close to reality.

Neddy opened his suitcase and retrieved the pamphlet given to him by Traveler. The one showing clusters of smiling, well-groomed boys on the deck of a ship and surrounding a distinguished bearded gentleman, who Neddy guessed was the ship's captain. It would be easy to assume that officer was regaling the boys with his many high-seas adventures setting their imaginations aflame as they prepared to sail from lives of poverty and loss to a new horizon of promise and unlimited opportunity.

As Neddy looked at the photos, he wondered where those boys were on the *Sea Empress* or if it even had a captain. If so, he certainly never ventured here in the bowels of this marine creature, lurching side to side, diving into then rising out of what was starting to feel like an endless sea.

After a chapter or two of geography, Neddy stashed the textbook and headed for the door, soon finding himself near the ladder leading to the upper deck, which was in deep shadow. Waiting again for an unguarded moment, he climbed the ladder and was on the upper deck. To his surprise, there was Mary about 30 feet away, standing at the rail holding his jacket.

He smiled and walked toward her. "Mary, so you finally ... Good, God!" he gasped, stunned by her cut lip and swollen jaw.

"'Tis nothing, I just ..."

"That's shite!" he interrupted. "You *did not* just fall. What in Jaysus's name ..."

"Not of yer concern a'tall," she started, but broke down, crumpling Neddy's jacket in her arms then nearly crumpling to the deck. "I dunno, I dunno. Last night, again ..."

"Again?" Neddy practically pleaded. "What about again?"

"Two nights ago ..."

"The bruise on yer forehead ..."

"Aye ..."

"Who? WHO??!!"

"I dunno," Mary struggled for words, ashamed, frightened. "I was asleep an' then he was there ... in th' dark. On me. A terrible heft. He tore at me dress ... grabbed me hair ... tried to kiss me ... his stinkin' breath ... hairy face ... he was so strong ... but I'm sure I cut him wit' me knife. Cut 'im, I t'ink, on his hand. Maybe an arm. Then he punched me."

"Why din'tya tell me after the first time?"

"Tell what? An' to a stranger? I just met ya. Knew nothin' of ya," she cried. "Besides, I thought 'twas ended, 'specially after I kneed him in th' bollocks and he ran away."

They stood silently. Mary held out Neddy's coat. "Here. 'Tis done."

"Mary, I'm so ..."

"Aye," she said quietly, then walking to the door and heading back to the compartment for women and families, she muttered, "Aye."

Neddy's entire body buzzed with a current of helplessness, of impotence, of anger. He was furious by the time he reached his bunk and threw the mended suit coat on the mattress and climbed in after it. Eamon was sleeping already, having the ability not only to fall asleep amid the early evening chaos of the men's compartment, but to fall asleep anywhere, anytime, under any condition. In fact, years later while living in Toronto, Eamon awoke one morning to find a church two doors down from his apartment ... gone. He had slept through an eight-alarm fire that destroyed everything except his undisturbed night's sleep.

But Neddy found sleep elusive that night. Thinking again and again of Mary and the horror she must have felt. The violation. The raw fear for her life. Then his thoughts turned to his sisters and how vulnerable they would be without him to protect them. That fed into the helplessness of the moment. He knew he couldn't have prevented the attack or even protected his sisters if still at the home place. But today? Now? What good was he? In its wake, he couldn't even find words of comfort. "Mary, I'm so ..." He couldn't even come up with "sorry" or "How can I help?" Neddy finally drifted off until Mick, standing on the rail of Eamon's bunk, was face to face with him.

"Hey, runt," he shook Neddy awake. "Runt, wake up. Ya gotta see this."

Dropping to the floor, Neddy reached in to wake Eamon, but was shaken off with a snarl and followed Mick through the compartment door, to the ship's bow and up the ladder to the deck above.

CREEEEEACCCCCCK!!! A gargantuan flash of lightning turned the ship's silhouette to daylight, a near-blinding splash illuminating the ship's funnels wet with sea spray.

"Real Furnace of God lightning," Mick said, squinting into the booming aftershock, waiting for the rain that hadn't quite caught up to the electric herald. "That's what me ma always called the bigguns. Holy Furnace of God."

BRRRUMMMMM ... brrrummmmm ... brum!

"And there are the apostles," Mick added with a chuckle, as the thunder was close behind, making his trouser legs vibrate. "Strange what t'ings you remember."

"Furnace of God," Neddy repeated, thinking of Mary's attack, adding, "if the Almighty even exists."

"Say again?" Mick asked, not quite hearing him.

Neddy didn't reply, leaning against a bulkhead and looking out to sea, waiting for the next lightning strike. But the next one was farther away and the thunder came after a five count. Then came the next and an eight count before the thunder. "Movin' away from us," he said, "or we're movin' away from it."

BRRRRRUMMMMMMMMM.

After a moment, Neddy turned to Mick. "Can I trust you wit' somet'ing?"

"Depends, I guess," Mick answered.

"'Tis about Mary ..."

"Mary?"

"The cailin with me jacket ..."

"From Galway?"

"Aye," Neddy said. "I need yer word ..."

"Well, if yer braggin' about you an' ...," Mick joked, but seeing Neddy's cold stare, he said, "Aye. You've me word."

"'Tis bad. Real bad. Mary's been beat ...," Neddy began.

"Beat? Whaddya mean?"

"Last night and a night before that, someone beat her ... and worse," Neddy said.

"Who, fer Jaysus sake, WHO?"

"Dunno. *She* dunno. Came to her bed in th' dark."

"Christ."

"She fought and cut his arm an' drew blood. It happened before, but she kicked him in th' bollocks and he run off."

Mick was silent for several minutes until he asked, "So, what now?"

"Don't know as anyt'ing can be done."

"A sin, 'tis," Mick said, "a bloody sin."

"Aye."

The storm was fading fast as the flashes of light were followed by diminishing reports of thunder that soon became mere grumbles. Finally, only silent, intermittent flashes remained until dropping below the horizon, as the boys headed back inside and to bed once again. God and his furnace were gone.

16

In Plain Sight

The breakfast bell caught Neddy and Eamon, quite literally, napping at 6:55, but they still made the dining compartment so fast it seemed they were in line with meal pails and utensils at the ready as the bell's last clang echoed into the clamor of hungry immigrants.

Eamon was half a head shorter than Neddy and struggled to see past the shoulders of a man who stood six feet tall in front of him. "How long's the line?" he asked impatiently.

Neddy stood on his tiptoes and could see just beyond the shoulders in front of him. He strained to see the serving table ahead, but only caught a glimpse of The German and two other stewards ladling the daily gruel. Then he saw it. For a brief moment, The German brushed hair from his forehead with the back of his bandaged right hand. A bandage with a prominent brown stain.

In passing, Neddy had noticed the hand wrapped in a rag the day before during the commotion surrounding the rat's head incident. But now ...? Suddenly, Mick was rushing up to Neddy from the front, his pail of gruel in hand. "Ned! Ned!" he hissed in a loud whisper, "I just saw The German's ..."

"... Right hand," Neddy said, unable to look away from the serving table. "His right hand with the rag wrapped around it. Jaysus, Mary and Joseph."

Minutes later, he, Eamon and Mick were two spots away from the food vats, as Neddy's stare held fast on The German's bandaged hand, now nearly saturated with gruel. Then, holding out his meal pail, he asked, "What's wit' yer hand?"

"Cuttink potatoes for you fuckink Irish," he sneered.

"I thought you burned it on a stove," said the steward next to him.

"Stove, potatoes, who de fuck cares ... Fuck you," The German barked. "Move along. Eile! Schnell!"

Neddy stood fast. "No," he persisted, "How'd it happen?"

"Maybe I punch an Irishman," The German laughed.

"... or an Irish girl?" Neddy said flatly, his eyes unblinking, his face cold.

The German was motionless for an instant, then looked past Neddy to the next in line. "Move along, Schnell!"

Finding no place at a table, the three boys headed outdoors to eat.

"We gotta do somethin'," Mick said urgently.

"About what?" Eamon said, shoving a large lump of gruel into his mouth.

"Don't bother 'bout it," said Mick.

But Neddy thought for a moment and decided to tell Eamon the whole story.

"Fuckin' German pig! We've to tell th' captain," Eamon offered.

"Who'll do what?" Neddy said with a shrug. "D'ya t'ink the captain or th' crew gives a pig's shite what happens to any of us. They t'ink we're animals."

"Then maybe we need to act like animals," Mick offered.

"No, we have to t'ink of somethin' else," Neddy said.

What hatched over the next few hours wasn't so much a plan as a plot. A plot to beat The German senseless ... then cut off his balls and throw them into the ocean.

While Neddy brought Eamon and Mick into the conspiracy, he never let them in on the fact that he had resolved to act alone. After all, it was Mary who took him ... and only him ... into her confidence and would never condone him sharing her shame with others. No, any action had to be carried out by him alone.

Tracking The German and his movements became the trio's primary focus. Starting after the morning meal, they began their reconnaissance. First they located the galley – where The German left before a meal, and returned after a meal, then where he slept and ate. None of it particularly easy to achieve, given the restricted movement imposed on steerage passengers who were denied access anywhere on the ship except those areas designated for third class: Sleeping quarters, three small heads, the dining compartment and the gathering area on the bow.

That's why Neddy always took special care when heading topside to go where the crew wasn't or to conceal himself if they were near. The other boys co-opted Neddy's avoidance tactic of ducking behind air vents, scooting under ladders or squeezing into tight, dark recesses whenever they heard crew about. Finding locations, it turned out, was a relatively easy task. Nailing down times when The German was in those locations was more difficult until they established one, important pattern. As unlikely as it was, cleanliness – or at least what this obese, garbage stained cretin considered cleanliness – was the key.

After a full two days of shadowing The German as best they could, they were back at Eamon's bunk.

"All meals are th' same t'ing," Neddy began, as Eamon and Mick nodded in agreement. "He drags th' vats filled wit' what's left of th' swill he feeds us an' dumps it over th' side of th' ship."

There, The German sloshed sea water into the vats, stirring it with his ladle and dumping that overboard as well. Meal in. Meal out. But with one significant detour. After the dinner meal, he wouldn't start the process until just before dark. The reason, unknown to the boys, was beer.

The German loved beer. Even if it *was* inferior British and Canadian brews he considered weak sisters to the meatier German Bockbier or Doppelbock. But for now, beer was beer. And he drank his fill after dinner each night adding to the prodigious belly that challenged the stamina of buttons on his garbage-stained shirt and spilled over his waistband.

By the time he got to dragging the dozen or so vats from the galley to the rail, the deck was in near darkness, illuminated only by a narrow shaft of light coming from the galley's open door.

"T'night," Neddy said firmly. "T'night, we have a talk wit' Th' German after dinner." Eamon and Mick nodded and all three agreed to meet at the ladder on the bow once the sun began to set.

But when the appointed hour arrived, Neddy didn't show because he was already in place, crouching in the darkness of a large air vent on deck, balancing on its lip and bracing himself with both hands. His lunch-pail fork was in his rear pocket. The vent, just eight feet or so from the galley door gave him easy access to The German as he struggled with the vats, while hiding in its darkness gave him cover should unexpected crew wander by.

Back at the ladder, Eamon and Mick waited anxiously until Mick went back inside the sleeping compartment to search for Neddy.

Meanwhile, Neddy balanced himself on the air vent lip, fighting off a cramp in his right leg by carefully extending it outside the vent opening, shaking it about and retracting it just as the galley door opened illuminating the deck. He held his breath, tightening the grip of his left hand on the mouth of the vent and reaching around with his right hand to his back pocket and extracting his fork.

Then came a deep, guttural off-key voice slurring as it sang out, *"Ein prosit, ein prosit, der gemut-ta-clut ... gemutlichkeit. Ein prosit ..."*

Neddy flashed on his father's drunken returns to

the home place, singing and staggering his way to bed, but snapped back to the present when he heard the scraping of metal and a loud, bubbling belch followed by a coarse, deep laugh. "Das ist gut," The German congratulated himself on his prodigious release of gas. "Ja, gut!"

As The German dragged the first food vat across the deck, Neddy was out of the vent, quietly approaching him from behind, fork raised to attack. Without a word, he sprang, driving the fork deep in The German's shoulder at the base of his neck. But rather than falling, The German whipped around his massive body and grabbed Neddy by the arm. As he did so, the makeshift bandage flew from his hand, exposing a five-inch-long, scabbed-over gash running diagonally across his knuckles. Seeing it, Neddy brought around his other arm and slammed into The German's right cheek. But The German recovered quickly, disabling Neddy's free arm as well, immobilizing the boy's upper body with such force Mary's knife wound reopened, mixing blood into the fray.

Grunting wildly as he pushed Neddy closer to the rail, The German screamed, "YOU FUCKINK IRISH SCUM! YOU FUCKINK IRI ..."

In mid-sentence, his tirade became a gurgling growl as a huge arm began crushing his windpipe from behind. He began flailing insanely, releasing Neddy who lurched sideways, losing his footing on the wet deck, sliding toward the rail, flipping over it and in one desperate lunge clamping onto its steel cable with one, then another hand. With both legs thrashing in the wind like signal flags, Neddy managed to loop his left leg up and onto the edge of the deck long enough to muscle his right leg there as well. Then, with what strength he had left, pulling the rest of his body topside and to safety.

Mick, tightening his deadly headlock on The German, now joined the primordial screams of battle with a thunderous roar of his own. He started hammering The German's face repeatedly until his nose collapsed in a splash of blood and crushed cartilage. The German was silent as he and Mick dropped to the deck. The tangled bodies lay still for a moment until Mick, regaining his breath, slowly rolled to his side, sat up and looked down at The Unconcious German. Raising his right foot, he placed it against the body and kicked it overboard.

Neddy, still recovering, his heart well on a return trip from near explosion, stood at the galley door and looked in. The remaining vats waited. One by one, they pulled them out on deck and one by one, threw the contents into the ocean and rinsed them before returning them to the galley. They did this for all of them ... except four. Neddy tipped over one of them and left it leaning against the rail.

Mick and Neddy went into the galley and rinsed the blood from their clothes, fists and arms with salt water, then looked outside. First forward. Then aft. Seeing no one, Mick threw several buckets of sea water on the deck to wash off the large smears of blood The German left on his way overboard. Putting the buckets back in the galley, Mick dried his hands on his trouser legs, when Neddy froze.

Looking aft, there in the darkness, he saw a shadow still as death itself. As his eyes adjusted, the shadow took form. "Mary?" he whispered.

Mary emerged from the darkness into the partial light of the doorway and as she moved closer, Neddy caught the glint of a knife in her right hand.

Neddy and Mick weren't the only ones to take note of the bloody bandage on The German's hand. Not long after Neddy and the boys had confronted The German in the dining compartment, Mary had gone there with a farm girl from Donegal for a chance at breakfast. But upon seeing The German's hand as he hefted an empty gruel vat from the table, Mary bolted from the compartment, running toward the stern, past the galley and back to her sleeping compartment, where she flung herself into her bunk, clutching her knife, her back toward the bulkhead.

Now, standing silently in the aftermath, she looked at Neddy, then to Mick, turned and walked away without a word. The boys were equally silent as they descended the ladder to the bow and entered the steerage sleeping compartment. They split up, again without a word, and fell into their bunks.

Neddy was still shaking as he pulled the blanket over his shoulders, his eyes fixed in a numb stare as he faced into the darkness, listening to Eamon, snoring like an old truck motoring through dreamland.

Eamon had tired of waiting for Neddy and Mick. One never showed up and the other disappeared without a word. He waited nearly an hour before crawling into his bunk, oblivious to what he would sleep through this night. Never knowing that nothing in his life ... not even the fiery death of a nearby church in decades to come ... would match the raw, violent fury unleashed on the deck far above his head.

Morning came for Neddy before the sun rose. He was awakened by the thumping staccato of rapid footsteps on the deck above. A muffled voice issuing what sounded like orders in one moment. Rumblings of a group of men in the next, moving as a unit. Neddy slid from his bunk onto the floor and apprehensively headed for the compartment door when he saw Mick standing outside, head cocked upward, studying the sometimes erratic movements of crew members moving this way and that.

"I'm not surprised it happened to the fucking bastard," said one crew member walking by.

"Who drinks himself stupid and goes out on deck to dump garbage at night?"

"A dumb fucking kraut, is who."

The men laughed as they walked away.

Neddy and Mick looked at each other, silently watching the frenzy they created above them. From the moment last night's events began unraveling – and actually much earlier in the planning phase of their scheme -- they never once thought of the aftermath, let alone consequences for their actions. After all, they never planned to *kill* The German. They only wanted to make him suffer for what he did to Mary. And after they cut off his balls, he would be so humiliated, he'd never mention it to another living soul. Instead, he would live ball-less and in shame, regretting what he did for the rest of his life. But even if that plan had come off along with The German's balls, they hadn't considered the massive amount of blood involved in his castration.

Then everything went sideways and within minutes Mick was off loading a dead, drunk German from a ship in the middle of the Atlantic. Still high with a flash-flood of adrenaline, Neddy hatched the fiction that The Drunk German fell overboard. He told Mick to help him empty and rinse most of the vats and leave four on deck so it seemed he was in the middle of cleaning them. As an afterthought, he tipped one over while Mick grabbed the bucket and flushed the blood from the deck. Then there was Mary.

The crew's activity on the deck above had subsided when Mick broke the silence. "Fer Christsake," he said. "How th' fuck did th' girl know?"

Neddy shrugged. "You tell me."

"Jaysus, she saw th' whole t'ing," Mick said. "She saw th' killin'."

"... an' said not a t'ing," Neddy replied. "Not a t'ing."

"That still don't explain ..."

"I know, I know," Neddy said. "And about explainin' t'ings, how didja know I was goin' after Th' German by me-self? Ya don't hardly know me."

"I didn't know shite," Mick whispered back. "When ya didn't turn up, I thought ya musta changed yer mind. T'inkin' what I'd do if it was me, I went off me-self to do it. Then I sees ya, jumpin' on The German twice yer size, an' stickin' him wit' a fork like he's a lamb roast. I thought ya had it under control ... until ya didn't."

"Acting th' eejit, eh?"

"Aye," Mick agreed, "a full out geebag."

Eamon emerged and walked over to the boys, focusing on the deck activity above. "What th' hell is this?"

"Dunno," Mick lied, "but 'tis somethin' fer sure."

"Meal bell's about to go," Eamon said with a yawn. "C'mon."

After grabbing meal kits from their bunks, Neddy realized his fork was missing. "Christ!" he thought, leaning close to Mick's ear. "Me fork's gone," he rasped in a panic.

Reaching into his back pocket, Mick pulled out the utensil and handed it to Neddy. "Saved yer arse again," he smiled. "Here. Saw it stickin' out of 'im just before he went over. Even cleaned it fer ya. A man's gotta eat."

As they approached the food vats, Eamon noticed something different. "Where's Th' fuckin' German?"

"Hmm," said Neddy. "Dunno."

"Hey," Eamon yelled to the stewards behind the vats, "Where's Th' German?"

One responded, "None of your business."

But a second one said, "Overboard. They think he was drunk and fell off, so no Irish Chicken for you today." The stewards laughed as Eamon flashed a middle finger.

After receiving their ration of gruel, the boys headed outside to eat.

"Where'd ya go last night?" Eamon said leaning in. "Didja kill th' kraut?"

"Ach, no. 'Course not. Killin' wasn't th' plan now, was it? Never got a chance," Neddy said, calmly looking down at his pail and shoving a dripping spoon of gruel in his mouth. "I went up there but couldn't find 'im."

"Ya went wit'out me?" Eamon turned to Neddy.

"'Twas me fight, not yours," Neddy responded.

"An' what happened wit' you," Eamon turned to Mick.

"Went fer a walk," he said.

"A walk, Aye," Eamon repeated, smiling to himself. "A bloody walk."

"Aye," Mick replied, amused at Eamon's inadvertently accurate word choice.

The morning fog was lifting and the sun was breaking through the clouds. The Atlantic was exceptionally calm as the *Sea Empress* glided through the waves, leaving a foamy wash, a curtain of smoke and one German corpse behind her.

Since rising that morning, Neddy struggled with a bout of Catholic Guilt, that overarching rush of inadequacy, doubt and self-hatred hammered into the heads of all papists from the earliest stages of life. But the guilt didn't spring from his involvement in The German's murder. It was rooted in his complete lack of contrition, a cornerstone of penance and forgiveness meted out in chains of prayer as mental flagellation by priests in the confessional. No. The German's death didn't trouble him in the least, but the thought of Mary watching The German's violent end became an obsession.

What was his next step? Was there a next step? Was she repulsed by his violent nature, which is why she armed herself with a knife in the first place?

But his inner turmoil evaporated as he glimpsed Mary making her way through the tangle of humanity in the men's steerage compartment. As she approached his bunk, Neddy was up like a shot, dropping to the floor just in time for her to reach out and embrace him. She held him tightly, almost as tightly as his mother had in their goodbyes several days past.

Then, without releasing her hold on him, Mary whispered, "Thank you." When she finally let go ... slowly, softly ... she said, "After dinner," then walked away.

Neddy stood by his bunk for a long while, then sat on Eamon's empty bunk for a think. Several minutes later, he cruised topside to enjoy the warm sunshine's counterpoint to the bracing wind as the *Sea Empress* navigated the downside of its northern arc toward Canada. Insinuating himself into the throbbing mass along the railing, all straining for fresh ocean air, Neddy flipped his suit coat collar up around his neck and felt Mary's mend where it had been torn by Mick. His hand lingered there a moment and he smiled.

"Not long now," said Eamon as he sidled up beside Neddy, elbowing out a rather, short, scrawny teen in a moth-eaten sweater, who pushed back briefly, but just as quickly gave up the fight.

"Two days, by me guess," Neddy responded. "Least that's what we're told."

"An' we always believe what we're told, don'cha know," Eamon grinned.

"Aye. 'Specially by Th' Church."

"Ya got th' leaflet, too?"

"Oh, aye," Neddy said. "I'm still lookin' fer the smilin' boys and th' captain. Need to have a wee talk to him about th' shite smell. 'Tis what most reminds me of the home place, but shite from cows an' pigs smells much better."

"GET AWAY OR I'LL CLUB YA!!" came a shrill voice farther down the deck, followed by an equally loud protest, "'TWASN'T ME!!" Just as quickly, Neddy saw a woman's fist rise above the crowd's heads, coming down hard then rising again, falling, then up again only to be stopped by another hand mid-flight. "SAID, T'WASN'T ME, WOMAN!!"

"TOUCH ME AGAIN AND ..."

"ACH!" the man's voice responded, "WHO'D WANT TO ..."

The crowd laughed and the skirmish ended.

Although Neddy scanned those on deck several times,

hoping Mary might show, she never did. And after a while, the boys soon retired to their bunks. Eamon for a nap. Neddy to read.

He fished out *Gulliver's Travels* from his suitcase, keen as ever for an escape to strange lands like Lilliput where a friendly giant extinguished a palace fire by unleashing his willy and pissing out the flames. While he thought that was funny, his greatest satisfaction with that particular passage was the knowledge it would scandalize Sister Assumpta, who obviously never read the book before making it available to parish children back home.

Mick came up to the bunk carrying a sizable length of rope. Neddy looked down and asked, "What's that?"

"Me fishin' line," Mick said proudly.

"Fishin' line? Th' fuck, ya say," Neddy grinned.

"Aye," Mick affirmed, "Me fishin' line. An' here's me hook." Taking something from his trouser pocket, he showed Neddy his dinner fork bent and fashioned into a three-pronged hook resembling a miniature trident. "I already dropped the line over th' side to see if it reached the water ... an' it does."

"Where'd ya get it?"

"Took it off th' mast before th' sun come up t'day."

"The mast??!! How ..."

"Used to climb trees at th' home place all th' time," Mick explained. "Climbin' th' mast was almost as easy, but a wee bit slippery."

Neddy rolled back in the bunk, convulsed with laughter for several seconds before finally sitting up to catch his breath. "And just what will ya use fer bait?"

"I was t'inkin' I'd use Eamon."

Hearing his name through the trailing end of his nap, Eamon yawned, "What are ya on about me?"

"Do ya know how to swim?" Mick asked, triggering another laughing jag at Eamon's expense.

"He don't," Neddy laughed between snorts.

"Me neither," Mick joined in, laughing harder than the other two.

"So, yer a fine one to be hangin' yer arse off a boat in th' ocean," Neddy said.

"What are ye on about?" Eamon said, finally shaking off his nap and being told about Mick's impending venture as a fisherman.

"Maybe we should start callin' ya St. Peter ..." Eamon offered.

"Or Jonah," said Neddy, "cause ya might just hook a whale."

At dinner, the boys took chunks of rancid fish from their portions of that night's stew and held them back as bait. Mick threw in a few bits of potato "in case the fish are Irish." The grand plan was to catch enough fresh fish so they didn't have to suffer the swill served up by the ship.

They waited until late afternoon, just as the sun began to set, and eased their way in and out of shadows to the poop deck aft. Looking out for crew members and satisfied no one was about, they dropped the rope over the port side, careful not to get the line tangled in the propeller wash. Then Mick tied a separate piece of rope securely to the rail and around his waist.

"Wait!" Eamon shouted, pointing off to starboard.

"Look! Look there! Is that land? Is that Canada?"

Mick, his hand across his brow to block the sun as he squinted toward the horizon. "I t'ink 'tis ... what'd he say? ... New-Found-Land. I heard a fella say we'd pass by t'day or ..."

"New-Found-Land," Neddy chimed in. "Aye ... AYE! Read about it in me geography. 'Tis an island not far from Canada." Then, "Oh, shite! Mary! I'm to meet her past dinner." And he was gone.

Mary was at their spot with her back toward Neddy as he approached her from behind. Far enough away for her to hear him without being startled, Neddy shouted, "Waitin' fer someone, are ya?"

She turned, her face illuminated by a deck light, and for the first time since they met, she smiled broadly. "Aye, someone."

At first, there was an awkward silence, then disjointed attempts to speak as co-conspirators meeting to discuss the aftermath of a well-executed plot. Both began speaking at the same time, entangling their thoughts in short, twisted phrasing.

"You go," Neddy said.

"No, you," said Mary.

"Last night," he began. "How'd ya know t'was him?"

"Th' hand," she started. "I saw th' rag around his hand at meal time. Th' dried blood on it. His size. Big, ugly face hair. I knew he was th' bodach ... a day ago. Me brother gave me th' knife to protect me-self, travellin' alone, and I'll be damned if I didn't use it on 'im."

Although Mary's face was tranquil, almost serene in the murder's aftermath, her eyes were sharp as the point of her blade. Cold. Determined. Unrepentant.

Silence again until, after a moment's thought, Neddy asked with a slight grin, "Will ya be usin' the stabber as a house maid?" Mary laughed.

"Maybe to cut string off a parcel," she offered, "or somethin' more dangerous like scarin' away a mouse."

"Now that's a picture," Neddy said. "Ya walkin' through th' grand house in th' dark in yer housemaid uniform, yer blade out, huntin' a wee mouse, protectin' yer grand owners."

They laughed briefly, but fell silent again, listening to the sound of propeller wash, a soothing hypnotic whoosh as if air were being let out of the darkest day of their journey. "The killin'," Neddy lowered his voice. "Is it a worry fer ya? I mean … 'tis a mortal sin."

"Aye, and what he did to me 'twas a mortal sin," she said. "'An eye fer an eye, is it not? One mortal sin answered wit' another."

"I thought I'd kilt a man back at th' home place," Neddy casually confessed. "A bad sort who did bad t'ings to little boys. Left 'im bloody and screamin' after I smashed his face with me glass."

"And did ya."

"Smash his face?"

"Did ya kill 'im?"

"Nah," Neddy said, "but no rent was paid on th' home place after."

"What does rent …?"

"A long story," Neddy waved her off gently. After a moment's contemplation, he added darkly, "One day, his bollocks will be cut off."

"Did he …"

"No," Neddy interrupted. "Never give him a chance. Smashed …"

"… the glass in his face," She seemed to understand Neddy's reluctance to provide more detail and said nothing more, when a dull scraping sound came from behind, getting louder as it approached. They spun around but could see nothing in the dark.

"Hey!" yelled Mick, emerging into the dim light, "Look what we fished outta th' water." Trailing behind him on the deck was the tangle of his makeshift fishing rig that had hooked, as unlikely as it was, a water-logged deck plank to which a rusted cleat caked with barnacles was attached.

Mary, who fished her entire life with her brothers on a local lough, immediately identified the object. "'Tis part of an old boat."

"G'wan," said Mick skeptically. "Part of a boat? This boat? Jaysus!"

"Nah, not this plank. I seen dozens of 'em on small boats," Mary said, grabbing hold of the decking, dropping it and drying her hand on the side of her skirt. "Called a cleat. Ya tie ropes 'round it."

"Can ya eat it?" Neddy quipped, looking down at the debris smiling.

Puzzled, Mick replied, "Eat it?"

"Aye," said Neddy, tapping the cleat with his foot. "'Twas th' plan, was it not? Catchin' t'ings to eat? I'll tell ya right now, I won't be eatin' that t'ing any time soon. B'sides, 'tis a day or so to Canada. Maybe the food's better there."

"Couldn't be worse than this shite," added Eamon,

joining the group.

They all agreed, as Mick and Neddy gathered the fishing gear and the day's catch and threw the entire mess overboard.

17

God Laughed

Mick awakened to thunder and torrential rain that sounded like a massive rake repeatedly scraping the length of the ship's hull and deck above them. The men's sleeping quarters were cold and damp with the inherent darkness punctured only by what little light came in through portholes or from the flare of naked light bulbs here and there throughout the compartment. But it wasn't the rain that woke him. Or the thunder. It was a guttural, growling chorus of vomiting and crying that intensified during the night as seasickness swept from bunk to bunk to bunk, as the acrid stench of expelled, partially digested food reached Mick's nostrils and forced his eyes open.

While not seasick himself, Mick was ... and always had been ... a sympathetic vomiter. With just the sound of others retching, the splash of it hitting the ground or even a hint of vomit in the air was enough to send him into a convulsive fit of dry heaves ... or worse. This morning it was *or worse* as Mick leaned out of his bunk and let fly a river of stew from last night's dinner. It hit the floor, forming several forking rivulets that flowed away from his bunk and back again. With that sight, he convulsed, vomited again then fell into a rhythm of dry heaves before rolling back into his bunk, just as the passenger above him let fly a waterfall of spew that barely missed his head. Hearing his neighbor's foul contribution outside the bunk, Mick nearly fell sick again, but with great effort quelled the vile tide, swallowed hard and closed his eyes.

Eamon ... now green as Ireland itself ... was no better off than Mick, but Neddy was only mildly affected with a bit of nausea, although he gripped the rails of his bunk firmly to prevent his body from rocketing off the straw mattress and going airborne as the old ship hammered through the waves.

To passengers of all classes, the *Sea Empress*, now approaching its final slog to the Canadian coast, seemed less a ship and more like a huge cradle furiously rocked by the hand of God. That image must have been shared by a sizable contingent of souls in steerage as prayers of deliverance were offered up in a desperate hosanna to the heavenly father. Still, the cradle rocked as the people prayed and God laughed.

The breakfast bell came and went with almost no one venturing outside their bunks. Many of those not sickened by the hours-long ride away from the gates of hell dared not navigate between the stacks of bunks for fear of cracking open a skull after slipping in the ooze that seemed to be everywhere. But as the ship emerged from the storm, settling into a gentle, almost soothing glide by mid-afternoon, those not weakened by the virulent assault on their digestive tracks took tentative steps out of the sleeping compartment's fouled air and into the chilled, recuperative breeze on the bow.

Neddy was one of the first to do so, wearing the dark wool trousers, Aran sweater and muslin shirt he packed along with his traveling suit and books. His only socks by this time were almost stiff enough to stand alone and his shirt was stained with stew and a large scuff of rust, where it constantly brushed against his meal pail to and from the dining compartment. After little more than a week aboard, the meal pail, fork, spoon and cup were covered with rust from being rinsed with cold sea water dispensed from six cold-water faucets in a narrow washroom serving the 730 people in steerage. There also was a single hot-water faucet that surrendered on day two. The passenger-to-faucet ratio kept most people from trying to use the washroom at all. In Neddy's case, he wiped his meal kit with a handkerchief Moira slipped into the suitcase with rosary beads as her son prepared to leave the farm. Now, however, even the handkerchief was caked with stew and gruel, almost unrecognizable as such. The rosary was untouched.

But Neddy had it better than either Eamon or Mick, who resorted to using their shirttails and sleeves to remove debris from their pails, which were nearly useless. Only by eating half rations, careful not to scrape the pail's bottom or sides with their utensils, could the boys avoid the strong taste of corrosion as they ate.

18

Confession

Standing near the prow, which was slowly filling with people in varying stages of recovery, Neddy saw something he hadn't seen since leaving Belfast Harbor. Seagulls. Not quite a flock, but a half dozen, maybe eight, at different altitudes and attitudes, gliding in random directions while tracking the ship's path. Off the stern, the gulls flapped wildly then hovered over the propeller wash, diving randomly into the foam for sea life churned to the surface by the two huge diesel engines.

"Tomorrow," came Mary's voice near Neddy's right shoulder, as Mick and Eamon drifted off to leave them alone.

"Or early the day after," Neddy said, turning and looking at her black hair whipping about her head.

Brushing the curls off her face and securing them against her scalp with a left hand, Mary asked, "Are ya scared?"

"Nah," Neddy shot back, but just as quickly conceded, "Aye ... a bit."

"Never been to a place like Philadelphia city," Mary said, "and I know nothin' of this rich John B. Kelly family I'll work for 'cept they're Irish ..."

"Well," Neddy smiled, "at least they've that goin' fer them."

Mary smiled. "... and never been far from the home place, 'specially this far."

"Who has?"

"Never been away from me brothers ..."

"Or me sisters," he said. "Or me Ma."

"How 'bout your Da?" She wondered as Neddy never mentioned him.

"Not much to miss there," Neddy said. "Spent most times at The Hen ... a pub ... like I had no Da a'tall most times."

"Me Da as well," she said. "Me Ma wasn't much better."

"Me Ma was ... *is* ... a saint, she is," Neddy said, "An' me sisters ..."

"Maybe scared's not the right word fer it," Mary

recalculated. "Maybe not sure of me-self is more like it. Maybe just not knowin' much 'bout this new life that's supposed to be so grand. D'ya t'ink it will be?"

"Grand? Not sure how grand farmin' in Canada will be," Neddy said. "There's dirt an' cows an' pigs an' hay an' ... s'pose it'd be the same as th' home place. But not knowin' a soul ..."

"Aye," Mary agreed. "'Tis bein' alone that stops me as well. But it also starts me t'inkin' I'm already alone. Fer a long time."

"Not with six brothers," said Neddy.

"I lied about bein' close," she confessed. "Haven't seen but one fer two years. Nor me Ma or Da. Not since they sent me to the sisters and now I'm away fer good."

"Sisters ...?"

"I've been to th' Magdalenes," Mary said stoically.

"Magdalenes? Th' laundries? I heard me sister Rose talk about 'em. But thought 'twas rubbish. They're real?"

Since 1795, the Magdalene Laundries were all too real for hundreds of thousands of Irish girls sent away to virtual slavery in prison-like conditions, under the guise of rehabilitating "fallen women" and with the full blessing of the Irish government and Catholic Church. They were banished by their families for having sex or giving birth outside of wedlock or for undefined moral turpitude or loose morals or ... as in Mary's case ... for spite or simply being a normal young girl aware for the first time of her blossoming womanhood.

"'I' was a boy at school I fancied," Mary began, "an' he fancied me. We'd have a wee snog here an' there, nothin' more than that. Wouldn't t'ink of it 'til I was married. But his Ma, a real eejit with a face on her like a plate of mortal sins, hated any girl sniffin' about her lad. She goes to th' parish priest and says I'm a hoor who's not leavin' her son be and temptin' him into sin. The priest tells me Da – who slashes his knickers if a priest looks sideways at 'im – an' says I'm a shame on th' family. Me Da didn't even tell me I'm goin' when nuns show up at me door an' I'm away to th' laundry near Dublin. One day I'm home. Th' next I find me-self in hell, up to me elbows in a wash tub."

"Fer how long?"

"A year, maybe more. I dunno fer sure. They took me name, blocked me brothers. Me parents were too skuttered on stout to care. The church stole me life, but me brother Malachy thought of a way to solve th' problem. I didn't know the problem was me. Later, he tells me that fer days, he stood outside th' gate of a side yard at th' laundry, where nuns let us go a bit each mornin'. When he sees me there, he whistles like he always did and I sneak over t'inkin' he's come fer me."

Her face darkened. "But he's not there to take me home. He's come to tell me about th' Church's Canada scheme to send me away. When th' nun sees us, she comes up and start's cuffin me somethin' terrible with a switch and screamin' I'm a hoor an' on me way to the divil. Malachy did nothin'. Just walked off.

"I was hopin' Malachy did what he thought best fer me, but now I'm t'inkin' all of them thought they'd be better with me in Canada and not in Ireland shamin' 'em. That was th' last I seen of 'em 'til Malachy shows up at th' boat in Belfast.

"I'm in the queue and he walks up. Gives me four shillings and the knife. 'It'll keep ya safe,' he says." She slowly pulled the knife from under her shawl and looked down at it in her open hand. "'Tis all I've left of Ireland."

Neddy couldn't look away. From Mary's tears. From her blue eyes rimmed in red. From her gentle mouth. All of it framed by hair as dark as a stallion's mane. He finally reached out, softly folded her small hand around the knife handle, which she returned to its hiding place. He then put an arm around her shoulders and carefully arranged the shawl up around her neck. She moved closer, leaning into his tentative embrace, an embrace he had rehearsed in his head with any number of girls back home, but never had the courage to follow through. She turned slightly, kissed him on the cheek and they remained there on the bow, long past the dinner bell and into the evening when they finally said good night.

Traveler waited on the far side of sleep.

Neddy was just inside the barnyard gate when Traveler stopped a bit farther down the farm lane, leaned over and plucked a deep pink clover bloom growing out of a week-old cow pie. He put the flower to his nose, sniffed it and took off his panama hat. He carefully slid the flower into the hat band and replaced the hat on his head.

"You just never know where beauty lies," he smiled at Neddy. "You may even find a flower in a pile of shit. Remember that and always keep looking. You'll never stop being surprised."

"What now?" Neddy scratched his head as he watched Traveler examining the roadside quietly, finding another flower, leaning down and coming up with the bloom between the thumb and index finger of his right hand. Placing the buttercup under his chin, he asked Neddy, "So, do I like butter?"

"Bridget," Neddy smiled wistfully. "Bridget liked butter."

"She did indeed," Traveler said, placing the buttercup next to the clover bloom in his hat band. "And Bridget liked more than that. Did you know she loved ladybugs best?"

"I did," said Neddy.

"Did you know she used to name them?"

"I did not," Neddy said surprised.

"Did you know her favorite ladybug name was Neddy? It was the only name she ever used. She called them all Neddybugs because she wanted you with her even when you weren't around. She was your little flower ..."

"Aye," Neddy said, pain rising in his voice. "Me, little flower."

"Now there are two to consider," Traveler said, relighting his cigar, "and both are rising out of this shit pile of a boat."

Neddy considered that for a moment. "Mary?"

"Bingo!" said Traveler, flashing a thumbs up. "Mary certainly is a flower of a girl, but you must prepare to lose her. Tomorrow. She'll be gone on the docks. While not the same way, as Bridget, she'll be on her way to Philadelphia and you'll be going to Ottawa."

"I didn't think ..."

"... didn't think that would happen?" responded Traveler. "How could it not? Your fates, your paths are different despite how you feel about each other. Sad, but true and truly sad. Life's a bitch."

Neddy was silent until, "But you said two flowers."

"I did, didn't I," Traveler agreed. "The other flower is

a small package and it's up to you to see it's delivered to St. George's Home for Ireland's Castoffs."

"Huh? St. George's Home fer ..."

"... Ireland's Castoffs," Traveler repeated. "A nickname you'll give it for all the boys who went there ... then weren't there ... then were there again and again. Oh, and wait until you meet Mother Frances Euphemia." Traveler rolled his eyes, sticking a finger down his throat and faking a dry heave. "She's a real beauty with the disposition of a reptile. Don't talk back to her."

Neddy awoke, eyes wide and staring at the mildewed planks of the bunk above his head, thinking of the thatch mouse back home. He rolled to his side, then swung his legs over the bunk rail and dropped to the floor. Eamon was stirring as well and as both boys collected their meal kits, Mick joined them to get an early jump on the final breakfast of the voyage. Halfway to the meal compartment, the breakfast bell rang. But there was something oddly out of place.

As they walked through the dining compartment door, they were greeted by the distinct aroma of ... bacon. For a moment, Eamon thought he was still asleep, but when he saw the serving tables at the far end of the compartment, the food vats were missing, replaced by large, flat metal pans mounded high with, yes, bacon. And sausages. And bread. And eggs. Black pudding, potatoes and even baked beans.

"Good morning," a uniformed steward announced through a bright-red *Sea Empress* megaphone while standing atop a chair in one corner of the compartment. "This is the last day of your journey to Canada and we want you to be your best self because you won't be admitted to Canada if you're unclean and in bad spirits. They don't permit dirty or angry people in."

"What's this about?" Mick said to Neddy.

"Dunno," Neddy responded, straining for a better look.

"When you return to your sleeping area," the steward continued, "you will find soap in the bottom bunk to be shared with your neighbors above. You're to wash up with water you'll get when you leave here. Remember, Canadians believe cleanliness is next to Godliness and everyone is clean in Canada."

"Bejaysus and Uncle Willy," Eamon whispered to Mick. "Are they tryin' to wash away me Irish?"

Actually, the motives were far more straightforward as many unrepentant shipping lines were seriously concerned with the stain of steerage, their major profit center. That concern sprang, not from any sense of morality, mind you, but from fear of damage to their bottom lines from reform-minded humanitarian do-gooders, liberal government officials and journalists. Should they find and expose long-ago-condemned medieval living conditions at this late date, they posed an existential threat to a shipping line's public image and, in turn, its revenue stream.

By this time, reforms were suggested, but not legislated, in an anemic effort to exorcize the lingering spectre of *Irish Coffin Ships* of the mid-19th century. Instead, many lines pursued a brand-saving sleight of hand "to turn a hoor into a nun," as Mick put it, in the final hours of a transatlantic voyage, finally treating their third-class passengers with something as close to humanity as budgets permitted.

Accepted maritime accountancy of the time held that

a modicum of spending at the end of a voyage to assuage
the savage beasts was sound fiscal policy. After all, the *Irish
livestock* traveling in steerage had such limited intellects, they
could only retain so much information at a time. Usually,
no more than a day's worth. All else would be forgotten. Of
course, such thinking was short-sighted being borne out by
the sinking of the Titanic and other steerage catastrophes.
People do, indeed, remember. And they talk.

Yet these disingenuous appeasements in the name of
public image persisted.

Despite the bounty in front of them, the boys and
everyone else were mindful how their rusted meal kids would
taint the food. Plotting a strategy as he approached, Neddy
pulled out his handkerchief and lined his pail with what
was now a filthy rag that was soon laden with two sausages,
bacon strips, potatoes, eggs, bread and a ladleful of baked
beans in a gastronomic mess at the bottom of the kit. After
all, he reasoned, coming into contact with old food on his
handkerchief was preferable to rust any day. Then, rather
than using his rusted fork or spoon, he dug in with his right
hand (like a Yahoo, he thought), shoveling the chaos of courses
into his mouth.

Without handkerchiefs, Mick and Eamon still took
Neddy's lead when they held out their rusted kits to be filled.
They dispensed with their rusty utensils and used their hands
in an effort to avoid the taste of rust ... for the most part.

After the meal, which they consumed near the ship's
bow, they found at least a dozen large vats of fresh water
and were instructed by stewards to rinse their kits (for most,
the first time), and to dump the used water into empty vats

that were identical, Neddy thought, to those involved in the nighttime incident with The German. Once relatively free of food residue, the kits, which held about a quart, became wash basins back at their bunks.

The fact that Neddy and Eamon hadn't shaved for more than a week was barely evident as neither of them needed to shave before, during or after the voyage. On the other hand, Mick looked like a simian nightmare and could be mistaken as much older than his 17 years, especially with his hairline already in full premature retreat.

As for washing with soap and water after eight days, it was not really outside the routine they observed at home. Weekly baths, whether they needed them or not, were more the custom than the exception. The same held true for their two outfits of clothing. Except for the rust stains and crusted food on the extra shirt and trousers he brought along with his suit, Neddy didn't look much different from his appearance on the farm.

After washing up as best they could with the limited tools provided, the boys moved topside to air dry. They spent most of the next few hours on deck watching the still indistinct Newfoundland coast on the far horizon dodge in and out of a persistent fog starboard. The air was crisp but had lost the bite of the more northern latitudes.

"Jaysus, Mary, Joseph an' the Holy Ghost! Is that an iceberg?" Mick cried, believing that if you're going to take the Lord's name in vain, you may as well invite the entire family.

"Christ, it is," said another passenger, whose white beard whipped about his neck as he almost lost his cap while leaning over the rail. "But 'tis far off, so we're not about to be another Titanic," he said.

The boys laughed uncomfortably. Very uncomfortably because while the Irish, as a people, invented gallows humor, there are limits. Standing on a ship and seeing an iceberg near Newfoundland was one of them.

As daylight softened to dusk, the number of inbound and outbound ships seemed to multiply by the hour, starting as far-off, indistinct forms near the horizon and becoming fire flies cruising on the water's surface as their deck lights ignited against the night sky.

The dinner bell rang and it was another feast. Lamb stew ... *with real lamb* ... potatoes and carrots, onions, garlic and parsley. Not the "slurry," as Eamon called it, of the previous eight days. There were scones, substantial fresh-baked wheat breads with crisp crusts, plum jam and stewed fruits. There was abundant coffee and tea, but best of all, there was enough food for everyone in steerage, so meal service lasted nearly two hours. The repast was so joyous for so many that the stew's thick, aromatic broth was enthusiastically consumed despite the pungent rusty overtones produced by drinking it directly from the befouled meal kits.

By meal's end, the ship's bow was alive with *steeragers*, as one Irishman calling himself Lofty had so named his fellow passengers. The distant ships, now on the port side, had been joined here and there to starboard by soft lantern lights from remote cottages in inlets along Newfoundland's southern coast just east of the Port Aux Basque lighthouse as the ship approached the Gulf of St. Lawrence.

Just before dawn, the bow was full to overflowing, not just with steeragers, but with the giddy anticipation of their journey's end. Many cheered and pointed. Others cried and offered up prayers of thanks. Parents held children in their arms, while some hoisted toddlers on their shoulders. Most stood silently, letting the coastal breeze wash over them like a greeting, as trawlers laden with nets, lobster traps, fishermen and the hope of bountiful catches headed out to sea as their Scottish, English, Irish and French ancestors had done for many generations before them.

As the sun rose and the topography grew steadily clearer, Neddy and Mary, Mick, Eamon and the other hundreds in all classes of the ship saw the waves breaking on the rocky shoreline of Canada for the first time.

With that in plain view, Neddy was torn between melancholy and exhilaration. Melancholy for leaving the only home and family he ever knew. Exhilaration as Canada stopped being a pamphlet's promise and became the reality of a new life, new adventures in a new country that, at first glance, seemed not so much different from the one he left.

But the excitement was short-lived as land slowly disappeared in the vastness of the gulf and many feared they were headed out to sea again. Next were the Magdalen Islands, a diffuse archipelago of rocky spits off to port, that came and went in less than an hour. But growing ever larger on the horizon was Anticosti Island, whose tree-covered cliffs and hills shot hundreds of feet above the surf that encircled them like a lace collar.

"Holy shite!" exclaimed Mick, thinking of the Donegal coast. "They've taken us back to Ireland."

"Nah," said Neddy, recalling photos of Nova Scotia, New Brunswick and environs in his geography book, "'tis Canada."

Then conceding, "But, Jaysus, it does look a wee bit like Ireland, it does."

19

May 19, 1921

The *Sea Empress* skimmed the coast of the island until Anticosti, too, slid out of sight behind them. This time, however, the mouth of the St. Lawrence River was dead ahead and with it, all manner of activity on and off the water.

On both sides of the ship, there were scattered settlements, fishing inlets and remote safe harbors lined with docks and small marine craft of every pedigree. In the fishing villages, there was activity everywhere as horse-drawn wagons were loaded and unloaded. People went about the routines of their work day amid plumes of black smoke that trailed trucks motoring dirt roads north along the river banks, inland to other settlements or south toward Montreal, still several hours away.

On board the *Sea Empress*, the throng of bow riders became an undulating tide, flowing in and out of the sleeping compartments, gathering their children, their parents and everything else they brought to the New World. Photos of loved ones most would never see again. A mirror. A brooch. A favorite hammer. Knitting needles, a straight razor. A cloth doll, the farewell gift from a sobbing grandmother. Even a rusted bicycle bell that didn't work, and carefully preserved dried buttercups.

For the past several hours, stewards throughout the

ship made regular announcements with the mechanical cadence of an engine. It seemed that every ten minutes or so, they reinforced the corporate message that everyone should appear happy or at least appreciative that Canada was letting them into "a land of milk, honey and great opportunity." Then as if lecturing recalcitrant children, they chided, "Dour countenances will be frowned upon by your hosts and could end badly for those who pout," up to and including expulsion and deportation.

Other announcements provided collection points at the port for specific groups of passengers. Miners headed to the Sudbury Basin of Ontario to help extract recently discovered deposits of copper and nickel. Laborers recruited to build Ontario's provincial network of highways made possible by the Canada Highways Act of 1920. Girls and women as domestics and cooks. Families heading west to homestead in the Canadian prairie provinces of Manitoba and Saskatchewan. Loggers to British Columbia. Fishermen to the maritime provinces. And boys indentured as free labor to Catholic farm families throughout Ontario and Quebec.

River traffic grew steadily the farther south the *Sea Empress* went. Passing Quebec City with the elegant Le Chateau Frontenac hotel perched on a promontory above the river, many passengers thought they had seen the first of many castles they would find in Canada. Then came Montreal with its ribbons of smoke rising from factories dominating the horizon near the port where the *Sea Empress* would make landfall.

The ship's bridge cut the engines about two miles north of the docks. For fifteen minutes or so, it glided ever slower into an awaiting school of tug boats that sidled up to the *Sea Empress* like pups to a mother's teats. At that point, the ship was guided to the pier and made fast with a half dozen mooring lines sent ashore and fixed there to a series of bollards along the water's edge. The lines were winched tight to secure the mooring and gang planks were lowered for disembarkation.

JOHN HEAGNEY

PART III
Canada

JOHN HEAGNEY

20
Timmy

The men's sleeping compartment was emptying fast as steeragers – including boys destined for different Catholic hostels or receiving homes – grabbed their belongings and headed topside. After gathering the remnants of life aboard, minus the rust-caked meal kit at the foot of the straw mattress, Neddy took one last look in the bunk, then dropped to the floor. He was about to head to the door when he noticed a shadowy figure against a bulkhead in the far corner of a lower bunk. The figure was crying softly.

Neddy approached slowly, ducking down to see a small boy who could not have been older than six or seven, his arms wrapped about his legs folded up to his chin.

"Hey, boyo," Neddy said softly, "are ya ready to go?"

"I dunno where," the boy sniffled. "I want me Da. He'd know."

Beside the boy, Neddy saw his small suitcase with a red tag. He reached in and smoothed it to better read the writing: "T. Lordan, St. George's Home, Ottawa, Canada c/o Mother Frances Euphemia."

"Tommy," Neddy guessed.

"Timmy," the boy corrected him.

"Timmy, can ya come wit' me?" Neddy said, knowing by the tag that Timmy's father wasn't on the ship but back in Ireland unable to care for the boy either because of illness, destitution, jail ... or likely worse.

"Aye," Timmy whispered as he scooted toward the edge of the bunk and put his right hand in Neddy's, grabbing the handle of his suitcase with the other. Together, they headed out of the sleeping compartment into the sea of bodies headed for Canada.

First- and second-class passengers were permitted to disembark first, many of them to awaiting families, friends or business associates on the dock. As a perfunctory examination of paperwork and such had been performed by Canadian officials on the ship, the process was brief and uncomplicated.

Neddy held Timmy's hand firmly. "How'rya?" he asked, glancing down at the boy.

"I canno' see," said Timmy, face to face with an impenetrable phalanx of adult behinds.

Neddy leaned down and hoisted the boy to eye level just high enough to see past most heads that seemed to Timmy to go on forever. All the while, Neddy searched the crowd for Mary, who had gone to the women's compartment to gather her belongings.

Next off was steerage and the crush of 730 passengers potentially scattering like leaves in the wind across the docks. But what threatened at first to become a chaotic torrent of humanity was corralled by the efficient orchestration of Canadian bureaucratic planning. Each person met. Each group addressed. Each segment diverted to the proper conveyance. Each immigrant easily classified and steered to waiting trains ready to transport them to their ultimate destinations.

For those without specific assignments or work contracts, the families, the single women, the elderly, the adventurers and dreamers, there would be help finding jobs … even if they were short-term … temporary housing with meals and places to bathe after processing.

At least on the surface, the system seemed foolproof. But despite the precise operational design, there remained small pockets of chaos and loss. A parent separated from her child. A special doll ripped from the hand of a toddler. A lost or stolen suitcase containing what little money a woman had. A shoe lost, leaving its owner partially barefoot with no replacement. A hat flipped from a head and trampled. Eyeglasses knocked off and crushed in a surge of the crowd. A train ticket dropped on deck, swept into a scupper and blown overboard. And somewhere in the crush to leave the ship, Neddy still couldn't find Mary as he was caught in the river of bodies swept inexorably toward dry land. Closer to the railing, then to the gangway, then to the pier, he struggled against the human tide, holding Timmy tighter, looking everywhere, seeing nothing but anxious faces intent on starting life anew.

A number of nuns and postulants stood like white sentries on the pier holding signs, scanning the crowd for suitcases with colored tags keyed to various hostels and receiving homes for boys descending the gangplank. Blue tags for Dr. Barnardo's Home. Yellow tags for St. Vincent's Rescue Home. White tags for Stephenson's National Children's Home. Red for St. George's and so on. Temporary human dispensaries in different cities or towns or provinces. Some religious, others secular, all operating with the blessing of and subsidies from the British and Canadian governments.

A young, thin-lipped postulant with a ruddy complexion and wire-rimmed glasses pointed at Neddy and directed him to move right. Not sure what she wanted him to do, he stopped like a small island as the stream of passengers swept past him and Timmy.

Mick pushed through the crowd and grabbed Neddy's sleeve. "Over there," Mick pointed.

Neddy spun around to where Mick's finger pointed. "Mary!?"

"No. th' sign!" Mick yelled above the crowd. "The sign sayin' St. George's Home. By th' buildin' ... *there!*" Neddy focused about 30 yards away on a large white placard with green lettering atop a pole held by a squat, moon-faced nun almost as wide as she was tall with a brooding and rather officious air about her. She slowly surveyed the crowd, having already harvested about a half dozen small boys who stood near her, all looking bewildered or scared. Small suitcases by their feet arranged in a semi-circle that needed a few more bags to be complete.

For a moment, Neddy's attention shifted. "Where's Eamon?" Neddy asked Mick anxiously.

"Over there," Mick hooked a thumb toward another nun and another sign that read, "St. Vincent's Rescue Home"

"Eamon!" Neddy yelled. "Over here!"

Eamon made a move in Neddy's direction, when the nun holding sway over the St. Vincent's group, collared him, pushed him back with the other boys there. She glowered at Neddy. "Keep to your own self, boy!" she warned. "He's where he needs to be."

"He belongs with us," Neddy thought, but within minutes Eamon's small contingent was shuffled away down the pier with two nuns in tow to a waiting trolley that would take them to St. Vincent's, elsewhere in Montreal.

Watching the St. Vincent group consume Eamon which in turn was consumed by the larger mass of people on the waterfront, Neddy felt deflated and helpless. But Timmy remained by his side, holding on to his hand, and ever stalwart Mick was like a stone wall, less for his resolve than his massive size when standing next to the other boys and Mother Frances Euphemia. Neddy, Timmy and Mick approached the nun, a clipboard in her hand as she accounted for her charges. With the trio that just arrived, she was at 12 ... a boy short. While her postulants continued to patrol the pier for the missing lamb, Mother Frances Euphemia (called FE – for Fucking Eejit – by the older boys behind her back), looked up slowly from her list, pushed her glasses back to the bridge of her nose and demanded, "Names?"

Neddy spoke up first. "Neddy ... uh ... Bernard McKenna, and this is ..."

"Tut tut," she scolded. "Did I ask you for the boy's name? I asked for yours and only yours, did I not?"

Neddy nodded.

"Are you a donkey, boy? Is that how you address me?"

Neddy thought for a second before replying, "No, sister."

"*Mother*," she countered. "*Mother* Frances Euphemia."

"Yes, Mother Frances Euphemia."

"Yes, Mother will do," she said.

"Yes, *mother*," Neddy said with a sigh.

"Am I bothering you?" Mother FE asked sharply.

"No, mother," Neddy replied.

"Glad to hear it, Bernard," Mother FE said sarcastically, turning her attention to Timmy. "And you, boy. Your name?"

Looking up, Timmy moved closer to Neddy and said nothing.

"I asked you a question," Mother FE said, her voice with more of an edge to it.

"Th' wee'un's knackered ...," Neddy said.

Mother FE took a step toward Neddy and smacked him in the face. "Was I talking to you? No! I was talking to the boy."

"His name is Timmy."

She slapped Neddy again. "Welcome to Canada," he thought, not moving or giving an inch. He didn't react at all, but held Timmy tighter. After Bridget died, Neddy had lost all respect and fear of *the habit* and the unquestioned authority it wielded back home. His eyes narrowed and he said, "Read th' boy's tag."

The nun was enraged. "You *brazen article!*" she growled, drawing back her hand for another blow, when a much larger hand stopped its forward motion.

"No need fer that, sister," said Mick, looking square in the nun's face as he released her and stepped back.

"Mother," the nun sneered, making a mental note of the Irish animal who dared to touch her.

"Mother," Mick repeated flatly. "And me name is Micheal Cormick."

It was the first time Neddy heard his full name, so he leaned in with a smile and whispered, "Gladta meet ya,

Micheal Cormick." Mick smiled and gave a small nod of acknowledgment.

At that moment the two postulants approached the group with another small boy ... number 13 ... between them. "Found him in Barnardo's," said one referring to a hostel in Quebec.

"His tag stood out like a beacon," the other laughed. "Not too bright, this one."

"None of them are," the first one chimed in. "Name's Sean O'Dwyer."

Checking the boy's name off her list, Mother FE said, "Put him with the rest and let's get a move on. We're running late."

Gathering up the boys like a trio of border collies herding sheep, Mother FE and the postulants with rosary beads clacking and veils billowing behind them, took the group of boys to the train terminal, where the *Canadian-Pacific Western Special* waited ready to embark on the two-hour journey to Ottawa.

One would think that after a life-changing transatlantic voyage aboard an ocean liner, the boys would find a train ride anticlimactic. But as this was their first journey by rail, their excitement as they approached the platform and the monstrous black locomotive was joyous and unrestrained, much to the complete annoyance of the nuns.

"Silence!" barked Mother FE as the boys buzzed. "BE QUIET THIS INSTANT!!"

Several yards away, a conductor's "All aboard!" echoed off the girders and glass of the terminal's roof. From all directions came the clamor of travelers by the hundreds spilling onto the platforms and into the waiting train cars. Blasts of steam shot from idling engines like impatient dragons, and train bells sang out at uneven intervals as trains prepared to travel west and north and south and east, then rolled away from the terminal.

But the boys bound for St. George's were silent as Mother FE walked down the line collecting their train tickets. About a half dozen younger boys, especially two brothers of six and 10 years of age, struggled to understand what was needed because one could barely read and the other couldn't read at all. Mick and Neddy quickly stepped in, locating their tickets then placing them in their hands.

"Do you plan to wipe their behinds as well?" Mother FE sniped at Neddy as she snatched the ticket from his hand, turned and approached the Track 2 conductor at the steps of Car Number 3 in the nine-car train.

The boys climbed the steps with their suitcases as one postulant guided them through the door and the other seated them to the right of the center aisle in the first eight rows two by two with three spots reserved for the nuns. Neddy, still holding Timmy's hand, moved quickly to a window seat in the fourth row.

Fascinated by the adventure, but already scared senseless of retribution from the nuns, most of the boys stiffly watched the comings and goings of boarding passengers without moving their heads. The elderly woman leaning on a cane and wearing a small flat bonnet with a single sad flower emerging from a soiled satin-ribbon hat band. Close behind a younger man, wearing a worn bowler and missing an upper front tooth, guiding her by the elbow to steady her unsure gait. The mother and father with four children in tow, all ragged, all haggard like so many others at the end of one journey and the start of another. The girl cradling a baby swaddled only in a torn woman's blouse.

"We're off to a new home, Pack ... um ... Timmy," Neddy smiled at the boy, brushing a bit of dirt from his tiny sweater. "T'won't be long now."

With Timmy settled, Neddy turned to the window, taking in the anxious swarm on the platforms waiting for train departures. Then as the *Western Special* jerked forward, tightening the linkage, straining until all nine cars aligned and began easing out of the terminal, he squinted into the sunlight as the journey to Ottawa began. In that moment and for countless moments in the future, he thought of Mary, swept from the *Sea Empress* in that tide of passengers, in a separate direction, to a separate life, yet forever bound to him by a terrible shared secret born on a dark night at sea.

Moving across the Island of Montreal, the train crossed the Riviere des Prairies to the Island of Jesus, then over Riveiere des Mille Isles to St. Eustach Sur le Lac. Farms and pastures, hamlets, villages and verdant countryside sped by. At the Lake of Two Mountains, views became panoramic, spanning a majestic 20 miles of gently sloping mountains with mantels of Balsam Fir and Black Spruce flowing from their pinnacle down to the lake's reed-rimmed shorelines where reflections of clouds danced and disappeared in the water.

Just an hour or so into the trip, Timmy and several other boys had fallen asleep, lulled by the rhythmic chatter of the wheels and the subtle sway of the train, heads bobbing at first then finally resting on the suitcases in their laps. At the rear of the group, Mother FE also dozed, emitting a low purring snore. With chin pressed against the wimple of her habit, the nun's head appeared disembodied as if sitting atop a large, white serving platter.

Some boys sat quietly or whispered to each other almost imperceptibly to be out of the nuns' earshot, while still others seemed content to watch the world glide by. Neddy and Mick, sitting rows apart, were in the latter group.

Mick was struck by how much of the passing scenery made him think of home while other long swaths were unlike anything he had seen before. Every so often, he would glance at the side of Neddy's head hoping he would turn around, but he never did. Instead, Neddy studied everything he saw, trying to square reality with the images he had constructed in his head with the help of his geography book during the days and weeks leading up to his departure.

West of St. Hermes, the train traced a route along the Rouge and North rivers, crossing the latter at St. Andrews East. Heading past Carillon, the rail line swung north into Ontario and followed the east bank of the Ottawa River until crossing at Grenville and entering the Opeongo foothills of the Laurentian Mountains. Next came Hawkesbury with its massive paper mill. The tiny town of L'Original. Treadwell. Then, finally, Ottawa, resting on the Ontario-Quebec border.

Despite being Canada's capital, Ottawa was a touch more than a third the size of Belfast. However, it was the legislative epicenter of Canada's ambition to be a commercial and industrial player on the world stage. But such ambitions were yet to be played out by the time Neddy McKenna arrived in a baker's dozen of Catholic boys from far flung areas of an Ireland still reeling from the Great Famine and its devastating exodus of more than a half century ago.

The *Canadian-Pacific Western Special* arrived at Ottawa's Union Station as scheduled and rolled to a stop with a sigh of air-brakes and an exhalation of steam like a middle-distance runner crossing the finish line. The nuns gathered the boys as they, in turn, gathered their belongings, each boy emerging on the platform, then forming a small, orderly cohort that headed for the trolleys.

21

St. George's Home

The boys couldn't help but gape at the station's Beaux-Arts-style vaulted and barrel ceilings, its domes and towering arched windows, the rows of stately columns and the expansive marble floors stretching before them like a polished-stone meadow.

"Stop rubber-necking and keep moving," Mother FE ordered as the boys continued to gawk despite the nun's threatening tone. Never had they seen such a structure on so grand a scale. Although Dublin and Belfast had buildings and cathedrals to rival or exceed the station's grandeur, the boys hadn't traveled much beyond the small hamlets and villages near their homes before crossing the Atlantic. For them, this was, indeed, a *New World*.

The group piled onto the wooden benches in an electric street car outside the station and a few minutes later were dropped off at a stop on Wellington Street, where a group of men stood across the road. Upon seeing the children, one picked up a stone and yelled, "Gutter rats!! Go the fuck home, you scum!!" As the other men hissed and jeered, the first chucked the rock, which sailed over a postulant's head and into a hedge lining the sidewalk. She glared at the men, but said nothing, being well-acquainted with the verbal abuse Home Children in her charge suffered. For a number of them, however, verbal abuse would be the least of it.

Quickly re-forming into their tight little band, they walked another two blocks without incident to 1153 Wellington Street. The St. George's Receiving Home.

The three-story hostel for British Home Children was encircled by a wide wraparound porch with lathe-turned wooden posts and balusters. It was painted deep green with black shutters years ago and was well past due for another coat or two. Scattered sections of the fascia on its six gables and turret as well as the lacy Victorian gingerbread trim were decaying in spots and missing in others.

For most daylight hours, half the structure was shrouded in shade from large oak, pine and elm trees so that much of the interior was starved of natural light, made worse by the extensive black-oak paneling and woodwork throughout the common areas and bedrooms. But the real darkness was generated by Mother FE and the other Sisters of Mercy who operated the home under the auspices of the Catholic Church, overseeing every aspect of its operation and the lives of boys and girls who lived there temporarily.

The nuns were the ultimate arbiters of good and evil, acceptable and unacceptable, meting out favor or punishment, many times altering the direction of a child's life on a whim or in a fit of anger.

As Mother FE stopped at the foot of the front walk and directed the boys toward the large Victorian house at the end of a vast front lawn, Neddy fell out of line with Timmy in tow. "This grand house is where we'll live," Neddy explained, unsure whether or not he might be overselling their situation. "'Tis th' grandest place ever, don't ya t'ink?"

"Aye," said Timmy tentatively, thinking of the tenement on the south side of Dublin around the Liberties that he shared with his father, older sister Ann and his Aunt Marie.

"Mr. McKenna! Come along," shouted Mother FE, as the two boys, raced after the others, leaping up the front steps two at a time and into the house's foyer.

Neddy, Mick, Timmy and the other new arrivals clustered at the base of the home's stairway as about a dozen other children awaiting disbursement in the days to come inspected them from the second- and third-floor landings. Mother FE looked down at her clipboard, jotting down offenses committed by several new boys like dark spots on their souls, and devising short- and long-term consequences.

Then, one by one, she called their names in alphabetical order: "James Cassidy, Micheal Cormick ..." She paused, jotted a notation next to his name and continued. "... William John Doherty, John Fitzgerald; (the brothers) Christopher Gallagher, James Gallagher; George Roe, Frank Russell, Hugh Lavery, Timothy Lordan ..." Another notation. "... Bernard McKenna ..." Notation. "... Sean O'Dwyer, Daniel Penny."

The St. George's Receiving Home processed as many as 400 Home Children each year with no more than 40 at a time, a way station on their path to Catholic farms in Ontario and Quebec. Stays at the home varied as did the number of boys who came back after failed placements. Some were placed numerous times. Some were lost in the system after leaving. A few placements ended in death.

Some children were at the receiving home a week or two before placement. Older boys might last mere days, especially if they looked like good strong labor stock.

Before any of that could take place, new arrivals had to be prepared. With the boys' medical condition approved on board the ship before disembarkation, the home's top priority was personal hygiene. Getting them bathed, deloused, fed and clothed in the home's uniforms of dark trousers, muslin shirt and black sweater. They also were given new shoes ... or at least used shoes in good condition as close to the boy's actual size as availability allowed.

But first, the baths. Following a scathing 1903 government review of what was then called New Orpington Lodge, the temporary hostel for Home Children was renamed St. George's Receiving Home and completely renovated ... including a large communal bathroom.

None of the boys had ever seen a bathroom, let alone one with tile flooring and five bathtubs filled with hot water from faucets. "Remove your clothing and get in," said Mother FE matter of factly to the complete horror of the first five boys who were instantly paralyzed, looking nervously at each other. *"Now!"*

Disrobing in public under any circumstance was anathema to every God-fearing, self-loathing child of the church. But in front of a nun? It roared past a mortal sin into the realm of sacrilege and eternal hell fire, exactly where Mother FE was most comfortable.

If Catholic children understood anything, it was fear of and obedience to the front-line standard bearers of Christ: Nuns and parish priests. So, when Sean O'Dwyer, the stray from the pier in Montreal, began undoing his shirt, the others slowly followed suit, then slid into the water. When finished, they dried themselves with towels stacked on a nearby bench and stood naked as a nun sized them up, rummaging through piles of underwear, uniform shirts, sweaters and trousers on a table to find their size. After they dressed, the nun told them to take their suitcases and wait downstairs in the foyer.

Neddy, Mick, and Timmy were the final group ushered into the bath. And like all the boys before, Timmy and Neddy were reluctant to start undressing as Mother FE watched. But not Mick. Without hesitation, he removed his shirt, exposing a heavily muscled chest covered with a carpet of red hair. Then, looking squarely into Mother FE's eyes, he removed his trousers without shame or a need for atonement. While the nun saw unbridled belligerence, what Neddy saw reminded him of Malachy Ryan's prized draft horse back home.

After dressing, they followed Mother FE down the staircase to rejoin the rest of the group. It was time for sleeping assignments. The nun took up her clipboard and began calling names mostly in alphabetical order. "Cassidy, Dougherty, Fitzgerald, the Gallagher boys, Roe, Russell, Lavery, O'dwyer and Penny to St. Bernadette's," she said, directing the postulant called sister Miriam the task of showing the boys to their dormitory on the third floor. "The rest of you , follow me."

As the first group of boys climbed the staircase, a few looking back at those left behind, Mother FE and the postulant led Mick, Neddy and young Timmy through a short hall at the end of which was a lone doorway. She stopped to flick a light switch on the wall, opened the door revealing stairs to the cellar, turned without a word and left.

"You'll sleep here," said the postulant, pointing to the cellar and motioning with her head for the boys to descend the stairs. Just as on the ship, the cellar was lit by a bare light bulb emitting a harsh splash of unfiltered light that threw jagged shadows everywhere. The rough rock walls were whitewashed, but the floor was hard-packed dirt, reminding Neddy of his farm's cottage ... except it was underground, damp and the only natural light came through a small window near the low ceiling. Along the far wall was a furnace and beyond that were five cots separated by small crates doubling as end tables between them. On the beds were folded coarse sheets, blankets and pillows without covers. There were two chamber pots in a corner.

Looking about the space as he tossed his suitcase on a bed, Neddy was baffled. "'What'd we do fer this?" he asked. "I was sure th' mother had it in fer us."

"Aye," Mick agreed. "but instead, we get posh beds and this place all t'ourselves. Whadya t'ink there Timmy?"

Timmy took a seat on the edge of a bed and thought he had never seen such a fine place to sleep. "I like it, I do," he smiled.

"Five beds fer th' three of us," said Neddy, amazed at their good fortune. Then the light was switched off, leaving them in the dark. They also were left unfed as the other boys headed to dinner a half hour later. Neddy would soon reassess their situation.

The communal dining room was lit by a half dozen milk-glass pendant lights suspended from its 12-foot-high ceiling. It contained five long tables and benches, arranged like pews, that accommodated 10 boys each. From the oil-cloth table coverings to the brown linoleum flooring, the room was utilitarian, as no-nonsense as the aproned postulants serving meals from steaming containers of food near the kitchen.

"Get your knives and forks as you get in line," instructed the postulant Miriam as the children joined the service line. As they moved along, their plates were filled with thinly sliced beef, potatoes, cabbage, carrots, gravy, a thick slice of buttered bread ... and a glass of milk from a nearby farm, which seemed fitting for a room of mostly farm boys. At the end of the line, a postulant anointed for traffic control, directed children to the tables, fully populating one before moving on to the next. As each table filled, Mother FE was there to lead the 10 young souls saying grace in an assembly line of thanks and supplication.

Following dinner was free time, an hour or so when boys could congregate in the home's enclosed back garden. It was devoid of grass, long ago trampled to death by thousands of shoes belonging to Home Children on their way to somewhere else. Then again, the purpose of the garden ... and indeed the home itself ... *was* containment, not unlike a stockyard. A place for herds of what the nuns called waifs and strays, gutter children and street arabs. They were to be detained only as long as needed until they could be shipped off to be someone else's problem.

Lying on his bed, Neddy could hear a commotion outside. He grabbed a crate, pulled it to the partially opened cellar window and stood on it for a look.

"See anyt'ing?" asked Mick, getting up and joining him.

"Aye," said Neddy. "Everyone 'cept us."

"Let us go," Mick said to Timmy heading off in the dim light from the cellar window with Neddy bringing up the rear. But reaching the top of the stairs, they found the door locked. "What th' hell ...?"

Moments later, Neddy was back at the window, where he saw a boy from the train a few feet away and pounded on the glass to get his attention. Bending down, Hugh Lavery recognized Neddy and smiled. "What're ya doin' down there? Missed ya at dinner," he said.

"Dinner?"

"Aye," Hugh responded, "and a grand one at that."

"What dinner?" Neddy repeated.

"The one you won't be eating, Mr. Smart Alek," said Mother FE as she pushed Hugh away from the window. "See what impertinence got you and the other two? Nothing to eat. Maybe you'll think twice next time." Then she was gone.

Neddy stepped off the crate and the three boys returned to their cots, lying there quietly except for Timmy, who whimpered softly into his pillow.

After the sun set, the cellar was completely dark and quiet until the boys heard the jangle of keys atop the stairs and the light was switched on, momentarily blinding them. Looking up, they saw the hem of the postulant's white habit as she quietly descended the stairs. "Shhhhh," she whispered, carrying a small basket and setting it down on an empty cot. "Don't say anything or Reverend Mother will hear you."

She quickly unloaded bread, several plates of food and a small container of milk as well as forks and knives. "I'm sorry the food is cold, but I had to grab what I could without getting caught. When you're done, hide what's left behind the furnace."

Just as quickly, she was climbing the steps as the boys thanked her.

"I don't agree with her methods," the postulant responded. "But please don't say anything about this."

The boys nodded, watching her disappear and lock the door. After the boys inspected their utensils for rust and finding none, they began eating.

The light remained on for another half hour or so until the postulant secretly returned to turn it off as the rest of the home shut down for the evening.

The following morning, each child was responsible for washing clothes they brought with them to prepare for Catholic families who would adopt them to live on farms across Ontario and Quebec. A large iron pot was set up on bricks and a fire built under the pot to heat water. Then six large galvanized tubs were arranged nearby, three of them containing hot soapy water and rub boards. The other three contained rinse water. Standing around the first tub, boys were shown the process of dipping their clothes in the soapy water then vigorously scraping them back and forth over the rub board before transferring them to the rinse tubs. Clothes lines ran back and forth across the rear garden where the clean clothes would hang to dry.

As the process was about to begin, Mother FE called to Mick, motioning for him to follow her into the home. Turning to Neddy, he said, "What th' hell does she want?"

It was the last time Neddy saw him.

Hours later, back in the cellar, Neddy and Timmy stood at Mick's empty cot, noticing his suitcase was gone. At the same time, several floors above, Jimmy Gallagher was looking for his brother.

"Sister?" he asked one of the postulants. "Have ya seen me brother, Chris? I can't find 'im or his bag."

"You'll have to ask the Reverend Mother," she said, nervously walking away.

Mother FE refused to reveal anything, but Christopher had been sent to a small dairy farm about 12 miles outside of Lindsey in central Ontario. Two days later, Jimmy was on a train bound for the Gatineau area of Quebec where a Cathoic farmer named Cadieux forced him to sleep in a barn during the province's coldest winter on record. He would lose a foot to severe frostbite.

It would take 53 years for Chris to track down his brother, who died just two months after their reunion.

The selections and departures of what church officials called *these treasures of the church of God* happened several times daily, six days a week as clusters of freshly washed and uniformed boys were paraded like prize animals before farmers and farmers' wives who applied to take them in. While the motives of many Catholic families were less than pure, focusing more on the possibilities of free farm labor, a few sought children with the best of intentions, although without the best or most honest information.

22

The McKeowns

Early the next day, Con and Bess McKeown sat in St. George's main parlor after driving the 40 miles from their farm near Winton. Wearing a drop-waist dress with white polka dots on a field of navy blue, Bess was a sturdy woman in her mid-20s with short straw-blonde hair tucked under a white cloche hat. Her face was bronzed and set off by kind green eyes that captivated Con the moment they were introduced to each other as teens by her older brother Edgar.

Back then, Con was already more than six feet tall with an engaging smile, lean muscular build and a confident gait. Now, Con was a little less lean and his once forest of hair more a thicket. He was wearing an open-collared white shirt and pleated trousers held in place by red-and-black-striped suspenders. Normally, he wore denim overalls, a plaid shirt and his favorite porkpie hat on the farm, not unlike the one worn constantly by Edward McKenna, but this *was* a special occasion.

They stood as Sister Miriam entered the room trailed by a half dozen boys like a gaggle of goslings following their mother. As the McKeowns sat on a small flowered settee, the nun arranged the boys in a row by height, shortest to tallest, each setting down a small suitcase next to where he stood.

One by one, the nun called their names and one by one the McKeowns reviewed information about each boy given them when they arrived.

Bess seemed to linger on one boy in particular: Timothy Lordan, described as an orphan from Dublin.

"Hello, Timothy," Bess said, leaning so her face was close to his, but not so close to make him uncomfortable.

"Timmy," he said. "Me name's Timmy."

"Well, Timmy," Bess started again, "can you tell me what happened to your mother and father?"

"Me mum's in heaven," he began, "but me Da's comin' to take me home."

"Your da? You mean your father ...?" Bess said, glancing at the nun.

"Aye ... an' me Aunt Marie."

Interrupting, Sister Miriam began to explain, "A lot of children are still dealing with the loss of a parent ..."

"But me Da ain't lost," Timmy protested quietly. "Jes feelin' poorly. He told me I'm to be home b'fore long, he says. Not long a'tall."

Turning to the nun, Bess said, "I don't understand ..."

"The boy ..." Sister Miriam started to explain.

"The boy says his father and his aunt are coming for him, isn't that right, Con? But it says here he's an orphan and in my mind that means he doesn't have parents ..."

"I have me Da and Aunt Marie," Timmy protested, his voice on edge. "Me Da's sick is all. Jes sick an' he's ... he's comin' fer me when he's better."

Bess reached out to calm the boy, but he pulled away, running to the far end of the room.

The nun ushered the other boys into the hallway, returning a moment later.

"Sister, this doesn't sound right," Bess said, gathering her belongings as she stood. "Not right at all. He says he's not orphaned ..."

Sister Miriam sputtered, "I ... um ..."

"We drove all this way," Con said, "... but the boy ..."

"Let me get the Reverend Mother ..."

"I think we need an explanation," Bess said. "The boy ... Timmy ... seemed quite sure his father and his aunt were alive ... so why ...?"

"Well, are they alive or aren't they?" Con asked pointedly. "We will need proof that he is or isn't an orphan ..."

"I'll get the Reverend Mother," Sister Miriam said as she left the room.

But by the time she returned with Mother FE, the McKeowns were already across the front porch and walking toward the street.

"What's going on here?" She demanded, scanning the room that was empty except for Timmy cowering behind a chair in the corner.

"As I explained, Reverend Mother," Sister Miriam said, "the boy says his father and an aunt are alive and that his father's coming to take him home ..."

"Foolishness," Mother FE huffed, turning to Timmy, "Come here, boy!"

But Timmy didn't move.

"I said come here!!" she repeated. But when Timmy remained still, she stormed across the room, grabbed his arm and slapped his face, eliciting a yelp as he began to cry. Then dragging him to the center to the room, "When I give you an order ..."

"What are you doing?" demanded Bess, standing in the doorway with Con. "What are you *doing*?? Let go of him."

Releasing Timmy's arm, lurching upright and forcing a smile, the nun tried to explain, "Sometimes, these boys ..."

The McKeowns had reached the street when Bess turned to Con, "Did you see his little face? He was scared. Did you see that?"

"I did," Con agreed. "Let's go back and see if we can get to the bottom of this."

But the bottom lay across the Atlantic in the labyrinth of government bureaucrats on two continents, and the offices of the Catholic Emigration Association, where the decision concerning Timmy's status had been made.

Bess ignored the nuns, as she knelt down about five feet from Timmy and smiled softly. "Timmy," she began, "do you like it here?"

"No," he answered in an almost inaudible whisper, wiping his nose with a sleeve.

Looking at Con, who nodded his approval, she asked, "Would you like to come and stay with us?"

Timmy thought for a moment before asking, "And Neddy, too?"

"Neddy?"

"Another boy from the ship," Sister Miriam offered as Mother FE winced.

"Well, I don't ..." Bess began.

"Can we meet him?" Con asked to Bess's surprise.

Mother FE nodded toward Sister Miriam, who left the

room and returned minutes later with Neddy and his suitcase.

"Bernard, this is Mr. and Mrs. McKeown," Sister Miriam said handing several sheets of paper to Con. Timmy ran to Neddy and threw his arms around his legs, as Neddy placed a hand atop his head.

"Neddy, is it?" Con asked, studying the paperwork of Bernard McKenna, then casually inspecting the boy.

"Aye," Neddy responded.

"Yes, sir," Mother FE interjected.

"Aye, sir."

"It says here you have worked on a farm?"

"Aye, with me family."

"Are they still there?" Bess asked, sliding a frozen glance at the nuns.

"They are," Neddy said.

"So why are you here?" Con asked.

"Times're hard in Tyrone an' me Ma and Da have a time with seven of us to feed ..."

"Tyrone? My grandfather was from Tyrone. Strabane."

"G'won ..." Neddy smiled.

"No, it's true," Con said. "Came over in '87." The two fell silent until Con spoke. "Would you like to work on a farm?"

"I guess," Neddy said. "'Tis all I know."

"Well, we have a farm about an hour outside Ottawa," Bess said.

After another brief silence, "Timmy put in a good word for you," Con said as Neddy looked down at the boy, then back at Con.

"I can't go 'til I know Timmy's safe," said Neddy, who

really didn't have a say in the matter, the nuns were thinking.

Looking at Con who nodded for Bess to continue, she said, "Neddy will be coming, too." Then looking at Timmy. "Would that be OK?"

Timmy nodded.

Con turned to the nuns. "What do we have to sign?"

Although the McKeowns had wanted to adopt a child, the forms they signed were de facto labor contracts. They called for the children to be supplied room and board as well as fair payment for their labor, an area for which St. George's was notoriously deficient. While many receiving homes working with other agencies required farm families to pay children as much as $15 per month above and beyond room, board and clothing, St. George's repeatedly allowed farmers, particularly French farmers in the Gateau area of Quebec, to pay no more than $2 a month and as little as nothing.

Stories were not uncommon of children forced to toil as many as 12 hours a day. Some ran away. Others -- unable to endure the isolation of remote farms, sexual abuse, living conditions and beatings – committed suicide. All of it due to a lack of oversight. The children were simply forgotten to death.

To St. George's, the Catholic Emigration Association and the Catholic Church itself, a child's welfare was subordinate to preservation of The Faith. Getting immigrant children into the homes of married Catholics, no matter their temperament or motivation, was of paramount importance.

On the surface, the McKeowns reached that religious threshold. They attended mass every week (more out of habit than commitment), although communion was taken less often. They donated to the poor and observed Catholic customs including eating fish on Fridays and eating just one full meal on Ash Wednesday. What church officials didn't know was the McKeowns' practice of what Bess called *Soft Catholicism* that respected most Church beliefs but tempered them with humanist reason and compassion. That would explain Bess's outrage at Mother FE's violent outburst against Timmy because they opposed corporal punishment in all its forms.

Con and Bess looked over the documents and signed one each for Timmy and Neddy, who grabbed their suitcases.

"Goodbye, my dear children," Mother FE smiled as Con, Bess, Timmy and Neddy headed for the door, "God bless you all."

Bess was tempted to say something, thought better of it and ... like Con and the boys ... left without a word.

Timmy and Neddy settled into the bed of the 1919 Chevrolet Model T on whose chassis Con had installed a wooden truck bed. Con and Bess sat in front on the open cab's bench seat. Turning around and looking at the boys' St. George's uniforms, Bess said, "Before we head home, we need to get you some clothes." Then she turned to Con. "Let's go to Murphy-Gamble on Sparks Street."

"OK, fellas," Con called back to the boys as he put the truck in gear, "hold on tight to the front seat and don't let go." As Con eased off the clutch and hit the gas, the truck stuttered forward and they were off with Neddy tightly gripping the seat frame and Timmy tightly gripping Neddy.

An hour later, the boys were outfitted in new shirts, trousers and new leather shoes. The rest ... jackets, gloves, socks, sweaters and underwear ... were neatly bundled in brown paper tied with string inside a large wooden box that served as the truck's trunk. However, their strange excitement with this retail adventure soon darkened as the McKeowns pulled to a stop outside St. George's. Bess was out of the truck and approaching the home's front porch, when Mother FE came out to greet her.

"Here," said Bess, handing the nun a neatly folded pile of St. George's uniforms. "Neddy and Timmy won't be needing these ..."

"You didn't have to ..." said the nun.

"Oh, but I did," Bess interrupted. "I had to bring them back to say I hope you treat the boys who get these far better than I saw you treat Timmy this morning." With that, she walked back to the truck without another word, leaving Mother FE alone on the porch and speechless for the first time in ages.

Moments later they were flying out of the city at a 25-mile-per-hour clip and the boys were watching the farmland skirt by in a swirl of road dust on an early Ontario afternoon. After less than two weeks and an ocean voyage, Neddy was headed again to a farm, but on the other side of the world.

The air was filled with perfume from the fresh-cut hay scattered in large rolls and smaller rectangular bales across amber fields of chaff and stubble. But rather than Ireland's ancestral patchwork of tiny pastures neatly segmented by stacked-stone walls, this landscape was broad and rambling and young, sliced neatly by wire fencing and occasional barbed wire. Individual fields seemed to go on forever, disappearing behind hills only to re-emerge farther on when the topography crested nearer the horizon.

A domed red silo zoomed by like a cardinal's miter on the run. Cows and sheep by the hundreds grazed in tree-lined meadows. Tractors kicked up plumes of dirt preparing the rich earth for summer planting to be harvested come fall.

This country, this terrain spoke of energy and freedom and possibilities, but its vastness also filled Neddy with an empty yearning for the familiar embrace of Ireland and loved ones. For tea and a turf fire. For Bridget and Packy, if only the memory of places they loved. For Ma. For Rose and the girls.

For the first time since his leaving, Neddy felt alone, especially with the loss of Eamon and Mick ... and Mary. Just as his situation appeared on the upswing, his emotions were at their lowest. What started on the ship as an ocean of hope for a new life, now was a flood of self-doubt.

About a half hour into the road trip, Timmy told Neddy he had to pee, a message Neddy relayed to Con, who pulled to the side of the road. "Go ahead, son," Con smiled. "There's a bush over there."

Timmy ran to relieve himself as Neddy opened his suitcase and retrieved his suit jacket as the afternoon chill settled in. He opened Timmy's suitcase, finding only a well-worn stuffed bear, a small shirt and trousers, so that when the boy returned, Neddy slipped his jacket over Timmy's shoulders and pulled up the collar around his neck. As he did so, Neddy felt Mary's repair. His hand lingered there as he thought of the missed goodbye and of not knowing where she went or if she reached Philadelphia City.

Was Mary in the grand house? Was she happy with a new life not of her choosing? Then, he thought of Mick. Then of The German.

Timmy nuzzled closer to Neddy who wrapped an arm around him, gripping the seat frame firmly. Bess turned to look at the boys with only a twinge of misgivings about embracing *two* young strangers and bringing them home. Con kept his eyes on the road, which curved slowly under a canopy of trees as he eased off the gas. The truck slowed as it approached an open white wooden gate and turned in. Before them was a long dirt farm lane shaded by towering maple trees interrupted occasionally by pines and willows. To the left was a golden field of oats spreading to a distant stand of trees. Ahead the farm lane stretched another 50 yards before dropping from sight as it sloped down a hill to a tractor shed and a huge brown barn.

The truck eased to a stop in front of a two-story farmhouse with clapboard siding and a broad front porch that wrapped around its left side. The house was painted a gentle cream with dark green shutters, matching trim and a green roof with scalloped shingles surrounding a large brick chimney.

Two chickens were in the front yard. One roosted on a porch railing while the other pecked the ground near the side of the house, where a chicken coop was about 100 feet away. Neddy had never seen anything like it as the coop was painted to look just like the farmhouse, right down to the green roof and green shutters flanking its doorway.

"That's Mavis," Bess pointed to the roosting chicken, "and the one over there is Blanche."

A brick path led from the farm lane, splitting in two as it encircled a bird bath, then reformed and continued to the porch steps. Con shut off the truck engine and turned to the boys. "Welcome home," he said. "Grab your suitcases."

Neddy took his jacket off Timmy's shoulders as the two boys jumped down from the truck bed and stood looking at the house.

"Well, c'mon," Bess said over her shoulder as she led the way. "You must be hungry."

The porch was wide and deep with four high-backed rattan rocking chairs serving as punctuation for the six front windows. At the center was a front door with cut-glass sidelights that opened to an entry hall, where a staircase with oak railing and white balusters led to the second floor. To the left was a dining room and to the right a parlor, where Neddy immediately noticed books inside several large cases along one wall. What he couldn't see were two other bookcases dominating two more walls. The kitchen was through a door at the end of the hall, where Bess led the boys.

"Let's get you something that will tide you over until dinner," she said, directing them toward the kitchen table as she retrieved plates, silverware and napkins from a sideboard, then a platter of chicken, a loaf of bread and a pitcher of milk from the oak ice box along a side wall. She disappeared momentarily into another small room off the kitchen and returned with a jar of blackberry preserves when she saw the boys still standing. "Sit, sit," she said, pulling out a chair and taking a seat. "This is your home now."

"Will me Da know where I am?" Timmy asked.

Bess paused. "That's something we have to find out," she said as Con entered the room and hung up his hat.

"But for now," Con said reaching for a drumstick, "let's get you settled and learn a little bit about each other."

What started with stiff, intermittent exchanges slowly evolved into cautious conversation as Neddy shared tidbits about the farm, his sisters, his mother, but not of Bridget or Packy and certainly not Traveler. Maybe another time, he thought. Timmy was even less forthcoming answering questions from Con and Bess with nods or simple yeses and noes. Maybe another time, the McKeowns thought.

It was a start.

As the meal ended, Bess cleared the dishes and said, "Would you like to see where you'll sleep?"

"Aye," the boys responded together.

"It's going to be an early day tomorrow, so we'll be turning in right after dinner," Con said as Bess and the boys headed up the stairs. At the end of the landing, Bess opened the door to a room darkened by a pull-down shade that she raised. With a slight tug, she also opened the window. When the room filled with shaded afternoon light, the boys could see more clearly there was a wide bed with a short-spindled headboard against one wall and a dresser with a mirror against another. Bess switched on the small milk-glass ceiling light fixture, further illuminating a multi-color hooked rug covering wide-plank oak flooring at the foot of the bed.

"Sorry you'll have to share a bed," Bess apologized, a bit embarrassed, "but we didn't plan on bringing *two* boys home."

"At th' home place, there were seven of us sharin' a straw bed in th' loft," Neddy said.

"Seven in one bed?" Bess gasped.

"Well, 'twasn't so much a bed as a few wee blankets on a straw mat with pillows."

"Oh, my ..."

"At St. George's 'twas better with five in th' cellar ... three of us and two chamber pots," he joked, but Bess didn't laugh.

"*The cellar??*"

"Aye," said Timmy. "It was posh."

"I should say not," Bess fumed. "Well, all of that is over." She reached down and pulled back the coverlet to expose the bed's white sheets. "I'll be making you some proper night shirts but until then, you'll have to sleep as you are."

Turning to leave, she had an afterthought. "And the bathroom is down the hall."

"What's a night shirt?" Timmy whispered to Neddy, who just smiled.

For Neddy, the day's events were almost too much to digest. Electric lights. Wood floors. A real bed. Indoor toilet. Shelves of books in the house. New shoes. A birdbath. An icebox. And maybe a little brother.

After a fine dinner of pork chops, mashed potatoes, green beans, gravy and apple pie, after the evening settled in, after Bess and Con said their good nights, Neddy lay awake as he had done many nights at the home place. Listening to the chill evening breeze and cricket song accompanied by the easy breathing of a child asleep next to him in bed. Again, he missed home and thought of his sisters as he slowly drifted off to meet Traveler.

"Nice people," Traveler said, sitting on the barnyard wall in Tyrone.

"I guess," Neddy said, not sure why he was holding a scythe and standing on the deck of the *Sea Empress*.

"You *guess* they're nice? What's wrong with you, boy?!" Traveler said sliding off the wall and pulling his sunglasses down to the tip of his nose, staring blankly at Neddy. "You've hit the jackpot and don't even know it."

"They seem good sorts," Neddy conceded, "but I miss me Ma and th' girls."

"And they miss you," Traveler said. "That's why you need to write them. To let them know you're OK. Especially your mother. A few days back, she received a letter that you had sailed for Canada. That's all it said: 'I have much pleasure in informing you that your son sailed for Canada on the *H.M.S. Sea Empress.*' Period. Write to let her know you landed and are OK.

"Oh, and the big news? Things could be going well for the rebels in Ireland."

"Yer talkin' I.R.A.?"

"Among others," Traveler said. "But there's still trouble ahead. The damned Irish can't make up their minds what they want."

Neddy thought of his father, but quickly changed direction. "What news have ya of Mary?"

"She's a maid in Philadelphia," Traveler replied playfully. "She's working hard and hasn't stabbed anyone. That's all I can say."

"All ya can say or all ya know?" Neddy asked.

Traveler ignored the question. "However, I can tell you to watch Con. You can learn a lot from him ... and Bess, too. There's a storm coming for them ... and for Timmy. Hold on tight like his life depends on it because it does. Don't let go! Don't let go of Timmy!!"

"Timmy?" Neddy shouted out loud as he shook himself awake.

"What?" Timmy mumbled.

"Nothin'," Neddy said. "Go back to sleep."

23

Lessons

Neddy thought he was the first up that morning as he descended the stairs, but the smell of coffee and bacon convinced him otherwise. He was about to walk to the kitchen when he heard Con talking in the parlor.

"Yes," he said as Neddy carefully glanced around the corner, trying to conceal himself, and saw Con on the telephone. "His name is Timothy Lordan. Uh-huh ... no ... it's spelled L-o-r-d-*A*-n. Yes, that's right. From Dublin. I just know he came over with a group of boys paid for by the Catholic Emigration Association. Yes. St. George's Home. Yes. Anything will be appreciated. Let me know."

As Con hung up the phone, Neddy hurried to the kitchen, where Bess was at the stove cracking eggs into a pan, when Con walked in a few moments later. "Just about to come and get you boys," he said.

"Timmy's stirrin' already," Neddy reported.

"Good," said Con, "there's plenty to do today and I'll need your help."

"Doin' what?" said Timmy, entering the kitchen.

"Farm work," Neddy responded.

"Farm work," Con repeated. "Neddy, your paperwork

says you have experience with chickens and pigs ..."

"And cows ..." Neddy added, turning to Timmy and milking an imaginary udder.

"Well, let's start with chickens today," Con said. "And Timmy ... you can work with Miss Bess."

After breakfast, Con and Neddy left by the back door, heading down a wide clover-lined lane toward the diminutive creme-and-green replica of the farmhouse and about 30 leghorns that scattered in a commotion of feathers. Neddy couldn't help a comparison to the desperately unpainted coop near his father's weapons cache back home and their puny flock of Sussex hens. But as they neared, then passed the coop, Con redirected him toward a clearing about 100 yards distant.

"Ya said I'd be workin' wit' chickens," Neddy said, confused.

"You will," Con smiled, leading the way. "Just not these." As they walked, Con turned to the boy. "So, tell me about your farm."

"'Tis not nearly so grand as this," Neddy began. "Th' home place's nothin' to barrack about, t'be sure. But me clan worked it fer donkey's years. Me Granda and his Granda and his. A barn, some cows, pigs, chickens an' bog."

As they entered the clearing, Neddy's mouth fell open as he saw the McKeowns' broiler house for the first time. Spanning nearly 60 yards in one direction and 20 more in another, the broiler house was bisected by a 20-foot-tall main structure crowned with a red Dutch-Colonial-style roof into which a row of six large skylights was inserted. Extending from its sides were low one-story wings where roughly 500 White Rock, Cornish and Label Rouge broiler chickens flapped and cackled and bothered about in the bright sunlight.

The broiler house exterior was painted grey-white to give it a patina of civility instantly betrayed by the inescapable bouquet of bird droppings and barnyard. The central structure's door was flanked by two windows and protruding from the wings were semicircular runs fanning out like two 30-foot aprons from the foundation. Segregated by breed, the chickens were kept apart in the runs by wood dividers and the entire area was covered by what could only be described as a pergola of chicken wire.

As Neddy and Con approached, a bulldog of a man with a swagger undeterred by a slight limp emerged from the broiler house, pulling off his work gloves.

"Neddy, this is Tom Wilson," Con said.

"How do," said Tom with smile, stuffing the gloves in his back pocket and thrusting out his right hand.

"Tom, this is Neddy McKenna, just arrived from the auld sod."

"How's th' craic?" Neddy said, taking Tom's hand and judging him to be of good character based on his firm handshake.

"Where in Ireland?" Tom asked.

"Tyrone, near Cookstown," Neddy said.

"Just like yer granddad," Tom said to Con. "My great grandfather came over from Mayo during the famine."

"Tom is our farm manager," Con explained, "and he's going to show you the ropes this morning. I've got other business to attend to, so I'm putting you in Tom's capable hands. OK?"

"Aye," said Neddy, thinking it strange that a farmer

would have a farm manager.

But while Con, indeed, was a third-generation farmer, he also was a man of commerce. His full name was Cornelius Donald McKeown III, whose grandfather Cornelius, referred to as *The Mick,* emigrated to Ontario from County Tyrone via Montreal in 1887. Unlike Neddy, however, he arrived with his teenage son Corny and his wife Sarah on the *R.M.S. Gaelic Princess* as second-class passengers looking for greater opportunity. Already a successful flax farmer in Ireland, Cornelius saw the promise of growth and greater wealth in burgeoning regions of Canada and decided to stake his claim there.

A decade later, his Ontario farm had grown to more than 300 acres producing various grain crops as well as cattle and poultry. But it was through a friend of a friend, Willet Miller, Ontario's chief geologist, that Cornelius learned of vast silver deposits discovered about 100 miles north of North Bay in 1902. Through various business connections he had made in Ottawa, Cornelius invested in a fledgling mining operation in an area named Cobalt. The discovery of what was known as *poor man's gold* proved to be the goose that laid the silver egg for Cornelius, who began spending more and more time juggling his investments.

Eventually, Corny took over full operation of the farm following the death of his mother, expanding it to more than 600 acres during World War I to help the war effort. But unlike other farmers in the region, Corny didn't actually farm most of the acreage. Instead, he leased it to other farmers who wanted to cash in on what was certain to be a grain-price bonanza during the war. Corny was content collecting rents and taking a cut of profits from each harvest. And while many farmers decided to borrow heavily to purchase their own land and more efficient farming equipment, Corny paid cash for everything like his father before him, recalling The Mick's oft repeated advice, "If you don't have it, don't spend it."

Corny's strategy worked as planned for several years until the unplanned tragically intervened. While on an inspection of mine sites in northern Ontario, Corny and his father were passengers in a truck that lost its footing on a remote access road, skidded sideways and toppled into a ravine. The three bodies were found four days later.

It was 1916. Con was married, a new father and a part-time student at the Ontario Agriculture College when he was told of the deaths. Suddenly, he wasn't just a student, husband and father, he was the family patriarch at the age of 22. Stunned almost to the point of paralysis, Con also knew he didn't have the luxury of grieving. The McKeowns never did. Not when his grandmother died of tuberculosis. Not when Corny's wife Mary Ellen, Con's mother, died along with her newborn during childbirth. Not now. Not with so much riding on a clear mind, uncluttered by emotion and loss.

Con had learned well. With guidance from loyal business partners, a family lawyer and Con's lifelong apprenticeship at the elbows of his father and grandfather, the holdings of the McKeown family scarcely missed a beat. Early on, he discovered a personal penchant for identifying people who could benefit the operation. People like Tom Wilson, the first hire he made after taking over the farm.

Although it may have seemed superficial to most, Con was drawn to Tom initially by his robust red beard that cascaded from his face like a thick fur scarf. While it was a calling card that could be off-putting, anyone who took the time to engage with him quickly discovered the depth of Tom's agricultural knowledge. Con was richer because of that knowledge and now Tom would share it with young Neddy McKenna.

"Mr. Con says I'm to work with chickens," Neddy began, "but this coop is more posh than th' cottage I lived in with me family."

"Well, rather than comparing it to your farm, try thinking of it as a factory," Tom explained. "A chicken factory. The broilers outside are six to eight weeks old and just about ready for market. In a year, we rotate about 5,000 to 6,000 birds in and out."

"What d'ya mean *rotate*?"

"Sell," Tom said. "We sell them to poultry processors who slaughter the chickens and prepare them for sale in towns and cities all over Ontario and Quebec."

Shaking his head, Neddy was amazed. "We had six at a time at th' home place. Maybe 35 a year fer eggs an' meat, an' I was ... what didya call it ... th' only processor. Feed th' layin' hens an' chop off their heads when we needed chicken to eat."

"Well, these are just for meat," Tom explained. "Much heavier with more muscle. The laying hens are back in the chicken coop by the house. We use those eggs for eating and cooking, and what we don't use, we donate to St. George's Home and the poor in and around Ottawa."

"A chicken factory," Neddy mused. "Never heard such a t'ing."

"Well, this is going to be part of your job," Tom

explained. "Feeding them, making sure they have water ..."

"Aye," Neddy said, "like th' home place."

"But for 500 birds at a time," Tom stressed. "Do you think you can handle it?"

Neddy thought a moment and surveyed the operation. "By me-self?" he asked.

"No, we'll work this together," Tom said, pulling a blue-and-white bandana from his back pocket and wiping his forehead. "It's a big job, so if you don't think ..."

"Nah, nah," Neddy said, "I'll do me best."

"That's all I can ask," Tom said. "Let's start here."

Late into the afternoon, save for a half-hour lunch, Tom put Neddy through the paces. Familiarizing him with the equipment. The bins of feed and checking lines for the water troughs. Cleaning the beds. Looking for signs of disease in the birds. "Over there is the sand bin for bedding," Tom said. "I'm sure you'll catch on fast."

Back at the farmhouse, Bess spent hours explaining farm life to Timmy, who knew nothing outside the tenements of Dublin before finding himself in the British government's custody. Although the boy had never been on a farm ... and barely knew they existed ... he was amazed by everything he was shown.

"You mean to tell me you've never heard of a blueberry or raspberry?" Bess asked, cocking her head slightly as if taking a microscopic look at the boy who claimed berry ignorance after she announced they would pick them a bit later for a pie. It was a ground-up education, but he was eager to learn.

In fact, the only resistance to anything introduced to

the boys involved a new bed that arrived at the farmhouse just as everyone sat down to lunch one day in early June.

"Oh, look, boys," Bess shouted as she glanced out the window and ran from the kitchen. "The new bed is here."

Neddy, Timmy and Con got up from the kitchen table and looked out the window to see Bess supervising the bed's unloading and giving instructions where it was to go.

The boys ran to the foot of the staircase as the deliverymen and the bed came into the house. Bess told the men to put it in the upstairs bedroom at the end of the hall, several doors down from where the boys slept.

"Now you can each have your own room," she smiled excitedly. But looking at the boys, she saw only concern on their faces. "What's wrong?"

Timmy spoke first. "D'ya mean I'm not to stay wit' Neddy at night?"

"Yes," Bess said. "Isn't that wonderful? Your own bed in your own room."

"But we like th' way 'tis," Neddy quietly protested.

"Aye," said Timmy, eyeing the bed not quite with dread, but certainly with apprehension.

"Really? But your own room!" Bess said, surprised that she hadn't even considered such a possibility. Thinking for a moment, she added, "Then, why don't we put the new bed in your room so you can still be with each other but with more room to sleep?"

The compromise seemed reasonable to the boys, especially because each of them had been awakened at one time or another by an elbow to the face, a knee in the back or a stray midnight yowl in the ear that scared the bejesus out of one or the other. They looked at each other without a word and nodded in unison at Bess.

That night, as they lay awake in the dark, Timmy asked, "Are ya there, Neddy?"

"I am," he responded. "Don't ya worry yer head. I am."

24

Searching

In a few weeks, Neddy and Timmy were easing into life with the McKeowns, as Timmy learned more and more about, well, everything. Even Neddy, purportedly the more worldly of the two, had trouble at first with the tiny room four feet wide and two feet deep inside their bedroom.

"It's called a closet," a bemused Bess explained as Neddy stood holding the door open. "It's for your clothes ..." (No reaction from Neddy) "... to hang them, store them until you wear them again." While he would catch on as his wardrobe expanded with the changing seasons, his curiosity about other things seemed to increase as time passed. Particularly curiosity about the McKeowns and their secrets.

He happened upon several more phone calls placed or received by Con, who never discussed their nature, even with Bess as far as he knew. At least one more concerned Timmy. Finally, after dinner on a mid-June evening, when it was Timmy's week to help Bess wash dishes, Neddy walked into the parlor, where Con was reading a newspaper. As Neddy entered the room, Con looked up. "Hey, Sport," said Con, who seemed to tag anyone he liked with that greeting. "What's up?"

"First, I didn't mean to be list'nin' in, but ..."

"But?" Con said, lowering the paper.

"But I've heard you talkin' about Timmy ..."

"On the phone?"

"Aye," said Neddy, almost too embarrassed to admit eavesdropping.

"There's nothing that concerns you," Con said gently, "but ... soon enough ... soon enough ..."

Neddy wasn't sure how to react to Con's dodge but took it to mean he wasn't to pursue the line of questioning further. "Aye," he said.

"Anything else?" Con asked.

"Yer books ..."

Con paused to look at his bookcases filled to overflowing with agricultural text books, volumes of fiction and non-fiction, a small oak humidor even though Con didn't smoke, a cast-iron figurine of a black Newfoundland dog, framed photos of people Neddy didn't know and several neat stacks of periodicals. "You like books, don't you? Miss Bess says you have a few."

"Aye," Neddy brightened. "*Gulliver's Travels* and me geography book.

"And what did you think of old Lemuel's journeys?"

"Ya read *Gulliver's Travels*?"

"Indeed I have," said Con, folding the newspaper and placing it on a side table. Getting up, he walked to a bookcase, looked for a moment and pulled out his copy of the Swift classic. "I think I read this for the first time when I was about your age."

"I've read it about three times," Neddy said with no intention to boast.

"You like it that much?"

"Aye," said Neddy.

"Do you have a favorite part?"

"When Gulliver puts out th' palace fire by peeing on it with his willy."

Con laughed. "When I was your age, that was my favorite part, too."

Neddy smiled. "But I also liked all th' t'ings he done an' th' places he went."

"Ever heard of a book called *Huckleberry Finn*?"

Neddy shook his head.

"I think you might like it," Con said, scanning titles in the bookcase, pulling out a leather bound volume and handing it to Neddy. Taking the book from Con, Neddy ran his hand slowly over the cover, then examined wording on the binding that said, *The Adventures of Huckleberry Finn,* then just the name *Clemens*.

"It was written by an American named Samuel Clemens who went by the name of Mark Twain," Con said. "It takes place about 80 years ago and is about a boy roughly your age who fakes his own death to escape his evil father and travels for months down the Mississippi River on a raft. Pretty exciting."

Neddy opened the book and carefully looked at the title page where a teenaged Con had written: *From the library of Con McKeown*. "Can I read it?" Neddy asked.

"You can have it," Con said.

"Ya mean ..."

"Yes, to own," Con said.

Not since he snatched *Gulliver's Travels* off the stack of books at school did Neddy feel such joy. Looking up slowly from the book and pausing to compose himself, he whispered, "T'ank you, Mr. Con."

As Neddy turned to leave, Con called after him, "About the phone calls. In good time, you will know everything ... and so will I."

For the time being, however, the calls would remain a mystery until all details were confirmed. Nearly a month ago, Con put in motion a hunt for facts surrounding Timmy Lordan. Was he or wasn't he an orphan? Were his father and aunt alive or weren't they? To help in the search, Con turned to his wife's brother, Edgar, a well-connected bureaucrat in Ottawa who had been quite useful cutting red tape for the McKeowns on a number of very lucrative projects over the years. In fact, it was through Edgar, who was 15 years older than his sister, that Con had met and married Bess.

This time, Con tasked Edgar with divining the nature of Timmy's separation from his family and how he ended up in Ottawa. Because of his position and being a devout Catholic, Edgar was friends with many church officials and clergy throughout Ontario and beyond. Particularly valuable was his relationship with the firebrand priest John Joseph O'Gorman, an ardent supporter of the Canadian and British efforts in World War I for which he received the OBE.

Hit by shrapnel while evacuating wounded from *no man's land* in France, Father O'Gorman was sent to recuperate in Ottawa, where he was tended to by a volunteer nurse named Bess McKeown.

And while the priest believed strongly that Ireland should be afforded at least the same dominion status enjoyed by Canada and Australia, the McKeowns felt just as strongly that Ireland should be free. As such, they supported the rebellion from afar by secretly donating to the Finian Brotherhood in the United States, which openly helped finance the rebels.

Concurrently, Father O'Gorman – who had studied in England, Germany, Belgium and France -- crisscrossed the Atlantic to champion his cause with members of Parliament.

Once Edgar informed the priest of this shared affinity for a free ... or at least freer ... Ireland, he was more than happy to take up a personal cause for friends and compatriots. Meanwhile, Edgar continued on a parallel track with the archdiocese and governments on both sides of the ocean.

25

The Truth

As Edgar's efforts entered a second month, June became July and July became brutal. For three weeks solid, daytime temperatures soared into the upper 80s, sapping the energy of two- and four-legged creatures alike, while scorching the few crops Con planted that season. Rainfall dropped below average, turning meadows into anvils of grass pounded into straw by an unrelenting sun. No clouds. No wind. Just thick, idle air.

Many nights, the boys abandoned their bedroom, escaping to the farmhouse porch until mosquitoes chased them inside to the cool tile floor of the sunroom off the parlor.

Con was up earlier than usual, sitting on the porch watching the day take shape. The crimson sun rose above the distant pines lining the field of wilting oats to unveil another empty sky as blue as cornflowers and no promise of rain.

Neddy stirred first in the sunroom, peering through the glass panes above his head, thinking he had never seen so many sunny days in his life ... or so much heat. He sat up and yawned, gathered his cotton nightshirt around him and walked toward the entrance hall, where he heard voices from the porch.

"Edgar says he has news," Con said to Bess who carried two cups of coffee to the porch, handing one to him. "He wants to come out today to deliver it in person."

"Today? What news?" asked Bess, taking a sip from the cup, then, "Oh ..."

"Yeah," Con nodded. "Said he'll be here about 11."

Squinting into the sunrise and shading her eyes with a hand to her brow, Bess said, "Another scorcher."

"Appears to be," said Con.

After breakfast and for the next several hours, everyone went about their usual morning chores, slowed somewhat by the rising temperature. Bess and Timmy started off gathering eggs from the chicken coop, checking feed, water and the bedding. Neddy headed off to the barn down the hill, opening the metal barnyard gate and releasing the forty or so cows into the small nearby pasture. And Con met with Tom to discuss what needed to be done to get past the heat wave. Afterwards,

Tom and Neddy were at the broiler house for the monthly deep cleaning.

About 11:15, Edgar pulled into the farm lane driving his Gray-Dort sedan whose red paint was almost completely obscured by road dust. He got out of the car firmly gripping a briefcase and headed up the walk to Bess and Con waiting for him on the porch.

He shook Con's hand and kissed Bess on the cheek as they retired to the parlor where Con slid the oak pocket doors closed. Bess and Con sat on the parlor sofa.

"I don't know where to begin," Edgar said sitting down in a leather library chair, flipping the briefcase latch and extracting a thick manila folder. "So, let's get to it. Timmy is an orphan ... but ..."

"But ..." Bess interrupted anxiously.

"Let him finish," urged Con.

"... but only recently."

"I don't understand ..."

"Bess ..." said Con, putting his hand softly on top of hers.

"It's complicated," Edgar started again. "When you picked him up at St. George's, Timmy wasn't an orphan and that's the tragedy of it ..."

"Oh, dear Lord," Bess sighed.

"His father, Thomas Lordan, was a laborer who fell ill with severe bronchitis and couldn't work. But he was alive. His parish priest told him the church and government could care for the boy and his sister until he recovered, so he agreed."

"But what about Timmy's Aunt Marie?" Con asked.

"Marie Flynn wasn't his aunt; she was the father's lady friend who lived with them," Edgar explained. "She wanted to take the children, but the church would have none of that sinful relationship and Tom was so intimidated by the parish priest, he didn't protest."

"But rather than care for the children, the church sent them to be processed by the Catholic Emigration Association as part of its Home Children program that ships poor and orphaned children like Timmy ..."

"... and Neddy ..." said Bess.

"... and Neddy to Canada, Australia and New Zealand either for adoption or as indentured servants ... with or without their parental consent."

"What about Timmy's father?"

"Without his consent," Edgar said as Bess put a hand to her mouth.

"This is horrible," she said, barely able to speak.

"There's more," said Edgar. "Timmy's father thought he had recovered enough to regain custody of the children, but when he approached the parish priest, he was told that Timmy and his sister were gone. Shipped off to new homes and out of Ireland.

"But that was just part of it. About the same time, Timmy's father also learned he didn't have bronchitis. It was tuberculosis. Very advanced tuberculosis," Edgar said, closing the folder. "He died about a month ago."

Con and Bess just stared blankly at nothing in particular. Con at a bookcase. Bess at the carpet. Without looking up, Bess broke the silence. "What now? How do you tell a seven year old that his father isn't coming to take him home? That his aunt isn't really his aunt? That his father is dead?"

"Gently. Carefully. With all the love you have," said Edgar.

"How could this happen?" Con asked, placing an arm around Bess's shoulder, pulling her closer.

"That's the truly troubling part," said Edgar. "My contacts in Birmingham said the practice of taking poor children out of homes deemed by the Church as unacceptable is common practice, even if the parents are still alive. Parents don't learn their children are gone until it's too late.

"It wasn't one overzealous priest or one low-level church official who decided to label Timmy an orphan. This is systemic and has been for decades."

"Those poor parents," said Con.

"Those poor children. Poor Timmy," Bess whispered.

Con took a deep breath, letting it out like the hiss from an escape valve. "The nuns," he said. "The nuns at St. George's hid the truth ... making us accomplices."

"Unwitting accomplices, yes, but accomplices nonetheless," Edgar agreed. "From what we uncovered, it appears this charade ..."

"... travesty," Bess added.

"... travesty has affected thousands of children and the families who took them in," Edgar said, closing the folder and placing it on a lamp table.

"How can they get away with this?"

"They're the church and the British Empire, two of the strongest powers on earth."

Suddenly, Bess asked, "What of the daughter? Timmy's sister?"

"We're still looking, but haven't been able to find her,"

Edgar said. "Australia, probably. New Zealand, maybe. Even South Africa is a possibility. We just don't know."

"And how many children?" asked Bess, anger rising in her voice.

"Thousands. Tens of thousands. No one knows for sure," Edgar said, closing his briefcase. Standing, he extended his hand to Con.

"Stay for lunch," offered Bess.

"Thanks, but I've got to get back." He hugged his sister. "I wish I had happier news."

"Well, there is a bright side, I guess," said Con. "We can now consider Timmy and Neddy our own. But the papers we signed were little more than labor agreements."

"Yes, there's that," Edgar said. "I'll obtain the proper paperwork so you can begin adoption proceedings for Timmy."

"And Neddy?" Bess asked.

"I think that's up to the three of you," Edgar said. "But I'm certain you will handle this in the best possible way for him and you. Make the most of it. I know you will."

With that, Edgar headed down the front walk to his car and before getting in, he turned a final time and said, "God bless."

As Edgar's car disappeared down the farm lane and through the gate, Neddy steered one of the farm's tractors up the lane's incline from the barnyard and stopped outside the farmhouse. He shut down the engine, jumped off and took several long strides up the front walk.

"Seems like you're really getting the hang of it," said Con, standing on the porch.

"Aye, a might," said Neddy, his shirt drenched in sweat as he removed his cap, wiped his forehead with it and stuck it into the back pocket of his overalls. "Tom says we start plowin' th' east field tomorrow, if I'm up fer it."

"And are you?" Con asked.

"Aye," Neddy smiled. "Aye."

"In this heat, I'd take things slow," Con warned. "You don't want to overdo it."

"Not a'tall," Neddy said. "Hard work'll never kill ya."

"Where's Timmy?" Con asked.

"Tom's showin' him th' hives," Neddy said, "and how honey's made."

"Miss Bess and I need to talk to you," said Con, motioning Neddy inside.

For the next hour, the three of them sat at the kitchen table as Bess and Con slowly unfolded the fabric of Edgar's investigation, thread by painful thread. Neddy found it all difficult to believe, yet at the same time believed every word of it.

While Bess tearfully laid out revelation after revelation, Neddy wasn't surprised by the off-handed brutality of it all. Except for the sheer scope of the Lordans' betrayal and the betrayal of thousands more like them, how was it different from the criminally pious complacency of Sister Assumpta calmly ignoring the dire circumstances leading to Bridget's death? All of it a reprise of tragic theatre with different players on different stages played out over decades.

More than once, he and his family had been caught up in the Church's deceit. Months ago, he had struggled to reconcile the reality of steerage and St. George's with the smiling countenance of the well-dressed boys aboard a ship on the free-passage leaflet given him by Traveler. The church knew it was a lie, yet had no issue with perpetuating it to the desperate and unsuspecting.

"We needed to find out the truth," Con explained, "but couldn't say anything to you until we knew. That's what the telephone calls were about. Can you understand?"

"Aye," Neddy said, not fully understanding. "And now, ya want me to tell Timmy ..."

"*Oh, no,*" Bess said emphatically, "that's the *last* thing we want. It has to come from us and we still don't know how or when to tell him."

"But we *will* figure it out," Con added.

Bess got up from the table and walked to the entry hall after she heard the screen door slam ... then burst out laughing. There stood Timmy still wearing a beekeeper's helmet and veil that consumed his small body almost to his waist.

"Bzzzzz, bzzzzzz," Timmy buzzed, "I'ma bee. Watch out 'r I'll sting ya."

"Oh, please don't sting me, Mr. Bee," Bess responded, recoiling in mock horror. But Timmy was already on his way to the kitchen, flapping his arms like wings while trying to stabilize the helmet to keep it from sliding off.

"Bzzzzzzzzzzzzz," he threatened as Con and Neddy laughed.

"Where's your honey?" Neddy asked.

"In me beehive, but ya canno' have none."

"And why not?" asked Con.

Timmy couldn't think of a reason, so he flapped his

wings and ran back through the house. "Bzzz, bzzz, bzzz ..."

"He's a good pupil," Tom said, removing his cap as he closed the screen door behind him. "And a good lad."

Shuffling into the kitchen, Timmy was buzzed out and in capitulation to the heat had removed the beekeeper's regalia. "When me Da comes to take me home, can I show him th' bees?" Timmy asked.

Con, Bess and Neddy glanced at one another before Bess said, "Why don't we have lunch and talk about it later."

"Hey, I've got an idea," said Con. "It's so hot out, why don't we have a picnic at the swimming hole?" The diversion worked.

"Can we?" asked Timmy.

"Aye," said Neddy.

"Great idea," said Bess, who began assembling picnic fare from the ice box, pantry and cupboard, including a bounty of yesterday's fresh baked goods.

The swimming hole was a large pond fed by McKeown Creek where it flowed into the Ottawa River about 100 yards from the farmhouse. The pond was created years ago when Con's father Corny dammed the stream and installed a windmill to pump water for chickens in the broiler house and irrigate the flax fields planted by Cornelius after his arrival in Ontario. As a side benefit, the pond served as a shaded summer retreat for Con and his parents who picnicked, swam or lazed in the shade of hundred-year oaks, while watching wildlife and the sails of merchant ships glide by on their way to Ottawa.

Almost from their arrival at the farm, Neddy and Timmy escaped to the swimming hole whenever they could slip away from their chores in the late afternoon. And during the early days of this scorching summer, the swimming hole became a second home.

But approaching the pond today, they saw it was nearly drained by the drought with its warm, murky water barely reaching Timmy's knees.

"Looks like we won't be swimming today, Sport," Con said to Timmy as Neddy helped him out of the water. Even when the pond was full, Timmy hugged its banks still unsure of his swimming ability, although he was less timid since Neddy began small lessons weeks earlier. Still, Timmy wasn't quite comfortable with mud squishing between his toes as the only water he had waded into before was a concrete drainage ditch not far from his home in Dublin.

Con helped Bess spread a large tablecloth on the ground and placed the wicker picnic hamper in the center. Soon they dined like royalty with napkins and cutlery and glasses. There were cold roast beef sandwiches, chicken drumsticks, potato salad, tomatoes, radishes, sliced cucumbers and hearts of celery. Also on the menu were several types of hearty breads with butter, raisin cookies, blueberry turnovers, apples and two thermos bottles. One filled with coffee. The other with milk.

"You've outdone yourself," Con said, taking a sizeable bite of a drumstick.

When the meal was over, a slight breeze lifted off the water. Albeit a warm breeze, it was welcomed nonetheless as they sat in the shade watching the afternoon float by.

Neddy could see that Timmy was still disappointed by the lack of pond water and came up with an idea. "Let us build a fort," he said.

"What's that?" said Timmy.

"'Tis a hidin' place," Neddy explained. "A secret place used by th' likes of Willie Brennan. D'ya know him?"

"Aye," said Timmy as every Irish lad had heard of the famous highwayman's exploits since the cradle.

"Well, in this book I'm readin', there's a lad named *Huckleberry Finn* an' his mate, Jim, who are like Willie Brennan and end up hidin' in a cave." Shooting conspiratorial looks from side to side, he added, "but there are no caves about, so we've to build one. 'Tis called a fort."

Jumping up and running to the edge of the clearing, Neddy grabbed a few tree branches and urged Timmy to do the same. They ran into the brush emerging with sticks and branches and twigs of all shapes and sizes until they had amassed a large pile. "'Tis a good start," said Neddy as Bess and Con looked on in amusement. Every so often, Con would look up from the book he was reading as Bess napped intermittently in the shade.

Using reeds and wild grass as twine, Neddy lashed the brush into a crude leaf-covered hut big enough for him and Timmy to crawl into. "D'ya t'ink were safe from th' king's men?" Neddy asked, scanning the distance with wild-eyed apprehension.

"Aye," said Timmy, joining the quest for invisible dragoons. "They canno' find us here."

For more than an hour, they darted in and out of the fort battling unseen enemies and always emerging victorious until Con, saying he was from headquarters, informed them it was time to retire from the field.

JOHN HEAGNEY

Skirmishes continued on the way back to the farmhouse where daily chores took the place of sorties. Cows were brought in. Chickens fed. And the farm manager reported on what had happened while the battles raged by the river.

26

Birthday

The phone rang late in the afternoon. Bess answered and ran outside to find Con, who was mowing the grass on the side of the house. "It's over!" she yelled as she ran. "There's a truce signed in Ireland. A truce."

Con dropped the handle of the mower and ran to embrace her. "The violence is finally over," he shouted.

Not quite. The Irish War of Independence, indeed, ended with the July 11, 1921 truce, and was formalized with the Anglo-Irish Treaty on Dec. 6 of the same year. But that was only the end of the Irish killing the British. Just six months after the treaty was signed, the Irish started killing the Irish during an 11-month civil war that finally ended in 1923. But enough of that. Today was a time for celebration, even if it was fleeting.

As Neddy approached the farmhouse, the last of his chores complete, he could hear John McCormack singing *Mother Machree* on the Gramophone. Walking through the front door, he saw Con, Bess and Tom dancing in the parlor, where several empty Guinness bottles were on the floor. A bottle of Jamieson was opened on a side table.

"It's a celebration," Con said as Neddy walked in. "So have yourself a beer."

It was the first time Con or Bess had invited him to drink alcohol of any kind, although Tom shared his flask every once in awhile with a solemn oath extracted from Neddy to never to tell the McKeowns.

Grabbing a Guinness by the neck and flipping it open with a church key, Neddy hoisted the bottle and proclaimed, "Happy birthday to me!"

Laughing, Tom said, "Birthday? It's not your birthday."

"But *'tis* me birthday," Neddy said taking a pull on the stout.

The dancing stopped as McCormack crooned, "*... Sure, I love the dear silver that shines in your hair, and the brow that's all furrowed and wrinkled with care ...*"

Bess lifted the needle from the record and the room fell silent. "Today's your birthday?"

"Aye," said Neddy, "July 11. Fer 16 years. 'Tis me birthday sesh, no?"

"No," said Con quietly. "We ... uh ... were celebrating the cease fire in Ireland. The war's over. Haven't you heard?"

"Uh, aye. Aye, I did," Neddy smiled trying to hide his embarrassment, raising his bottle and offering a traditional Irish toast, "Slainte!"

"I'm so, so sorry, Neddy," Bess said, walking up to Neddy and throwing her arms around him. "We'll make it up to you ..."

"No worries," Neddy said.

It was a quiet dinner that night as Neddy found himself thinking of home and his family more than he had in months.

Birthdays were always happy occasions with friends and food and, of course, bumping, where the birthday boy was held upside down by an adult and his head bumped on the floor. One bump for each year. That, of course, hadn't been done to Neddy since he was a wee lad, so for several years before he died, Packy was a stand-in for Neddy who bumped his little brother in his place.

Bess again apologized for the terrible oversight and again Neddy told her not to worry about it. As he said his goodnights, he was about to head up the stairs when Con called him into the parlor.

"A special day," he said, "for Ireland, but for you as well."

"'Specially fer Ireland," Neddy offered.

"No, especially for you. Sixteen is an important year," Con said, turning to the three parlor walls of bookcases. "Pick a book."

"What?"

"Pick a book," Con repeated. "Any one you want for your birthday."

"I don't ..." Neddy said, overwhelmed.

"Quite a daunting task, I agree," Con said, getting up and standing next to Neddy in front of his personal library. Studying the spines momentarily, he reached out and pulled a book from the shelves. "Here, try this. *Around the World in 80 Days* by Jules Verne."

Neddy was immediately captivated by the title and wrapped his hands around it.

"I think you'll like Phileas Fogg," Con said, then noticed Neddy's confusion. "He's the main character and world traveler. A 19th century Gulliver, but to real places."

"So was Huck," Neddy said with a smile.

"I guess you're right," said Con, returning the smile. "I also wanted you to know that from now on, you can read any book I have in here. Come in any time. The only thing I ask is that you treat each book with respect and return it in the same condition you found it. Books are to be cherished like old family members who have given you joy, who have taught you things or taken you to places or other times in history. Books, Neddy, are forever and can be enjoyed over and over again."

"I understand, Mr. Con," Neddy said. "G'night an' t'ank you."

When he entered the bedroom, it was already dark, so Neddy got undressed and crawled into bed without turning on the light. As he settled in, a small voice across the room said, "Neddy?"

"Aye," he responded.

"Happy birthday."

27

Furnace of God

Several hours before dawn, Neddy heard the first rumble roll out of the north. Several minutes later, another. Then silence. He waited a long time for another, but finally fell back to sleep. Then, in the pre-dawn light an hour later, he heard another sound outside the open bedroom window. A nearly imperceptible night visitor. First tapping then a steady hiss until enough water gathered into a series of rivulets on the window glass, dripping on the windowsill.

He threw back the sheet and went to the window.

Con and Bess were also at their window, hoping they weren't being teased by a false siren promising more than she was willing to deliver. They watched, hoping for relief that had been elusive for so long. They prayed for the crops. They prayed for their neighbors. Please, please ... rain.

Then it stopped. Just a taunt of precipitation, enough to resurrect the aroma of petrichor and crush their expectations.

BRUMMMMMM ... CREEEEEACCCCCCK!!!

The morning sky exploded white, then fell silent as if the whole world were holding its breath. In the next moment, it exhaled in a monstrous blast of wind and rain, making limbs of the massive oaks outside the farmhouse whip frantically like the raised arms of the possessed at a revival meeting. The rain came down in horizontal sheets making the entire house shudder. The porch's screen door pounded open and shut, open and shut as if desperately seeking sanctuary inside the house before being ripped from its hinges and sailing through the front yard.

CREEEEEACCCCCCK!!! The rain pounded the dirt in a million tiny explosions. In the farm lane. In the fields. On the roof. On the cows, the chickens, the pigs ... and one small boy. CRAAAAAAACKKKKK!

"Furnace of God," Neddy thought back to Mick on deck during the electrical storm at sea. Hearing Con and Bess in the hall, he turned to join them when he looked at Timmy's bed. It was empty.

"Timmy," he called, going to the closet. "Timmy?" But the closet held only the boys' clothing ... except for Timmy's shoes. They were missing.

Neddy walked to the hall, "Have you seen Timmy?" he asked the couple, still in their night clothes. Before they could answer, he was in the bathroom. Timmy wasn't there.

"What's wrong?" Bess asked.

"I dunno," Neddy replied, heading toward the staircase. "Maybe nothin'."

Joined by the McKeowns downstairs, Neddy continued the search, "Timmy?" in the kitchen. "Timmy?!" in the parlor and sunroom. "Timmy!!??" from the front porch and into the side yard, where they saw Tom leaning into the torrent as he approached the house.

"Have ya seen Timmy?" Neddy, yelled above the storm.

"Wha?" Tom replied, leaning in to hear.

"Timmy, Timmy!! Have ya seen 'im?"

"Can't say for sure," Tom said, clamping his cap to his head with a free hand. "Think I saw someone headed down there." He pointed in the direction of the swimming hole.

"Jaysus!!" Neddy blurted and started running. Barefoot and still in his nightshirt, he bolted toward the river with Bess and Con trailing behind, screaming as he ran. "Timmy? TIMMY!!!"

About 50 yards from the swimming hole, he began sloshing through increasingly deep water. First to his ankles, then mid-calf, then to his knees. The flash flood had barreled down the parched stream bed, a watery locomotive gaining speed as it went, sweeping up loose vegetation, debris and anything on its route to the river.

"TIMMY!! TIMMY!! TIMMY!!," the three of them screamed.

"Damn you, *Jaysus*," Neddy bellowed, suddenly awash in the irrational guilt of being unable to save Packy and Bridget. "Not again! Not again, *damn you!!*"

In the distance, Neddy squinted through the deluge, glimpsing something white whipping in the gale. Drawing closer, he saw it was a nightshirt ... worn by a small boy. "*TIMMY!!!*" he screeched.

"*NEDDY!!!,*" the boy cried, as Neddy, Bess and Con struggled through the waist-high water. Con stumbled and fell, dragging Bess into the water with him. Neddy finally got a clear look at Timmy clinging to a tree limb bouncing in and out of the river water.

"Stay where y'are," Neddy yelled. "Hold on!"

Neddy could see the boy tighten his grip on the limb as he finally reached him, grabbing Timmy around the waist just as the limb snapped, dropping both of them into the turbulent river current. With the impact, Neddy's grip on Timmy loosened and the boy began slipping away. But Neddy's arm shot across Timmy's chest and under both arms just as the river rolled them under the water's surface, then shot them back up. The current carried them another forty feet as Neddy thrashed wildly looking for anything he could use to pull them ashore. Suddenly his foot hooked around a submerged tree root protruding into the river along the bank. They stopped and the water raged around them as if they were rocks in a riverbed, threatening to pull them into the shipping channel.

"NEDDY!!" Con screamed from a small rise along the shore, pulling a long tree branch behind him. "Grab this!!" Raising the branch high in the air, he cast it like a fly-fishing rod holding one end firmly and slapping it into the water downstream from the boys, just out of Neddy's reach.

"Timmy," Neddy shouted, "Grab me around me neck."

As Timmy secured his stranglehold, Neddy unhooked his foot from the tree root and shot toward the outstretched limb. The current suddenly began pulling them away from the riverbank as Neddy dove for the limb ... and clamped a hand on it. "NOW," he shouted to Con. "Pull it NOW!!"

Con and Bess slowly retracted the limb, praying it would hold long enough to bring the boys to safety. Neddy's foot brushed silt for a moment, then he was up to his ankle, then he was kneeling in mud. The McKeowns waded out to the boys, grabbing them both and pulling them from the water. All of them collapsed to the ground as the boys coughed up river water and the McKeowns breathed heavily with exhaustion. Recovering and finally breathing deeply, Neddy whispered, "Not again, ya bastard. Not this time."

Finally, Con rolled to his side, wiped rain from his face, then pushed himself up to a sitting position. "Timmy," he said sternly, "what the hell were you doing down here?"

Timmy began to cry, never having heard Con angry. "Th' fort," he said. "I was worried 'bout our fort."

"Your *FORT*??!!" Con said, his anger about to crest until Bess firmly grasped his forearm. He took a breath. "Don't you know how dangerous it is to come out in a storm like this by yourself? You could have ..."

"You could have been hurt," Bess interrupted. "All of us could have been hurt. Do you understand?"

Sniveling, Timmy whispered, "Aye," as Neddy reached around the boy's shoulders and pulled him close.

The rain continued falling heavily, but the wind and

lightning had subsided as the four of them found high ground and began walking back toward the farmhouse.

Entire fields turned to lakes and dirt roads to streams. Cattle and chickens were scattered, as were countless tree limbs, milk cans, wheelbarrows and more. But aside from some debris, a toppled birdbath and a disembodied screen door in the front yard, the farmhouse had weathered the storm and so had Neddy, Timmy and the McKeowns who walked by the chicken coop, climbed the side porch steps and entered the kitchen.

Dripping water that formed a small lake on the kitchen floor, everyone was instructed by Bess to change into dry clothing, bring down their nightshirts and reassemble for breakfast. Timmy kicked off his waterlogged shoes and Bess stuffed them with old newspapers before placing them on the stove to dry.

When the boys hadn't returned from changing, Bess went upstairs to find both of them stretched out on Neddy's bed, still in their wet nightshirts and asleep. She quietly stripped the quilt from Timmy's bed and softly covered the boys. As she left the room, she turned to look at them then closed the door and went downstairs.

"They're exhausted," she said to Con who had poured both of them a cup of coffee.

"We're all exhausted," Con said, taking a sip. "But we better rest up today because there's plenty to do tomorrow."

"Oh, I forgot," Bess said. "The auction."

Near the end of each month, property auctions took place in Ottawa as foreclosed farms were placed on the block. Hundreds of Canadian farm families were being displaced by the agricultural depression following World War I as wartime demand for grain and other agricultural products evaporated and prices plummeted. Many farmers, caught with vast stores of unsold harvests couldn't produce income to pay loans taken out against their farms to buy land or equipment during the war boom. Foreclosures rocketed.

With diverse financial holdings including the silver mines and a generations-old philosophy of paying cash for everything, Con was debt-free. And in foreclosures, he saw opportunity. For the past several years, he made regular pilgrimages to the auctions in Ottawa to scoop up farms foreclosed throughout the area for pennies on the dollar. It also was a chance for Bess and the boys to see the big city, eat at a restaurant, take in a moving picture or two and do a little shopping. Neddy had his eye on a new thing called radio and was keen to get a crystal-radio set to build.

The McKeowns were paying Neddy 18 dollars a month, well above the minimum required by the indenture agreement they signed. Good money for a 16-year-old considering that food, lodging, clothing and everything else he needed were also paid for by them. In many cases, room, board and clothing were deducted by farmers who took in Home Children, violating the indenture agreements. Without oversight, the children had no income at all.

At 6 a.m. the next day, Bess, Con, Neddy and Timmy piled into the one luxury Con had allowed himself: A new Hudson closed-body sedan that not only had a windshield, but side windows that blocked wind and rain. The boys – who had never seen let alone driven in such a marvel – were kings of the road as they pulled out of the farm lane and headed off to

Ottawa.

The skies had cleared, with towering fair-weather clouds stretching to the horizon. At least for the time being, yesterday's storm also broke the back of the heat wave as temperatures dropped into the high 60s during their drive into the city.

They arrived just in time for breakfast at the Canadian Café, after which Con walked to Thomlinson Auctioneers on Albert Street near Elgin, where a monthly property foreclosure sale took place. The main hall of the Victorian auction house contained 30 or so folding chairs arranged in a tight rectangle on the oak plank flooring. Prospective bidders were scattered here and there, along with a half dozen banking officials with the paperwork necessary for deed transfers. As Con was a regular at these sales, he was afforded a reserved seat in the front row.

The bidding started with commercial land inside and outside city limits, most nearly worthless slices adjacent to railroad rights of way. Some under water. Others land-locked without road access. Residential tracts were next, then homes in foreclosure. Finally came agricultural tracts and farms.

Because bidding was sluggish this month, Con was able to pick up three properties in the general area surrounding his farm. A fourth was the 24-acre Conway farm 16 miles south of his property. With only marginal interest in the available properties, Con purchased them from lenders for between 16 and 28 cents on the dollar. A good haul for a half day investment of time and just 90 minutes of bidding.

Leaving the auction, Con walked the few blocks to the offices of Trexler Frend and Raymond, the McKeown family attorneys, where he had arranged to meet Harold Trexler, a senior partner of the firm.

"Harold, I want everything drawn up by the first of the week," Con said, handing him the deeds. "I'd like to inform the families no later than Wednesday."

28

Kate

First thing Monday morning, Harold pulled up in front of the McKeown farmhouse with the documents Con requested. He dropped them off and left.

Early Tuesday, Con and Bess steered their Hudson down the dirt lane leading to Kate and Frankie Conway's farm and parked in front of the modest frame farmhouse. As they reached the porch, Con stopped to tear down the prominent eviction notice nailed to a porch post. Knocking on the front door, they were greeted by a slight young woman dressed in a dove-grey smock dress with a pink flowered apron tied neatly about her trim waist. Her red hair flowed easily to her shoulders, framing a face as refined and soft as a porcelain doll with a light dusting of freckles. Only her sullen eyes made Kate seem older than her 25 years.

The past five years had taken a terrible toll, starting with news that her husband Frankie had been killed in the Third Battle of Ypres in Belgium just a month after being conscripted, leaving her with an infant daughter and a farm to run in 1917.

Although raised on a farm, Kate had only rudimentary

knowledge of the farming business and within months was overwhelmed by the sole responsibility and unflagging grief. Near desperation, she implored her brother Robert, 18 years her senior, to move in with his wife and two teenaged sons to help keep the farm afloat. However, by the time her nephews were old enough, they enlisted in the army, taking with them the bulk of her workforce. After the war, she was dealt another blow as the boys decided they wanted more out of life than farming. Nathan settled in Toronto as an auto mechanic, and Elwood as an apprentice chef in Marseille on the southern coast of France.

Like so many other farmers, Kate and Frankie had amassed debt to keep up with demand for more crops during the war. When the war ended and grain prices plunged, she quickly fell behind in payments and foreclosure soon followed.

"Good morning, Mr. McKeown," said Kate, face to face with the visit she dreaded since hearing of the farm's sale several days before. "I heard you now own my farm. We can be out ..."

Bess interrupted. "May we come in?"

She opened the screen door and ushered the McKeowns into the tiny, dimly lit parlor, where Robert got up from a wood rocker and shook Con's hand. There was an old upright piano against the stairwell on the far wall, a worn flowered settee, an overstuffed mohair easy chair with cigarette burns in one arm, a round end table on which sat a brown ceramic lamp with tassel-fringed lampshade. Kate's old mutt Blaze got up, tail wagging as slowly as his approach and sniffed in the visitors' general direction. Assured they weren't a threat and that he had fulfilled his duty as family guardian, he returned to his original spot on the hook rug, circled once, plopped down and closed his eyes.

"As I was saying," Kate began, "we can be out ..."

"We're not here to evict you," Bess said. "We're here to help."

Kate didn't understand. "Help?"

"We did satisfy the loan in the auction earlier this week," said Con, "but not to take possession of your farm. What are neighbors for if those who are better off can't help those who are struggling?"

"That's why we want you to sign an agreement," Bess said.

"An agreement? What kind of agreement?" Kate asked.

"An agreement," said Con, "to pay us back for the purchase price of your farm ..."

"But I can't pay," Kate quietly protested. "It's the reason I was foreclosed."

"... to pay us back for the purchase price of your farm ... *when* you can and *only* when you can."

Kate still didn't comprehend the offer and looked to Robert for help, but he just shrugged, as confused as she was.

"When you and your brother get back on your feet, you can start paying us whatever you can afford. But when you can't afford to pay, you don't pay us anything."

"You're giving me back my farm?"

"Not exactly," Con said. "We'll still own it until you've paid us back ... no matter how long that takes. A year. Ten years. It doesn't matter. Only if you decide to leave will we take possession or sell it."

Kate who had been sitting on the edge of the chair slowly eased back, letting herself sink into the cushion. "Why?" she finally asked.

"We've been fortunate," Bess said. "Many are not. After all, neighbors should take care of neighbors if they can, don't you think? We'll pay the taxes and won't charge you interest, but there *is* a stipulation. We are private people, so you and your brother can't tell anyone we have done this."

"But I want to tell the world," Robert blurted out.

"*No one.*" Con said firmly. "This is an agreement between us. Tell anyone and the agreement will be cancelled. Understand?"

"Yes," said Kate.

"Understood," said Robert.

Con handed them the agreement. "Once you have looked it over and signed it, bring this to our place this weekend."

With that, the McKeowns stood, shook hands with Kate and Robert, got in their car and headed to the other three farmers on their list.

29

Heaven

The drought was over as temperatures moderated through August and even more in September. Gentle, nourishing rains came with blessed frequency as if a contrite Mother Nature felt compelled to offer an extended mea culpa for her ferocity on that tempestuous July morning near the swimming hole.

The fields were again golden blankets of oats and wheat, deep-green corn stalks full of silken cobs and the promise of a fine harvest to come. Sugar maples and sycamores began doffing their summer finery for the crimsons, yellows and umbers of fall, as two boys reclined in the shade by the Ottawa River this Sunday afternoon, fishing poles poised above the water.

Timmy was unusually quiet, tossing stones into the river currents.

"You'll be scarin' fish doin' that," Neddy said flatly, staring unfocused on the distant riverbank.

Timmy didn't respond, continuing to throw stones in the water until, "'Tis me Da."

"What about your da?," Neddy responded.

"I ... I don't t'ink he's comin'," Timmy said.

"What makes ya say that?"

"'D'ya t'ink he could be in heaven?"

Neddy was taken aback by the question and fought the temptation to tell Timmy the truth outright because while the McKeowns had taken full ownership of the task, they had failed to follow through. "Heaven?"

"Aye," said Timmy. "He once tol' me he wanted t'be in heaven wit' me Ma, so he wouldn't be sick no more."

"How'd ya feel if yer da was in heaven?"

"Sad," Timmy said.

"Me sister Bridget an' brother Packy are in heaven," Neddy said, prompting Timmy to turn and look directly at him. "An' they were sick, too."

"Were you sad?"

"Aye," Neddy said. "Terrible sad an' still am. But I'm happy they're not sick no more. They're in heaven an' happy every day bein' together. Do ya t'ink if yer da was in heaven wit' yer ma, they'd be happy too?"

Timmy didn't get a chance to answer as his line went taut and the fishing pole bowed in a perfect arc nearly touching the water's surface, "I gotta fish!" he yelled.

"Hold on tight," said Neddy, "an' don't pull too fast ..."

Timmy gripped the rod firmly and started scooting back on his rear end from the shore inch by inch, pulling gently until the line emerged with the passing tree branch it had hooked on the river bottom. Looking at the tangle, Neddy quipped, "We won't be eatin' this tonight now, will we?"

Timmy smiled for the first time that afternoon while cutting the line as Neddy began gathering their belongings. "What say we head back?" Neddy said. "'Bout time fer dinner."

A short time later as they entered the kitchen through the back door, Bess was peeling and slicing potatoes, sliding them into a large pot of water on the stove. "So how are my great fishermen?" she asked.

"Not great a'tall," said Neddy.

"An' no fish," said Timmy.

"Well, dinner will be ready soon, so go on and wash up," Bess said, adding, "and Timmy, don't forget your lessons tonight."

All summer, Bess had been reading to Timmy from an old set of McGuffey Readers Con bought at a Toronto book store years ago. And in quiet moments before chores or in the early evening between dinner and bed, she and Timmy worked on the McGuffey Primer to give him a working knowledge of

the alphabet, rudimentary reading and arithmetic skills. Last
month, she enrolled him in an English-language parochial
school affiliated with St. Andrew's parish in Winton.

In the bathroom upstairs, Timmy rubbed a bar of soap
between his hands and said to Neddy, "Miss Bess says I'm fer
school next week."

"Whatd'ya t'ink of that?" asked Neddy.

"Dunno," said Timmy. "Never been."

"I liked school," Neddy said, "'specially geography."

"Are ya goin', too?"

"Nah," said Neddy. "I'm past it. Too old, I guess."

It was Neddy's turn to help in the kitchen, so after
dinner, he had a chance to talk with Bess as Timmy was with
Con and McGuffey in the parlor.

"Timmy's askin' 'bout his da," Neddy said, drying a
platter and placing it on the kitchen table. "Today, while
fishin', we had a talk and he's worried his da won't be comin'
fer 'im. I t'ink 'tis time …"

"I know, I know," said Bess, hands bracing the lip of the
sink. "But the timing has to be right and we have to handle
this with care." But Bess was such a perfectionist that her
search for the ideal solution sometimes triggered a serious
bout of inertia.

Neddy wanted to step in. "Timmy has t'be told, an' I
t'ink I've a way to do it. Can I give it a lash?"

In the few short months Neddy had been part of her
life, Bess grew to consider him bright, sensitive and sensible
beyond his years. Moreover, his loving relationship with
Timmy was more that of an older, wiser brother than simply
two independent souls thrown together by happenstance. She

was certain, Neddy would do what was right ... and best for Timmy. "Be careful," she cautioned. "I'll talk to Mr. Con."

Neddy wouldn't wait for Con's blessing.

The next morning, Timmy quietly entered the kitchen and sat at the table without his usual bright greeting. Bess sensed something was off. "Morning, Timmy," she said cautiously. "Anything wrong?"

"Me Da's not sick," Timmy announced solemnly.

"What?" Bess immediately feared that Neddy's plan had somehow misfired and Timmy would expect his father any day now, setting him up for a brutal crush of reality. "He's ... he's not sick?"

"He's in heaven wit' me Ma," Timmy said as Neddy appeared in the doorway.

"In heaven?"

"Aye," Timmy confirmed almost dispassionately. "In heaven wit' me Ma an' they're both happy. Neddy says so ..."

"Aye," said Neddy from the doorway. "In a dream last night, Timmy's da an' ma came ta me from heaven an' told me they were happy an' that they loved Timmy very much."

"An' I wasn't ta worry me head no more," Timmy said, "because you are ... are ..."

"... fine people," Neddy prodded, "who love ..."

"... who love me very much," said Timmy.

Bess sat down and gently drew Timmy closer until she wrapped her arms around him, but was concerned by the boy's complete lack of emotion. "I'm sad that me Da isn't comin'," he continued, "but Neddy says I should be happy he's not sick. I 'spose but ..."

"You'll always have your father and mother in your

heart," Bess whispered, holding him closer, "and they'll always be a part of you ..."

"I know," Timmy said, "Me Ma told Neddy that, too."

Stroking Timmy's hair, Bess looked at Neddy and smiled, not just affirming his kindness and affection, but thanking him without words for doing what she could not.

At that moment, Con and Tom came in from outside. "What's for breakfast?" Con asked.

"Me Da's not comin'," Timmy said before Con had time to hang up his hat and jacket. "He's in heaven."

Not sure how to react or what to say, Con glanced helplessly toward Bess, whose expression told him the situation was under control. "Timmy's parents came to Neddy in a dream last night," Bess explained, as Con quickly connected the dots.

Timmy nodded, "They tol' Neddy they're happy an' I'm to be happy too."

"I'm ... sorry to hear ..." Con struggled. "It's sad that ..."

"Aye," Timmy said, "but me Da's not sick, so I 'spose I'm happy an' sad together."

Con nodded but said nothing and the kitchen fell silent.

Clearing his throat, Tom began, "We best get ..."

"Um ... yes ... plenty to do today," Con joined in and everyone began to move. Bess to the stove. Neddy to set the table. Con to hang up his hat and jacket. Timmy getting a hair-tousling head rub from Tom as he sat at the table next to him. Slowly the conversation turned to the tasks at hand.

"Neddy, you'll be coming with me for firewood, while Tom gets the pickers started in the apple orchard."

Bess chimed in, "Don't forget, Neddy, I'll need your help

this afternoon with some of the canning and hams."

How could he possibly forget anything about canning and hams, having intimate knowledge of transporting and stocking hams and jar upon jar of preserves from root cellar to root cellar under circumstances Bess couldn't begin to imagine? "Aye," said Neddy, taking a last bite of potatoes and finishing his tea.

Soon, Neddy and Con started off. Con behind the wheel of the Chevrolet Model T truck while Neddy followed in the farm's 12-20 Rock Island Heider tractor to haul the larger deadfall logs to a clearing where they could be cut into manageable lengths and stacked on the flatbed.

About a half hour from the farmhouse, they arrived at a field cleared of trees in the spring and earmarked for winter wheat. The uprooted trees and heavy brush had been mounded at the far end of the field waiting to be cut, split, stacked and set ablaze in the farmhouse fireplace to dull the bite of long nights during Ontario's coming winter.

Neddy maneuvered the tractor into place as Tom, returning on horseback, dragged chains from the truck bed. Con secured one end to the tractor's three-point hitch then while Tom wrapped the other around a fallen oak with an eleven-inch diameter. Neddy grabbed the shifter, slammed the tractor into gear and with no more effort than clearing its throat to hurl a single belch of black smoke skyward, the tractor dragged the 18-foot long tree into the open.

They repeated the process for the next six hours or so until more than a dozen trees of varying lengths and widths lay scattered on the ground like wooden carcasses to be carved by dragon-toothed crosscut saws into five- and six-foot lengths. One by one, the logs were stacked on the flatbed and secured with chains for the return to the farmhouse.

Although the home's central heat was supplied by the large coal furnace in the cellar, firewood added another layer of warmth when the family set up winter headquarters in the parlor for frigid evenings that would stretch from November to the doorstep of April.

While firewood was the focus of this particular morning, it was just a brush stroke in a vast landscape of preparations for the coming winter that coincided with autumn's harvest season.

During the ensuing month and a half, the McKeowns' farm was alive with tractors and combines, threshing machines, wagons, teams of horses and scores of men and women harvesting crops they had planted on the leased tracts.

On more than two dozen other fields of the McKeown's 600 acres, Tom and Con oversaw a small army of migrant farm workers harvesting corn and wheat, oats, flax and soybeans, storing the agricultural bounty in a half dozen large silos. It was an enterprise that overwhelmed Neddy who thought often of the farm in County Tyrone that barely kept his family alive.

Nonetheless, he took to the pace and hard work, embracing the long hours, now extending into ever shorter days of sun and encroaching cold. By late October, daily high temperatures in Ontario were struggling to hold onto the 60s. A month after that, the 40s would be a fond and warming memory.

For now, however, the harvests were nearing an end and autumn days were reaching their peak of ripeness with sweet, flavorful afternoons of pumpkin skies and celestial red-apple sunsets. Neddy brought in the last of the cattle for the night and went to the barn checking on feed for the pig pens when he heard it. A whimper near the corner of an empty stall lit by a lingering shaft of sunlight. Approaching the stall, Neddy caught sight of a teddy bear and a small arm holding it.

"Timmy?" Neddy probed as the boy withdrew into the shadows. "Timmy, why'rya cryin'?"

After a short silence, Timmy said, "I'm not cryin'."

"Aye. Aye, you're not cryin'," Neddy said. "So, what *are* you on about then?"

"'Tis ...," he began, "'tis me Da."

"Your da?"

"I miss 'im terrible," Timmy confessed. "I know he's in heaven an' he's not sick ..."

"But ya can't stop t'inkin ..."

"Aye," Timmy said. "Not all th' time, but ..."

"I know, I know," Neddy said, sitting down in the hay next to him. "'Tis like he's here ... but not."

"Aye," Timmy nodded.

"D'ya know what that is?"

"No."

"'Tis our people in heaven t'inkin' 'bout *us*," Neddy said. "Carin' fer us an' wantin' us t'be happy an' go on wit' our lives. 'Tis th' same wit' me. Bridget sometimes is on me one shoulder an' Packy on th' other, tellin' me they miss me, too. I'm t'inkin that's what yer da is doin'."

"He's on me shoulder?" Timmy said, craning his neck to get a better look.

"Oh, ya canno see 'im," Neddy smiled. "He's an angel an'

so's yer ma. But ya can *feel* 'em all around because they love ya from heaven as much as you love them."

Recalling what Bess told him months ago, Timmy said, "... an' they'll be in me heart forever."

"Aye," said Neddy, wondering if his hypocrisy with Timmy was acceptable under the circumstances. He believed none of it. For years, he had flirted with heresy in Ireland, growing increasingly resentful of his Catholic education in and out of the classroom. The resentment pushed him to the edge of a spiritual chasm with Bridget's illness and its awful aftermath. But it was the Church's banishment of an innocent girl like Mary to a life of toil, degradation and exclusion, as well as its contemptibly casual theft of innocents like Timmy to be doled out for slave labor by the likes of Mother FE that spawned the irreparable schism between Neddy and Catholicism.

The McKeowns struggled with Neddy's refusal to attend mass after the first month under their roof, chalking it up to adolescent rebellion. But it seemed the stronger they argued for Neddy's adherence, the more they examined their own attendance and how it existed more by force of habit than anything else. Ultimately, while they didn't fully understand his unwillingness to participate in what he called, "a terrible dishonesty," they made peace with his decision.

Others in the largely Catholic community weren't so easily appeased and Neddy became the focus of religious gossips ready to resent without facts and condemn with absolute certainty. Chief among them was Millie Ryan, a wisp-thin milliner from Winton, who was at the epicenter of St. Andrew's lay leadership. She was known throughout that part of the province for her flinty demeanor, inflated sense of self worth and an upturned nose perfect for sniffing out dirt on those around her.

Although called Millie from childhood, she now insisted on being called Miss Millicent so that the name of her self-titled hat shop – *Miss Millicent's Chapeau Emporium* – would always be on the lips of those who knew her or talked about her. In her mind, that was everyone, although behind her back, she was Miss Millipede to most.

Neddy watched the shaft of light in the stall fade and disappear, and said to Timmy, "Always remember your ma an' da are in yer heart forever."

Brushing off the barn straw, the boys walked up the rise in the farm lane and into the house just as the sun set. Bess was at the kitchen table reading the latest *Saturday Evening Post* as a large pot simmered on the stove. "A bit longer until dinner," she said. "Thought we'd do something special tonight: Irish stew. It's a recipe brought over by Mister Con's grandmother, so you go wash up."

"Neddy," Con called from the parlor, having heard Bess talking to the boys in the kitchen. "Can you come here?"

As Neddy entered the parlor, fireplace flames choreographed an erratic dance of shadow and light around the room, making Con's collection of books and, indeed, Con himself flicker. Still dressed in the day's work clothes, his legs stretched before him and his feet facing the warming flames, Con closed the book he was reading and said, "C'mon in, Sport. Have a seat." Neddy settled on the rug near the fire. "You've been enjoying the books, haven't you?"

"I have," said Neddy, "an' th' *National Geographics*."

"Quite a world we live in, isn't it?"

"Aye, 'tis," said Neddy.

"I want to tell you how proud I am of the work you've been doing here," Con said. "It seems there isn't a job you *can't* do ... and do it well."

"I like th' work fine," Neddy said.

"With the harvest all but done, it's time to focus on getting ready for winter ..."

"Aye," said Neddy, "Tom's been tellin' me all 'bout it, an' we've winter wheat to plant in a week."

"Do you know Mrs. Conway, a few farms over? I think you met at church, when you were still going to church," said Con, hoping a little guilt would prompt a return to the flock. It didn't.

"Aye, th' widow woman?"

"That's her," said Con. "She's been having a time of it recently and things just got worse. Her brother, who's been helping since her husband Frankie was killed in the war, well, he was repairing the farmhouse roof and fell. Broke his leg, putting Mrs. Conway in quite a fix."

"Poor critter," Neddy said, shaking his head.

"That's where you come in," said Con.

"Sorry?" Neddy said

"I need you to start checking in on her a few times a week to see if she needs help. You know, things she might not be able to do by herself. You've driven the flivver in the shed before, so you can use that to go back and forth."

"But don't ya need me here?"

"I do," Con assured him, "but most of the heavy lifting here has been done and in a few weeks or so, we'll just need to do maintenance, bookkeeping and planning for the spring. Mrs. Conway has no one to help her and I couldn't think of anyone I'd trust with this more than you."

Neddy not only felt a burst of pride and purpose, but a sense that Con no longer considered him just the extra Irish boy they brought home from St. George's home. Con trusted him ... like a man ... to do *man's work*. "When do I start, Mr. Con? I have a few jobs to do come mornin', so how's th' afternoon?

"That's fine, Neddy," Con said, then as an afterthought, "And by the way, you don't have to call me mister. Just Con will do."

Neddy smiled as he went upstairs to wash for dinner. He heard Timmy in the bedroom and after drying his hands, poked his head in the room. Timmy was sitting on the edge of his bed, looking out the window at the night sky and holding his stuffed bear. He was still, seemingly deep in reflection. Everyone needs moments like this, Neddy thought, leaving without a sound, descending the stairs and walking to the porch.

The evenings were getting colder, but without wind, the night air was clean and crisp and absent the bite that would come soon enough. Going to the end of the front walk, Neddy turned to look at the farmhouse. The porch light was reflected in the birdbath's water and a warm glow spilled from windows on the first floor, dimly illuminating the ground outside. He watched Bess at the kitchen table and the top of Con's head above the back of his easy chair in the parlor. Looking up, he could make out the faint face of a small boy looking down at him. They waved to each other.

Neddy thought of home and the warmth of family. Of Ma baking soda bread, while he and the girls huddled around a turf fire with hot tea on a winter's night. He thought of Bridget sitting on his lap, her head resting against his chest. How Packy would drive him to distraction mimicking his every movement until, frustrated, he'd yell at his younger brother to stop.

His letters home let everyone know about his latest adventures, but he was hard pressed to express in writing the emptiness in his heart. It was so Irish of him, he thought, and true to a rigid standard of masculinity passed down through generations of McKenna fathers to McKenna sons. McKenna mothers and daughters were different. Rose and Ma wrote less about the mechanics and milestones of daily farm life, instead opening their veins and spilling their yearnings for a son and brother so far way. By *their* letters, Neddy knew he was missed and deeply loved.

Watching the fireplace smoke rise and disappear, the crickets chirping in the dark and the stars like pin lights in the heavens, Neddy also knew Ontario, this farm, was home. Different and foreign, yet familiar and welcoming as his family in Ireland. Con more of a father than Edward. Timmy, a lost brother rediscovered.

"Neddy! Tommy!" Bess called. "Time for dinner."

They settled at the table with the pot of stew taking center stage. Bess stood, ladling steaming portions into bowls, handing them out with a thick slice of crusty bread resting on top. A far cry from the rancid slop given him on the ship.

As Con reached for the stew, he noticed an apple pie cooling on the stove and began thinking of dessert before the first spoonful of dinner reached his lips. Bess immediately noticed Con's look of longing.

"You'll finish your stew before you get pie," Bess chided him as she would a child.

"But, Ma ..." Con whined, winking at the boys, who joined in.

"Pleaaaase ..." Neddy begged smiling broadly.

"Me, too," Timmy chimed in.

"Eat!" Bess commanded. "Eat what's good for you ... *first.*"

After dinner ... and the pie ... they all retired to the parlor for a familiar ritual that would carry them through the winter. Neddy retrieved firewood to stoke the fireplace blaze started before dinner. Bess and Timmy pored over school books. Neddy read under the floor lamp to the right of the hearth or fiddled with the crystal set he had built with Con. Finally, Con either read farming periodicals, a new book or made ledger entries and completed other paperwork. Before going to bed, Con descended the cellar stairs and shoveled coal into the maw of the coal furnace to warm everyone until morning.

Outside, the wind kicked up, jostling the trees and rippling water in the birdbath. A lone owl hooted near the boys' bedroom and in the harvested oat field across the farm lane, a fox snagged a careless rabbit for an evening meal. And on the other side of sleep, Traveler arrived at the McKenna farm.

Traveler sat on the edge of the farmhouse porch, leaning against the railing, blowing smoke rings. Panama hat pushed back on his head, he studied Neddy who was at the barnyard gate outside the home place in Tyrone.

"Well, this scenario is interesting," he said, flicking a long ash off his cigar. "Two farms for the price of one. I guess this is your unconscious saying you're torn between two worlds. Something of a cliche, don't you think?"

"I don't know that word ... cleer shave? ... means," Neddy confessed, "but, aye. I'm forever t'inkin' about this farm an' th' home place."

"And the outside world, of course," Traveler pointed out. "So many places. So little time. So many ... um ... adventures to come. In fact, something's coming up tomorrow."

"An adventure?"

"Of sorts," Traveler said. "More a lesson in human nature, actually. And as that lesson unfolds, I want you to be thinking of Mary ..."

"I t'ink about her all th' time ..."

"... thinking of Mary and her nightmare at home. The nightmare of hate and how fast it can consume your life and those around you. Watch Con. You're about to learn from him that dealing effectively with hate doesn't always require violence. Violence comes easy. Too easy sometimes. Sometimes as easy as stabbing a German with a fork. Using your head, my boy, takes a great deal of effort and can be much more satisfying."

"I don't ...

"Oh, you will," Traveler interrupted. "Take care, Neddy. A disruption is coming, so gird your loins against millipedes and the acid they spray."

"What?"

30

Traditions

Timmy was awakened by Neddy mumbling something about "millipedes" but rolled over and slept until morning. By the time Timmy opened his eyes, Neddy was already dressed and at the kitchen table with Con, Bess and Tom.

"I've rung Mrs. Conway and let her know you'll be helping out," Con said. "She remembered you from church, so she at least knows what you look like."

"How long should I stay?" Neddy asked.

"You can go over when your chores are done this morning," Con said, "Stay until right before dark because you don't have much experience driving at night. Be home before that. Here's the key."

When Neddy finished his last chore, he walked to the shed and climbed behind the wheel of the Model T Ford. He inserted the key, pulled the emergency brake all the way back to put the transmission in neutral, pulled down the spark lever near the steering column and adjusted the gas lever. He then walked to the front of the car, grabbed the crank, pushed it in and gave it a quick jerk. He ran back to the driver's seat, then made a few more adjustments as the flivver sputtered awake. And just like that, he was past the farm house and through the farm's white gate.

"What did he mean by gird me loins against millipedes?" Neddy thought about his dream as he drove.

"Gird? What lesson? Sweet Jaysus, why was Traveler always wit' th' riddles an' clues? Why not just be straight wit' me?"

It was a 30-minute drive to the Conway farm where Neddy stopped outside the farmhouse, walked across the porch to the front door and knocked.

"I'm here," called a woman's voice from the side of the house, and a moment later, Kate emerged wearing a broad-brimmed straw hat, garden gloves and a flowered dress almost entirely obscured behind one of the reddest aprons Neddy had ever seen. She wore sensible shoes, white socks and an engaging smile. "You must be Eddie," she said.

"Neddy," he corrected her, recalling that Mary had made the same mistake when they met aboard the *Sea Empress*. "Neddy McKenna. I t'ink Con let ya know ..."

"Neddy, of course. Yes, yes, he did," she said, swiping an unruly lock of red hair from her forehead with the back of her hand. "Have you eaten?"

"Aye," said Neddy, "I have."

"Then let's talk about what needs to be done," Kate said motioning toward the front door. "Go ahead, go in."

As Neddy entered the parlor, the first thing he saw was Robert's right-leg cast up to his knee with his bare toes protruding from the plaster. His fall broke the tibia and he would be out of action for as much as four months.

"How do. I'd get up, but ..." Robert said shrugging as he motioned to his leg.

"No worries," said Neddy as Kate directed him to the kitchen where he removed his cap and took a seat at the table.

Their previous meeting at church months ago was fleeting and cordial as Kate was distracted by her young daughter tugging her toward the church door. At the time, Neddy focused more on the child's desire to leave, wishing he could join her. As for Kate, he vaguely recalled a stressed young mother. Nothing more. Nothing less.

But today, he was in an unfamiliar farmhouse, sitting across a kitchen table from an older woman in need. By older, he didn't mean *old*, but just older than him. Despite her advanced years, he thought, Kate still seemed sort of ... well ... young. Her face was pleasant, unlined and uncomplicated, set off by deep green eyes and wavy red hair like Bridget's. And she smelled like flowers.

"Your hair reminds me of me sister," he blurted out before even realizing he was speaking. He could feel the rush of heat to his cheeks.

"Um, thank you," Kate said self-consciously, brushing the same recalcitrant curl from her forehead she had harnessed outside moments before.

"I didn't mean ..." he fumbled.

"No, no," she assured. "It's okay. Lots of people seem fascinated by red hair."

Just then, Kate's sister-in-law, Vera, walked in with Kate's daughter, Jenny, who was wearing a light blue pinafore over her calico dress. It had a gathered waist and two large pockets into which she thrust her tiny hands. Like her mother, Jenny had red hair.

"Hello," said Vera, placing a hand on the child's shoulder. "This is Jenny."

"Jenny? 'Tis a grand name," said Neddy.

"Jenny," said Kate, "this is Mister Neddy. He's going to be helping us for a while."

Jenny didn't speak as she looked down at her dark blue Mary Janes.

"She's shy with strangers," Vera offered, "but gets over it pretty fast. Say goodbye to Mister Eddy."

"Neddy," said Kate. "Mister Neddy."

Kate had lied to Con about remembering Neddy. Truth was, she ever so vaguely remembered the brief encounter at church, and had heard mention of the McKeowns' two Irish lads, one which was called *"The Heathen"* in a few of Miss Millipedes rants outside church before Sunday mass. In any event, Kate didn't think Neddy was ill-mannered and evil at all. In fact, he was polite and downright respectful. He also seemed up to the task of farm work. While he wasn't what you would call tall, the dense shock of blackish-brown hair atop his head made him appear taller. He was, in her initial assessment, solid. Good strong shoulders and arms. A confident stride that spoke of a strong back as well. He seemed amiable, though maybe a bit reserved, not unusual for a first meeting.

"Probably most important is the roof," Kate said, referring to the one thing that launched her need for help ... and her brother-in-law through the air ... in the first place. Neddy had some experience working on the chicken coop roof and asked Kate where he could find a ladder. They walked to a shed by the side of the house where an extension ladder was on the ground, leaning against a wall.

"Lead th' way," Neddy said, hoisting the ladder on one shoulder as Kate started back toward the house. Once she explained the problem, Neddy went to the Ford and returned with a tool chest.

An hour and two pounds of nails later, he climbed down and returned the ladder to its original resting place. He knocked on the kitchen door and announced, "'Tis done," surprising Kate, who again called from the vegetable garden, "I'm here."

"'Tis done," Neddy repeated. "Anyt'ing more?"

"I'm afraid there's plenty to do," Kate said, "but you've done enough today. Can I get you something to drink? Water? Lemonade?"

"T'anks fer askin'," Neddy said, "but no. I best be goin', but I can be back, say, Friday?"

"Yes, that would be fine," Kate said, extending her hand for a shake, "and I'll have time to organize my thoughts better."

Neddy shook her hand and was impressed by the firmness of her grip, immediately deciding she was of good character. But unlike the death-grip challenge he had with Mick on the ship, he just as quickly released her hand that, while sturdy, had surprisingly soft skin. "Then, Friday 'tis."

By the time Neddy reached home, Con had already received a phone call from Kate. "Good job," Con said from the parlor as Neddy walked by.

"Sorry?" Neddy responded.

"Got a call from Miss Kate who said you did a fine job on her roof today," Con said, looking up from his desk.

"I'm t' go back Friday, if that suits," Neddy said.

"Suits me just fine," Con said.

And it suited Kate just fine as well. Neddy was an enthusiastic worker, never questioning a task, never unable to complete one. If he was unsure of a job at first, he would ask Robert or Con or Tom for advice or would find a book or periodical in Con's library that might shed light on how to approach it.

Even as October became November and working late in the day devolved into a challenge of endurance and a race against the thermometer, Neddy bundled himself in ever increasing layers of warm clothing, sometimes so entombed, he could barely bend his arms or legs. Still, he soldiered on. There would be times when Kate had to practically drag him from a job site despite his assurances that he needed just a few more minutes.

Between Neddy's duties at the Conway farm, there remained chores at the McKeowns', not the least of which was joining the crew to plant winter wheat.

By early December, Neddy's resolve was being tested daily with a winter already beyond his comprehension as low temperatures stalled in the bone-numbing teens at night and early morning.

As Con predicted, activity at the McKeown farm slowed to an easy hum of maintenance. Feeding stock. Checking systems at the broiler house. Mending fences. Repairing windmills. Making sure the barn was secure. For Con, it also was time to reconcile the ledgers for farming and mining operations with his accountants in December. Then, in late January or early February, he would take the seven-hour train ride north to his silver mines in Cobalt meeting with mine managers, talking to miners and reviewing mine operations, leaving the farm in Tom's capable hands.

Of course, with Neddy splitting time between the two farms, making up to three round trips through the bitter cold each week, maintaining the old Tin Lizzy also was a priority.

But he had learned enough about engine maintenance and repair working on the Hudson, the tractor and flatbed truck that fiddling with the simple guts of the old Ford was easy enough, although the bitter cold made everything that much more difficult.

With Christmas just weeks away, even the all-consuming cold couldn't prevent Con, Bess, Neddy and Timmy from kicking off the holiday season with a traditional Christmas tree pilgrimage on the Feast of the Immaculate Conception to an area of Balsam fir in the northwest corner of the farm. Mounting the flatbed, the four of them ventured into the cold, outfitted like arctic explorers with thick wool scarves wrapped about their necks and faces; leather mittens; fur hats with ear flaps; long underwear; multiple pairs of socks; layers of sweaters and heavy boots to the point that no one from the outside world could have identified them from a most-wanted poster.

As the truck crunched to a stop on the frozen dirt road, the boys leapt to the ground and ran into the trees. Bess, barely able to form words in the freezing air, yelled after them, "Make it fast boys before we freeze to death."

"Timmy, you pick it," Neddy instructed, as Timmy wasted no time.

Too tall. Too short. Too thin. "That one," Timmy pointed to what Neddy thought looked like a perfect specimen. Burrowing into the snow and crawling under the lowest boughs, Neddy positioned the cross-cut saw, taking the tree down in five minutes, then, with Con's help, dragging it to the truck and hoisting it on the flatbed.

Although the McKeowns had their own set of family

traditions, they were more than happy to include those brought by the boys from Ireland. For Neddy, it was potato-and-onion stuffing for the goose on Christmas day, and a Christmas candle that burned throughout the holidays. For Timmy it was making paper chains for the tree and bringing home a few good-luck strands of straw from the church's nativity scene after midnight mass on Christmas Eve.

For the McKeowns, McKennas and Lordans, Christmas Eve midnight mass was as much a generational constant as the holiday itself. As the day approached, Con and Bess grew concerned how Neddy's rejection of The Faith might affect the usually joyous celebration. But on Christmas Eve morning, as the McKeowns and the boys sat down to breakfast, Neddy was the first to broach the subject.

"What time are we fer mass t'night?" he said off-handedly to the table.

"What time are *we* leaving? Bess repeated cautiously. "Does that mean you're coming with us?"

"Oh, aye," Neddy said casually as if that were never in doubt.

Con and Bess looked at one another, then at Neddy. "You're coming to mass?" Con said as if trying to lock in the confirmation.

"Aye," Neddy said, lowering his spoon. "I know 'tis important fer ya, so 'tis important fer me as well. Bein' a special time an' all."

Bess reached across the table, placing her hand on Neddy's. "Thank you so much," she said. "You don't know how much this means to me ... and Con."

"I t'ink I do," said Neddy with a smile. "I do, indeed."

And, indeed, at 11:00 that night, they were in the Hudson on their way to St. Andrew's Roman Catholic Church in Winton, leaving time for greetings and conversations before mass. Like every Catholic town in Canada and Ireland, the Catholic church in Winton was the grandest, most elaborate, most prominent structure for miles around ... until the next Catholic town with its own church that was the grandest, most elaborate, most prominent structure for miles around.

From its narthex to its transept, St. Andrew's looked nothing like a country church. From concept to consecration, it was designed as a diminutive gothic cathedral. With pontifical gilding on everything from chalices to baptismal fonts to stations of the cross, the church was the domain of Father William Egan, now resplendent in gold brocade vestments for the holidays. Soaring above the nave's mosaic-tile floor, the ceiling was a golden blanket of power and glory held high toward heaven by intersecting limestone gothic arches spreading like angel wings above a marble, gold and silver altar where its tabernacle housed the holy host of the living Christ. But for a physical manifestation of Jesus, visitors need only look left of the altar for a larger-than-life statue of a blue-eyed son of God, dressed in a luxurious gold-trimmed toga instead of the more likely woolen tallith of a simple Jewish carpenter, whose birth was being celebrated tonight.

The altar was adorned with evergreen branches and holly boughs full of red berries. To the right of the altar was a galaxy of votive candles on the floor leading to a large creche strewn with straw on which there were nearly life-sized plaster cattle, sheep, wise men, Mary and Joseph huddled around an empty manger, awaiting the arrival of the plaster Savior, who materialized on Christmas Day. Even Con never understood why Mary was up and about with everyone else when logic dictated she would be in labor and in no condition to entertain guests.

While Catholic churches at this time didn't officially reserve pews for important people in the parish, unspoken tradition held that the first several rows were reserved for certain families. The O'Briens, the Fourniers, the McKees ... and the McKeowns among them. Bess, Con, Neddy and Timmy began taking their seats in a first-row pew when Timmy saw the creche and broke from the group. He quickly reached the nativity scene, leaning down and carefully pulling a piece of straw from the floor.

"What do you think you're doing, boy?!" huffed Miss Millipede in a loud whisper, rushing toward Timmy from a side aisle and demanding, "Put that back this instant!"

Seeing the apparently distraught woman racing toward Timmy, Neddy was almost immediately at his side, "Takin' a bit o'straw from th' church's nativity is what's done in Ireland," he said, trying to calm the woman.

"Well, we're not in Ireland, are we?" she sniped, a bit louder than she intended, drawing the attention of nearby worshipers.

"Aye," Neddy agreed, "but we are in th' house of God, are we not? And didn't Jaysus bless th' children?"

"Not children who steal," she said. "And what right does a heathen like you have to quote Our Lord?

"He's no heathen," came another approaching voice. "He's more Christian than many people here tonight whether or not he goes to church."

Neddy spun around to see Kate, just as Con and Bess arrived.

"Is there a problem, Miss Ryan?" Con demanded quietly but with enough frost that his displeasure was evident.

"Timmy took a piece of straw from th' nativity," Neddy explained. "'Tis what's done at Christmas in Ireland."

"I'm familiar with the tradition," said Con, "but Miss Ryan obviously is not."

"But, this is not …" she sputtered.

"Miss Ryan," Con persisted, his eyes narrowing, "do you think the baby Jesus will miss that piece of straw?"

Locked silently in Con's gaze, Miss Ryan slowly disengaged and returned to her pew without replying, as Kate and the McKeown party did the same. Before sitting down, Neddy glanced back at Kate, who nodded at him as she rejoined Robert, Vera and Jenny just in time for the mass to begin.

The service wasn't over soon enough for Neddy, who learned after years of practice that it was easier and less stressful to mask his boredom and discomfort than explaining it after the fact. As mass ended, Bess leaned over and said, "Wasn't that a beautiful service?"

"'Twas," Neddy agreed. "Didya like it, Timmy?"

"Aye, 'specially when th' priest set his wee bucket afire," he said, referring to the burning of incense in the thurible during the liturgy.

They all laughed, collecting their cold-weather gear from the pew for the drive home. As they approached the vestibule, Father Egan greeted worshipers heading out into the night where a gentle snow had begun to fall, muffling the sound of cars, trucks and carriages as they left the church grounds. Beside him at the door were several nuns and lay leaders including Millie Ryan.

"God be with you," Father Egan said, alternating between shaking hands and slashing an air crucifix with two fingers of his right hand. Noticing the McKeowns five families down the line, Miss Ryan excused herself and walked away by a side aisle.

Neddy was the first to notice. "And she's off escapin' on her broom," he whispered to no one in particular, but Bess picked up on the comment immediately.

"Neddy," she scolded, "it's Christmas. Be kind."

"Aye," he frowned. "Right ... Right. What I said 'bout th' broom was wrong of me. What I meant was she'll disappear in a puff o' black smoke." Bess gave him a playful punch to the arm, smiled and extended her right hand to the priest.

"God be with you, Bess, Con ... and Timmy," he said, ignoring Neddy.

"And God be with you, Father," said Neddy, brushing off the slight and shaking the priest's reluctant hand just as it was about to form another crucifix. Neddy recoiled slightly, quickly releasing the priest's hand that was as flaccid as a cow's udder. Father Egan nodded cooly and blessed the next family.

The ride back to the farm took a bit longer than the trip to church as Con carefully navigated the increasingly snow-covered road. By the time they arrived shortly before 1:30, the boys were sufficiently tired. Wishing all a good night and *Nollaig shona dhuit*, the Irish Happy Christmas greeting, they climbed the stairs and into bed.

Downstairs, Con and Bess went to a locked storage box in the kitchen and retrieved two red stockings (dropping an orange and other trinkets into each) as well as several wrapped packages, placing them under the tree before exchanging small gifts between them. For Bess it was a bottle of the latest perfume from France.

"The woman at Murphy-Gamble said it was all the rage in Paris," Con said, anxiously watching Bess unwrap the box.

"*Channel Number Five?*" Bess said, purposely mispronouncing the name, removing the stopper and placing it under her nose. She rolled her eyes. "Oh, my. It's wonderful." Putting a hand to Con's cheek, she added, "Now open mine."

Con unwrapped the small box with *Hamilton* on the lid. He looked at Bess before opening it, then lifted the lid to reveal a *Tonneau*, an impressive gold wristwatch with an art-deco-inspired rectangular case. "I was told it's all the rage in Toronto," she joked.

"Merry Christmas, sweetheart," Bess said to Con.

"Merry Christmas," Con replied, putting his arm around her waist, pulling her close and kissing her slowly on the mouth.

"Why don't we go upstairs," she whispered, taking him by the hand. "I have another present for you up there."

Christmas morning was clear and frigid and brilliant as the sun ignited last night's snowfall into a reflective mantle of white light flooding into the sunroom, where the McKeown Christmas tree stood. As it turned out, Timmy's tree selection was, indeed, a perfect shape, although significantly larger inside the house than it appeared in the middle of the field. Nonetheless, it was a celebration of paper chains and popcorn garlands, multi-colored glass balls and a lifetime of memories. Small framed photographs of loved ones past, mementos of childhood, small ceramic figurines, tinsel and blinking electric lights. And at the top of the tree, where tradition dictated a star, the McKeowns placed a silver star-shaped picture frame engraved with the name *Neil*, containing the photo of a toddler dressed in a child's sailor suit and cradling a toy boat in his arms.

Timmy stood at the bedroom window and took in the dazzling white landscape as far as the eye could see. Fields, trees, bushes, even the Hudson parked in front of the house, covered with the stuff.

"Neddy, come look," Timmy squealed as Neddy threw back the bed covers and joined him. At the window, Neddy recalled the winter of 1917 when a foot of snow fell on the farm, trapping the family inside the cottage for days and bringing most of Northern Ireland to a stop. Peering from the window, he also recalled snowball fights with his sisters and building a snow fort with Packy. Returning to the warmth of the cottage, the children found their mother piling fresh-baked scones on a platter and pouring cups of hot tea. They huddled by the peat fire laughing and telling stories for hours, warmed not just by the fireplace glow, but by their love for each other as the wind swirled snow into drifts, whipping through the barnyard and into the night.

"Nollaig shona dhuit, Packy," Neddy said, putting a hand gently on the boy's head.

"Packy?" the boy replied. "I'm Timmy."

"'Course y'are." Neddy corrected himself. "Nollaig shona dhuit, Timmy. Let's see what Santy brought."

With that, the boys shot down the stairs, past the parlor where a fire blazed, and into the sunroom. There, Con and Bess sat drinking their morning coffee next to a small table on which there was a painted-china hot chocolate pot with four fancy cups and a plate of brightly decorated Christmas cookies.

"Merry Christmas," Con and Bess said together as the boys responded in kind.

"Get a cup of hot chocolate," Bess urged, "and let's just see what Santa got for you two last night." Neddy poured the chocolate for both boys, who each grabbed a cookie and sat on the rug beneath the tree. Bess pointed to a red-and-white striped package. "Timmy, I think that's yours." His eyes widened in disbelief as he looked at Bess. "Go ahead. It's yours."

Timmy carefully removed the wrapping paper, undoing its folds as if the paper were the gift itself, finally revealing the orange label on a brown box that read: *Lionel Electric Trains. Standard of the World Since 1900.* He couldn't believe it. The magnificent toy trains he had admired in an Ottawa store window months ago were actually sitting under the tree. "Santy brought this fer me?"

"Sure did, Sport," said Con, "and later, we can set them up."

"Open that one," Con said to Neddy, pointing to a flat package wrapped in green.

When Neddy removed the ribbon and the paper, the bold silver lettering and matching silver globe of the earth on a red-clay-colored cover screamed: *Rand-McNally Dollar Atlas of the World.*

"Now you can locate all the Canadian provinces, all the U.S. states and every country in the world," Con smiled, "as you plan your future world travels, Mr. Gulliver." But Neddy already was immersed in the book, leafing through the color plates, skimming text and only peripherally hearing Con.

"T'ank ya so much an' God bless us, everyone," he added, having just read Dickens' *A Christmas Carol* the week before. They all laughed, including Timmy, although he wasn't sure why.

Neddy left the sunroom and returned a few moments later, carrying two wrapped packages bought with money he had saved from his 18 dollar monthly indenture stipend. He handed one to Bess, the other to Con. Attached to the packages were holly twigs with red berries and small cards with a child's crayon-and-pencil inscriptions. The larger of the two was addressed to *Miss Bess.*

Happy Christmas from Timmy and Neddy, the card read as she unwrapped the box that contained a new electric toaster called a flipper for the way it toasted bread. "Oh, this is just what I wanted," Bess gushed. "How did you know?"

"And now, you, Mr. Con," Timmy said.

Con opened the card, read it and smiled as he unwrapped the Gillette safety razor shaving kit in the black velvet box complete with three extra blades.

"You won't be cuttin' yerself all th' time," said Neddy.

"First I have to learn how to use it," said Con, a lifelong straight razor enthusiast. "Maybe you got me this just in the *nick* of time." Con winked but no one got the joke.

"There are two more gifts for you boys," Bess said. "Over there by the side table."

Neddy got up and retrieved the parcels, handing Timmy the smaller one earmarked for him. In it were several heavy cotton shirts, two sweaters, a pair of corduroy trousers as well as four pairs of long underwear. "You'll be needing these for the next few months," Bess explained.

Neddy opened his to find a neatly folded grey tweed three-piece suit. There also was a white dress shirt with three round-edge detachable club collars and a bow tie. At the bottom of the parcel was a pair of cap-toed brown oxford shoes and two pairs of socks.

"At some point, you'll want to look your best all the time for the ladies," Con said, as Bess shot him a look of disapproval, "so I just wanted to prepare you for that."

Neddy appreciated the effort, but felt mildly insulted, certain he always looked fine, not yet understanding the difference between *farm* fine and *everywhere else* fine. That aside, he loved the suit, long ago having outgrown the outfit he wore to Canada. In fact, before discarding that jacket, he cut off the small swatch of repaired collar fabric to help him remember Mary.

Neddy never had a Christmas like this before, at least as far as gifts were concerned. And while he missed his family, Neddy couldn't deny the McKeowns had filled this holiday with so much warmth – and, yes, even love – it helped in some measure to mitigate his homesickness.

Timmy's memories of Christmases past were less distinct. Although the loss of his father and his absence at yuletide remained in sharp focus, Timmy found comfort and safety with the McKeowns. As he and Con sat on the sunroom floor that afternoon, assembling the train set, Neddy helped Bess with the Christmas goose, preparing the potato stuffing using his mother's recipe for champ as its foundation. Later still, as the goose roasted, Neddy read the Rand-McNally atlas in the parlor, while Bess cracked open *Mansfield Park* from the eight-volume Jane Austen set of books Con "suddenly remembered" buying her for Christmas.

It was a memorable day. A memorable Christmas that everyone would recall in years to come as they looked back on one of the last times they all were happily, contentedly, warmly ... together.

Two days later, after finishing his chores in mid-afternoon, Neddy got in the Ford and started off for the Conway farm. For December, the temperature was a very moderate 35 degrees as the sun continued to melt the Christmas Eve snow from the roads, leaving them wet and clear.

Driving down the Conway farm lane, Neddy noticed a strange car parked outside the house and pulled in behind it. Knocking on the front door, he glanced in the porch window to see Millie Ryan seated in the parlor. As Kate opened the door, Neddy said, "If you've company I can call back."

"No, no," came Miss Ryan's shrill voice, "I was just leaving." Standing and walking to the door, she brushed past Neddy without looking at him, then called over her shoulder, "Remember, dear, what I said."

Kate slowly shook her head as her guest drove off. "Please come in."

Stepping into the parlor and noticing Robert wasn't in

his usual roost, Neddy inquired, "Where's your brother?"

"Toronto with Vera," she replied. "Took the train Christmas afternoon to visit their son Nathan and his family."

"And Jenny?"

"Taking a nap," Kate said, sitting in the over-stuffed parlor chair and exhaling loudly. "That woman ..."

"Miss Millicent?"

"Miss Millipede is more like it."

Neddy froze the instant he heard the name Traveler had mentioned in his dream. "Miss ... um ... Millipede?"

Kate laughed. "That's what people call her behind her back. What a busybody."

"About that," Neddy began. "T'anks fer what ya said at mass th' other night."

"What? Oh, that," she said with a dismissive wave of her hand. "She had no right to talk to you, Timmy or anyone else that way."

"Din't bother me none," Neddy said, "'cause I am a bit of a heathen fer not goin' to mass."

"Not going to church doesn't make someone a heathen," she said. "To me, a heathen is someone who goes to church and thinks they're better than those who don't."

"Well, t'anks anyway," he said. "I just dropped by to see if there's somet'ing ya need done."

"I do," she said, "but it's too late in the day to start now. It's cold outside, would you like tea or coffee?"

"Nay, don't go to any trouble."

"No trouble at all," she said.

"Tea would be grand," he said, taking off his cap and sliding off his overcoat, which he draped over the chair back.

As Kate rose and went to the kitchen, afternoon sunlight filled the doorway, backlighting her so that Neddy could see every gentle curve of her silhouette through the pink cotton dress she wore. He was embarrassed and looked away, but couldn't do so when she returned with two cups of tea and a plate of cookies. As she leaned over to place the small tray on a living room table, Neddy caught a glimpse of her cleavage and, in the moment, nearly knocked over his cup.

"Whoa," she laughed. "That was close."

"Aye," said Neddy, fumbling to right the cup, hoping he hadn't been caught gawking in the general area of mortal sin. "I'm a bit of a full haymes at times."

"Full what?"

"A haymes ... a mess," he explained, embarrassed. After an awkward moment, he asked. "How was yer Christmas?"

"For Jenny, it was fine," Kate smiled. "Children, love Christmas. They're so innocent."

"And you?"

"It's a rough time of year," she said, lowering her eyes. "Lots of memories."

"I'm sorry," Neddy said, "I din't mean to ..."

"No, no, it's all right," she said. "I'm fine."

They began sipping the tea in silence, but soon were discussing projects large and small. Some needed immediate attention while others could wait until warmer weather or the spring. The sun was starting to set when Jenny walked into the room, rubbing her eyes from her nap.

"There's me Jenny girl," Neddy said, opening his arms toward the child, who walked slowly to him and leaned into his chest. He picked her up and parked her on his lap. "How're ya, lass?"

"Fine," she yawned.

He handed a cookie to Jenny and said, "Hope 'tis ok?" Kate nodded. "Well, if there's nothin' more, I'm away 'til t'morrow. About one o'clock?"

"Yes," said Kate, picking up Jenny and walking Neddy to the door.

Approaching the Ford, Neddy looked down the farm lane and saw the same car that had been parked in front of the house when he arrived. He watched for a moment until the car suddenly pulled away.

31

Damage

With the holidays fading, January invaded Ontario in like a Nordic marauder, slamming the region with temperatures so brutal, Neddy was certain he wouldn't survive the month, let alone until spring. A stretch of six days leading up to the Epiphany barely reached 10 degrees with each night sliding well below zero. For two of those days, the power went out and the furnace struggled to warm the house, forcing everyone in the McKeown household to take up round-the-clock residence near the fireplace. Several heavy blankets were nailed to the opening between the parlor and unheated sunroom, and the parlor pocket doors were kept closed at all times to prevent fireplace heat from escaping the room while storm windows took up the slack. Meals were cooked in the fireplace whenever possible and winter clothing was worn at all times inside the house.

When the weather finally broke and power returned, Con, Neddy and Tom drove the property to assess damage. In all, they lost three head of cattle ... two Holsteins and an Angus steer. Although most chickens were spared, about 20 didn't survive.

The Christmas snow was gone by now and the roads were clear enough for Neddy to drive to the Conway farm. "Use the Hudson," Con told him. "Too cold for the Ford."

The enclosed Hudson did, indeed, provide a buffer against winter's raw blasts, but with car heaters still 10 years in the future, heavy clothing was essential for any trip by auto. When Neddy pulled up in front of the Conway farmhouse, he was met by Kate's brother Robert.

"I think it best, if you don't come around for a while," Robert said, leaning against a porch post, his leg stiffly poised at an angle to the right. "Kate's feeling poorly and I'm starting to get around a bit more so ..."

"Is Kate about?" Neddy asked as he started up the path to the porch.

"No," said Robert, holding up his hand as if to stop Neddy. "Not right now. Sorry." With that, he turned and went inside.

Neddy stared at the house for a few minutes before getting back in the Hudson and driving away.

Bess, Con and Tom were at the kitchen table when Neddy came home. "What's wrong?" Bess asked, seeing Neddy's bewildered expression.

"Not sure," Neddy said.

"How's Miss Kate?" Bess asked.

"Dunno. Her brother blocked me from seein' her."

"What do you mean blocked?" Con leaned forward in his chair.

"Robert stood on the porch an' wouldn't let me pass, sayin' Kate was feelin' poorly."

"That's strange," Bess commented. "Maybe I should call her to see if she needs anything." Bess went to the phone and dialed Kate's number, hanging up and waiting for her to answer on the party line. A few moments later, she picked up to see if Kate was on the line. She wasn't. Several more tries netted the same result. "I may have to go over tomorrow after church."

The next morning, Bess was at Kate's house when she returned from Sunday mass, but again, it was Robert who answered the door.

"I'm here to see Kate," Bess began. "I didn't see her at mass today; is she sick?"

"No, she's not sick, but she's not seeing anyone today. Thank you for asking," Robert replied, then abruptly closed the door.

Returning home, Bess again tried for most of Sunday and Monday to reach Kate by phone but no one answered.

It wasn't until shortly after noon on Tuesday that the situation became clear when Tom approached Bess near the chicken coop. "I think I may have an answer to what's happening with Kate Conway," Tom said, letting a bag of fertilizer slide from his shoulder to the ground. "I was at the feed store in Winton this morning and overheard Bill Slater and Harry Whiticker talkin' when I hear Kate's name."

"And ...?"

"And ... well ...," Tom hesitated.

"And, well, *what*!?" Bess bristled.

"They were sayin' terrible things about her ... and Neddy. That's when I went up to 'em and said where the hell did they hear such a thing? They shut up real quick and wouldn't say nothin' more, but I was toe to toe with 'em, not backin' down or nothin'. That's when they said their wives heard it from the hat lady."

"The hat lady? You mean Millie Ryan?"

"Yep, Miss Millipede."

"Tell me what they said, Tom,"

"I don't think you should hear ..."

"Damn it, Tom, *tell me*," she almost growled like a mother bear protecting her cub.

"They said she and Neddy are havin' relations. And they're havin' 'em with her daughter in the house and all. That they're carryin' on and are goin' to hell."

Bess was livid. She fumed all the way down the farm lane to the barn where Neddy was repairing a stall. "Is it true?" she said to Neddy, startling him. "Is it *true*?"

"Is what true?" Neddy shot up from a crouch.

"Are you and Kate Conway involved? Are you and Kate ..."

"*What?*" Neddy said, setting down the hammer and nails, suddenly convinced he, indeed, had been caught looking down Kate's dress and seeing her cíocha.

Bess laid out in detail what Tom had told her and, in turn, Neddy ... horrified on the one hand and relieved on the other ... told her about his last visit to the Conway farm and how Millie Ryan was there when he arrived. He said she was sitting in her car at the end of the farm lane when he left about an hour later and "left in a hurry when she seen me."

"So, you and Kate didn't …"

"Jaysus, Mary and Joseph … *NO!!* There's not a t'ing true about it," he almost pleaded.

"I believe you," Bess said, relieved herself.

Con had gone to Ottawa on business that day, but when he came in shortly before dinner, Bess laid out the sordid tale Tom had shared with her. Early that evening, Con – one of St. Andrew's major benefactors – placed a phone call to Father Egan, then spent the better part of an hour at his desk in the parlor. The next morning he was in the Hudson and headed to *Miss Millicent's Chapeau Emporium* in Winton.

Con McKeown was known throughout the Ottawa region as a kind and fair businessman farmer. Someone who treated everyone with respect and a person willing to help neighbors in need. Ask anyone and they would tell you he was a square dealer, a straight talker, a person to respect and a faithful churchgoer. Most of all, Con McKeown was known as an extremely private man who fiercely protected those he loved.

Today, Millie Ryan would learn just how fierce he could be.

A group of prominent women from the town and parish had assembled in Miss Millicent's shop to map out a social gala for the Winton centennial in the spring. Tea in delicate China cups and dainty finger sandwiches had no sooner been served when the shop door opened and a blast of winter sent doilies and hat feathers swirling about the room. Mary Whiticker, attempting to keep her hat from joining the maelstrom, dropped a cucumber sandwich on the floor.

Con removed his hat and stopped next to Mrs. Whiticker. He leaned down, picked up the sandwich and replaced it on the small plate she was holding.

"Good afternoon, ladies. Is Miss Ryan about for a word?"

Before they could answer, she emerged from the back room with a plate of petit fours. Seeing Con, Miss Ryan turned white as the bread of her sandwiches and nearly dropped the plate. "Why ... why ... Mr. McKeown," she cooed, "what a pleasure ..."

"Don't flatter yourself," he said coldly. "This is not a social visit."

The mood in the room became as cold as the winter outside. The group of women froze, heads slowly pivoting to see Miss Millicent's reaction. But Nora Slater, sensing a possible eruption of some significance, turned in her seat to leave.

"No, no, ladies," Con said with firm politeness, "please be seated. This won't take long at all." Mrs. Slater eased back into her chair.

"You call yourself a good Christian, don't you?" Con began, taking a step toward Millie, who retreated a step in response.

"Everyone knows I am," Miss Millicent said, throwing back her shoulders defiantly.

"Then bearing false witness against your neighbor should ring a bell," he said. "Or how about Proverbs 10:18. He that hideth hatred with lying lips, and he that uttereth a slander, is a fool."

"I don't ..." Millicent sputtered.

"You don't what? You know damned well why I'm here ..."

"Mr. McKeown, there's no need for ..."

"Vulgarity?" Con completed her sentence. "The only vulgarity here is you. What in God's name possessed you to be so vile to innocent people? What possessed you to attack a poor widow, whose husband died in the war? What possessed you to attack a poor Irish farm boy who came to this country alone looking for nothing more than a new life? What possessed you to smear them with a vicious lie?" Miss Ryan was silent.

Diverting his attention momentarily, Con focused on the small circle of women. "And you, Mrs. Whiticker and Mrs. Slater, you're no better than she is by repeating the lie without taking time to learn the facts. To learn that Neddy McKenna has been going to Kate Conway's farm two to three times a week for months to lend a hand while Kate's brother mends a broken leg. Did you know I was the one who sent him?

"Well it all ends now, ladies," Con said, taking another step, as Millie put down the plate. "All of you will apologize. You will apologize in person to Kate Conway and Neddy McKenna before the end of this week. You will apologize to every person you spoke to about this despicable incident and you will apologize in writing in the church bulletin this coming Sunday."

As expected, there were expressions of shock and indignation all around. Seeing the outrage, Con continued. "If you don't apologize, several things will happen. Mrs. Whiticker and Mrs. Slater, please inform your husbands that my fields will be unavailable to them to lease this spring. No planting then. No harvests come fall.

"As for you, Miss Ryan, you not only will be removed as chairwoman of St. Andrew's Lay Council, but you will be removed from the council altogether."

"You can't do that," she huffed.

"But Father Egan can and he's assured me he will," Con said, pulling a folded sheet of paper from his pocket before starting to read aloud. "Here's the letter all of you will sign:

"*Dear members of St. Andrew's Parish:*

"*It is with deep regret that we admit being party to untruths about two innocent people who live in our parish. Without a basis in fact, we spread a lie about a young man and young woman having illicit relations, when no such relationship actually existed.*

"*The young man in question was simply helping a widow during her time of need and should be praised for his charitable nature.*

"*We are ashamed of our actions and ask The Lord, Father Egan and all parishioners of St. Andrew's to forgive us as we vow to never commit such sins again.*"

The room was quiet as a confessional, except for the sound of wind gusting outside.

"I'll leave this with you and a copy with Father Egan who anticipates your signatures," he said to the group. "Please make the right decision."

With that, Con left the women in disarray, drove to the St. Andrew's rectory, then headed home.

By Friday, Millie Ryan continued to stew about Con's visit and brash ultimatum, convinced he was bluffing. Convinced, that is, until the phone in her shop rang midmorning.

"Miss Millicent's Chapeau Emporium," she announced.
"How can we make you more beautiful?"

"Miss Ryan," the voice on the other end of the line said,
"This is Father Egan."

"Why, yes, Father," she gushed, "How may I help you?"

"We are going to print this week's church bulletin
this afternoon," he explained, "and we haven't received your
signature on the letter of contrition."

"Excuse me?"

"The letter of contrition given to you by Mr. McKeown,"
the priest repeated. "You're to sign it so we can include it
in this week's bulletin. Mrs. Whiticker and Mrs. Slater have
signed. We've been waiting for you."

"I hadn't planned on signing such a foolish document,"
she told him confidently.

"That wouldn't be prudent," Father Egan cautioned,
"for someone who wishes to remain on this parish's lay
council."

"But I'm the chairwoman," she insisted.

"I'm afraid that's no longer the case, Miss Ryan," the
priest said. "Mrs. O'Brien has been given that post. Signing
the letter, as any good Catholic would under the current
circumstances, will only ensure your continued membership
on the council."

Without a word, Miss Millicent removed the receiver
from her ear and stared incredulously at it as if trying to see
the expression on the priest's face through the telephone
wires.

"Miss Ryan," the priest inquired, "are you still there?

Miss Ryan?"

"I'll leave right now for the rectory to sign the letter," she whispered, hanging up the phone, throwing it across the room and scattering several mannequin heads displaying the latest fashions from Montreal.

By the end of Saturday, Millie Ryan and her two cohorts had made trips to the McKeown and Conway farms to apologize in person to Neddy and Kate. They also made special trips of contrition to each household where the lie was spread. Miss Millicent, particularly, nearly choked on every word.

Sunday morning, the McKeowns and Timmy arrived early as usual for the nine o'clock mass and quickly became aware of an unusual buzz among the parishioners. Many were engaged in animated discussions in small groups, others in pairs while some stood by themselves ... all reading the church bulletin. Even a few nuns were huddled like conspirators around the bulletin whispering and shaking their heads. Ellen McCorkle approached Bess as she was about to enter the nave.

"I never believed a word of it," confided Mrs. McCorkle, one of the parish's most notorious wags. "Not a word. A terrible thing. They should be ashamed."

"I'm certain they are," Bess nodded, just as sure that Mrs. McCorkle also spread the lie, but didn't get caught. Looking away dismissively, Bess searched for signs of Kate Conway, Robert or Vera, but found none. As Bess, Con and Timmy proceeded to their pew, face after face turned toward them and nodded or smiled or in some other way acknowledged their presence. Yet, no Kate.

Then it occurred to Bess someone else was missing.

"Have you seen Millie Ryan?" she asked Con.

"Haven't really been looking for her."

"She's not here," Bess said.

"I thought the church air smelled fresher," Con smiled, getting an elbow to the ribs from Bess. It was then that Con realized he hadn't seen Mary Whiticker or Nora Slater either, although their husbands were among the congregants. The reason became clear when mass ended and the McKeowns were putting Timmy in the Hudson's back seat.

"Con, have you a minute?" came Bill Slater's voice over Con's right shoulder. Turning around, he saw Bill and Harry Whiticker near the Hudson's rear bumper.

"What can I do for you gentlemen?" Con asked as Bess opened the front passenger door and got in.

"We're sorry about what happened," Harry said.

"Yes, very sorry about our wives and their wagging tongues," added Bill.

Con looked at them both for a long moment before saying, "We first heard about this vicious lie, not from your wives, but from what Tom Wilson overheard you saying in the feed store. In my mind, you're just as guilty."

The men looked embarrassed like two boys caught kicking a dog. Finally, Bill spoke. "But you said if our wives signed ..."

"I know what I said," Con cut him off, "and I'm a man of my word ..."

"That you are," said Bill.

"I agree," said Harry.

"I'm a man of my word," he began again, "so when your wives signed the letter, they fulfilled their part of the bargain, so I'll fulfill mine. When you're ready to sign a lease, come by the farm."

"Thank you," said Bill.

"Thanks, Con," said Harry extending his right hand.

"Con," Bess called from inside the car, "can we start home? We're freezing."

Con considered Harry's hand, then looked at both of them before sliding behind the wheel, leaving the hand hanging in the wind.

On the way home, the McKeowns drove to the Conway farm. Bess walked to the farmhouse door and knocked. Again, it was Robert who came out. Bess handed him the church bulletin and said, "Give this to Kate. I hope it helps." She walked back to the car and they drove away.

Robert looked at the bulletin's front page and beneath a message from Father Egan, he saw a letter addressed to St. Andrew's parishioners and signed by Millicent Ryan, Mary Whiticker and Nora Slater. After reading it, he shared the bulletin with Vera and they hurried to the kitchen where Kate was making breakfast for Jenny.

"Bess McKeown wanted you to have this," he said. "You need to read it."

Kate began reading and slowly sat down at the kitchen table. As she read, her eyes filled with tears.

"Why are you crying, Mommy?" asked Jenny, looking to the adults for answers.

"Mommy just got good news," Vera answered, gently guiding Jenny to a kitchen chair and serving her the fried eggs and toast Kate had been preparing.

"That's right, honey," Kate added. "People cry when they're happy, too."

But Kate's tears were not so easily explained. While they certainly were tears of relief, they also were tears of anger and confusion. As Jenny finished her breakfast, Vera ushered her into the parlor, leaving Kate and Robert alone.

"I don't understand what I've done to these women for them to hate me so much," she said, dabbing her eyes with a dish towel. "To hate Neddy so much. How can people be so cruel?"

"For some people, cruelty is as easy as breathing," Robert offered. "But there are so many more good people in the world like Bess, Con, Neddy ... and you. Remember that."

It wasn't until a friend's telephone call early Monday morning that Kate learned of Con's intervention with Millie Ryan last week, resulting in the church bulletin's letter. As soon as she hung up, she quickly dressed and was on her way to the McKeown farm.

"Why, Kate, what a pleasant surprise," said Bess, answering the knock on her front door. "Come in. Come in."

Kate removed her overcoat and hat, sitting down on the parlor's settee.

"I don't know where to begin, except to tell you and Mr. McKeown how incredibly grateful I am to you both for what you did for ..." Kate said, choking back tears.

"It was the right thing to do when people go out of their way to hurt others," said Bess, moving beside Kate and wrapping an arm around her shoulders. "If we don't help each other, who will?"

"You have been so kind already," Kate said, "what with the foreclosure and sending Neddy when Robert broke his leg. I don't know how I ever can repay you."

"Repay us? Posh!" Bess sat back, gently grabbing Kate's shoulders and looking her square in the face. "You'll repay us by continuing to raise that beautiful little girl and by just being who you are."

Bess hugged her.

"I can't thank you enough," said Kate.

"You already have."

"Is Neddy somewhere about?" Kate asked.

"I think he's out by the chicken coop," said Bess. "Do you want him for something?"

"Just to talk," Kate said.

Neddy was coming out of the coop with a shovel and broom when he saw Kate approaching from the house. They hadn't seen each other since before the gossip started snaking its way through the area, and he was happy to see her.

"Kate," he said approaching her. "I was to call on ya about startin' work again ..."

"About that," Kate began. "Um ... Robert's leg has been healing much quicker than we thought and ... he's ... getting around much better."

"Gladta hear it," Neddy smiled.

"So ... he has started doing a few more jobs ... others can wait until spring."

"Aye ..." Neddy said, not quite sure where Kate was heading.

"So ... there's no need to take you away from your work here ..." she said, avoiding Neddy's now quizzical look.

"'Tis no bother a'tall," Neddy countered.

"I think you should ... concentrate your efforts ... here ..."

"But I don't mind ...," Neddy said cautiously, not sure what might come next.

"Neddy, I don't need your help anymore," Kate said firmly, then gently pleading, "Please."

By the pained look on Kate's face, he began to grasp what was happening ... and why. "Aye ... right," he said clearing his throat, knowing that pressing the issue was at an end. Then silence. Neddy looking at Kate. Kate looking anywhere but at Neddy.

He pulled up his collar against the sleet that had begun to fall. Kate adjusted her scarf. Wrapping her arms in a self-embrace, she said, "But if I do need help, you'll be the first one I'll call."

"Grand," Neddy replied, forcing a smile. "So ..."

"I must be getting home before the weather gets worse," she said.

"Aye," Neddy agreed. "It can come on quick."

Nothing more was said and Neddy could do nothing but watch Kate walk to the house, where she exchanged pleasantries with Bess before leaving for home.

32

The Fire

Bystanders said the blaze started in a store room and spread quickly throughout the shop, fed by an array of fragile fabrics and fancy hats. It raged so completely that almost nothing in *Miss Millicent's Chapeau Emporium* was salvageable.

Millie Ryan arrived in her nightgown and overcoat in time to see windows shatter and the roof collapse with a growl, exploding in a font of sparks that shot into the winter night. Firefighters from the Winton Volunteer Fire Co. arrived in the company's lone ladder truck when the fire already was a lost cause, and fought not only the flames, but the truck's fire hose, which constantly froze solid in the subzero temperatures.

Standing across the street, Neddy watched it all.

"Make you feel better?" asked Traveler, sidling up beside him.

Neddy smiled broadly, never breaking his contented gaze, "Aye. Much better."

"OK, we got that out of your system," said Traveler, instantly relocating Neddy's dream from the charred hat shop to the home place in Tyrone.

The abrupt shift in scenery, however, left Neddy rattled, which said something, given the often surreal dreamscapes concocted by his subconscious.

"Did that really happen?" Neddy asked.

Standing in the farm lane, Traveler sniffed his flowered shirt. "Whew!" he scowled, it'll take months to get the smell of smoke out of this silk." Then turning to Neddy, "Oh. Did it happen? The fire?"

"Aye, the fire."

Smiling, Traveler responded, "Um ... no."

"But the smoke on your shirt?!"

"Cigar smoke," he answered calmly. "Nasty stuff. Worse than a shop fire."

After a brief silence, Neddy began looking about curiously. As much as he still missed home, the once-crisp outlines of the cottage and barnyard, the trees behind the barn, even the barn itself seemed slightly blurred, less distinct than he remembered from previous dreams. By the look on Neddy's face, Traveler recognized the symptoms.

"Your memories are starting to fade," He said, pulling a fresh cigar from his trouser pocket. "It happens when you start making new, fresher memories. It happens with places, with experiences, even with people. That's why it's important to stay in touch with your past to soften the blow. Get new pictures in letters ..." Traveler knew guilt when he saw it. "Haven't written home in a while, huh?"

"I've been ..."

"Busy. Oh, I get it. Things to do, places to go, people to meet," Traveler said as Neddy avoided looking at him. "I've told you before, write your Ma. Write Rose."

"I know," Neddy mumbled.

"So, *do it.* Write those you care about, and even people here," Traveler said, hoisting himself on the barnyard wall and crossing his legs. "After all, you'll be leaving before you know it."

Neddy finally looked up, surprised. "Really?"

"Really?" Traveler said. "That shocks you?"

"Well ... no," Neddy conceded. "I guess not. I've but two years on me indenture ..."

"Oh, I'm talking well before that," Traveler said. "You'll be faced with a tough choice very soon and you'll have to decide which way your life will go. Some might say, it's a pivotal moment. I'd call it that. It's the here and now versus the future. The easy road or the road to adventure. Sounds simple, but it ain't. Make sure you use your head ... and not just your heart. Personally, adventure sounds good to me."

33

Course Correction

Kate would never call Neddy again as the winter grew darker and colder, and the McKeown household burrowed deeper into their stores of preserves, smoked meats, fresh chicken, and evenings around the fire immersed in books and school work.

Con was preparing for his usual trek to Cobalt in early February, when an afternoon phone call came from Paul Moretti, chief of the assay office at Triple C Mines, named by Con's father for Cornelius, Corny and Con McKeown when he incorporated the venture.

"I really hate to drop this on you at the last minute," said Paul, as Con rolled his eyes at Bess, prompting her to mouth the word, "What?" Con shrugged as Paul explained, "My assistant just quit without notice and I'm swamped with work. I guess the work is good news, but if we can't get it done ..."

"I understand," Con said. "So what do you need from me?"

"I've started looking around," Paul said, "but there's pretty slim pickins here. Can you look for at least a temporary replacement until I can get someone permanent up here? Ottawa should have more prospects, don't you think?"

"How long will you need a temporary assistant?"

"Oh, I don't know," Paul said. "A month. Maybe a bit more. Just someone to help us get over the first quarter rush. In the meantime, I'll look for a permanent replacement with ads in the Toronto and Montreal newspapers as well as *Canadian Mining Journal.*

"Let me see what I can find," he said, hanging up the phone.

Halfway through the call, Con already had his candidate.

"Bess," Con said, getting up from his desk, "can I see you in the kitchen?"

Closing the door behind them, Con turned to Bess and said, "The call was from Paul at Triple C."

"I gathered that," Bess said. "What did he want?"

"His assistant quit and left him high and dry. He wanted to know if I could find him temporary help until he could locate a replacement."

"And?"

"Neddy," Con said. "What would you think about giving Neddy a chance?"

"How long would he be gone?" Bess asked.

"Paul says maybe a month. Six weeks, tops."

Bess thought for a few seconds. "Do you think he could handle it?"

"To be honest, I don't have a doubt," Con shot back. "He's one of the hardest workers I've ever seen and he's a quick learner. Look how he tackled the broiler house and rebuilding that windmill in the fall."

"That's true," Bess said, "but doesn't Paul need experienced office help?"

"A job's a job," Con said, "and what Neddy doesn't know off the top of his head, he researches it or asks questions until he finds the answer. I'm sure he'd do the same in the Cobalt office."

"Why not ask him?" Bess suggested. "Things are slow here, so I'm fine with it."

Returning to the parlor, the McKeowns approached Neddy who was on the floor reading *The Invisible Man* by H.G. Wells under the lamp by the fireplace.

"Neddy?" said Con. Neddy closed the book and sat up. "I have what I think could be a great opportunity for you. How would you like to work for about a month at our assay office in Cobalt?"

"What office?" asked Neddy.

"The assay office," explained Con. "They're in charge of examining the ore coming out of the mines up in Cobalt to determine the quality and quantity of silver it contains. You would help our chief assayer, Paul Moretti, until he can find a replacement for his assistant who quit."

Neddy seemed overwhelmed at first, "But don't you need me here?" he asked.

"We probably will come the middle of March," said Bess, "but right now, we're hunkered down for the winter and there's not much going on. You may as well try something new. Consider it a new adventure."

Weighing the offer momentarily, Neddy said, "If you need help more there than here, aye."

"Not to put too much pressure on you," Con smiled. "We leave tomorrow morning."

The materials Con needed for his trip were almost

complete and Bess helped assemble clothing he'd need in and out of the mines. As for Neddy, his Christmas suit would come in handy as would all of his winter clothes, but he needed a proper suitcase. The cardboard carry-on from his transatlantic journey had been relegated to the back of the boys' bedroom closet. It was falling apart and its precious contents had been transferred by Neddy months ago to the top drawer of his bedroom dresser, where they would stay ... save for the Rand-McNally atlas ... during his venture north.

Bess emerged from the attic with a large, dust-covered leather suitcase bearing the monogram *cMcKd II* for Cornelius Donald McKeown II, Con's father, Corny. "This should do for your trip to Cobalt," she said, running a dust cloth over its surface before hoisting it on Neddy's bed.

Neddy opened it, flipping back the partition and inspecting the pockets. He had never seen such a wonderful valise. In fact, he had never seen the inside of any valise not made of cardboard before now.

Timmy stood wide-eyed as Neddy and Bess began arranging clothing this way and that inside the bag. "Big enough to pack you, too," Neddy said, grabbing the boy and swinging him into the lid, then tickling him. His jolly little laugh tickled Neddy in return, reminding him of Bridget's giggle. "Ya do know I'll be back," Neddy assured Timmy.

"Aye," said the boy, rolling out of the lid and onto the bed. "Miss Bess says you'll be back in two shakes of a lamb's tail."

"An' so I will," Neddy responded.

After packing, Neddy and Timmy went downstairs for dinner, where Con gave Neddy a rundown of what he could expect when they left for the 8 a.m. train in Winton the next morning and arrived in Cobalt tomorrow afternoon.

They all retired to the parlor for a shortened evening of reading and a few games of rummy, which Timmy had grasped so easily and deftly that he won at least half the hands before they turned in shortly after eight.

The Hudson was loaded and ready to go at seven thirty the next morning, and the four of them drove to Winton Station, where there were hugs and kisses and goodbyes as the locomotive hissed and wheezed trackside. As the train pulled out of the station, Bess and Timmy waved goodbye on the platform, watched the train disappear in the distance and walked back to the Hudson for the drive home.

As for Neddy, he settled into heaven or at least the closest thing he had ever seen this side of it. The first-class compartment Con reserved for the seven-hour trip was spacious enough for four people and rich enough, he thought, for King George himself. With its plush maroon mohair seats, foot rests, headrests and huge windows, Neddy couldn't help comparing this magic carpet to what certainly must have been a cattle car that carried him from Montreal to Ottawa. Best of all, without Mother FE and the nuns, the company was far superior and the conversation much more enjoyable.

Neddy was fascinated by the McKennas' family history, which Con laid out in great detail. How his grandfather came from Ireland and got a life-changing tip about silver being discovered near Lake Temiskaming about 300 miles north of Winton. How he and Bess met. Even how his father and grandfather tragically died together.

Neddy talked of life on the farm, his sisters and his

mother, but never once mentioned his father. Con noticed, suddenly realizing Neddy *never* talked of his father in any of their previous discussions. Not once.

"I don't mean to pry," said Con, "but you never talk about your father. Is he still alive?

Neddy fell silent, turning momentarily to look at the passing scenery. "Not much to say," he said flatly. "'Twasn't much of a father."

"So, he died?"

"No," Neddy said without elaborating.

Con let the subject drop.

They sat quietly for a time until Con returned to discussing the mines and Neddy's contribution to their operation. After that, they began reading as the passing panorama sped by.

About four hours into the journey, it was time for lunch in the dining car with its white table linens, fine china, silverware and crystal glassware. Con asked if he could order for them and Neddy, not recognizing a single thing on the menu except for the words beef and chicken, acquiesced. There was Bearnaise this and Wellington that, puree of something else and your basic flambe of who knows what. All of it incredible. But when the waiter, through mysterious alchemy, drowned thin, delicately folded pancakes (Con called them "crepes") in a sauce he divined from melted sugar, fresh-squeezed orange juice, a family-sized dollop of butter and something Neddy heard as "cure-a-sow" then set it aflame, the boy almost bolted from the table in terror. But seeing Con's approving smile at the tableside blaze, he remained seated.

"Not exactly farm food, is it?" Con said, slicing into

the buttery concoction. "But I like to indulge myself as compensation for being away from home on these trips. Besides, I couldn't eat like this much more than a few days a year."

"I've not seen or eaten anyt'ing like this in me whole life," Neddy said, putting a citrus-soaked slice of crepe into his mouth.

By the time mid-afternoon tea service and scones ended, the train was hurtling toward the final leg of the trip. In less than an hour or so and they would pull into Cobalt, where the meals would be hearty but pedestrian and the temperature already hovered near zero. For now, however, they luxuriated in the warmth of the train as Con gave Neddy a few more details.

"Paul will meet us at the station," Con told Neddy, "then we'll check into the hotel and the three of us probably will have dinner so Paul can give you more information about your duties starting tomorrow."

Neddy didn't say much, listening instead and trying to mentally organize as much information as possible. Then came talk of money.

"We'll be starting you at $30 a week for the first two weeks, then see how that goes," Con said.

"Don't ya mean $30 a month, which is grand," Neddy corrected Con.

Con smiled. "No, that's $30 a *week* to start. But don't worry, we'll also continue paying your $18 a month indenture stipend, totalling $35," Con could see Neddy struggling to do the math in his head and added, "That's about 29 pounds a week."

Never in his life had he imagined such a staggering amount of money ... a staggering amount of *his* money. How could just one person spend it all? What would he do with it? The sum was overwhelming in itself, but the thought of 29 pounds ... every ... week ... was almost beyond his comprehension.

"Ever heard of income tax?" Con asked, knowing Neddy probably had not. "The government is going to keep some of that, so you'll probably receive a bit less each week."

"Brilliant. Just grand," Neddy smiled broadly. "I'm over th' moon." His thoughts turned to the farm and his family. Wouldn't they be proud of him? Wouldn't they ...? "That's it!" he thought. He could send the overflow of his financial windfall home to help the family. To provide for them in a way Edward never could ... or would.

The train slowed as it neared the Silver City Station in Cobalt. As the train eased to a stop, Neddy could see light snow flurries partially obscuring the station sign and a lone figure standing in the window of the depot office.

When Con and Neddy left the train, the figure emerged with his hand extended toward Con.

"Paul, my friend," Con said, grasping the man's hand and giving it a hearty shake. "How are you, Sport? I'd like you to meet your temporary assistant Neddy McKenna."

With that, Neddy's hand shot out and Paul clasped it firmly, assuring Neddy he was someone of good character.

"Glad to meet you, Eddie," said Paul.

"That's Neddy," Con corrected him.

"Sorry," said Paul. "Neddy. Let's get you two out of the cold and into the hotel," Paul said, grabbing the suitcases and walking to the Lexington seven-passenger sedan with the Triple-C Mining Ltd. logo on its front door.

The Prospect Hotel was a short drive along Bay Street and offered the best accommodations in town. A four-story wooden structure, it was built during the first Cobalt silver rush in 1903 and completed before paved roads or sidewalks. Then again, that was the nature of Cobalt at the time, a raw and raucous frontier boom town with as many miners' tents as actual buildings.

But as troy ounces grew to tons of silver pulled from the ore-rich ground, the town's population exploded to more than 10,000 souls seeking their fortunes. Streets were paved, telephone lines strung and regular train service brought miners from as far away as British Columbia, Nevada and even South Africa. There were hotels and saloons, a Red Cross Hospital, stores, public schools, banks and an opera House. Even a professional hockey team called *The Cobalt Silver Wings* played for the National Hockey Association, a forerunner of the NHL. And civic pride could be found in the town's unofficial anthem written in 1910 by L.F. Steenman :

The Cobalt Song

For we'll sing a little song of Cobalt
If you don't live there, it's your own fault.
Oh, you Cobalt!
Where the wintry breezes blow.
Where all the silver comes from
And you live a life and then some.
Oh, you Cobalt!
You're the best old town I know.

There were business men and con men. Fancy women and church ladies. Priests and pugilists. Drunks, gamblers and dreamers. And now came a 16-year-old farm boy from Northern Ireland who had never seen such a cacophonous collision of humanity.

Later, at dinner, Paul provided Neddy a broad overview of his duties in Triple C's administrative office including filing, running paperwork back and forth to the crew bosses, logging-in ore samples to be assayed, ensuring assay reports were mailed to Con in a timely fashion, and otherwise being the go-to for anything else Paul needed accomplished on a given day.

Con could see Neddy was approaching information overload as Paul ran down the expanding list. Con looked at him as if to say ease off the gas a bit.

Paul responded, "But you'll have a few days to get acquainted with everything and will work with someone in the office who will run you through the paces."

"I wouldn't worry," said Con. "Neddy is a quick study and can do anything you ask of him."

"Aye," Neddy agreed. "I'll do me best."

"I'm sure you will," said Paul.

Snow fell gently at first the next morning. Con and Neddy finished breakfast as Paul pulled up in front of the hotel. They got in the company car and drove to the Triple C offices about a quarter mile away.

"Once you get a few hours of training under your belt, we'll have lunch about two or so," Con said to Neddy on the way. "Then we'll get you settled in the rooming house where you'll be staying."

The administrative offices were situated on a side street in a three-story, deep-crimson Victorian row house with yellow trim and an orange turret, a survivor of the disastrous 1909 fire that destroyed more than 150 buildings in the town. The house's color pallette stood in vibrant contrast to the increasingly heavy snowfall that now covered the bushes and street outside like a billowy white quilt.

Stamping their feet free of snow on the front porch, they entered the offices and hung their coats and hats on the coat rack inside the door then walked into what had been the reception area of a veterinary clinic until the vet died of rabies about 15 years ago. That irony was one reason Con's father, Corny, bought the place. He had a seriously warped sense of humor, which Con, in many respects, inherited.

Paul was a tall, heavy-set Italian with thick raven hair and perpetual beard stubble. His eyes were glistening nuggets of coal reduced to black beads behind his thick-lensed, dark-rimmed glasses, draped around ears thatched with black hair. He was the administrative brains behind the operation and had little experience with mining before joining the company ten years ago. Now, he oversaw three college-trained chemists in the assay lab, a payroll clerk, a typist ... and a temporary assistant on his first day.

While Con went upstairs to his office and began examining mining reports and ledgers, Paul squired Neddy around the office and lab, introducing him to pleasant, but indifferent staff momentarily distracted from their daily tasks. Only Gil Smythe, the bookish payroll clerk from Detroit, looked up from his ledger long enough for a brief, pleasant salutation.

"Welcome to Cobalt, Neddy," Gil said, shaking Neddy's hand and impressing all with his ability to get the boy's name right. "Hope you brought plenty of long underwear."

"Aye, four pair," Neddy laughed, having approved of Gil's handshake. "Packed 'em me-self."

"Ah, an Irish lad," Gil remarked. "Always wanted to travel there."

Earlier that day, before leaving the hotel, Con warned Neddy there would be a flood of details to remember, urging him to take notes. And during the office tour, Neddy jotted down tidbit after tidbit with a pencil and pad he brought with him. When the walkthrough was over, he had six pages of notes. By about three that afternoon, Con returned downstairs and said to Neddy, "Let's call it a day and get something to eat."

The lunch was hot and substantial, but nowhere near the elegant fare on rails from the day before. Still, Neddy enjoyed a return to meat and potatoes that seemed more in line with a mining town than haute cuisine, though he didn't know that's what it was called.

"How was you first day, Sport?" Con said, sipping his coffee.

"There's much to learn," Neddy admitted, "but I'm up fer it."

"That's what I like to hear," Con said.

When they finished lunch, Con took Neddy to *The Bess Boarding House in Town*, known simply by most as *The Bess*, a six-bedroom house he purchased and named after his wife years ago as an investment and a place to put up friends and business associates who might visit Cobalt. Three rooms were rented to long-term boarders and the house was run by Anna Obliski, an affable Polish immigrant and one hell of a cook.

Anna was in the kitchen as usual, supervising a large pot of Bigos, a hearty hunters stew of cabbage and sauerkraut, kielbasa, bacon, beef, onions and a variety of wild mushrooms that had been on the stove since noon and was deep into its six-hour journey to dinner with fresh-baked, hard-crusted rye bread.

The Bess cost $6 a week and served two meals a day ... breakfast and dinner ... while a daily bag lunch could be supplied for an additional $1 a week.

"Neddy, this is Anna Obliski and she runs the place," Con said, as Neddy thrust out his hand to Anna. "He'll be my guest for his time in Cobalt, so it won't be necessary to collect rent from him."

"T'anks fer th' offer, Con," Neddy said suddenly. "I appreciate it, I do. But I'll pay me rent. If I'm here to do man's work, I'll pay me own rent like a man." His father's words had no sooner spilled from his lips than he wanted to rephrase them into something he could call his own.

Con smiled as he dug into his wallet and pulled out $7, handing it to Anna. "That's to cover Neddy until he gets his first paycheck," he said.

"T'anks," Neddy said to Con. "I'll pay ya back."

"Consider it a thank you for coming here on such short notice," Con said, turning to leave. "I'll be here for another day or two, but will be busy tonight. I'll check in with you before I go, however. I'll have your bag sent over from the hotel in a while."

Although Neddy had just finished lunch, his mouth watered as soon as he walked into the delightful cloud of Bigos that filled the entire house. With introductions over, Anna showed Neddy his second-floor bedroom that was comfortably furnished without the more substantial decor of The Prospect. The brass bed's thick mattress was covered by a large quilt and wool blanket, while thick dark-green velveteen draperies hung at the window. There was an armoire in one corner and a chest of drawers opposite the foot of the bed. The bathroom, Anna explained, was down the hall and was shared with the other two rooms on the floor.

The parlor at *The Bess* was dominated by a large fireplace with a marble-trimmed firebox. A glass chandelier in the middle of the ceiling illuminated the room. There were several table lamps as well as a curtained bay window overlooking the street. A game table and chairs sat in one corner of the room and three upholstered chairs were arranged on either side of a six-foot-high oak bookcase well-stocked for use by boarders and guests.

As Neddy examined the book titles, he heard, "Well, hello," from behind.

Looking up, he saw Gil Smythe, still bundled in an overcoat and hat standing in the entrance hall. As he removed his gloves, Gil smiled, "What are you doing here?"

"I guess I'm to be livin' here fer a time," Neddy said, standing up.

"So, we'll be house mates, then," Gil said. "I've been here for about six months now. Best deal in town ... or should I say *Bess* deal in town. Wait until you taste the food. Incredible, if you like Polish."

"Don't t'ink I've ever," Neddy confessed.

"Lots of potatoes," Gil said, "so being Irish, you'll love it."

They both laughed as Gil excused himself and went upstairs to put away his outer gear and dress for dinner. Neddy went back to the bookcase and pulled out a book written by an author he knew: Mark Twain. As fate would have it, *The Innocents Abroad* was the quintessential travel book of the 19th Century and the best-selling volume of Twain's long career. Still in his Christmas suit, Neddy sat in an easy chair by the fire and began reading as he had done so many nights at the McKeown farm. Whether he knew it or not, for the moment, Neddy no longer looked like the Irish farm boy and indentured servant. Miles and hours away on his first day in Cobalt, he looked like he belonged.

34

A Damaged Marionette

The heart monitor continued its metronomic ping as it had done for days. His blood pressure, breathing and other vitals were in order. The sun was just cresting the parking lot trees as Patrick crossed the hospital lobby with his wife Karen, rode the elevator to the fourth floor and entered the intensive-care unit. "We came as fast as we could," Patrick said, walking into the room, where anesthesiologist Dr. Sunjay Vindaya and a nurse stood next to the bed.

"He should be waking up anytime now," said Dr. Vindaya, who had started reversing the induced coma. "We monitored a

steady reduction in brain swelling for the past 24 hours. His vitals
remained strong, so we decided the danger was passing."

Patrick couldn't stop thinking how fragile his father
looked, lying there like a damaged marionette, attached by wires
and tubes to monitors and a tangle of other electronics, his pale
veined arm being nourished by a drip bag of pharmaceuticals, and
his white hair a chaotic halo on the bed pillow. Karen wrapped her
arm about her husband's shoulder as Patrick began, "We should
have known this would happen. We should have put our foot
down when he refused to consider assisted living."

"Falls are quite common with the elderly," the doctor
responded, "especially given your father's condition ... "

"My father's condition? The brain swelling? That
happened after the fall."

"I think you should talk to Dr. Feinberg."

The old man's eyes fluttered open.

35

Gil

After a week, Neddy was hitting his stride. Between the
steady fusillade of questions he fired at Gil and the 18 pages
of notes taken since his arrival, Neddy already had mastered
several aspects of the job and was nearly certain about a few
more.

Gil, as it turned out, was a great asset, sharing not only
his knowledge of the operation, but as a companion during
meals when they talked of home, of places they'd been and
places they wanted to visit, as well as other life experiences. In

fact, Neddy was surprised with how easy it was to share with Gil so many subjects he rarely talked about for no other reason than he never considered them worth discussing.

"I've heard good things from Paul," Con said, standing on the train platform with Neddy as the morning train to Winton and Ottawa prepared for departure, having stayed longer than usual because of a few labor issues. "Keep up the good work."

"I havta admit, bein' a culchie, I was afeared at first," Neddy said, "but then I says, aw, give it a lash. I didn't want to let ya down."

"Well, you were the only one who worried," Con said, placing a hand on Neddy's shoulder. "You're a smart boy and this is your chance to let everyone know what I knew from the day you came home with us. Continue working hard and I'll see you when you come home."

"T'anks fer believin' in me, Con."

"Just remember to believe in yourself," he replied. "That's what really counts."

A porter loaded Con's bag on the train and Con followed onboard. Moments later, he was at the window of his compartment watching Neddy and the station disappear in clouds of smoke and steam as the train pulled away.

Walking back to the office, leaning into a frigid gale, Neddy couldn't believe the depth, breadth and near depravity of the oppressive cold. The highs during the past week hadn't reached 20 degrees and it was unsafe to venture out in the sub-zero blasts at night. With a fur hat pulled low to his eyebrows and two scarves binding his face to the top of his cheeks, only his eyes, which he worried might freeze, were exposed to the relentless cold before he crossed the porch and hung his clothes in the entrance hall.

No sooner had Neddy started to thaw when Paul shouted from his office, "I need you to run these schedules up to shafts nine and 13 this morning."

"And while you're there," added Gil, "pick up time sheets from Thompson, Billings, and get one from Shuhler in number six."

Turning around and reconstructing his winter suit of armor, Neddy grabbed the schedules and truck key and was on his way to the Triple C mines on Cobalt Lake where he arrived 45 minutes later

"You're the new kid, aren't ya," said Tom Billings, a slab of a shift boss dressed in a rumpled, vested suit, bowler hat, a well-chewed cigar butt jabbed in a corner of his mouth, but no overcoat. Neddy, looking like a walking clothes closet, asked him for the time sheet. Giving Neddy the once-over as he handed him the paper, Billings grumped, "From the looks of you, you won't last long." He then threw his head back and laughed, it seemed, to the soles of his boots. "Don't pay me no mind. Just havin' a bit of sport with you. Welcome, aboard."

"I'm just here 'til they find a full-timer to take me place," Neddy explained, but Billings was already walking off to his shift crew waiting for the day's orders.

The dirt road linking the various mines was a cantankerous, uneven slash of frozen dirt and rock undulating like waves on an angry sea. And like a boat on that sea, the truck rocked and dove and groaned from bumper to bumper as Neddy grasped the wheel, navigating it slowly toward the next safe harbor.

With schedules delivered and time sheets in hand, Neddy headed back to the office as the sun finally broke through what he thought had been an unrelenting cloudy sky. But even with bright sunlight illuminating the surrounding hillside and lake, the town of Cobalt, its buildings and people remained steadfastly grey to the pit of their souls. Certainly, he was well acquainted with the pallor of Ireland's colder months, but at least Irish fields and meadows and glens remained green year round, dulling the sharp edges of winter. Here, there was nothing but sharp edges that went on forever, cutting through the thickest layers of clothing and to the very heart of the human spirit.

Back at the office, Neddy polished off the stack of folders Paul wanted him to file, and posted several reports to Con. Gil was also winding down, making final entries in the daily ledger when he looked up from his desk and said to Neddy, "Why don't we head over to Verner's?"

"Verner's? What's that?"

"It's the saloon around the corner," Gil said. "We can have a beer. Maybe shoot some pool or darts. A group of us go there sometimes after work to unwind."

"Ya mean a pub?"

"Yeah, a pub."

"Maybe another time," Neddy said, pulling on his coat. "I'm knackered from runnin' around today."

"Sure," said Gil. "Another time."

Neddy returned to *The Bess* and had a fine dinner of Anna's perogies stuffed with onions and potatoes topped with sour cream and bacon, which, curiously had him thinking not so much of Poland as of Ireland and his mother's remarkable champ.

After dinner, Neddy settled by the parlor fire, continuing his vicarious travels with Twain's innocents, when Gil walked in. "Ya missed a brilliant dinner," Neddy said.

"I grabbed a bite at Verner's," Gil said, unwrapping his scarf and stashing it in a sleeve of his overcoat. "You missed a good time."

"Next time," Neddy said, returning to his book.

"What'rya reading?"

"*Innocents Abroad* by Mark Twain."

"Great book about travel."

"Aye."

"Have you ever wanted to go to some of those places?"

Neddy smiled. "I fancied vistin' Lilliput once."

"Me, too," Gil grinned. "*Gulliver's Travels?*"

"Aye. 'Twas th' first real book I read."

"I've read it, oh, I don't know ... maybe five times."

"I've read it only three times, the last bein' on th' ship from Ireland."

"Always wanted to go there."

"Lilliput?"

"No, Ireland."

Although Neddy didn't consider Ireland a compelling subject for discussion, Gil was obsessed with everything Irish. The countryside. The people. The war of independence. The Giants Causeway. The bogs and mountains. And especially Neddy's account of his brush with the British army (while omitting certain details).

Neddy, on the other hand, couldn't imagine what life in a big city like Detroit might be like. Although he had a taste of cities when he left Ireland and arrived in Canada 10 days later, Detroit was nearly twice the size of Belfast and already an industrial giant with the burgeoning auto industry.

"I lived most of my life in Detroit," Gil explained, "and it just wasn't enough. My father wanted me to come to work in his cabinet shop, but I just couldn't see myself being a cabinet maker or a carpenter for the rest of my life."

"I t'ink I know what ya mean, but I never knew nothin' but th' farm all me life, 'til I read *Gulliver's Travels* ..."

"What a great book!" Gil said.

"His adventures were brilliant, I thought, until I find out they weren't real. But a ... uh ... mate ... told me there were places like them in th' real world ..."

"I know what you mean," Gil said. "That's why I left home and I've been moving around now for three years. How old are you?"

"I'm 17 in July."

"I was 17 when I went out on the road," Gil said, then assuming a conspiratorial tone, added, "I'm starting to get *the itch* again, but don't tell anyone."

"The itch?"

"Yeah, you know. The urge to move to the next place, the next adventure. And being a payroll clerk isn't my idea of adventure."

"What is?" Neddy asked.

"Being a cowboy out west," Gil said, whirling an imaginary lariat above his head. "Yeehaw!! Can't you just see it? Or how about a river boat captain. Or learning to fly airplanes?"

Neddy just looked at Gil for a long moment, finally

commenting, "Never thought none about it much, 'cept fer Huck Finn ... and when I got me atlas fer Christmas."

"You've got an atlas?"

"Aye," said Neddy. "An atlas of th' whole world. Even Canada."

"I'd like to see it some time."

Although Neddy traveled great distances under incredible circumstances and experienced good and unimaginable evil along the way, he envied Gil's path. In the three years or so since leaving Detroit, he had seen Alabama's gulf coast and had been to Alaska. He rode the rails across the Great Plains and landed in a mining town of northern Ontario. He had been a cook in a lumber camp, a truck driver in Idaho, and a ticket taker for the New York City subway system.

"A lot of jobs," Neddy said.

"But don't you get it? It's not about the jobs. It's the going. It's the seeing," Gil said, leaning closer to Neddy by the fire and whispering, "It's the freedom of going where you please, when you please. Being the captain of your own destiny."

Neddy's thoughts turned to Traveler. Isn't self-determination what he had been hinting at all along? Making choices independent of what others want or expect? Being, as Gil just said, "captain of your own destiny."

"So, ya just go?"

"You bet," said Gil. "Go when the mood strikes and find a new adventure. Look, you'll be old for a long time. More years than when you're young. And when you're old, life gets complicated. I looked at my father. He never went anywhere. He just worked and got married and had kids and worked some more. At 20, I've done more than he'll ever do and have more experiences than he can imagine. I'll probably get married some day. Probably have kids and a steady job. But not now. Not when I've got … *the itch*."

Neddy wasn't sure if he had the itch, but since leaving Ireland, moving from Tyrone to Montreal to Ottawa to Winton to Cobalt, there's been a desire to see what's beyond the next fork in the road. Maybe that *is* the itch.

"I dunno," Neddy said. "'Twas hard leavin' Ireland and me family."

"But you left, didn't you?"

"Aye, but I had no choice?"

"Of course you did," Gil said, leaning back in his chair. "You always have a choice. How did you get here?"

"Con said I was to fill in 'til …"

"Did he hold a gun to your head?"

"Don't be daft," Neddy responded.

"So, you made the decision to come to Cobalt?"

"I did."

"Mr. McKeown gave you a choice to go or to stay and you decided to go."

"Aye, but I also owed it to him to go."

"What did you owe him?"

"Him an' Miss Bess, that's his wife, took me in right off th' boat. Me 'an a lad named Timmy."

"Didn't you say something about working on his farm?"

"Aye."

"You were earning your keep?"

"Aye an' gettin' 18 dollars a month," Neddy said proudly.

"You worked for less than five dollars a week? So you

were his employee. His low-paid employee. You worked and he paid you. How do you owe him anything?"

Neddy had never thought of the arrangement in quite those terms and wasn't sure he wanted to think that way now. The McKeowns fed him, clothed him, gave him a bed in their home, gave him books and advice and, most recently, went to battle with people trying to harm him. That wasn't an employer. That was family.

"Con an' Miss Bess're grand people, who took a culchie from Ireland, a strainséir, into their home," Neddy said. "They treat me kind an' teach me all sorts of t'ings I didn't know b'fore. They give me books an' treat me better than me own Da. Aye, I do owe them."

"But don't you owe something to yourself, as well?" Gil said. "I've only known you for a few days, but we've talked a lot about our lives, right?"

"Aye."

"Well, from what I can see, most of what you've done has been for other people. You hid guns at the farm to save your father. You left Ireland because your family was poor. You went home with the McKeowns because Timmy wanted you to go. You came to Cobalt because Mr. McKeown wanted you here. Ask yourself how many times in your life did you do something without once considering how if would affect other people? Another question is how many of the things you've been asked to do was for your benefit and not for the person doing the asking? I'm not telling you to be ungrateful for what Mr. McKeown and his wife have done for you. They sound like great folks. I'm just asking: What do *you* want out of life?"

"I ... um ... dunno," said Neddy, who had held back stories of his father sacrificing him to Squire Loughran to avoid paying rent, as well as the entire shipboard incident with The German. But combined with everything else Gil laid out, Neddy knew there was more than a kernel of truth in what he said. "I guess I never give it a thought."

"Time's a wastin' especially when there are places like this to see," Gil said, pulling a folded pamphlet from his hip pocket and handing it to Neddy. *Miami by the Sea*, the cover announced over the photo of a svelte young woman posing in the sand and wearing a scandalous bathing suit that barely covered her knees. Palm trees lazed overhead while white clouds floated above the deep blue ocean in the background. *A beautiful resort city affordable for all*, the copy teased.

"Where'd ya get this?" Neddy asked, transfixed by the young woman's form.

"I sent away for it from an advert in the *Toronto Star*."

"Does this really exist?" asked Neddy, turning the brochure over, studying the pictures of boating and fishing and more young women in those bathing suits lying on a beach under a large striped umbrella.

"You bet," said Gil, "and I'm goin'. Wanna come?"

"Me?"

"Am I talking to anyone else?"

"I could never ..."

"And why not?"

Neddy couldn't think of a reason. And while his silence wasn't an endorsement of the idea, it also wasn't an outright rejection. He simply had never been faced with such a proposal. Of course, there was the immigration scheme that brought him to Canada, but he had been *compelled* by his parents ... and by Traveler ... to leave. It certainly wasn't something of his own device. Neither was Gil's offer, but it was done so without pressure or expectation. It *would be* a decision made completely on his own. Maybe the first independent decision of his life.

"'Tis somethin' to t'ink on," he said, returning to his book as Gil went upstairs to his room.

36

Ramona

During the next few weeks, the brochure became the centerpiece of an ongoing joke between Gil and Neddy. Whenever Gil saw an opening, he would take it.

Picking up the office phone and speaking into the mouthpiece, Gil would act as if someone were on the line. "Neddy," he'd say, "it's Ramona calling you from Miami." Or he would stand in the hall outside Neddy's room at night and, in a falsetto voice, croon, "Oh, Romeo, this is Ramona. I'm naked and waiting in the hall to take you back to Miami with me."

For all the joking, however, Gil's campaign was having an effect. Neddy would open the Rand-McNally Atlas at night and finding Florida would look not just at Miami, but other cities around the state. Clearwater. Tampa. Palm Beach. Boca Raton. Tarpon Springs. All such exotic names, especially his favorite during this brutal winter, Frostproof. Each, he assumed, with their own pretty women in scandalous swimsuits.

Gil was reading a *National Geographic* one evening when Neddy walked into the parlor. "So how're ya gettin' there?" Neddy mused. "Rand-McNally says 'tis nigh onto 2,000 miles. That's a terrible long walk."

"The train," Gil said, not looking up from a story about wild horses in Montana. "We would go by train."

"*We? We'd* have none of it," Neddy said flatly. "This is *yer* daydream." Then after a brief pause ... "How much would that cost?"

"About $50," Gil said matter of factly. "I've researched it. It would take two days."

"Ya must be ossified," said Neddy, calculating in his head that he had cleared roughly $175 since he started work, after paying for room, board and other small expenses as well as sending money home to his family.

"I have about $125 put away," Gil said, "so I'm ready at any time. After train fare, I would have about two weeks salary once we arrive in Miami to find work and start saving for the next move."

"But we ... uh ... *you* would have to eat on th' train. That would cost more."

"Not if we pay Anna five dollars to pack us some eggs and bread and sausages and perogies and cake. We can pick up four quarts of Molson's from Verner's for two dollars and get tea and coffee on the train."

Neddy was amazed. It seemed there was no contingency Gil hadn't thought through.

Putting down the magazine, Gil looked at Neddy standing in front of him. "So, you coming or not?"

Neddy shrugged and went back to his room where

he opened his Rand-McNally Atlas. For the longest time, he studied the map of North America, tracing an imaginary route from Ontario to Florida as if he could obtain through osmosis an answer to his dilemma from the printed page. None was forthcoming. He thought of writing Rose for counsel, but getting an answer could take more than six weeks and he probably didn't have the time.

Neddy returned downstairs, but Gil had gone to bed, so he did the same.

37

Maybe Days

Oncologist Helen Feinberg was direct. "As your father's swelling brain began to recede, a brain scan discovered a glioblastoma, a rather large malignant brain tumor, in the cerebellum," the doctor explained, adding somberly, "and it's inoperable."

"Inoperable?" said Patrick, reaching for Karen's hand. "How do you know? Isn't there something? Chemo? Radiation? How about ... ?"

"A glioblastoma is a particularly virulent form of cancer," the doctor said, glancing down at the old man's chart. "Very aggressive. Fast growing. Therefore, treatments are unavailable."

Patrick felt as if the air had been sucked from his lungs. He looked at Karen who had started to sob softly, then turned to the oncologist, "How long?"

"A week ... maybe days," the doctor said, removing a business card attached to the old man's chart. "I suggest you

think about getting your father's affairs in order and contact
this organization." The doctor handed Patrick the card. It read,
"Sacred Heart Hospice of the Suncoast."

38

Where It's Warm

By his sixth week in Cobalt, Neddy had fallen into a
routine. Office work, while cleaner and warmer than manual
labor in the winter, was, to his mind, monotonous. From clock
in to clock out, the duties were essentially the same with little
or no variation. Ever. At least farming, by its very nature, held
surprises every day. Whether good or bad, at least they were
different.

On this particular day, Neddy decided to ask Paul
how the replacement search was progressing, to which Paul
responded, "It's coming along. I have two candidates arriving
next week. One Monday and another Thursday."

Neddy was not disappointed. He didn't even have
mixed emotions. It was time to leave Cobalt and, difficult
as it may be, quite possibly Ontario. Neddy had reached a
fulcrum and as he eased away from it, found himself strangely
comfortable with his decision, although breaking the news to
the McKeowns and Timmy was another matter.

Neddy and Gil began planning in earnest, mapping out
a game plan, not only for their departure from Cobalt, but
from Ontario. During his research, Gil found they would be
taking the train from Ottawa south. So it was decided that
Neddy would travel to Winton while Gil remained in Cobalt,

continuing to work and earning as much money as possible
until he heard from Neddy.

The only remaining question was when.

Gil urged Neddy to leave, but he refused to make a move
until a replacement had been found and Paul was comfortable.
Neddy even might stay on to help break in the new hire. It was
not the ideal situation for Gil, but he acquiesced. In the end,
the plan was put in motion when Mr. Thursday was hired by
Paul and was available to start immediately. Better still, Paul
thanked Neddy for the offer, but he would not be needed to
ease the transfer into his duties as the candidate had similar
job experience.

However, Gil was more of a gentleman than he may
have let on and felt compelled to give Paul at least a week's
notice before leaving. Paul appreciated that, and as Gil had
been a great employee, he asked after his plans. Neddy and
Gil decided nothing would be shared until Neddy had time to
break the news personally to Con and Bess.

"Nothing special," Gil told Paul. "I just have this itch
that needs to be scratched. Maybe I'll head south where it's
warm."

On his last day in Cobalt, Neddy called the McKeowns
to let them know he was returning to the farm on the 2 p.m.
train. His journey back to Winton made him think of the
final ride through the Tyrone countryside bound for Belfast
nearly a year ago. While he didn't have the same connection
to Ontario he had with Northern Ireland, he still felt the sting
of melancholy, realizing that for now and for the foreseeable
future, this would be the last of his Ontario adventure.

Colder than he could have imagined and aside from

Cobalt's somber disposition, the Ontario winter at its best had been a stunning crystalline landscape from snow-infused woodlands to its sparkling frozen lakes alive with skaters and ice fishermen. But those, too, had become memories as spring thawed lake ice, chased snow from all but the highest hills and lured the oaks and poplars and sycamores to life with its resurgent warmth. For now, the countryside was nothing more than fleeting passenger-train moments as Neddy headed toward a new tomorrow.

By late afternoon, the low-hanging sun blinked wildly through the blur of trees until sliding behind the mountains, leaving the stage for twilight. Neddy's second-class return passage was not the opulent delight of the arrival in Cobalt, but the seating was accommodating and meals were still served on white table cloths.

Moonrise had taken place an hour ago when the train pulled to a stop at the empty Winton Station platform. Neddy grabbed his suitcase and stepped from the train, looking south, then hearing a voice from the north.

"Neddy!" Bess yelled. "Down here."

He smiled, waved and walked toward her, as Con and Timmy rounded the side of the depot and approached. "Good to have you home, Sport," Con said, taking hold of the suitcase handle as they started for the Hudson parked nearby.

"How'rya, boyo?" Neddy asked Timmy, smiling broadly and scooping the boy into his arms with a hug. "Have ya been good?"

"Aye," said Timmy, throwing his arms around Neddy's neck.

Arriving at the farm, Neddy felt a warmth he had

missed for nearly two months. Not the warmth of the farmhouse or the fireplace in the parlor, but the warmth of family. Of belonging. The very spirit engendered by mutual respect and kindness. But at the same time, he knew this moment was coming to an end ... for now.

Neddy carried his suitcase to the boys' bedroom and dropped it on the bed. He changed out of his travel clothes and went downstairs, where Bess, Con and Timmy were in the parlor, sitting in the glow and crackle of a fire.

"So," said Bess, "tell us about your adventure. How did you like Cobalt?"

"'Tis hard to describe," Neddy began. "Cold. Terrible cold."

"That's Ontario in winter," Con smiled. "If you don't like the cold, don't worry. Wait long enough and it'll get even colder."

"Aye," Neddy laughed. "Nothin' like it in Ireland. Never saw nothin' like Cobalt neither. A rough town t'was."

"Certainly no one goes to Cobalt on holiday," Con said.

"But I met grand people there," Neddy said. "Paul was a class gaffer ..."

"Paul was what?" Bess asked.

"A good boss," Con translated.

"... and Anna was brilliant."

"Great cook, isn't she?" Bess said. "Especially her perogies."

"Ach, aye," Neddy said, closing his eyes to visualize the heavenly Polish dumplings. "I could have eat 'em every day 'til I died. But I did miss your rhubarb pie."

With that, Bess got up and went to the kitchen, returning a moment later holding a metal pie plate. "Just for you," she said, holding the plate under Neddy's nose. "Rhubarb pie. Want a slice? I've put on water for tea."

Following Bess back to the kitchen, Con asked Neddy, "Did you make it to Verner's?"

"Never did," said Neddy, thinking of years wasted in a pub by his father, "but me mate, Gil, would go."

"Your mate, Gil?"

"Oh, aye," said Neddy, "we got on from th' start."

"Interesting guy," Con said. "From Detroit, I believe."

"Aye ... an' lots of other places," Neddy said, sitting himself at the kitchen table and cutting into his slice of pie.

"Here's your tea," said Bess, serving everyone at the table.

"This ... is ... brilliant," Neddy said, relishing the lip-puckering tang of rhubarb in his first forkful. Then, looking at Timmy, he reached into his trouser pocket. "Almost forgot. I brought you this."

"A stone?" Timmy said, slowly examining the facets of its shiny surface.

"Not just a stone," said Con. "It's a silver nugget and very special."

Taking a fresh look at it, Timmy turned the nugget over and over in his hands, watching it sparkle in the electric light.

"Twas pulled from th' ground in Cobalt," Neddy explained, "an' it said, 'Take me to Timmy."

"Stones don't talk," Timmy frowned, raising the stone close to his lips and whispering, "Hello?" Then he put the nugget to his ear. "Nothin' a'tall."

"Must be sleepin'," Neddy winked at Bess and Con.

"Yes, that must be the case," echoed Con.

As the evening evolved, Neddy laid out his daily office routine, his trips to and from the mines and how his nights reading by the parlor fire always reminded him of those spent in front of the McKeown hearth. His only regret was having to leave behind the half-read copy of Twain's *The Innocents Abroad.*

As Neddy spoke, Con sensed a sub-text in his storytelling. Something indistinct. Something not quite frustration or displeasure with the experience. It was more like ... restlessness.

Later, as Con and Bess turned off the lights and settled into bed, Con said, "I think Neddy is planning to leave."

"What? No. What makes you think that?"

"Did you hear him tonight and how often he talked about the atlas?"

"It sounds like he really likes it," Bess recalled.

"No, it was more than that," Con said. "When he talked, he wasn't talking so much about *the book* as he was about the *places in it.* More like looking at the Sears catalog and picturing yourself in one of the homes they sell. It was more ... what's the word ... aspirational."

"I didn't get that at all," Bess concluded.

"Maybe you're right," Con said, rolling to his side. "Maybe I'm imagining things."

In the boys' room, Neddy had unpacked much of the suitcase's contents including the Rand-McNally atlas. As Timmy fell asleep, Neddy flicked on the flashlight he kept bedside and pulled the covers over his head to read as he had done so many nights before. Opening the atlas, he turned first to the North American map, then to the map of Florida, once again visualizing the long journey and adventures that lay ahead. He also thought again of the young woman in the swim suit beneath the palm trees. And then, strangely enough ... Mary.

That night, he dreamed of palm trees, but beneath them was Traveler, dressed appropriately for once in his flowered shirt and Panama hat.

"Big day coming," smiled Traveler, flicking a cigar ash into the white sand beneath his lounge chair. "Got it all figured out, don't you?"

"Not quite," Neddy said. For one thing, Neddy had trouble reconciling Traveler reclining on a rattan beach lounge, while himself was dressed in his Christmas suit, fur hat and standing bunkside on the *Sea Empress*.

"Yeah," said Traveler, looking around. "This *is* confusing, but I don't ask questions. It's *your* dream. Haven't quite decided how to break the news to them, have you? Don't worry, you'll come up with something. Oh, one more thing before you wake up. Miami girls in bathing suits? They're real and they just *lovvvvvve* men with Irish brogues. Even boys with Irish brogues. Dangerous business, those American women. They're fast, so be very, very careful not to get scorched. And I'm not talking about sunburn."

39

Not Forever

Like more mornings than he could count, Neddy was pulled from his dream by the smell of frying bacon. He looked over at Timmy still asleep with his stuffed bear held tightly to his chest by one arm while the other was shoved under his pillow. The blanket had slipped to the boy's waist, so Neddy reached over and gently adjusted it to his shoulders, causing Timmy to stir without waking.

The thought of leaving Timmy was soul crushing and would have been unthinkable even six months ago. But now, while sad at the prospect, Neddy knew he would leave a boy deeply loved by the McKeowns and who, in turn, loved them back. Besides, he thought, his leaving wasn't forever.

Neddy dressed and went down to breakfast to find Bess alone in the kitchen.

"I was about to come up and get you," she smiled. "Had a busy day yesterday, so today you can just relax."

"Where's Con?"

"He had a business meeting in Winton early this morning, but should be back in an hour or so," she explained. "How do you want your eggs? Sunny side up, as usual?"

"Aye," said Neddy, "that would be grand."

A cool, easy breeze underscored the whistling chirp of a cardinal and a grackle's slow staccato outside the kitchen window confirming to Neddy that spring, indeed, had arrived. Tips of gladiolus and tulips were cresting the garden soil and the first leaves of the season dressed trees over the farm lane in pale green lace. Neddy heard the crunch of road dirt seconds before the Hudson stopped outside the farmhouse and Con walked through the front door and into the kitchen.

"Hey, Sport," he said, removing his hat. "All recovered from the trip?"

"Aye," said Neddy, finishing the last of the bacon and turning his attention to a thick slice of toast and strawberry jam. "Slept like the dead."

"So what are your plans for today?"

"Thought Timmy an' me would go down to th' swimming hole later."

"A bit cold for that, don't you think?" Con chuckled.

"Just to go there is all. But, first," Neddy got serious, putting down his toast. "I need a talk with you and Miss Bess about something."

"You're leaving, aren't you?" Con said abruptly, sliding onto a kitchen chair as Bess stopped cleaning the breakfast dishes and looked hopefully at Neddy, praying it wasn't so.

Neddy was stunned at first, but took a deep breath. "Aye," he said calmly. "Me and Gil." Looking quizzically at Con, he then asked, "How did'ya know?"

"I've had it in the back of my mind almost since you arrived," Con confessed. "You always seemed, so ... so unsettled. Like you wanted to be somewhere else."

"I don't t'ink that's so ..." said Neddy rather

unconvincingly. "You an' Miss Bess're grand people ... an' have been kind an' ..."

"I never doubted that you had affection for us ... and you know we love you ..."

"Aye ..."

"But it had less to do with us and more to do with you," Con explained. "You seemed to want more ... of everything. I first saw it when you talked about *Gulliver's Travels*. That's why I gave you *Huck Finn*. A book about a boy's traveling spirit to see if that fed into what I saw as wanderlust ..."

"Wander ...?"

"Wanderlust is the need to see new places, to find new things, to see the world."

"Oh," said Neddy like a child whose most-guarded secret had been uncovered.

"Last night, when you talked about the atlas, *the way* you talked about it, I knew you weren't talking *about the book*, but *places in the book*."

By now, Bess was at the table, holding back tears and silently listening to the reality she had hoped wouldn't come but was sitting across from her in the kitchen.

"We're fer Florida by train," Neddy said. "An' we've planned everyt'ing out."

"Florida?!" Bess gasped. "So far. So, so far away. Why there?"

But it was Con who answered, "Why not?" Again, Neddy was surprised Con knew his thoughts so well, but Con was guessing, all the while hoping he was wrong. "What will you do when you get there?"

"Look fer work," said Neddy.

"And money?" asked Bess. "What will you do for money?"

"I've $125 after th' train ticket," Neddy explained, "then we'll get jobs. We even paid Anna t'cook extra food fer th' train ride."

"Got it all planned out, huh?" Con said. "Did you also consider that you have time left on your indenture to us? About two years, I figure."

"I have," said Neddy, reaching into his pocket and handing several folded bills to Con. "Here's $36 dollars fer two months an' I can send th' rest as I make money."

Con looked at the money and said, "I'm sure you're good for it."

Timmy came into the kitchen and Bess met him at the door. "And what do you want for breakfast?"

Still rubbing his eyes, he said, "Pancakes."

Neddy stood. "I'm off ta talk to Tom, if that'll do ..."

Con waved him toward the back door and went to the parlor.

A half hour later, Neddy returned to find Timmy and Bess in the parlor reading. "Miss Bess," he said, "can I talk to Timmy?" She nodded as Neddy and Timmy headed off toward the swimming hole. They walked past it and came to rest on the banks of the Ottawa River. Neddy was the first to pick up a stone, trying to skip it across the water's surface. It hopped three times and sank. Timmy picked one up, fired and watched it sink immediately to the bottom."

"Here," said Neddy. "Hold it like this."

For the next ten minutes, stone after stone sailed through the air as Neddy adjusted Timmy's stance, approach and the angle of his arm. Finally, Timmy tossed a winner and watched it take one ... two ... three ... then four hops before sinking.

"Brilliant!" yelled Neddy. "Ya learn fast."

Timmy picked up another rock and skipped it three times. "Timmy, I need to tell ya somethin' and I don't want ya to be sad."

"What?" asked Timmy cautiously.

"I'm ta leave' fer a time."

"But ya just got home," Timmy protested.

"Not like that," Neddy said. "I'm ta be gone fer a long time ..." Timmy had a sudden rush of fear that Neddy saw in his eyes. "But I'll be comin' back ..."

"Me Da said he'd be back ..."

"'Tis not like that a'tall," Neddy assured. "I'll be away, but I'll be sendin' letters ... an' pictures ... an' there's telephones ... so we can talk ..."

"Why are ya goin'? asked Timmy, "I don't want ya to leave ..."

"I know, I know," said Neddy, pulling Timmy close, wiping his tears and then his own. "I know. It'll be hard at first, but I'll be back. I promise."

They held each other for a long time before Neddy stood, took Timmy by the hand and started back toward the farmhouse.

Dinner, then the evening in the parlor were understandably somber. Little was said except that Neddy offered to pay for the suitcase and Con declined, telling him to take it as a going-away present.

"So," Bess said, quietly putting a bookmark into *Sense*

and Sensibility, "when will you be leaving?"

"I've time still," Neddy said. "There's work to be done here before ..."

"We could use the help," Con lied. "I lined up a few jobs ..."

"Aye," Neddy agreed.

Bess smiled.

40

April 17, 1922

During the next few weeks, Neddy worked with Bess and Timmy in the vegetable garden, preparing the beds for summer berries, tomatoes and, of course, rhubarb. Other times, he was with Con and Tom plowing for the spring planting season, tuning up the tractor and working on the windmills.

They shared meals and laughed and talked, worked side by side and slept under the same roof during those final days, trying their best to relish the time together, filling roles in a play they knew had entered its final act.

Neddy made the call to Gil in Cobalt late one afternoon a month after his return to Winton. They agreed to meet in Ottawa the next day.

Later, everything was as it always had been. Dinner. Reading by the fire. Early to bed.

Then it was morning. Everyone got up and went about their normal routine, if not mechanically. Get dressed. Make breakfast. Eat breakfast. The only new element was

Neddy packing for the final time. As Timmy watched, Neddy carefully packed every bit of his clothing for cold weather and warm as well as his personal treasures and books, then closed the suitcase and took it downstairs.

As Tom took Timmy to gather eggs, Con and Bess asked Neddy to join them in the parlor.

"We wanted to talk to you alone before starting off for Winton," Con said, inviting Neddy to sit in the easy chair next to his desk. "First of all, Neddy, let me tell you that Bess and I are so proud of you and the man you're becoming. Although we had no idea what we were getting into more than a year ago when you came home with us, you have brightened our lives more than you know. For that, we're grateful."

"'Tis me who's grateful," Neddy said, "takin' on two Irish lads from St. George's when all ya wanted was one ..."

"We never told you about Neil," Con's voice was barely a whisper.

"Neil?"

"Our son," Con said, reaching into his wallet, retrieving a photo of a toddler dressed in a child's sailor suit and cradling a toy boat in his arms. He handed it to Neddy. "We lost Neil during the Spanish Flu and our world collapsed."

"We tried to have another child," Bess added, "but it wasn't in God's plan. Then we heard about St. George's ..."

"Me, too," Neddy said quietly. "Me brother, Packy died from the flu."

"I never knew you had a brother," Con said as Bess put an arm around Neddy's shoulder.

"Aye, a brilliant lad who was buildin' a bicycle ..." Neddy stopped. He swallowed hard and tried to speak again, but began to quietly sob for his brother for the first time in years as Con struggled to hold the edge on his emotions.

"We saw Neil in Timmy," said Con, composing himself, "and knew that while God didn't want us to have a child of our own, He was giving us a chance to change another boy's life for the better ..."

"But ya never counted on me, did ya?" Neddy smiled gamely.

"When we saw how Timmy clung to you in St. George's parlor," Con said, "we somehow knew it was a package deal. One couldn't come without the other, but we couldn't have imagined what would happen next."

"Not only did God want us to help Timmy, He sent you as a road map," said Bess, rubbing Neddy's hand. "He wanted you to show us what Timmy would become. A smart, hard-working, loyal and loving young man. And we love you because of it. You've worked so hard and learned so much, we're confident that whatever you do and wherever you go, you'll continue to make us proud."

Con leaned closer to Neddy. "That's why we're releasing you from your indenture." Picking up an envelope from his desktop, Con said, "Here's your thirty six dollars. Add it to your travel fund. And here's another fifty dollars to make sure you've got a little more of a pad if you can't find work."

Neddy could do nothing but stare at the money in his hand, even as it blurred and lost focus through his tears. He looked at Con and Bess, barely able to say, "You didn't have to ..."

"But we wanted to do this for you because of all you've done for us and Timmy," Con said. "After you arrived, Bess and I set up bank accounts for you and Timmy and have been putting away $25 a month for your futures. I checked on it this morning and your account has about $250 in it. I will keep it there for you to use if and when you need it in Florida. All you have to do is call me on the telephone and I'll wire money to you."

Neddy stood and so did Con. Neddy stuck out his hand and Con stuck out his. But when their hands met in a firm handshake, Con pulled Neddy close and hugged him. As they released each other, Neddy turned to Bess, who took both of his hands in hers and kissed them gently before hugging him.

Moments later, they were in the Hudson. Bess and Con in the front seat, Neddy and Timmy in the back. No one spoke all the way to the Winton Station, although Neddy turned to look at the "For Rent" sign in what used to be *Miss Millicent's Chapeau Emporium.*

There were tears and embraces on the train platform as a conductor yelled, "All aboard."

Bess embraced Neddy again, then handed him the small wicker basket lined with a cloth napkin she held on her lap during the drive to Winton. "Something for your trip," she said, whispering in his ear, "I love you."

Then it was Con's turn. "Here," he said, "some reading for the train ride."

Neddy glanced down and saw the book's title: *The Innocents Abroad.* When he looked up, he assured, "'Tis not the last you'll see of me."

"Is that a promise or a threat?" Con replied as they both struggled to laugh.

Timmy never took his eyes off Neddy as if trying to

capture and preserve every inch of him. Neddy kneeled beside Timmy, touching his face gently. "Hey, boyo," he whispered. "Don't ya bother none about me goin' 'cause it's not forever. B'sides, I've to come back an' see y're takin' good care of Mister Con an' Miss Bess. Promise me you'll be doin' that?" Timmy nodded. "I love ya, Timmy."

Timmy didn't say a word, but threw his arms around Neddy's neck instead.

Neddy stood and looked around one last time. At Bess. At Con. At Timmy. He grabbed his suitcase and climbed aboard the train, uncertain, but confident in his choice.

The locomotive bell rang out as linkage connecting the four passenger cars slammed into place and the train began to move. Neddy looked out the window watching as his Canadian family became smaller and Winton was reduced to the size of Lilliput.

And as the train gained steam, Neddy picked up the basket from the seat beside him, unfolded the napkin to find four scones and a half dozen cookies.

41

Wheat from the Chaff

The old man died in his sleep under hospice care after regaining consciousness, but not full awareness. There was no pain. He just slipped away with his son and daughter in law seated by his bedside as the sun rose into another blistering Florida day.

Ahead, were the formalities of the estate. Not a huge one, but certainly a comfortable one by most measures. There were stocks, some bonds, several life insurance policies, an eight-year-old Buick and a house filled with the accumulations of an 89-year-old. Of all he left behind, Patrick and Karen dreaded clearing the old man's house the most.

With estate appraisers coming by the end of the week, they stood in the foyer, overwhelmed in all directions, but their eyes focused immediately on ... the books. Lining one entire wall of the living room was a floor-to-ceiling bookcase filled with hundreds of books his Mom and Dad had read during their lifetimes. But there also were bookcases in almost every other room of the house. Histories. Biographies. Mysteries. Romances. Textbooks. All alphabetized, categorized and loved. One guest room bookcase was filled with National Geographic magazines, all in date order up to the most recent issue.

Trying to devise a plan of attack, Patrick and Karen eventually decided that the old man's bedroom was a logical starting point. They would donate to charity all his clothing, at least those articles without indelible food stains, and begin "separating the wheat from the chaff," as Karen called it.

They started with his dresser on which there were three family portraits. The first was a gold-framed wedding picture of Patrick's mother and father, next to another photo of Patrick, Karen and the kids. The third was a faded photo of Patrick's grandparents, bowed with age, standing outside their small cottage in Tyrone. There was a clock radio and a small ceramic bird. Inside the dresser, they found five pairs of underwear, several watches – some working, some not. Seven pairs of reading glasses, a belt, nearly a dozen travel-size packets of tissues and a few vials of expired pills. On the night stand, several more

National Geographics. Toiletries and towels in the bathroom. Shoes and slippers scattered everywhere. Hanging on the wall above his bed was an oil painting of an anonymous beach with check-mark brush strokes representing seagulls, the type of artsy schlock hawked to tourists on the islands during a Caribbean cruise. On another wall, two antique gilded picture frames containing wildlife watercolors.

Next stop was the closet. Crammed with clothing of all fabrics and eras, wools, polyesters, silk, cotton. Even seersucker. Patrick was certain some of it predated his birth including a powder-blue double-knit polyester tuxedo with outsized velvet lapels in a dry-cleaner's plastic bag on a wire hanger. In the back of the closet was a rumpled pile of clothing mounded two-feet high almost obscuring the cedar chest beneath it.

Patrick remembered the chest from his childhood, when it served as a coffee table in the living room. He gathered the clothes pile, took it to the bed and dumped it there, returning to the chest. He opened it. "Hey, honey, come here."

They looked down at its carefully arranged piles, bundles and boxes, as neat as the rest of the closet was chaotic. Patrick pulled out what looked like the collar of a woolen jacket with a two-inch stitched repair. There was a small envelope containing a withered flower – a buttercup – preserved in wax paper. There also was an old bicycle bell, which he flicked, but it didn't ring. Putting the bell down, he moved on to a cigar box filled with a boarding pass from the R.M.S. Sea Empress, a few dog-eared official-looking papers and a small faded photograph of a long-ago teenager wearing an ill-fitting three-piece suit, a wrinkled shirt with the points of its frayed collar pinched together by a collar bar. Completing the ensemble was a thin necktie with an attempted forehand knot. Patrick couldn't decide if the boy's expression was bewildered or sad, but he was certain the look of determination was something that never faded from his father's deep-set eyes.

There were his father's passport and United States naturalization papers. Next in the chest was a neat stack of six books and two photo albums bound together with twine. One book was a copy of Gulliver's Travels. The others were an old geography text book, two by Mark Twain – The Adventures of Huckleberry Finn and The Innocents Abroad – Jules Verne's Around the World in 80 Days and a well-read, but well-loved Rand-McNally Dollar Atlas of the World whose cover looked remarkably fresh despite its age. As Patrick undid the twine, he opened Gulliver's Travels and a piece of paper slid out. He unfolded it and looked at the pictures of well-dressed boys smiling and waving their caps on the deck of a ship. At the top of the page was the headline:

Canada Welcomes British Boys
FREE PASSAGES TO CANADA

Replacing the leaflet, he picked up Huckleberry Finn and opened it. Inside the cover was an inscription: "From the Library of Con McKeown."

Next, he turned his attention to a photo album he had never seen before. It was labeled "McKenna's Travels" and filled with nearly 50 pages of unfamiliar photos and picture postcards from a stunning array of destinations. From Toronto to Saskatoon, Victoria to Banff, Costa Rica to Cuba, San Diego to Bangor, Maine. Postcards picturing vast fields of wheat in Manitoba to logging operations in the Northwest Territory.

Turning the pages randomly, Patrick stopped on an old photo of two young men – one of them his father -- in bellboy uniforms, arms draped over each other's shoulders labeled: "Me and Gil in Miami." There was the shot of six miners identified as "the lads of Mayo, Yukon Territory." Glued to the page below was a leaflet announcing a boxing card. Three fights down from the main event were the names Dugan vs. McKenna.

Another photo focused on a young woman in a maid's uniform, head thrown back in laughter, her face partially obscured by wind-blown black hair.

"Is that Mom?" Patrick asked Karen.

"I can't be sure ..." Karen said, moving in for a closer look, " but ... yes, I think it is." The photo was labeled "My favorite traveling companion."

There was a train ticket to Nome, Alaska, and a snapshot of his dad as a middle-aged man standing with a family identified as "Dr. Timothy 'Timmy' Lordan, Delores and Timmy Jr. in Winton, 1949." It was clipped together with another picture of an older couple in front of a farmhouse. It was labeled "Con and Miss Bess, 1939." There also was an obituary for Cornelius David McKeown III from 1953. On a newspaper clipping about Tokyo was a notation, "Some day."

The other album was more familiar with its hand-lettered title scrawled in gold ink: "Life's Great Adventure." Beneath the title was the inscription: "As long as you can dream, nothing is cast in stone."

Patrick opened it and found a treasury of old photos, each carefully labeled in white ink on the black pages. Photos of his dad and mother with the inscription: "Mary and me on the North Rim of the Grand Canyon." There were shots of them at the Statue of

Liberty and Mount Rushmore. Huddled on a snowy shoreline as icebergs floated behind them off the coast in a photo identified as "Iceberg Alley, Bonavista, Newfoundland." Whale watching on a boat in the Pacific near Monterey, California. Another showed "Mary holding up the Leaning Tower of Pisa." The Black Hills of South Dakota and Telluride in the Rockies, Big Sur and Little Big Horn. Wearing bibs and eating lobsters at a picnic table in Maine, and sitting on the rocky coast of Nova Scotia. Lounging on a tropical beach and hoisting Pina Coladas toward the camera. A picture of his middle-aged father with six women, one markedly older than the others. The inscription read, "You <u>can</u> go home again: Ma and me at the home place with my sisters Rose, Nuala, Colleen, Sissy and Eileen." Then there was the photo of his Dad with a smile almost as wide as his outstretched arms, standing in front of a large pagoda. Its label read: "Gulliver in Japan 1978"

Returning the album to the chest, he saw three carefully labeled stacks of letters each neatly bound with satin ribbon. The first was labeled Ma and Rose. The second was identified as The McKeowns and Timmy. The third was identified as Mary.

Then Patrick chuckled as he pulled out a neatly folded red, flowered Hawaiian shirt, a yellowing Panama hat, a pair of huarache sandals and white linen trousers.

"Oh, lord!" he laughed, shaking his head. "Dad's 'this-is-why-I-moved-to-Florida' outfit that he bought when my folks retired here," Patrick recalled fondly. "He wore it all the time for years and didn't care how outrageous he looked." Protruding from a trouser pocket was a Cuban cigar and a pair of wire-rimmed sunglasses.

At the very bottom of the chest, under more moments of his father's life, he saw a small velvet box, which he carefully opened.

Inside was a commemorative loyalty pin and an inscription on the lid recognizing his father for 35 years of company service. It was inscribed to:

Bernard "Neddy" McKenna

Director, Travel Insurance Division

The Travelers Insurance Companies

42

Tiny Footsteps

Neddy stood in the middle of the farm lane. Pushing back the brim of his Panama hat, he scanned the path meandering toward the stream behind the chicken coop, then the upper field toward the Cowley farm. He looked down the lane in one direction, then the other, almost as if memorizing the landscape, tree by tree. The birches, the elms and hawthorns, junipers and oaks and scotch pines. He glanced down at his white linen trousers and flicked a thistle from the right leg. Nearby, sheep bleated randomly as sheep are prone to do. He straightened his red Hawaiian shirt with several swipes of a hand, brushed a fly from a yellow hyacinth printed there and lit his cigar. A skylark raced by on a wind gust that would carry it effortlessly to its home meadow.

Turning to his right, Neddy gazed at Mary by his side, pulling her close and kissing her gently, his arm around her waist, as the faint sound of footsteps approached them from the barnyard. Bridget rushed toward Neddy and threw her tiny arms around his legs. He smiled down at her and stroked the tight red curls touching her shoulders. Looking again toward the cottage, he saw Moira smiling in the doorway as she dried her hands on her apron.

Neddy looked left as someone approached far down the lane, but couldn't make out who it was. The figure came closer and Neddy saw it was a bicycle and rider. Closer still and the features were more distinct. The sleek, black Raleigh racing bike slowed, then stopped not five feet away.

"So, brother," Packy said. "Wher'll ya be goin' t'day? If yer ready, let's away."

Epilogue

At the family attorney's office, later that week, with the funeral over and legal paperwork finalized, Patrick was handed a letter.

"Your father instructed me to give this to you after all legalities were completed," the lawyer said.

Looking at his name, written in his father's executive scrawl, Patrick studied the envelope briefly before tearing it open. Here's what it said:

Dear Patrick:

If you're reading this, I'm dead.

I saw that once in a movie and always wanted to write it: "If you're reading this, I'm dead." So, here we are.

As you already know, I had a good life, considering where I started and where I ended up (and, no, I'm not talking about being dead). I'm talking about being here in Florida with you, Karen and the kids, living the dream. In fact, dreams are the reason I'm writing this letter.

I imagined finding your mother after losing her in Montreal, but once I did, the many decades we spent together went by so fast. Too fast. Since she died, I missed everything about her every day of my life. Many people believe we've been reunited in heaven, but I'm not entirely sure there is a heaven or hell. And I seriously doubt that if they do exist I would land in the latter, not the former.

But despite all the good things I've experienced, there were many times I looked back and asked myself what I would change. What if this had happened? What if that didn't? Wouldn't it be amazing if I could give advice to my younger self based on what I knew later in life?

Then, incredibly, it happened. I swear.

Although I never embraced the concept of time travel, I did entertain the fantasy. What time period would I choose if I could start over? If I could take all my knowledge and money (which you know by now wasn't a fortune, but allowed me to live very comfortably), would it be the 1950s when I could take what cash I had and invest the whole kit and kaboodle in IBM? Maybe the 1970s to get in on the ground floor of Walmart, or the '80s for Microsoft and Apple? Would I go back to relive the life I had with your mother? (Of that, you can be certain.)

This is going to sound deranged, but somehow I did, in one sense, travel back in time. I was allowed (by whom or what, I simply don't know) to go back to the beginning ... to Ireland on that little farm with my mother, father and the girls. Not to start over, but as a visitor in my boyhood dreams with the power to

*influence who I was to become. I was able to go back to change
what happened to my father. To prevent him being murdered
by the Brits when they found a cache of weapons he was hiding
for the I.R.A. in a root cellar on the farm. I was able to stop the
landlord who owned my parents' farm from raping me as a boy.
And I encouraged myself to leave the farm, to travel, to explore.
However, as much as I wanted to, I still couldn't prevent the deaths
of my brother Packy and sister Bridget from disease.*

*Of course, you have no idea what I'm talking about because
your grandfather wasn't gunned down by the British. And I never
told you about being raped ... because I wasn't. What's truly
baffling about the incidents in question was how I retained both
versions of the memory to my final breath. The before **and** after.
That, my boy, might explain what you thought were early stages of
dementia when I let slip the wrong memory. (I'd like to see you try
to keep something this bizarre straight!)*

*That's why I remember being a night visitor and being
visited by that visitor in my dreams as a boy. To be honest, I
thought I was losing my mind. I would fall asleep as an adult and
find myself outside the Tyrone farm barnyard watching myself
as a boy. Or aboard the ship that brought me to Canada. Or in
Canada on the McKeowns' farm.*

*At first, I was just an observer, like a moviegoer watching
an old film. But then, slowly, inexplicably, I became part of the
film. Young Neddy could see me and we began talking. Eventually,
I began giving advice on little things. Really insignificant stuff.
But before long, I found myself inserted in dreams just before
pivotal moments in my young life. Points in time I knew would
alter my course for better or worse. Stranger still, I was allowed
to intervene ... up to a point. As much as I wanted to provide*

every detail of the solution and the aftermath, all I could do was provide hints and warnings. There were obvious limitations to my interference, although I never found out why.

Every time I woke up from these dreams, something was different ... in the real world. At first, my influence only changed my life, but when I awoke one morning to find, on my dresser, a framed picture of my aged mother and father at the farm, I was stunned that I had changed their lives as well. My father was killed in 1921 by the British army when he was 42, yet because I warned my 15-year-old self ... in a dream ... to move I.R.A. guns he was hiding before the British raided the farm, I somehow saved my father's life in the real world.

I know I sound crazy. I entertained that possibility for a long time. Especially when I would wake up from one of these dreams and have an actual childhood memory of being visited in my dreams by someone who looked like I did as an old man. And why I was wearing my "This Is Why I Moved To Florida outfit" I have no idea.

One time, my younger self wanted to know my name but I was prevented from telling him. So, because I was attending a Travelers Insurance sales conference at the time, I said, "Traveler." It was all I could think of in the moment.

With more dreams came more actual childhood memories of dreams. Again and again and again. As I said before, I can't explain why this happened. All I know is it did.

You know I've never been religious or even what you could call spiritual. I never believed in ghosts or miracles. I wasn't much of a drinker and certainly never indulged in hallucinogens. Still, I went on these "trips" that left me with two conclusions:

First: While life is strange, the universe is stranger. Is there a God? Is there an afterlife? Who knows? (Although as you read this, I have definitive proof ... one way or the other.) However, I am certain of a random power in the cosmos that has a warped sense of humor, making all of us the butt of a massive cosmic joke. Once you embrace that, once you stop taking things so damned seriously, life becomes much more tolerable, even enjoyable. So, laugh as often as possible, especially in the darkest times. Love one another deeply and openly because as trite as it sounds, love, indeed, conquers all. Most important, read everything you can get your hands on to better understand your fellow travelers ... to separate the enlightened from the ignorant ... and appreciate life's inevitable moments of hilarious irony.

Second: Never stop moving toward the world's physical and philosophical horizons because as long as you can dream, nothing is cast in stone ... not even the past.

Love to you, Karen and the kids ... eternally,

Dad

Sin deireadh leis

JOHN HEAGNEY

Acknowledgements

Traveler is an homage to my father that wouldn't have been possible without the tremendous efforts of my family and friends on both sides of the Atlantic. The hours they spent reading, editing, counseling and suggesting changes in direction during its creation were, in many cases, invaluable. In fact, it was because of their critiques, encouragement and input that *Traveler* grew from a short story into a novella, finally emerging as a novel.

For their faith in this project, I am forever grateful that I have all of them in my life.

However, my most ardent critic, editor, fan and collaborator is my wife and soulmate, Linda, who suffered through the highs and lows of creating this book for the better part of two years. Without her astute insights, painfully brutal assessments and patience, *Traveler* would not have emerged in its final form.

JOHN HEAGNEY

Made in the USA
Columbia, SC
28 February 2024

32144503R10185